The Lost Valley

and Other Stories

Other books by Algernon Blackwood

Fiction

The Empty House and other Ghost Stories
The Listener and other Stories
John Silence: Physician Extraordinary (stories)
Jimbo: a Fantasy
The Education of Uncle Paul (children's novel)
The Human Chord (novel)
The Lost Valley and Other Stories
The Centaur (novel)
Pan's Garden: A Volume of Nature Stories
A Prisoner in Fairyland (children's novel)
Ten Minute Stories
Incredible Adventures (stories)
The Extra Day (children's novel)
Julius LeVallon: an episode (novel)
The Wave: An Egyptian Aftermath (novel)
Day and Night Stories
The Promise of Air (children's novel)
The Garden of Survival (novel)
Karma: A Reincarnation Play in Prologue (with Violet A. Pearn)
The Wolves of God and Other Fey Stories
The Bright Messenger (novel)
Episodes Before Thirty (autobiography)
Tongues of Fire and Other Sketches
Through the Crack: a Play in Five Scenes (with Violet A. Pearn)
Sambo and Snitch (children's novel)
Ancient Sorceries and Other Tales
The Dance of Death and Other Tales
Strange Stories
Dudley and Gilderoy: A Nonsense (children's novel)
Full Circle
Tales of Today and Yesterday
The Fruit Stoners (children's novel)
The Willows and other queer tales
Shocks
How the Circus Came to Tea
The Doll and One Other (two stories)

The Lost Valley

and Other Stories

ALGERNON BLACKWOOD

ÆGYPAN PRESS

The Lost Valley and Other Stories
A publication of
ÆGYPAN PRESS

www.aegypan.com

Table of Contents

THE LOST VALLEY 7

THE WENDIGO 51

OLD CLOTHES 91

PERSPECTIVE 119

THE TERROR OF THE TWINS 137

THE MAN FROM THE 'GODS' 143

THE MAN WHO PLAYED UPON THE LEAF 155

THE PRICE OF WIGGINS'S ORGY 171

CARLTON'S DRIVE 189

THE ECCENTRICITY OF SIMON PARNACUTE 195

The Lost Valley

I

Mark and Stephen, twins, were remarkable even of their kind: they were not so much one soul split in twain, as two souls fashioned in precisely the same mold. Their characters were almost identical — tastes, hopes, fears, desires, everything. They even liked the same food, wore the same kind of hats, ties, suits; and, strongest link of all, of course disliked the same things too. At the age of thirty-five neither had married, for they invariably liked the same woman; and when a certain type of girl appeared upon their horizon they talked it over frankly, agreed it was impossible to separate, and together turned their backs upon her for a change of scene before she could endanger their peace.

For their love for one another was unbounded — irresistible as a force of nature, tender beyond words — and their one keen terror was that they might one day be separated.

To look at, even for twins, they were uncommonly alike. Even their eyes were similar: that grey-green of the sea that sometimes changes to blue, and at night becomes charged with shadows. And both faces were of the same strong type with aquiline noses, stern-lipped mouths, and jaws well marked. They possessed imagination, real imagination of the winged kind, and at the same time the fine controlling will without which such a gift is apt to prove a source of weakness. Their emotions, too, were real and living: not the sort that merely tickle the surface of the heart, but the sort that plow.

Both had private means, yet both had studied medicine because it interested them, Mark specializing in diseases of eye and ear, Stephen in mental and nervous cases; and they carried on a select, even a distinguished, practice in the same house in Wimpole Street with their names on the brass plate thus: Dr. Mark Winters, Dr. Stephen Winters.

In the summer of 1900 they went abroad together as usual for the months of July and August. It was their custom to explore successive ranges of mountains, collecting the folklore and natural history of the region into small volumes, neatly illustrated with Stephen's photographs. And this particular year they chose the Jura, that portion of it, rather, that lies between the Lac de Joux, Baulmes and Fleurier. For, obviously, they could not exhaust a whole range in a single brief holiday. They explored it in sections, year by year. And they invariably chose for their headquarters quiet, unfashionable places where there was less danger of meeting attractive people who might break in upon the happiness of their profound brotherly devotion — the incalculable, mystical devotion of twins.

"For abroad, you know," Mark would say, "people have an insinuating way with them that is often hard to withstand. The chilly English reserve disappears. Acquaintanceship becomes intimacy before one has time to weigh it."

"Exactly," Stephen added. "The conventions that protect one at home suddenly wear thin, don't they? And one becomes soft and open to attack — unexpected attack."

They looked up and laughed, reading each other's thoughts like trained telepathists. What each meant was the dread that one should, after all, be taken and the other left — by a woman.

"Though at our age, you know, one is almost immune," Mark observed; while Stephen smiling philosophically —

"Or *ought* to be."

"*Is,*" quoth Mark decisively. For by common consent Mark played the *rôle* of the elder brother. His character, if anything, was a shade more practical. He was slightly more critical of life, perhaps, Stephen being ever more apt to accept without analysis, even without reflection. But Stephen had that richer heritage of dreams which comes from an imagination loved for its own sake.

II

*I*n the peasant's chalet, where they had a sitting room and two bedrooms, they were very comfortable. It stood on the edge of the forests that run along the slopes of Chasseront, on the side of Les Rasses farthest from Ste Croix. Marie Petavel provided them with the simple cooking they liked; and they spent their days walking, climbing, exploring, Mark collecting legend and folklore, Stephen making his natural history studies, with the little maps and surveys he drew so cleverly. Even this was only a division of labor, for each was equally interested in the occupation of the other; and they shared results in the long evenings, when expeditions brought them back in time, smoking in the rickety wooden balcony, comparing notes, shaping chapters, happy as two children, They brought the enthusiasm of boys to all they did, and they enjoyed the days apart almost as much as those they spent together. After separate expeditions each invariably returned with surprises which awakened the other's interest — even amazement.

Thus, the life of the foreign element in the hotels — unpicturesque in the daytime, noisy and overdressed at night — passed them by. The glimpses they caught as they passed these caravansarais, when gaieties were the order of the evening, made them value their peaceful retreat among the skirts of the forest. They brought no evening dress with them, not even "le smoking."

"The atmosphere of these huge hotels simply poisons the mountains," quoth Stephen. "All that 'haunted' feeling goes."

"Those people," agreed Mark, with scorn in his eyes, "would be far happier at Trouville or Dieppe, gambling, flirting, and the rest."

Feeling, thus, secure from that jealousy which lies so terribly close to the surface of all giant devotions where the entire life depends upon exclusive possession, the brothers regarded with indifference the signs of this gayer world about them. In that throng there was no one who could introduce an element of danger into their lives — no woman, at least, either of them could like would be found *there!*

For this thought must be emphasized, though not exaggerated. Certain incidents in the past, from which only their strength of will had made escape possible, proved the danger to be a real one. (Usually, too, it was some un-English woman: to wit, the Budapest adventure, or the incident in London with the Greek girl who was first Mark's patient and then Stephen's.) Neither of them made definite reference to the danger, though undoubtedly it was present in their minds more or less vividly whenever they came to a new place: this singular dream that one day a woman would carry off one, leave the other lonely. It was instinctive, probably just as the dread of the wolf is instinctive in the deer. The curious fact, though natural enough, was that each brother feared for the other and not for himself. Had anyone told Mark that some day he would marry, Mark would have shrugged his shoulders with a smile, and replied, "No; but I'm awfully afraid Stephen may!" And *vice versâ.*

III

*T*hen, out of a clear sky, the bolt fell – upon Stephen. Catching him utterly unawares, it sent him fairly reeling. For Stephen, even more than his brother, possessed that glorious yet fatal gift, common to poets and children, by which out of a few insignificant details the soul builds for itself a whole sweet heaven to dwell in.

It was at the end of their first month, a month of unclouded happiness together. Since their exploration of the Abruzzi, two years before, they had never enjoyed anything so much. And not a soul had come to disturb their privacy. Plans were being mooted for moving their head-quarters some miles farther towards the Val de Travers and the Creux du Van; only the day of departure, indeed, remained to be fixed, when Stephen, coming home from an afternoon of photography alone, saw, with bewildering and arresting suddenness – a Face. And with the effect of a blow full upon the heart it literally struck him.

How such a thing can come upon a strong man, a man of balanced mind, healthy in nerves and spirit, and in a single moment change his serenity into a state of feverish and passionate desire for possession, is a mystery that lies too deep for philosophy or Science to explain. It turned him dizzy with a sudden and tempestuous delight – a veritable sickness of the soul, wondrous sweet as it was deadly. Rare enough, of course, such instances may be, but that they happen is undeniable.

He was making his way home in the dusk somewhat wearily. The sun had already dipped below the horizon of France behind him. Across the open country that stretched away to the distant mountains of the Rhone Valley, the moonlight climbed with wings of ghostly radiance that fanned their way into the clefts and pine-woods of the Jura all about him. Cool airs of night stirred and whispered; lights twinkled through the openings among the trees, and all was scented like a garden.

He must have strayed considerably from the right trail – path there was none – for instead of Striking the mountain road that led straight to his chalet, he suddenly emerged into a pool of electric light that shone round one of the smaller wooden hotels by the borders of the forest. He recognized it at once, because he and his brother always avoided it deliberately. Not so gay or crowded as the larger caravansarais, it was nevertheless full of people of the kind they did not care about. Stephen was a good half-mile out of his way.

When the mind is empty and the body tired it would seem that the system is sensitive to impressions with an acuteness impossible when these are vigorously employed. The face of this girl, framed against the glass of the hotel verandah, rushed out towards him with a sudden invading glory, and took the most complete imaginable possession of this temporary employment of his spirit. Before he could think or act, accept or reject, it had lodged itself eternally at the very center of his being. He stopped, as before an unexpected flash of lightning, caught his breath — and stared.

A little apart from the throng of "dressy" folk who sat there in the glitter of the electric light, this face of melancholy dark splendor rose close before his eyes, all soft and wondrous as though the beauty the night — of forest, stars and moon-rise — had dropped down and focused itself within the compass of a single human countenance. Framed within a corner pane of the big windows, peering sideways into the darkness, the vision of this girl, not twenty feet from where he stood, produced upon him a shock of the most convincing delight he had ever known. It was almost as though he saw someone who had dropped down among all these hotel people from another world. And from another world, in a sense, she undoubtedly was; for her face held in it nothing that belonged to the European countries he knew. She was of the East. The magic of other suns swept into his soul with the vision; the pageantry of other skies flashed brilliantly and was gone. Torches flamed in recesses of his being hitherto dark.

The incongruous surroundings unquestionably deepened the contrast to her advantage, but what made this first sight of her so extraordinarily arresting was the curious chance that where she sat the glare of the electric light did not touch her. She was in shadow from the shoulders downwards. Only, as she leaned backwards against the window, the face and neck turned slightly, there fell upon her exquisite Eastern features the soft glory of the rising moon. And comely she was in Stephen's eyes as nothing in his life had hitherto seemed comely. Apart from the vulgar throng as an exotic is apart from the weeds that choke its growth, this face seemed to swim towards him along the pathway of the slanting moonbeams. And, with it, came literally herself. Some released projection of his consciousness flew forth to meet her. The sense of nearness took his breath away with the faintness of too great happiness. She was in his arms, and his lips were buried in her scented hair. The sensation was vivid with pain and joy, as an ecstasy. And of the nature of true ecstasy, perhaps, it was: for he stood, it seemed, *outside himself.*

He remained there riveted in the patch of moonlight at the forest edge, for perhaps a whole minute, perhaps two, before he realized what had happened. Then came a second shock that was even more conquer-

ing than the first, for the girl, he saw, was not only gazing into his very
face, she was also rising, as with an incipient gesture of recognition. As
though she knew him, the little head bent itself forward gently, grace-
fully, and the dear eyes positively smiled.

The impetuous yearning that leaped full-fledged into his blood taught
him in that instant the spiritual secret that pain and pleasure are
fundamentally the same force. His attempt at self-control, made instinctively, was utterly overwhelmed. Something flashed to him from her
eyes that melted the very roots of resolve; he staggered backwards,
catching at the nearest tree for support, and in so doing left the patch
of moonlight and stood concealed from view within the deep shadows
behind.

Incredible as it must seem in these days of starved romance, this man
of strength and firm character, who had hitherto known of such attacks
only vicariously from the description of others, now reeled back against
the trunk of a pine tree knowing all the sweet faintness of an overpow-
ering love at first sight.

"For that, by God, I'd let myself waste utterly to death! To bring her
an instant's happiness I'd suffer torture for a century — !"

For the words, with their clumsy, concentrated passion were out
before he realized what he was saying, what he was doing; but, once out,
he knew how pitifully inadequate they were to express a tithe of what
was in him like a rising storm. All words dropped away from him; the
breath that came and went so quickly clothed no further speech

With his retreat into the shadows the girl had sat down again, but
she still gazed steadily at the place where he had stood. Stephen, who
had lost the power of further movement, also stood and stared. The
picture, meanwhile, was being traced with hot iron upon plastic deeps
in his soul of which he had never before divined the existence. And,
again, with the magic of this master-yearning, it seemed that he drew
her out from that horde of hotel guests till she stood close before his
eyes, warm, perfumed, caressing. The delicate, sharp splendor of her face,
already dear beyond all else in life, flamed there within actual touch of
his lips. He turned giddy with the joy, wonder and mystery of it all. The
frontiers of his being melted — then extended to include her.

From the words a lover fights among to describe the face he worships
one divines only a little of the picture; these dimly-colored symbols
conceal more beauty than they reveal. And of this dark, young oval face,
first seen sideways in the moonlight, with drooping lids over the
almond-shaped eyes, soft cloudy hair, all enwrapped with the haunting
and penetrating mystery of love, Stephen never attempted to analyze
the ineffable secret. He just accepted it with a plunge of utter self-aban-

donment. He only realized vaguely by way of detail that the little nose, without being Jewish, curved singularly down towards a chin daintily chiseled in firmness; that the mouth held in its lips the invitation of all womankind as expressed in another race, a race alien to his own — an Eastern race; and that something untamed, almost savage, in the face was corrected by the exquisite tenderness of the large dreamy, brown eyes. The mighty revolution of love spread its soft tide into every corner of his being.

Moreover, that gesture of welcome, so utterly unexpected yet so spontaneous (so natural, it seemed to him now!), the smile of recognition that had so deliciously perplexed him, he accepted in the same way. The girl had felt what he had felt, and had betrayed herself even as he had done by a sudden, uncontrollable movement of revelation and delight; and to explain it otherwise by any vulgar standard of worldly wisdom, would be to rob it of all its dear modesty, truth and wonder. She yearned to know him, even as he yearned to know her.

And all this in the little space, as men count time, of two minutes, even less.

How he was able at the moment to restrain all precipitate and impulsive action, Stephen has never properly understood. There was a fight, and it was short, painful and confused. But it ended on a note of triumphant joy — the rapture of happiness to come.

With a great effort he remembers that he found the use of his feet and continued his journey homewards, passing out once more into the moonlight. The girl in the verandah followed his disappearing figure with her turning head; she craned her neck to watch till he disappeared beyond the angle of vision; she even waved her little dark hand.

"I shall be late," ran the thought sharply through Stephen's mind. It was cold; vivid wit keen pain. "Mark will wonder what in the world has become of me — !"

For, with swift and terrible reaction, the meaning of it all — the possible consequences of The Face — swept over his heart and drowned it in a flood of icy water. In estimating his brotherly love, even the of the twin, he had never conceived such a thing as this — had never reckoned with the possibility of a force that could make all else in the world seem so trivial. . . .

Mark, had he been there, with his more critical attitude to life, might have analyzed something of it anyway. But Mark was not there. And Stephen had — *seen*.

Those mighty strings of life upon which, as upon an instrument, the heart of man lies stretched had been set powerfully a-quiver. The new vibrations poured and beat through him. Something within him swiftly disintegrated; in its place something else grew marvelously. The Face had established dominion over the secret places of his soul; thence-forward the process was automatic and inevitable.

IV

*T*hen, specterlike and cold, the image of his rose before his inner vision. The profound brotherly love of the twin confronted him in the path.

He stumbled among the roots and stones, searching for the means of self-control, but finding them with difficulty. Windows had opened everywhere in his soul; he looked out through them upon a new world, immense and gloriously colored. Behind him in the shadows, as his vision searched and his heart sang, reared the single thought that hitherto had dominated his life: his love for Mark. It had already grown indisputably dim.

For both passions were genuine and commanding, the one built up through thirty-five years of devotion cemented by ten thousand associations and sacrifices, the other dropping out of heaven upon him with a suddenness simply appalling. And from the very first instant he understood that both could not live. One must die to feed the other....

On the staircase was the perfume of a strange tobacco, and, to his surprise and intense relief, when he entered the châlet he found that his brother for the first time was not alone. A small, dark man stood talking earnestly with him by the open window — the window where Mark had obviously been watching with anxiety for his arrival. Before introducing him to the stranger, Mark at once gave expression to his relief.

"I was beginning to be afraid something had happened to you," he said quietly enough, but in a way that the other understood. And after a moment's pause, in which he searched Stephen's face keenly, he added, "but we didn't wait supper as you see, and old Petavel has kept yours all hot and ready for you in the kitchen."

"I — er — lost my way," Stephen said quickly, glancing from Mark to the stranger, wondering vaguely who he was. "I got confused somehow in the dusk —"

Mark, remembering his manners now that his anxiety was set at rest, hastened to introduce him — a Professor in a Russian University, interested in folklore and legend, who had read their book on the Abruzzi and discovered quite by chance that they were neighbors here in the forest. He was staying in a little hotel at Les Rasses, and had ventured to come up and introduce himself. Stephen was far too occupied trying to conceal his new battling emotions to notice that Mark and the stranger seemed on quite familiar terms. He was so fearful lest the perturbations of his own heart should betray him that he had no power to detect anything subtle or unusual in anybody else.

"Professor Samarianz comes originally from Tiflis," Mark was explaining, "and has been telling me the most fascinating things about the legends and folklore of the Caucasus. We really must go there another year, Stephen. . . . Mr. Samarianz most kindly has promised me letters to helpful people. He tells me, too, of a charming and exquisite legend of a 'Lost Valley' that exists hereabouts, where the spirits of all who die by their own hands, or otherwise suffer violent deaths, find perpetual peace – the peace denied them by all the religions, that is. . . ."

Mark went on talking for some minutes while Stephen took off his knapsack and exchanged a few words with their visitor, who spoke excellent English. He was not quite sure what he said, but hoped he talked quietly and sensibly enough, in spite of the passions that waged war so terrifically in his breast. He noticed, however, that the man's face held an unusual charm, though he could not detect wherein its secret specifically lay. Presently, with excuses of hunger, he went into the kitchen for his supper, hugely relieved to find the opportunity to collect his thoughts a little; and when he returned twenty minutes later he found that his brother was alone. Professor Samarianz had taken his leave. In the room still lingered the perfume of his peculiarly flavored cigarettes.

Mark, after listening with half an ear to his brother's description of the day, began pouring out his new interest; he was full of the Caucasus, and its folklore, and of the fortunate chance that had brought the stranger their way. The legend of the "Lost Valley" in the Jura, too, particularly interested him, and he spoke of his astonishment that he had hitherto come across no trace anywhere of the story.

"And fancy," he exclaimed, after a recital that lasted half-an-hour, "the man came up from one of those little hotels on the edge of the forest – that noisy one we have always been so careful to avoid. You never know where your luck hides, do you?" he added, with a laugh.

"You never do, indeed," replied Stephen quietly, now wholly master of himself, or, at least, of his voice and eyes.

And, to his secret satisfaction and delight, it was Mark who provided the excuses for staying on in the chalet, instead of moving further down the valley as they had intended. Besides, it would have been unnatural and absurd to leave without investigating so picturesque a legend as the "Lost Valley."

"We're uncommonly happy here," Mark added quietly; "why not stay on a bit?"

"Why not, indeed?" answered Stephen, trusting that the fearful inner storm instantly roused again by the prospect did not betray itself.

"You're not very keen, perhaps, old fellow?" suggested Mark gently.

"On the contrary — I am, *very,*" was the reply.

"Good. Then we'll stay."

The words were spoken after a pause of some seconds. Stephen, who was down at the end of the room sorting his specimens by the lamp, looked up sharply. Mark's face, where he sat on the window-ledge in the dusk, was hardly visible. It must have something in his voice that had shot into Stephen's heart with a flash of sudden warning.

A sensation of cold passed swiftly over him and was gone. Had he already betrayed himself? Was the subtle, almost telepathic sympathy between the twins developed to such a point that emotions could be thus transferred with the minimum of word or gesture, within the very shades of their silence even? And another thought: Was there something different in Mark to — something in him also that had changed? Or was it merely his own raging, heaving passion, though so sternly repressed, that distorted his judgment and made him imaginative?

What stood so darkly in the room — between them?

A sudden and fearful pain seared him inwardly as he realized, practically, and with cruelly acute comprehension, that one of these two loves in his heart must inevitably die to feed the other; and that it might have to be — Mark. The complete meaning of it came home to him. And at the thought all his deep love of thirty years rose in a tide within him, flooding through the gates of life, seeking to overwhelm and merge in itself all obstacles that threatened to turn it aside. Unshed tears burned behind his eyes. He ached with a degree of actual, physical pain.

After a moment of savage self-control he turned and crossed the room; but before he had covered half the distance that separated him from the window where his brother sat smoking, the rush of burning words — were they to have been of confession, of self-reproach, or of renewed devotion? — swept away from him, so that he wholly forgot them. In their place came the ordinary dead phrases of convention. He hardly heard them himself, though his lips uttered them.

"Come along, Mark, old chap," he said, conscious that his voice trembled, and that another face slipped imperiously in front of the one his eyes looked upon; "it's time to go to bed. I'm dead tired like yourself."

"You are right," Mark replied, looking at him steadily as he turned towards the lamplight. "Besides, the night air's getting chilly — and we've been sitting in a draft, you know, all along."

For the first time in their lives the eyes of the two brothers could not quite find each other. Neither gaze hit precisely the middle of the other. It was as though a veil hung down between them and a deliberate act of focus was necessary. They looked one another straight in the face as usual, but with an effort — with momentary difficulty. The room, too, as Mark had said, was cold, and the lamp, exhausted of its oil, was beginning to smell. Both light and heat were going. It was certainly time for bed.

The brothers went out together, arm in arm, and the long shadows of the pines, thrown by the rising moon through the window, fell across the floor like arms that waved. And from the black branches outside, the wind caught up a shower of sighs and dropped them about the roofs and walls as they made their way to their bedrooms on opposite sides of the little corridor.

V

*F*our hours later, when the moon was high overhead and the room held but a single *big* shadow, the door opened softly and in came — Stephen. He was dressed. He crossed the floor stealthily, unfastened the windows, and let himself out upon the balcony. A minute afterwards he had disappeared into the forest beyond the strip of vegetable garden at the back of the châlet.

It was two o'clock in the morning, and no sleep had touched his eyes. For his heart burned, ached, and fought within him, and he felt the need of open spaces and the great forces of the night and mountains. No such battle had he ever known before. He remembered his brother saying years ago, with a half serious, half playful, ". . . for if ever one of us comes a cropper in love, old fellow, it will be time for the other to — go!" And by "go" they both understood the ultimate meaning of the word.

Through the glades of forest, sweet-scented by night, he made his way till he reached the spot where that Face of soft splendor had first blessed his soul with its mysterious glory. There he sat down and, with his back against the very tree that had supported him a few hours ago, he drove his thoughts forward into battle with the whole strength of his will and character behind him. Very quietly, and with all the care, precision and steadiness of mind that he would have brought to bear upon a difficult "case" at Wimpole Street, he faced the situation and wrestled with it. The emotions during four hours' tossing upon a sleepless bed had worn themselves out a little. He was, in one sense of the word, calm, master of himself. The facts, with the huge issue that lay in their hands, he saw naked. And, as he thus saw them, he discerned how very, very far he had already traveled down the sweet path that led him toward the girl — and away from his brother.

Details about her, of course, he knew none; whether she was free even; for he only knew that he loved, and that his entire life was already breaking with the yearning to sacrifice itself for that love. That was the naked fact. The problem bludgeoned him. Could he do anything to hold back the flood still rising, to arrest its terrific flow? Could he divert its torrent, and take it, girl and all, to offer upon the altar of that other love — the devotion of the twin for its twin, the mysterious affinity that hitherto had ruled and directed all the currents of his soul?

There was no question of undoing what had already been done. Even if he never saw that face again, or heard the accents of those beloved lips; if he never was to know the magic of touch, the perfume of close thought, or the strange blessedness of telling her his burning message and hearing the murmur of her own — the fact of love was already accomplished between them. That was ineradicable. He had seen. The sensitive plate had received its undying picture.

For this was no foolish passion arising from the mere propinquity that causes so many of the world's misfit marriages. It was a profound and mystical union already accomplished, psychical in the utter sense, inevitable as the marriage of wind and fire. He almost heard his soul laugh as he thought of the revolution effected in an instant of time by the message of a single glance. What had science, or his own special department of science, to say to this tempest of force that invaded him, and swept with its beautiful terrors of wind and lightning the furthest recesses of his being? This whirlwind that so shook him, that so deliciously wounded him, that already made the thought of sacrificing his brother seem sweet — what was there to say to it, or do with it, or think of it?

Nothing, nothing, nothing. . . ! He could only lie in its arms and rest, with that peace, deeper than all else in life, which the mystic knows when he is conscious that the everlasting arms are about him and that his union with the greatest force of the world is accomplished.

Yet Stephen struggled like a lion. His will rose up and opposed itself to the whole invasion . . . and in the end his will of steel, trained as all men of character train their wills against the difficulties of life, did actually produce a certain, definite result. This result was almost a *tour de force*, perhaps, yet it seemed valid. By its aid Stephen forced himself into a position he felt intuitively was an impossible one, but in which nevertheless he determined, by a deliberate act of almost incredible volition, that he would remain fixed. He decided to conquer his obsession, and to remain true to Mark. . . .

The distant ridges of the dim blue Jura were tipped with the splendors of the coming dawn when at length he rose, chilly and exhausted, to retrace his steps to the châlet.

He realized fully the meaning of the resolve he had come to. And the knowledge of it froze something within him into a stiffness that was like the stiffness of death. The pain in his heart battling against the resolution was atrocious. He had estimated, or thought so, at least, the meaning of his sacrifice. As a matter of fact his decision was entirely artificial, of course, and his resolve dictated by a moral code rather than by the living forces that direct life and can alone make its changes permanent. Stephen had in him the stuff of the hero; and, having said that, one has said all that language can say.

On the way home in the cool white dawn, as he crossed the open spaces of meadow where the mist rose and the dew lay like rain, he suddenly thought of her lying dead — dead, that is, as he had thus decided she was to be dead — for him. And instantly, as by a word of command, the entire light went out of the landscape and out of the world. His soul turned wintry, and all the sweetness of his life went bleak. For it was the ancient soul in him that loved, and to deny it was to deny life itself. He had pronounced upon himself a sentence of death by starvation — a lingering and prolonged death accompanied by tortures of the most exquisite description. And along this path he really believed at the moment his little human will could hold him firm.

He made his way through the dew-drenched grass with the elation caused by so vast a sacrifice singing curiously in his blood. The splendor of the mountain sunrise and all the vital freshness of the dawn was in his heart. He was upon the châlet almost before he knew it, and there on the balcony, waiting to receive him, his grey dressing gown wrapped about his ears in the sharp air, stood — Mark!

And, somehow or other, at the sight, all this false elation passed and dropped. Stephen looked up at him, standing suddenly still there in his tracks, as he might have looked up at his executioner. The picture had restored him most abruptly, with sharpest pain, to reality again.

"Like me, you couldn't sleep, eh?" Mark called softly, so as not to waken the peasants who slept on the ground floor.

"Have *you* been lying awake, too?" Stephen replied.

"All night. I haven't closed an eye." Then Mark added, as his brother came up the wooden steps towards him, "I knew — you were awake I felt it. I knew, too — you had gone out."

A silence passed between them. Both had spoken quietly, naturally, neither expressing surprise.

"Yes," Stephen said slowly at length; "we always reflect each other's pai — each other's moods —" He stopped abruptly, leaving the sentence unfinished.

Their eyes met as of old. Stephen knew an instant of quite freezing terror in which he felt that his brother had divined the truth. Then Mark took his arm and led the way indoors on tiptoe.

"Look here, Stevie, old fellow," he said, with extraordinary tenderness "there's no good saying anything, but I know perfectly well that you're unhappy about something; and so, of course, I am unhappy too." He paused, as though searching for words. Under ordinary circumstances Stephen would have caught his precise thought, but now the tumult of suppressed emotion in him clouded his divining power. He felt his arm clutched in a sudden vice. They drew closer to one another. Neither spoke. Then Mark, low and hurriedly, said — he almost mumbled it — "It's all my fault *really*, all my fault — dear old boy!"

Stephen turned in amazement and stared. What in the world did his brother mean? What was he talking about? Before he could find speech, however, Mark continued, speaking distinctly now, and with evidences of strong emotion in his voice —

"I'll tell you what we'll do," he exclaimed, with sudden decision; "we'll go away; we'll leave! We've stayed here a bit too long, perhaps. Eh? What d'you say to that?"

Stephen did not notice how sharply Mark searched his face. At the thought of separation all his mighty resolution dropped like a house of cards. His entire life seemed to melt away and run in a stream of impetuous yearning towards the Face.

But he answered quietly, sustaining his purpose artificially by a force of will that seemed to break and twist his life at the source with extraordinary pain. He could not have endured the strain for more than a few seconds. His voice sounded strange and distant.

"All right; at the end of the week," he said — the faintness in him was dreadful, filling him with cold — "and that'll give us just three days to make our plans, won't it?"

Mark nodded his head. Both faces were lined and drawn like the faces of old men; only there was no one there to remark upon it — nor upon the fixed sternness that had dropped so suddenly upon their eyes and lips.

Arm in arm they entered the chalet and went to their bedrooms without another word. The sun, as they went, rose close over the tree-tops and dropped its first rays upon the spot where they had just stood.

VI

*T*hey came down in dressing gowns to a very late breakfast. They were quiet, grave and slightly preoccupied. Neither made the least reference to their meeting at sunrise. New lines had graved themselves upon their faces, identical hues it seemed, drawing the mouth down at the corners with a touch of grimness where hitherto had been merely firmness.

And the eyes of both saw new things, new distances, new terrors. Something, feared till now only as a possibility, had come close, and stood at their elbows for the first time as an actuality. Sleep, in which changes offered to the soul during the day are confirmed and ratified, had established this new element in their personal equation. They had changed — if not towards one another, then towards something else.

But Stephen saw the matter only from his own point of view. For the first time in his memory he seemed to have lost the intuitive sympathy which enabled him to see things from his brother's point of view as well. The change, he felt positive, was in himself, not in Mark.

"He knows — he feels — something in me has altered dreadfully, but he doesn't yet understand what," his thoughts ran. "Pray to God he need never know — at least until I have utterly conquered it!"

For he still held with all the native tenacity of his strong will to the course he had so heroically chosen. The degree of self-deception his imagination brought into the contest seemed incredible when his mind looked back upon it all from the calmness of the end. But at the time he genuinely hoped, wished, intended to conquer, even *believed* that he would conquer.

Mark, he noticed, reacted in little ways that curiously betrayed his mental perturbation, and at any other time might have roused his brother's suspicions. He put sugar in Stephen's coffee, for instance; he forgot to bring him a cigarette when he went to the cupboard to get one for himself; he said and did numerous little things that were contrary to his habits, or to the habits of his twin.

In all of which, however, Stephen saw only the brotherly reaction to the change he was conscious of in himself. Nothing happened to convince him that anything in Mark had suffered revolution. With the mystical devotion peculiar to the twin he was too keenly aware of his own falling away to imagine the falling away of the other. He, Stephen, was the guilty one, and he suffered atrociously. Moreover, the pain of his renunciation was heightened by the sense that his ideal love for Mark had undergone a change — that he was making this fatal sacrifice, therefore, for something that perhaps no longer existed. This, however, he did not realize yet as an accomplished fact. Even if it were true, the resolution he had come to, acted by way of hypnotic suggestion to conceal it. At the same time it added enormously to the confusion and perplexity of his mind.

That day for the brothers was practically a *dies non.* They spent what was left of the morning over many aimless and unnecessary little duties, somewhat after the way of women. Although neither referred to the decision to leave at the end of the week, both acted upon it in desultory fashion, almost as though they wished to make a point of proving to one another that it was *not* forgotten — not wholly forgotten, at any rate. They made a brave pretence of collecting various things with a view to ultimate packing. No word was spoken, however, that bore more closely upon it than occasional phrases such as, "When the time comes to go" — "when we leave" — "better put *that* out, or it will be forgotten, you know."

The sentences dropped from their mouths alternately at long intervals, the only one deceived being the utterer. It was not unlike the pretence of schoolboys, only more elaborate and infinitely more clumsy and ill-done. Stephen, at any other time, would probably have laughed aloud. Yet the curious thing was that he noticed the pretence only in his own case. Mark, he thought, was genuine, though perhaps not too eager. "He's agreed to leave, the dear old chap, because he thinks I want it, and not for himself," he said. And the idea of the small brotherly sacrifice pleased, yet pained him horribly at the same time. For it tended to rehabilitate the old love which stood in the way of the new one.

He began, however, to take less trouble to sort and find his things for packing; he wrote letters, put out photographs to print in the sun, even studied his maps for expeditions, making occasional remarks thereon aloud which Mark did not negative. Presently, he forgot altogether about packing. Mark said nothing. Mark followed his example, however.

During the afternoon both lay down and slept, meeting again for tea at five. It was rare that they found themselves in for tea. Mark today made a special little ritual of it; he made it over their own spirit-lam — almost tenderly, looking after his brother's wants like a woman. And the little meal was hardly over when a boy in hotel livery arrived with a note — an invitation from Professor Samarianz.

"He has looked up a lot of his papers," observed Mark carelessly as he tossed the note down, "and suggests my coming in for dinner, so that he can show mc everything afterwards without hurry."

"I should accept," said Stephen. "It might be valuable for us if we go to the Caucasus later."

Mark hesitated a minute or two, telling the boy to wait in the kitchen. "I think I'll go in *after* dinner instead," he decided presently. There was a trace of eagerness in his manner which Stephen, however, did not notice.

"Take your notebook and pump the old boy dry," Stephen added, with a slight laugh. "I shall go to bed early myself probably." And Mark, stuffing the note into his pocket, laughed back and consented, to the other's great relief.

It was very late when Mark returned from the visit, but his brother did not hear him come, having taken a draft to ensure sleeping. And next morning Mark was so full of the interesting information he had collected, and would continue to collect, that the question of leaving at the end of the week dropped of its own accord without further ado. Neither of the brothers made the least pretence of packing. Both wished and intended to stay on where they were.

"I shall look up Samarianz again this afternoon," Mark said casually during the morning, "and — if you've no objection — I might bring him back to supper. He's the most obliging fellow I've ever met, and crammed with information."

Stephen, signifying his agreement, took his camera, his specimen-tin and his geological hammer and went out with bread and chocolate in his knapsack for the rest of the afternoon by himself.

VII

Moreover, he not only set out bravely, but for many hours held true, keeping so rigid a control over his feelings that it seemed literally to cost him blood. All the time, however, a passionate yearning most craftily attacked him, and the very memory he strove to smother rose with a persistence that ridiculed repression. Like snowflakes, whose individual weight is inappreciable but their cumulative burden irresistible, the thoughts of *her* gathered behind his spirit, ready at a given moment to overwhelm; and it was on the way home again in the evening that the temptation came upon him like a tidal wave that made the mere idea of resistance seemed utterly absurd.

He remembered wondering with a kind of wild delight whether it could be possible for any human will to withstand such a tempest of pressure as that which took him by the shoulders and literally pushed him out of his course towards the little hotel on the edge of the forest.

It was utterly inconsistent, of course, and he made no pretence of argument or excuse. He hardly knew, indeed, what he expected to see or do; his mind, at least, framed no definite idea. But far within him that deep heart which refused to be stifled cried out for a drop of the living water that was now its very life. And, chiefly, he wanted to *see*. If only he could see her once again — even from a distance — the merest glimpse —! With one more sight of her that should charge his memory to the brim for life be might face the future with more courage perhaps. Ah! that *perhaps...!* For she was drawing him with those million invisible cords of love that persuade a man he is acting of his own volition when actually he is but obeying the inevitable forces that bind the planets and the suns.

And this time there was no hurry; there was a good hour before Mark would expect him home for supper; he could sit among the shadows of the wood, and wait.

In his pocket were the field-glasses, and he realized with a sudden secret shame that it was not by accident that they were there. He stumbled, even before he got within a quarter of a mile of the place, for the idea that perhaps he would see her again made him ridiculously happy, and like a school-boy he positively trembled, tripping over roots and misjudging the distance of his steps. It was all part of a great whirling dream in which his soul sang and shouted the first delirious nonsense that came into his head. The possibility of his eyes again meeting hers produced a sensation of triumph and exultation that only one word describes — intoxication.

As he approached the opening in the trees whence the hotel was so easily visible, he went more slowly, moving even on tiptoe. It was instinctive; for he was nearing a place made holy by his love. Picking his way almost stealthily, he found the very tree; then leaned against it while his eyes searched eagerly for a sign of her in the glass verandah. The swiftness and accuracy of sight at such a time may be cause for wonder, but it is beyond question that in less than a single second he knew that the throng of moving figures did not contain the one he sought. She was not among them.

And he was just preparing to make himself comfortable for an extended watch when a sound or movement, perhaps both, somewhere among the trees on his right attracted his attention. There was a faint rustling; a twig snapped.

Stephen turned sharply. Under a big spruce, not half-a-dozen yards away, something moved — then rose up. At first, owing to the gloom, he took it for an animal of some kind, but the same second he saw that it was a human figure. It was *two* human figures, standing close together. Then one moved apart from the other; he saw the outline of a man against a space of sky between the trees. And a voice spoke — a voice charged with great tenderness, yet driven by high passion —

"But it's nothing, nothing! I shall not be gone two minutes. And to save you an instant's discomfort you know that I would run the whole circle of the earth! Wait here for me — !"

That was all; but the voice and figure caused Stephen's heart to stop beating as though it had been suddenly plunged into ice, for they were the voice and the figure of his brother Mark.

Quickly running down the slope towards the hotel, Mark disappeared.

The other figure, leaning against the tree, was the figure of a girl; and Stephen, even in that first instant of fearful bewilderment, understood why it was that the face of the man Samarianz had so charmed him. For this, of course, was his daughter. And then the whole thing flashed mercilessly clear upon his inner vision, and he knew that Mark, too, had been swept from his feet, and was undergoing the same fierce tortures, and fighting the same dread battle, as himself. . . .

There seemed to be no conscious act of recognition. The fire that flamed through him and set his frozen heart so fearfully beating again, hammering against his ribs, left him apparently without volition or any power of cerebral action at all. *She* stood there, not half-a-dozen yards away from where he sat all huddled upon the ground, stood there in all her beauty, her mystery, her wonder, near enough for him to have taken her almost with a single leap into his arms; — stood there, veiled a little by the shadows of the dusk — waiting for the return of — Mark!

He remembers what happened with the blurred indistinctness common to moments of overwhelming passion. For in the next few seconds, that mocked all scale of time, he lived through a series of concentrated emotions that burned his brain too vividly for precise recollection. He rose to his feet unsteadily, his hand upon the rough bark of the tree. Absurd details only seem to remain of these few moments: that a foot was "asleep" with pins and needles up to the knee, and that his slouch hat fell from his head, filling him with fury because it hid her from him for the fraction of a second. These odd details he remembers.

And then, as though the driving-power of the universe had deliberately pushed him from behind, he was advancing slowly, with short, broken steps, towards the tree where the girl stood with her back half turned against him.

He did not know her name, had never heard her voice, had never even stood close enough to "feel" her atmosphere; yet, so deeply had his love and imagination already prepared the little paths of intimacy within him, that he felt he was moving towards someone whom he had known ever since he could remember, and who belonged to him as utterly as if from the beginning of time his possession of her had been absolute. Had they shared together a whole series of previous lives, the sensation could not have been more convincing and complete.

And out of all this whirlwind and tumult two small actions, he remembers, were delivered: a confused cry that was no definite word came from his lips, and — he opened his arms to take her to his heart. Whereupon, of course, she turned with a quick start, and became for the first time aware of his near presence.

"Oh, oh! But how so softly quick you return!" she cried falteringly, looking into his eyes with a smile both of welcome and alarm. "You a little frightened me, I tell you."

It was just the voice he had known would come, with the curiously slow, dragging tone of its broken English, the words lingering against the lips as if loath to leave, the soft warmth of their sound in the throat like a caress. The next instant he held her smothered in his arms, his face buried in the scented hair about her neck.

There was an unbelievable time of forgetfulness in which touch, perfume, and a healing power that emanated from her blessed the depths of his soul with a peace that calmed all pain, stilled all tumult — a moment in which Time itself for once stopped its remorseless journey, and the very processes of life stood still to watch. Then there was a frightened cry, and she had pushed him from her. She stood there, her soft eyes puzzled and surprised, looking hard at him; panting a little, her breast heaving.

And Stephen understood then, if he had not already understood before. The gesture of recognition in the hotel verandah two days ago, and this glorious realization of it that now seemed to have happened a century ago, shared a common origin. They were intended for another, and on both occasions the girl had taken him for his brother Mark.

And, turning sharply, almost falling with the abruptness of it all, as the girl's lips uttered that sudden cry, he saw close beside them the very person for whom they were intended. Mark had come up the slope behind them unobserved, carrying upon his arm the little red cloak he had been to fetch.

It was as though a wind of ice had struck him in the face. The revulsion of feeling with which Stephen saw the return of his brother passed rapidly into a state of numbness where all emotion whatsoever ebbed like the tides of death. He lost momentarily the power of realization. He forgot who he was, what he was doing there. He was dazed by the fact that Mark had so completely forestalled him. His life shook and tottered upon its foundations. . . .

Then the face and figurer of his brother swayed before his eyes like the branch of a tree, as an attack of passing dizziness seized him. It may have been a mere hazard that led his fingers to close, moist and clammy, upon the geological hammer at his belt. Certainly, he let it go again almost at once. . . .

And, when the tide of emotion returned upon him with the dreadful momentum it had gathered during the interval, the possibility of his yielding to wild impulse and doing something mad or criminal, was obviated by the swift enactment of an exceedingly poignant little drama that made both brothers forget themselves in their desire to save the girl.

In sweetest bewilderment, like a frightened little child or animal, the girl looked from one brother to the other. Her eyes shone in the dusk. Strangely appealing her loveliness was in that moment of seeking some explanation of the double vision. She made a movement first towards Mark — turned halfway in her steps and ran, startled, upon Stephen — then, with a sharp scream of fear, dropped in a heap to the ground midway between the two.

Her indecision of half-a-second, however, seemed to Stephen to have lasted many minutes. Had she fallen finally into the arms of his brother, he felt nothing on earth could have prevented his leaping upon him with the hands of a murderer. As it was — mercifully — the singular beauty of her little Eastern face, touched as it was by the white terror of her soul, momentarily arrested all other feeling in him. A shudder of fearful admiration passed through him as he saw her sway and fall. Thus might have dropped some soft angel from the skies.

It was Mark, however, with his usual decision, who brought some possibility of focus back to his mind; and he did it with an action and a sentence so utterly unexpected, so incongruous amid this whirlwind of passion, that had he seen it on the stage or read it in a novel, he must surely have burst out laughing. For, in that very second after the dear form swayed and fell, while the eyes of the brothers met across her in one swift look that held the possibilities of the direst results, Mark, his face abruptly clearing to calmness, stooped down beside the prostrate girl, and, looking up at Stephen steadily, said in a gentle voice, but with his most deliberate professional manner —

"Stephen, old fellow, this is — my patient. One of us, perhaps, had better — go."

He bent down to loosen the dress at the throat and chafe the cold hands, and Stephen, uncertain exactly what he did, and trembling like a child, turned and disappeared among the thick trees in the direction of their little house. For he understood only one thing clearly in that awful moment: that he must either kill — or not see. And his will, well-nigh breaking beneath the pressure, was just able to take the latter course.

"*Go!*" it said peremptorily.

And the little word sounded through the depths of his soul like the tolling of a last bell.

VIII

"*This is my patient!*" The dreadful comedy of the phrase, the grim mockery of the professional manner, the contrast between the words that someone *ought* to have uttered and the words Mark actually *had* uttered — all this had the effect of restoring Stephen to some measure of sanity. No one but his brother, he felt, could have said the thing so exactly calculated to relieve the choking passion of the situation. It was an inspiration — yet horrible in its bizarre mingling of true and false.

"But it's all like a thing in a dream," he heard an inner voice murmur as he stumbled homewards without once looking back; "the kind of thing people say and do in the rooms of strange sleep-houses. We are all surely in a dream, and presently I shall wake up — !"

The voice continued talking, but he did not listen. A web of confusion began to spin itself about his thoughts, and there stole over him an odd sensation of remoteness from the actual things of life. It was surely one of those vivid, haunting dreams he sometimes had when his spirit seemed to take part in real scenes, with real people, only far, far away, and on quite another scale of time and values.

"I shall find myself in my bed at Wimpole Street!" he exclaimed. He even tried to escape from the pain closing about him like a vice — tried to escape by waking up, only to find, of course, that the effort drove him more closely to the reality of his position.

Yet the texture of a dream certainly ran through the whole thing; the outlandish proportions of dream-events showed themselves everywhere; the tiny causes and prodigious effects: the terrific power of the Face upon his soul; the uncanny semi-quenching of his love for Mark; the ridiculous way he had come upon these two in the forest, with the nightmare discovery that they had known one another for days; and then the sight of that dear, magical face dropping through the dusky forest air between the two of them. Moreover — just when the dream ought to have ended with his sudden awakening, it had taken this abrupt and inconsequent turn, and Mark had uttered the language of — well, the impossible and rather horrible language of the nightmare world —

"This is my patient . . ."

Moreover, his face of ice as he said it; yet, at the same time, the wisdom, the gentleness of the decision that lay behind the words: the desire to relieve an impossibly painful situation. And then — the other words, meant kindly, even meant nobly, but charged for all that with the naked cruelty of life —

"One of its, perhaps, had better — go."

And he had gone — fortunately, he had gone. . . .

Yet an hour later, after lying motionless upon his bed seeking with all his power for a course of action his will could follow and his mind approve, it was no dream-voice that called softly to him through the keyhole —

"Stevie, old fellow . . . she is well . . . she is all right now. She leaves in the morning with her father . . . the first thing . . . very early. . . ."

And then, after a pause in which Stephen said nothing lest he should at the same time say all — ". . . and it is best, perhaps . . . we should not see one another . . . you and I . . . for a bit. Let us go our ways . . . till tomorrow night. Then we shall be . . . alone together again . . . you and I . . . as of old. . . ."

The voice of Mark did not tremble; but it sounded far away and unreal, almost like wind in the keyhole, thin, reedy, sighing; oddly broken and interrupted.

I'm yours, Stevie, old fellow, always yours," it added far down the corridor, more like the voice of dream again than ever.

But, though he made no reply at the moment, Stephen welcomed and approved both the proposal and the spirit in which it was made; and next day, soon after sunrise, he left the châlet very quietly and went off alone into the mountains with his thoughts, and with the pain that all night long had simply been eating him alive.

IX

*I*t is impossible to know precisely what he felt all that morning in the mountains. His emotions charged like wild bulls to and fro. He seemed conscious only of two master-feelings first, that his life now belonged beyond possibility of change or control — to another; yet, secondly, that his will, tried and tempered weapon of steel that it was, held firm.

Thus his powerful feelings flung him from one wall of his dreadful prison to another without possible means of escape. For his position involved a fundamental contradiction: the new love owned him, yet his will cried, "I love Mark; I hold true to that; in the end I shall conquer!" He refused, that is, to capitulate, or rather to acknowledge that he had capitulated. And meanwhile, even while he cried, his inmost soul listened, watched, and laughed, well content to abide the issue.

But if his feelings were in too great commotion for clear analysis, his thoughts, on the other hand, were painfully definite — some of them, at least; and, as the physical exercise lessened the assaults of emotion, these stood forth in sharp relief against the confusion of his inner world. It was now clear as the day, for instance, that Mark had been through a battle similar to his own. The chance meeting with the Professor had led to the acquaintance with his daughter. Then, swiftly and inevitably, just as it would have happened to Stephen in his place, love had accomplished its full magic. And Mark had been afraid to tell him. The twins had traveled the same path, only personal feeling having clouded their usual intuition, neither had divined the truth.

Stephen saw it now with pitiless clarity: his brother's frequent visits to the hotel, omitting to mention that the notes of invitation probably also included himself; the desire, nay, the intention to stay on; the delay in packing — and a dozen other details stood out clearly. He remembered, too, with a pang how Mark had not slept that memorable night; he recalled their enigmatical conversation on the balcony as the sun rose . . . and all the rest of the miserable puzzle.

And, as he realized from his own torments what Mark must also have suffered — be suffering now — he was conscious of a strengthening of his will to conquer. The thought linked him fiercely again to his twin; for nothing in their lives had yet been separate, and the chain of their spiritual intimacy was of incalculably vast strength. They would win — win back to one another's side again. Mark would conquer her. He, Stephen, would also in the end conquer . . . her. . . !

But with the thought of her lying thus dead to him, and his life cold and empty without her, came the inevitable revulsion of feeling. It was the anarchy of love. The Face, the perfume, the rushing power of her melancholy dear eyes, with their singular touch of proud languor — in a word, all the amazing magic that had swept himself and Mark from their feet, tore back upon him with such an invasion of entreaty and command, that he sat down upon the very rocks where he was and buried his face in his hands, literally groaning with the pain of it. For the thought lacerated within. To give her up was a sheer impossibility; . . . to give up his brother was equally inconceivable. The weight of thirty-five years' love and associations thus gave battle against the telling blow of a single moment. Behind the first lay all that life had built into the woof of his personality hitherto, but *beyond* the second lay the potent magic, the huge seductive invitation of what he might become in the future — with her.

The contest, in the nature of the forces engaged, was an unequal one. Yet all that morning as he wandered aimlessly over ridge and summit, and across the high Jura pastures above the forests, meeting no single human being, he fought with himself as only men with innate energy of soul know how to fight — bitterly, savagely, blindly. He did not stop to realize that he was somewhat in the position of a fly that strives to push from its appointed course the planet on which it rides through space. For the tides of life itself bore him upon their crest, and at thirty-five these tides are at the full.

Thus, gradually it was, then, as the hopelessness of the struggle became more and more apparent, that the door of the only alternative opened slightly and let him peer through. Once ajar, however, it seemed the same second wide open; he was through; — and it was closed — behind him.

For a different nature the alternative might have taken a different form. As has been seen, he was too strong a man to drift merely; a definite way out that could commend itself to a man of action had to be found; and, though the raw material of heroism may have been in him, he made no claim to a martyrdom that should last as long as life itself. And this alternative dawned upon him now as the grey light of a last morning must dawn upon the condemned prisoner: given Stephen, and given this particular problem, it was the only way out.

He envisaged it thus suddenly with a kind of ultimate calmness and determination that was characteristic of the man. And in every way it *was* characteristic of the man, for it involved the precise combination of courage and cowardice, weakness and strength, selfishness and sacrifice, that expressed the true resultant of all the forces at work in his soul. To him, at the moment of his rapid decision, however, it seemed that the dominant motive was the sacrifice to be offered upon the altar of his love for Mark. The twisted notion possessed him that in this way he might atone in some measure for the waning of his brotherly devotion. His love for the girl, her possible love for him — both were to be sacrificed to obtain the happiness the eventual happiness — of these other two. Long, long ago Mark had himself said that under such circumstances one or other of them would have to — go. And the decision Stephen had come to was that the one to "go" was — himself.

This day among the woods and mountains should be his last on earth. By the evening of the following day Mark should be free.

"I'll give my life for him."

His face was grey and set as he said it. He stood on the high ridge, bathed by sun and wind. He looked over the fair world of wooded vales and mountains at his feet, but his eyes, turned inwards, saw only his brother — and that sweet Eastern face — then darkness.

"He will understand — and perforce accept it — and with time, yes, with time, the new happiness shall fill his soul utterly — and hers. It is for her, too, that I give it. It *must* — under these unparalleled circumstances be right. . . !

And although there was no single cloud in the sky, the landscape at his feet suddenly went dark and sunless from one horizon to the other.

X

*T*hen, having come into the gloom of this terrible decision, his imaginative nature at once bounded to the opposite extreme, and a kind of exaltation possessed him. The stereotyped verdict of a coroner's jury might in this instance have been true. The prolonged stress of emotion under which he had so long been laboring had at last produced a condition of mind that could only he considered — unsound.

A cool wind swept his face as he let his tired eyes wander over the leagues of silent forest below. The blue Jura with its myriad folded valleys lay about him like the waves of a giant sea ready to swallow up the little atom of his life within its deep heart of forgetfulness. Clear away into France he saw on the one side where, beyond the fortress of Pontarlier, white clouds sailed the horizon before a westerly wind; and, on the other, towards the white-robed Alps rising mistily through the haze of the autumn sunshine. Between these extreme distances lay all that world of a hundred intricate valleys, curiously winding, deeply wooded, little inhabited — a region of soft, confusing loveliness where a traveler might well lose himself for days together before he discovered a way out of so vast a maze.

And, as he gazed, there passed across his mind, like the dim memory of something heard in childhood, that legend of the "Lost Valley" in which the souls of the unhappy dead find the deep peace that is denied to them by all the religions — and to which hundreds, who have not yet the sad right of entry, seek to find the mournful forest gates. The memory was vivid, but swiftly engulfed by others and forgotten. They chased each other in rapid succession across his mind, as clouds at sunset pass before a high wind, merging on the horizon in a common mass.

Then, slowly, at length, he turned and made his way down the mountainside in the direction of the French frontier for a last journey upon the sweet surface of the world he loved. In his soul was the one dominant feeling: this singular exaltation arising from the knowledge that in the long run his great sacrifice must ensure the happiness of the two beings he loved more than all else in life.

At the solitary farm where an hour later he had his lunch of bread and cheese and milk, he learned that he had wandered many miles out of the routes with which he was more or less familiar. He had been walking faster than he knew all these hours of battle. A physical weariness came upon him that made him conscious of every muscle in his body as he realized what a long road over mountain and valley he had to retrace. But, with the heaviness of fatigue, ran still that sense of interior spiritual exaltation. Something in him walked on air with springs of steel — something that was independent of the dragging limbs and the aching back. For the rest, his sensations seemed numb. His great Decision stood black before him, blocking the way. Thoughts and feelings forsook him as rats leave a sinking ship. The time for these-was past. Two overmastering desires, however, clung fast: one, to see Mark again, and be with him; the other, to be once more — with her. These two desires left no room for others. With the former, indeed, it was almost as though Mark had called aloud to him by name.

He stood a moment where the depth of the valley he had to thread lay like a twisting shadow at his feet; it ran, soft and dim, through the slanting sunshine. From the whole surface of the woods rose a single murmur; like the whirring of voices heard in a dream, he thought. The individual purring of separate trees was merged. Peace, most ancient and profound, lay in it, and its hushed whisper soothed his spirit.

He hurried his pace a little. The cool wind that had swept his face on the heights earlier in the afternoon followed him down, urging him forwards with deliberate pressure, as though a thousand soft hands were laid upon his back. And there were spirits in the wind that day. He heard their voices; and far below he traced by the motion of the tree-tops where they coiled upwards to him through miles of forest. His way, meanwhile, dived down through dense growths of spruce and pine into a region unfamiliar. There was an aspect of the scenery that almost suggested it was unknown — an undiscovered corner of the world. The countless signs that mark the passage of humanity were absent, or at least did not obtrude themselves upon him. Something remote from life, alien, at any rate, to the normal life he had hitherto known, began to steal gently over his burdened soul. . . .

In this way, perhaps, the effect of his dreadful Decision already showed its influence upon his mind and senses. So very soon now he would be — *going!*

The sadness of autumn lay all about him, and the loneliness of this secluded vale spoke to him of the melancholy of things that die — of vanished springs, of summers unfulfilled, of things forever incomplete and unsatisfying. Human effort, he felt, this valley had never known. No hoofs had ever pressed the mossy turf of these forest clearings; no traffic of peasants or woodsmen won echoes from these limestone cliffs. All was hushed, lonely, deserted.

And yet — ? The depths to which it apparently plunged astonished him more and more. Nowhere more than a half-mile across, each turn of the shadowy trail revealed new distances below. With spots of a haunting, fairy loveliness too: for here and there, on isolated patches of lawnlike grass, stood wild lilac bushes, rounded by the wind; willows from the swampy banks of the stream waved pale hands; firs, dark and erect, guarded their eternal secrets on the heights. In one little opening, standing all by itself, he found a lime tree; while beyond it, shining among the pines, was a group of shimmering beeches. And, although there was no wild life, there were flowers; he saw clumps of them — tall, graceful, blue flowers whose name he did not know, nodding in dream across the foaming water of the little torrent.

And his thoughts ran incessantly to Mark. Never before had he been conscious of so imperious a desire to see him, to hear his voice, to stand at his side. At moments it almost obliterated that other great desire. . . . Again he increased his pace. And the path plunged more and more deeply into the heart of the mountains, sinking ever into deeper silence, ever into an atmosphere of deeper peace. For no sound could reach him here without first passing along great distances that were cushioned with soft wind, and padded, as it were, with a million feathery pine-tops. A sense of peace that was beyond reach of all possible disturbance began to cover his breaking life with a garment as of softest shadows. Never before had he experienced anything approaching the wonder and completeness of it. It was a peace, still as the depths of the sea which are motionless because they *cannot* move — cannot even tremble. It was a peace unchangeable — what some have called, perhaps, the Peace of God. . . .

"Soon the turn *must* come," he thought, yet without a trace of impatience or alarm, "and the road wind upwards again to cross the last ridge!" But he cared little enough; for this enveloping peace drowned him, hiding even the fear of death.

And still the road sank downwards into the sleep-laden atmosphere of the crowding trees, and with it his thoughts, oddly enough, sank deeper and deeper into dim recesses of his own being. As though a secret sympathy lay between the path that dived and the thoughts that plunged. Only, from time to time, the thought of his brother Mark brought him back to the surface with a violent rush. Dreadfully, in those moments, he wanted him — to feel his warm, strong hand within his own — to ask his forgiveness — perhaps, too, to grant his own . . . he hardly knew.

"But is there no end to this delicious valley?" he wondered, with something between vagueness and confusion in his mind. "Does it never stop, and the path climb again to the mountains beyond?" Drowsily, divorced from any positive interest, the question passed through his thoughts. Underfoot the grass already grew thickly enough to muffle the sound of his footsteps. The trail even had vanished, swallowed by moss. His feet sank in.

"I wish Mark were with me now — to see and feel all this —"

He stopped short and looked keenly about him for a moment, leaving the thought incomplete. A deep sighing, instantly caught by the wind and merged in the soughing of the trees, had sounded close beside him. Was it perhaps himself that sighed — unconsciously? His heart was surely charged enough. . . !

A faint smile played over his lips — instantly frozen, however, as another sigh, more distinct than the first, and quite obviously external to himself, passed him closely in the darkening air. More like deep breathing, though, it was, than sighing. . . . It was nothing but the wind, of course. Stephen hurried on again, not surprised that he had been so easily deceived, for this valley was full of sighings and breathings — of trees and wind. It ventured upon no louder noise. Noise of any kind, indeed, seemed impossible and forbidden in this muted vale. And so deeply had he descended now, that the sunshine, silver rather than golden, already streamed past far over his head along the ridges, and no gleam found its way to where he was. The shadows, too, no longer blue and purple, had changed to black, as though woven of some delicate substance that had definite thickness, like a veil. Across the opposite slope, one of the mountain summits in the western sky already dropped its monstrous shadow fringed with pines. The day was rapidly drawing in.

XI

*A*nd here, very gradually, there began to dawn upon his overwrought mind certain curious things. They pierced clean through the mingled gloom and exaltation that characterized his mood. And they made the skin upon his back a little to — stir and crawl.

For he now became distinctly aware that the emptiness of this lonely valley was only apparent. It is impossible to say through what sense, or combination of senses, this singular certainty was brought to him that the valley was not really as forsaken and deserted as it seemed — that, on the contrary, it was the very reverse. It came to him suddenly — as a certainty. The valley as a matter of fact was — full. Packed, thronged and crowded it was to the very brim of its mighty wooded walls — with life. It was now borne in upon him, with an inner conviction that left no room for doubt, that on all sides living things — persons — were jostling him, rubbing elbows, watching all his movements, and only waiting till the darkness came to reveal themselves.

Moreover, with this eerie discovery came also the further knowledge that a vast multitude of others, again, with pallid faces and yearning eyes, with arms outstretched and groping feet, were searching everywhere for the way of entrance that he himself had found so easily. All about him, he felt, were people by the hundred, by the thousand, seeking with a kind of restless fever for the narrow trail that led down into the valley, longing with an intensity that heat upon his soul in a million waves, for the rest, the calm silence of the place — but most of all for its strange, deep, and unalterable peace.

He, alone of all these, had found the Entrance; he, *and one other.*

For out of this singular conviction grew another even more singular: his brother Mark was also somewhere in this valley with him. Mark, too, was wandering like himself in and out among its intricate dim turns. He had said but a short time ago, "I wish Mark were here!" Mark *was* here. And it was precisely then — while he stood still a moment, trying to face these overwhelming obsessions and deal with them — that the figure of a man, moving swiftly through the trees, passed him with a great gliding stride, and with averted face. Stephen started horribly, catching his breath. In an instant the man was gone again, swallowed up by the crowding pines.

With a quick movement of pursuit and a cry that should make the man turn, he sprang forward — but stopped again almost the same moment, realizing that the extraordinary speed at which the man had shot past him rendered pursuit out of the question. He had been going downhill into the valley; by this time he was already far, far ahead. But in that momentary glimpse of him he had seen enough to know. The face was turned away, and the shadows under the trees were heavy, but the figure was beyond question the figure of — his brother Mark.

It was his brother, yet not his brother. It was Mark — but Mark altered. And the alteration was in some way — awful; just as the silent speed at which he had moved — the impossible speed in so dense a forest — was likewise awful. Then, still shaking inwardly with the suddenness of it all, Stephen realized that when he called aloud he had uttered certain definite words. And these words now came back to him —

"Mark, Mark! Don't go yet! Don't go — without me!"

Before, however, he could act, a most curious and unaccountable sensation of deadly faintness and pain came upon him, without cause, without explanation, so that he dropped backwards in momentary collapse, and but for the closeness of the tree stems would have fallen full length to the ground. From the center of the heart it came, spreading thence throughout his whole being like a swift and dreadful fever. All the muscles of his body relaxed; icy perspiration burst forth upon his skin; the pulses of life seemed suddenly reduced to the threshold beyond which they stop. There was a thick, rushing sound in his ears and his mind went utterly blank.

These were the sensations of death by suffocation. He knew this as certainly as though another doctor stood by his side and labeled each spasm, explained each successive sinking of the vital flame. He was passing through the last throes of a dying man. And then into his mind, thus deliberately left blank, rushed at lightning speed a whole series of the pictures of his past life. Even while his breath failed, he saw his thirty-five years pictorially, successively, yet in some queer fashion *at once*, pass through the lighted chambers of his brain. In this way, it is said, they pass through the brain of a drowning man during the last seconds before death.

Childhood rose about him with its scenes, figures, voices; the Kentish lawns where he had played with Mark in stained overalls; the summer-house where they had tea, the hay-fields where they romped. The scent of lime and walnut, of garden pinks, and roses by the tumbled rockery came back to his nostrils. . . . He heard the voices of grown-ups in the distance . . . faint barking of dogs . . . the carriage wheels upon the gravel drive . . . and then the sharp summons from the opened window — "Time to come in now! Time to come in. . . !"

Time to come in now. It all drove before him as of yesterday on the scented winds of childhood's summer days. . . . He heard his brother's voice — dreadfully faint and far away — calling him by name in the shrill accents of the boy: "Stevie — I say, you *might* shut up . . . and play properly. . . ."

And then followed the panorama of the thirty years, all the chief events drawn in steellike lines of white and black, vivid in sunshine, alive — right down to the present moment with the portentous dark shadow of his terrible Decision closing the series like a cloud.

Yes, like a smothering black cloud that blocked the way. There was nothing visible beyond it. There, for him, life ceased —

Only, as he gazed with inward-turned eyes that could not close even if they would, he saw to his amazement that the black cloud suddenly opened, and into a space of clear light there swam the vision, radiant as morning, of that dark young Eastern face — the face that held for him all the beauty in the world. The eyes instantly found his own, and smiled. Behind her, moreover, and beyond, before the moving vapors closed upon it, he saw a long vista of brilliance, crowded with pictures he could but half discern — as though, in spite of himself and his Decision, life continued — as though, too, it *continued with her.*

And instantly, with the sight and thought of her, the consuming faintness passed; strength returned to his body with the glow of life; the pain went; the pictures vanished; the cloud was no more. In his blood the pulses of life once again beat strong, and the blackness left his soul. The smile of those beloved eyes had been charged with the invitation to live. Although his determination remained unshaken, there shone behind it the joy of this potent magic: life with her. . . .

With a strong effort, at length he recovered himself and continued on his way. More or less familiar, of course, with the psychology of vision, he dimly understood that his experiences had been in some measure subjective — within himself. To find the line of demarcation, however, was beyond him. That Mark had wandered out to fight his own battle upon the mountains, and so come into this same valley, was well within the bounds of coincidence. But the nameless and dreadful alteration discerned in that swift moment of his passing — that remained inexplicable. Only he no longer thought about it. The glory of that sweet vision had bewildered him beyond any possibility of reason or analysis.

His watch told him that the hour was past five o'clock — ten minutes past, to be exact. He still had several hours before reaching the country he was familiar with nearer home. Following the trail at an increased pace, he presently saw patches of meadow glimmering between the thinning trees, and knew that the bottom of the valley was at last in sight.

"And Mark, God bless him, is down there too — somewhere!" he exclaimed aloud. "I shall surely find him." For, strange to say, nothing could have persuaded him that his twin was not wandering among the shadows of this peaceful and haunted valley with himself, and — that he would shortly find him.

XII

*A*nd a few minutes later he passed from the forest as through an open door and found himself before a farmhouse standing in a patch of bright green meadow against the mountainside. He was in need both of food and information.

The châlet, less lumbering and picturesque than those found in the Alps, had, nevertheless, the appearance of being exceedingly ancient. It was not toylike — as the Jura châlets sometimes are. Solidly built, its balcony and overhanging roof supported by immense beams of deeply stained wood, it stood so that the back walls merged into the mountain slope behind, and the arms of pine, spruce and fir seemed stretched out to include it among their shadows. A last ray of sunshine, dipping between two far summits overhead, touched it with pale gold, bringing out the rich beauty of the heavily-dyed beams. Though no one was visible at the moment, and no smoke rose from the shingled chimney, it had the appearance of being occupied, and Stephen approached it with the caution due to the first evidence of humanity he had come across since he entered the valley.

Under the shadow of the broad balcony roof he noticed that the door, like that of a stable, was in two parts, and, wondering rather to find it closed, he knocked firmly upon the upper half. Under the pressure of a second knock this upper half yielded slightly, though without opening. The lower half, however, evidently barred and bolted, remained unmoved.

The third time he knocked with more force than he intended, and the knock sounded loud and clamorous as a summons. From within, as though great spaces stretched beyond, came a murmur of voices, faint and muffled, and then almost immediately — the footsteps of someone coming softly up to open.

But, instead of the heavy brown door opening, there came a voice. He heard it, petrified with amazement. For it was a voice he knew — hushed, soft, lingering. His heart, hammering atrociously, seemed to leave its place, and cut his breath away.

"Stephen!" it murmured, calling him by name, "what are *you* doing here so soon? And what is it that you want?"

The knowledge that only this dark door separated him from her, at first bereft him of all power of speech or movement; and the possible significance of her words escaped him. Through the sweet confusion that turned his spirit faint he only remembered, flashlike, that she and her father were indeed to have left the hotel that very morning. After that his thought stopped dead.

Then, also flashlike, swept back upon him the memory of the figure that had passed him with averted face — and, with it, the clear conviction that at this moment Mark, too, was somewhere in this very valley, even close beside him. More: Mark was in this chalet — with her.

The torrent of speech that instantly crowded to his lips was almost too thick for utterance.

"Open, open, open!" was all he heard intelligibly from the throng of words that poured out. He raised his hands to push and force; but her reply again stopped him.

"Even if I open — *you* may not enter yet," came the whisper through the door. And this time he could almost have sworn that it sounded within himself rather than without.

"I must enter," he cried. "Open to me, I say!"

"But you are trembling —"

"Open to me, O my life! Open to me!"

"But your heart — it is shaking."

"Because you — you are so near," came in passionate, stammering tones. "Because you stand there beside me!" And then, before she could answer, or his will control the words, he had added: "And because Mark — my brother — is in there — with you —"

"Hush, hush!" came the soft, astonishing reply. "He is in here, true; but he is not with me. And it is for my sake that he has come — for my sake and for yours. My soul, alas! has led him to the gates . . ."

But Stephen's emotions had reached the breaking-point, and the necessity for action was upon him like a storm. He drew back a pace so as to fling himself better against the closed door, when to his utter surprise, it moved. The upper half swung slowly outwards, and he — saw.

He was aware of a vast room, with closely shuttered windows, that seemed to stretch beyond the walls into the wooded mountainside, thronged with moving figures, like forms of life gently gliding to and fro in some huge darkened tank; and there, framed against this opening — the girl herself. She stood, visible to the waist, radiant in the solitary beam of sunshine that reached the chalet, smiling down wondrously into his face with the same exquisite beauty in her eyes that he had seen before in the vision of the cloud: with, too, that supreme invitation in them — the invitation to live.

The loveliness blinded him. He could see the down upon her little dark cheeks where the sunlight kissed them; there was the cloud of hair upon her neck where his lips had lain; there, too, the dear, slight breast that not twenty-four hours ago had known the pressure of his arms. And, once again, driven forward by the love that triumphed over all obstacles, real or artificial, he advanced headlong with outstretched arms to take her.

"Katýa!" he cried, never thinking how passing strange it was that he knew her name at all, much more the endearing and shortened form of it. "Katýa!"

But the young girl held up her little brown hand against him with a gesture that was more strong to restrain than any number of bolted doors.

"Not here," she murmured, with her grave smile, while behind the words he caught in that darkened room the alternate hush and sighing as of a thousand sleepers. "Not here! You cannot see him now; for these are the Reception Halls of Death and here I stand in the Vestibule of the Beyond. Our way . . . your way and mine . . . lies farther yet . . . traced there since the beginning of the world . . . together . . ."

In quaintly broken English it was spoken, but his mind remembers the singular words in their more perfect form. Even this, however, came later. At the moment he only felt the twofold wave of love surge through him with a tide of power that threatened to break him asunder: he *must* hold her to his heart; he *must* come instantly to his brother's side, meet his eyes, have speech with him. The desire to enter that great darkened room and force a path through the dimly gliding forms to his brother became irresistible, while tearing upon its heels came like a fever of joy the meaning of the words she had just uttered, and especially of that last word:

"Together!"

Then, for an instant, all the forces in his being turned negative so that his will refused to act. The excess of feeling numbed him. A flying interval of knowledge, calm and certain, came to him. The exaltation of spirit which produced the pictures of all this spiritual clairvoyance moved a stage higher, and he realized that he witnessed an order of things pertaining to the world of eternal causes rather than of temporary effects. Someone had lifted the Veil.

With a feeling that he could only wait and let things take their extraordinary course, he stood still. For an instant, even less, he must have hidden his eyes in his hand, for when, a moment later, he again looked up, he saw that the half of the swinging door which had been open, was now closed. He stood alone upon the balcony. And the sunshine had faded entirely from the scene.

It was here, it seems, that the last vestige of self-control disappeared. He flung himself against the door; and the door met his assault like a wall of solid rock. Crying aloud alternately the names of his two loved ones, he turned, scarcely knowing what he did, and ran into the meadow. Dusk was about the chalet, drawing the encircling forests closer. Soon the true darkness would stalk down the slopes. The walls of the valley reared, it seemed, up to heaven.

Still calling, he ran about the walls, searching wildly for a way of entrance, his mind charged with bewildering fragments of what he had heard: "The Reception Halls of Death" — "The Vestibule of the Beyond" — "You cannot see him now" — "Our way lies farther — and *together. . . !*"

And, on the far side of the châlet, by the corner that touched the trees, he suddenly stopped, feeling his gaze drawn upwards, and there, pressed close against the windowpane of an upper room, saw that someone was peering down upon him.

With a sensation of freezing terror he realized that he was staring straight into the eyes of his brother Mark. Bent a little forward with the effort to look down, the face, pale and motionless, gazed into his own, but without the least sign of recognition. Not a feature moved: and although but a few feet separated the brothers, the face wore the dim, misty appearance of great distance. It was like the face of a man called suddenly from deep sleep — dazed, perplexed; nay, more — frightened and horribly distraught.

What Stephen read upon it, however, in that first moment of sight, was the signature of the great, eternal question men have asked since the beginning of time, yet never heard the answer. And into the heart of the twin the pain of it plunged like a sword.

"Mark!" he stammered, in that low voice the valley seemed to exact; "Mark! Is that really *you?*" Tears swam already in his eyes, and yearning in a hood choked his utterance.

And Mark, with a dreadful, steady stare that still held no touch of recognition, gazed down upon him from the closed window of that upper chamber, motionless, unblinking as an image of stone. It was almost like an imitation figure of himself — only with the effect of some added alteration. For alteration certainly there was — awful and un-known alteration — though Stephen was utterly unable to detect wherein it lay. And he remembered how the figure had passed him in the woods with averted face.

He made then, it seems, some violent sign or other, in response to which his brother at last moved — slowly opening the window. He leaned forward, stooping with lowered head and shoulders over the sill, while Stephen ran up against the wall beneath and craned up towards him. The two faces drew close; their eyes met clean and straight. Then the lips of Mark moved, and the distraught look half vanished within the borders of a little smile of puzzled and affectionate wonder.

"Stevie, old fellow," issued a tiny, faraway voice; "but where are you? I see you — so dimly?"

It was like a voice crying faintly down half-a-mile of distance. He shuddered to hear it.

"I'm here, Mark — close to you," he whispered.

"I hear your voice, I feel your presence," came the reply like a man talking in his sleep, "but I see you — as through a glass darkly. And I want to see you all clear, and close —"

"But *you!* Where are *you?*" interrupted Stephen, with anguish.

"Alone; quite alone — over here. And it's cold, oh, so cold!" The words came gently, half veiling a complaint. The wind caught them and ran round the walls towards the forest, wailing as it went.

"But how did you come, how did you come?" Stephen raised himself on tiptoe to catch the answer. But there was no answer. The face receded a little, and as it did so the wind, passing up the walls again, stirred the hair on the forehead. Stephen saw it move. He thought, too, the head moved with it, shaking slightly to and fro.

"Oh, but tell me, my dear, dear brother! Tell me —!" he cried, sweating horribly, his limbs shaking.

Mark made a curious gesture, withdrawing at the same time a little farther into the room behind, so that he now stood upright, half in shadow by the window. The alteration in him proclaimed itself more plainly, though still without betraying its exact nature. There was something about him that was terrible. And the air that came from the open window upon Stephen was so freezing that it seemed to turn the perspiration on his face into ice.

"I do not know; I do not remember," he heard the tiny voice inside the room, ever withdrawing. "Besides — I may not speak with you — yet; it is so difficult — and it hurts."

Stephen stretched out his body, the arms scraping the wooden walls above his head, trying to climb the smooth and slippery surface.

"For the love of God! " he cried with passion, "tell me what it all means and what you are doing here — you and — and — oh, and *all three of us?*" The words rang out through the silent valley.

But the other stood there motionless again by the window, his face distraught and dazed as though the effort of speech had already been too much for him. His image had begun to fade a little. He seemed, without moving, yet to be retreating into some sort of interior distance. Presently, it seemed, he would disappear altogether.

"I don't know," came the voice at length, fainter than before, half muffled. "I have been asleep, I think. I have just waked up, and come across from somewhere else — where we were all together, you and I and — and —"

Like his brother, he was unable to speak the name. He ended the sentence a moment later in a whisper that was only just audible. "But I cannot tell you *how* I came," he said, "for I do not know the words."

Stephen, then, with a violent leap tried to reach the windowsill and pull himself up. The distance was too great, however, and he fell back upon the grass, only just keeping his feet.

"I'm coming in to you," he cried out very loud. "Wait there for me! For the love of heaven, wait till I come to you. I'll break the doors in — !"

Once again Mark made that singular gesture; again he seemed to recede a little farther into a kind of veiled perspective that caused his appearance to fade still more; and, from an incredible distance — a distance that somehow conveyed an idea of appalling height — his thin, tiny voice floated down upon his brother from the fading lips of shadow.

"Old fellow, don't you come! You are not ready — and it is too cold here. I shall wait, Stevie, I shall wait for you. Later — I mean farther from hear — we shall one day all three be together. . . . Only you cannot understand now. I am here for your sake, old fellow, and for hers. She loves us both, but it is . . . you . . . she loves . . . the best. . . ."

The whispering voice rose suddenly on these last words into a long high cry that the wind instantly caught away and buried far in the smothering silences of the woods. For, at the same moment, Mark had come with a swift rush back to the window, had leaned out and stretched both hands towards his brother underneath. And his face had cleared and smiled. Caught within that smile, the awful change in him had vanished.

Stephen turned and made a mad rush round the chalet to find the door he would batter in with his hands and feet and body. He searched in vain, however, for in the shadows the supporting beams of the building were indistinguishable from the stems of the trees behind; the roof sank away, blotted out by the gloom of the branches, and the darkness now wove forest, sky and mountain into a uniform black sheet against which no item was separately visible.

There was no châlet any longer. He was simply battering with bruised hands and feet upon the solid trunks of pines and spruces in his path; which he continued to do, calling ever aloud for Mark, until finally he grew dizzy with exhaustion and fell to the ground in a state of semiconsciousness.

And for the best part of half-an-hour he lay there motionless upon the moss, while the vast hands of Night drew the cloak of her softest darkness over valley and mountain, covering his small body with as much care as she covered the sky, the hemisphere, and all those leagues of velvet forest.

XIII

*I*t was not long before he came to himself again — shivering with cold, for the perspiration had dried upon him where he lay. He got up and ran. The night was now fairly down, and the keen air stung his cheeks. But, with a sure instinct not to be denied, he took the direction of home.

He traveled at an extraordinary pace, considering the thickness of the trees and the darkness. How he got out of the valley he does not remember; nor how he found his way over the intervening ridges that lay between him and the country he knew. At the back of his mind crashed and tumbled the loose fragments of all he had seen and heard, forming as yet no coherent pattern. For himself, indeed, the details were of small interest. He was a man under sentence of death. His determination, in spite of everything, remained unshaken. In a few short hours he would be gone.

Yet, with the habit of the professional mind, he tried a little to sort out things. During that state of singular exaltation, for instance, he understood vaguely that his deep longings had somehow translated themselves into act and scene. For these longings were life; his decision negatived them; hence, they dramatized themselves pictorially with what vividness his imagination allowed.

They were dramatized inventions, singularly elaborate, of the emotions that burned so fiercely within. All were projections of his consciousness, maimed and incomplete, masquering as persons before his inner vision, it began with the singular sensations of death by drowning he had experienced. From that moment the other forces at work in the problem had taken their cue and played their part more or less convincingly, according to their strength. . . .

He thought and argued a great deal as he hurried homewards through the night. But all the time he knew that it was untrue. He had no real explanation at all!

From the high ridges, cold and bleak under the stars, swept by the free wind of night, he ran almost the entire way. It was downhill. And during that violent descent of nearly an hour the details of his "going" shaped themselves. Until then he had formed no definite plans. Now he settled everything. He chose the very pool where the water coiled and bubbled as in a cauldron just where the little torrent made a turn above their house; he decided upon the very terms of the letter he would leave behind. He would put it on the kitchen table so that they should know where to find him.

He urged his pace tremendously, for the idea that his brother would have left — that he would find him gone — haunted him. It grew, doubtless, out of that singular, detailed vision that had come upon him in his great weakness in the valley. He was terrified that he would not see his brother again — that he had already gone deliberately after her.

"I *must* see Mark once more. I *must* get home before he leaves!" flashed the strong thought continually in his mind, making him run like a deer down the winding trail.

It was after ten o'clock when he reached the little clearing behind the chalet, panting with exhaustion, blinded with perspiration. There was no light visible; all the windows were dark; but presently he made out a figure moving to and fro below the balcony. It was *not* Mark — he saw that in a flash. It moved oddly. A sound of moaning reached him at the same time. And then he saw that it was the figure of the peasant woman who cooked for them, Marie Petavel.

And the instant he saw who it was, and heard her moaning, he knew what had happened. Mark had left a letter to explain — and gone: gone after the girl. His heart sank into death.

The woman came forward heavily through the darkness, the dew-drenched grass swishing audibly against her skirts. And the words he heard were precisely what he had expected to hear, though patois and excitement rendered them difficult —

"Your brother — oh your poor brother, Monsieur le Docteur — he — has gone!"

And then he saw the piece of white paper glimmering in her hands as she stood quite close. He took it mechanically from her. It was the letter Mark had left behind to explain.

But before Stephen had time to read it, a man with a lantern came out of the barn that stood behind the house. It was her husband. He came slowly towards them.

"We searched for you, oh, we searched," he said in a thick voice, "my son went as far as Buttes even, and hasn't come back yet. You've been long, too long away . . ."

He stopped short and glanced down at his wife, telling her roughly to cease her stupid weeping. Stephen, shaking inwardly, with an icy terror in his blood, began to feel that things were not precisely as he had anticipated. Something else was the matter. The expression in the face of the peasant as the lantern's glare fell upon it came to him suddenly with the shock of a revelation.

"You have told monsieur — all?" the man whispered, stooping to his wife. She shook her head; and her husband led the way without another word. The interval of a few seconds seemed endless to Stephen; he was trembling all over like a man with the ague. Behind them the old woman floundered through the wet grass, moaning to herself.

"No one would have believed it could have happened — anything of *that* sort," the man mumbled. The lantern was unsteady in his hand. The next minute the barn, like some monstrous animal, rose against the stars, and the huge wooden doors gaped wide before them.

The peasant, uncovering his head, went first, and Stephen, following with stumbling footsteps, saw the shadows of the beams and posts shift across the boarded floor. Against the wall, whither the man led, was a small littered heap of hay, and upon this, covered by a white sheet, was stretched a human body. The peasant drew back the sheet gently with his heavy brown hand, stooping close over it so that the lantern threw its light full upon the act.

And Stephen, tumbling forward, scarcely knowing what he did, without further warning or preparation, looked down upon the face of his brother Mark. The eyes stared fixedly into — nothing; the features wore the distraught expression he had seen upon them a few hours before through the windowpane of that upper chamber.

"We found him in that deep pool just where the stream makes the quick turn above the house," the peasant whispered. "He left a bit of paper on the kitchen table to say where he would be. It was after dark when we got there. His watch had stopped, though, long before —" He muttered on unintelligibly.

Stephen looked up at the man, unable to utter a word, and the man replied to the unspoken question — "At ten minutes past five the watch had stopped," he said. "That was when the water reached it."

By the flicker of the lantern, then, sitting beside that still figure covered with the sheet, Stephen read the letter Mark had left for him —

"Stevie, old fellow, one of us, you know, has got to — go; and it is better, I think, that it should not be you. I know all you have been through, for I have fought and suffered every step with you. I have been along the same path, loving her too much for you, and you too much for her. And I leave her to you, boy, because I am convinced she now loves you even as she first believed she loved me. But all that evening she cried incessantly for you. More I cannot explain to you now; she will do that. And she need never know more than that I have withdrawn in your favor: she need never know *how*. Perhaps, one day, when there is no marriage or giving in marriage, we may all three be together, and happy. I have often wondered, as you know . . ."

The remainder of the sentence was scratched out and illegible.

". . . And, if it be possible, old fellow, of course *I shall wait.*"

Then came more words blackened out.

". . . I am now going, within a few minutes of writing this last word to you of blessing and forgiveness (for I know you will want that, although there is nothing, *nothing* to forgive!) – going down into that Lost Valley her father told us about – the Valley hidden among these mountains we love – the Lost Valley where even the unhappy dead find peace. There I shall wait for you both. – MARK."

*S*everal weeks later, before he took the train eastwards, Stephen retraced his steps to the farmhouse where he had bought milk and asked for directions. Thence for some distance he followed the path he well remembered. At a point, however, the confusion of the woods grew strangely upon him. The mountains, true to the map, were not true to his recollections. The trail stopped; high, unknown ridges intervened; and no such deep and winding valley as he had traveled that afternoon for so many hours was anywhere to be found. The map, the peasants, the very configuration of the landscape even, denied its existence.

The Wendigo

A considerable number of hunting parties were out that year without
finding so much as a fresh trail; for the moose were uncommonly shy,
and the various Nimrods returned to the bosoms of their respective
families with the best excuses the facts of their imaginations could
suggest. Dr. Cathcart, among others, came back without a trophy; but
he brought instead the memory of an experience which he declares was
worth all the bull moose that had ever been shot. But then Cathcart, of
Aberdeen, was interested in other things besides moose — amongst them
the vagaries of the human mind. This particular story, however, found
no mention in his book on *Collective Hallucination* for the simple reason
(so he confided once to a fellow colleague) that he himself played too
intimate a part in it to form a competent judgment of the affair as a
whole. . . .

Besides himself and his guide, Hank Davis, there was young Simpson,
his nephew, a divinity student destined for the "Wee Kirk" (then on his
first visit to Canadian backwoods), and the latter's guide, Défago. Joseph
Défago was a French "Canuck," who had strayed from his native
Province of Quebec years before, and had got caught in Rat Portage
when the Canadian Pacific Railway was a-building; a man who, in
addition to his unparalleled knowledge of woodcraft and bush-lore,
could also sing the old *voyageur* songs and tell a capital hunting yarn
into the bargain. He was deeply susceptible, moreover, to that singular
spell which the wilderness lays upon certain lonely natures, and he loved
the wild solitudes with a kind of romantic passion that amounted
almost to an obsession. The life of the backwoods fascinated him —
whence, doubtless, his surpassing efficiency in dealing with their mys-
teries.

On this particular expedition he was Hank's choice. Hank knew him
and swore by him. He also swore at him, "jest as a pal might," and since
he had a vocabulary of picturesque, if utterly meaningless, oaths, the
conversation between the two stalwart and hardy woodsmen was often

of a rather lively description. This river of expletives, however, Hank agreed to dam a little out of respect for his old "hunting boss," Dr. Cathcart, whom of course he addressed after the fashion of the country as "Doc," and also because he understood that young Simpson was already a "bit of a parson." He had, however, one objection to Défago, and one only — which was, that the French Canadian sometimes exhibited what Hank described as "the output of a cursed and dismal mind," meaning apparently that he sometimes was true to type, Latin type, and suffered fits of a kind of silent moroseness when nothing could induce him to utter speech. Défago, that is to say, was imaginative and melancholy. And, as a rule, it was too long a spell of "civilization" that induced the attacks, for a few days of the wilderness invariably cured them.

This, then, was the party of four that found themselves in camp the last week in October of that "shy moose year" 'way up in the wilderness north of Rat Portage — a forsaken and desolate country. There was also Punk, an Indian, who had accompanied Dr. Cathcart and Hank on their hunting trips in previous years, and who acted as cook. His duty was merely to stay in camp, catch fish, and prepare venison steaks and coffee at a few minutes' notice. He dressed in the worn-out clothes bequeathed to him by former patrons, and, except for his coarse black hair and dark skin, he looked in these city garments no more like a real redskin than a stage Negro looks like a real African. For all that, however, Punk had in him still the instincts of his dying race; his taciturn silence and his endurance survived; also his superstition.

The party round the blazing fire that night were despondent, for a week had passed without a single sign of recent moose discovering itself. Défago had sung his song and plunged into a story, but Hank, in bad humor, reminded him so often that "he kep' mussing-up the fac's so, that it was 'most all nothin' but a petered-out lie," that the Frenchman had finally subsided into a sulky silence which nothing seemed likely to break. Dr. Cathcart and his nephew were fairly done after an exhausting day. Punk was washing up the dishes, grunting to himself under the lean-to of branches, where he later also slept. No one troubled to stir the slowly dying fire. Overhead the stars were brilliant in a sky quite wintry, and there was so little wind that ice was already forming stealthily along the shores of the still lake behind them. The silence of the vast listening forest stole forward and enveloped them.

Hank broke in suddenly with his nasal voice.

"I'm in favor of breaking new ground tomorrow, Doc," he observed with energy, looking across at his employer. "We don't stand a dead Dago's chance around here."

"Agreed," said Cathcart, always a man of few words. "Think the idea's good."

"Sure pop, it's good," Hank resumed with confidence. "S'pose, now, you and I strike west, up Garden Lake way for a change! None of us ain't touched that quiet bit o' land yet —"

"I'm with you."

"And you, Défago, take Mr. Simpson along in the small canoe, skip across the lake, portage over into Fifty Island Water, and take a good squint down that thar southern shore. The moose 'yarded' there like hell last year, and for all we know they may be doin' it agin this year jest to spite us."

Défago, keeping his eyes on the fire, said nothing by way of reply. He was still offended, possibly, about his interrupted story.

"No one's been up that way this year, an' I'll lay my bottom dollar on *that!*" Hank added with emphasis, as though he had a reason for knowing. He looked over at his partner sharply. "Better take the little silk tent and stay away a couple o' nights," he concluded, as though the matter were definitely settled. For Hank was recognized as general organizer of the hunt, and in charge of the party.

It was obvious to anyone that Défago did not jump at the plan, but his silence seemed to convey something more than ordinary disapproval, and across his sensitive dark face there passed a curious expression like a flash of firelight — not so quickly, however, that the three men had not time to catch it.

"He funked for some reason, *I* thought," Simpson said afterwards in the tent he shared with his uncle. Dr. Cathcart made no immediate reply, although the look had interested him enough at the time for him to make a mental note of it. The expression had caused him a passing uneasiness he could not quite account for at the moment.

But Hank, of course, had been the first to notice it, and the odd thing was that instead of becoming explosive or angry over the other's reluctance, he at once began to humor him a bit.

"But there ain't no *speshul* reason why no one's been up there this year," he said with a perceptible hush in his tone; "not the reason you mean, anyway! Las' year it was the fires that kep' folks out, and this year I guess — I guess it jest happened so, that's all!" His manner was clearly meant to be encouraging.

Joseph Défago raised his eyes a moment, then dropped them again. A breath of wind stole out of the forest and stirred the embers into a passing blaze. Dr. Cathcart again noticed the expression in the guide's face, and again he did not like it. But this time the nature of the look betrayed itself. In those eyes, for an instant, he caught the gleam of a man scared in his very soul. It disquieted him more than he cared to admit.

"Bad Indians up that way?" he asked, with a laugh to ease matters a little, while Simpson, too sleepy to notice this subtle by-play, moved off to bed with a prodigious yawn; "or — or anything wrong with the country?" he added, when his nephew was out of hearing.

Hank met his eye with something less than his usual frankness.

"He's jest skeered," he replied good-humoredly. "Skeered stiff about some ole feery tale! That's all, ain't it, ole pard?" And he gave Défago a friendly kick on the moccasined foot that lay nearest the fire.

Défago looked up quickly, as from an interrupted reverie, a reverie, however, that had not prevented his seeing all that went on about him.

"Skeered — *nuthin'!*" he answered, with a flush of defiance. "There's nuthin' in the Bush that can skeer Joseph Défago, and don't you forget it!" And the natural energy with which he spoke made it impossible to know whether he told the whole truth or only a part of it.

Hank turned towards the doctor. He was just going to add something when he stopped abruptly and looked round. A sound close behind them in the darkness made all three start. It was old Punk, who had moved up from his lean-to while they talked and now stood there just beyond the circle of firelight — listening.

"'Nother time, Doc!" Hank whispered, with a wink, "when the gallery ain't stepped down into the stalls!" And, springing to his feet, he slapped the Indian on the back and cried noisily, "Come up t' the fire an' warm yer dirty red skin a bit." He dragged him towards the blaze and threw more wood on. "That was a mighty good feed you give us an hour or two back," he continued heartily, as though to set the man's thoughts on another scent, "and it ain't Christian to let you stand out there freezin' yer ole soul to hell while we're gettin' all good an' toasted!" Punk moved in and warmed his feet, smiling darkly at the other's volubility which he only half understood, but saying nothing. And presently Dr. Cathcart, seeing that further conversation was impossible, followed his nephew's example and moved off to the tent, leaving the three men smoking over the now blazing fire.

It is not easy to undress in a small tent without waking one's companion, and Cathcart, hardened and warm-blooded as he was in spite of his fifty odd years, did what Hank would have described as "considerable of his twilight" in the open. He noticed, during the process, that Punk had meanwhile gone back to his lean-to, and that Hank and Défago were at it hammer and tongs, or, rather, hammer and anvil, the little French Canadian being the anvil. It was all very like the conventional stage picture of Western melodrama: the fire lighting up their faces with patches of alternate red and black; Défago, in slouch hat and moccasins in the part of the "badlands" villain; Hank, open-faced and hatless, with that reckless fling of his shoulders, the honest and deceived hero; and old Punk, eavesdropping in the background, supplying the atmosphere of mystery. The doctor smiled as he noticed the details; but at the same time something deep within him – he hardly knew what – shrank a little, as though an almost imperceptible breath of warning had touched the surface of his soul and was gone again before he could seize it. Probably it was traceable to that "scared expression" he had seen in the eyes of Défago; "probably" – for this hint of fugitive emotion otherwise escaped his usually so keen analysis. Défago, he was vaguely aware, might cause trouble somehow . . . He was not as steady a guide as Hank, for instance . . . Further than that he could not get . . .

He watched the men a moment longer before diving into the stuffy tent where Simpson already slept soundly. Hank, he saw, was swearing like a mad African in a New York nigger saloon; but it was the swearing of "affection." The ridiculous oaths flew freely now that the cause of their obstruction was asleep. Presently he put his arm almost tenderly upon his comrade's shoulder, and they moved off together into the shadows where their tent stood faintly glimmering. Punk, too, a moment later followed their example and disappeared between his odorous blankets in the opposite direction.

Dr. Cathcart then likewise turned in, weariness and sleep still fighting in his mind with an obscure curiosity to know what it was that had scared Défago about the country up Fifty Island Water way, – wondering, too, why Punk's presence had prevented the completion of what Hank had to say. Then sleep overtook him. He would know tomorrow. Hank would tell him the story while they trudged after the elusive moose.

Deep silence fell about the little camp, planted there so audaciously in the jaws of the wilderness. The lake gleamed like a sheet of black glass beneath the stars. The cold air pricked. In the drafts of night that poured their silent tide from the depths of the forest, with messages from distant ridges and from lakes just beginning to freeze, there lay already the faint, bleak odors of coming winter. White men, with their dull scent, might never have divined them; the fragrance of the wood fire would have concealed from them these almost electrical hints of moss and bark and hardening swamp a hundred miles away. Even Hank and Défago, subtly in league with the soul of the woods as they were, would probably have spread their delicate nostrils in vain. . . .

But an hour later, when all slept like the dead, old Punk crept from his blankets and went down to the shore of the lake like a shadow – silently, as only Indian blood can move. He raised his head and looked about him. The thick darkness rendered sight of small avail, but, like the animals, he possessed other senses that darkness could not mute. He listened — then sniffed the air. Motionless as a hemlock stem he stood there. After five minutes again he lifted his head and sniffed, and yet once again. A tingling of the wonderful nerves that betrayed itself by no outer sign, ran through him as he tasted the keen air. Then, merging his figure into the surrounding blackness in a way that only wild men and animals understand, he turned, still moving like a shadow, and went stealthily back to his lean-to and his bed.

And soon after he slept, the change of wind he had divined stirred gently the reflection of the stars within the lake. Rising among the far ridges of the country beyond Fifty Island Water, it came from the direction in which he had stared, and it passed over the sleeping camp with a faint and sighing murmur through the tops of the big trees that was almost too delicate to be audible. With it, down the desert paths of night, though too faint, too high even for the Indian's hairlike nerves, there passed a curious, thin odor, strangely disquieting, an odor of something that seemed unfamiliar — utterly unknown.

The French Canadian and the man of Indian blood each stirred uneasily in his sleep just about this time, though neither of them woke. Then the ghost of that unforgettably strange odor passed away and was lost among the leagues of tenantless forest beyond.

In the morning the camp was astir before the sun. There had been a light fall of snow during the night and the air was sharp. Punk had done his duty betimes, for the odors of coffee and fried bacon reached every tent. All were in good spirits.

"Wind's shifted!" cried Hank vigorously, watching Simpson and his guide already loading the small canoe. "It's across the lake — dead right for you fellers. And the snow'll make bully trails! If there's any moose mussing around up thar, they'll not get so much as a tail-end scent of you with the wind as it is. Good luck, Monsieur Défago!" he added, facetiously giving the name its French pronunciation for once, "*bonne chance!*"

Défago returned the good wishes, apparently in the best of spirits, the silent mood gone. Before eight o'clock old Punk had the camp to himself, Cathcart and Hank were far along the trail that led westwards, while the canoe that carried Défago and Simpson, with silk tent and grub for two days, was already a dark speck bobbing on the bosom of the lake, going due east.

The wintry sharpness of the air was tempered now by a sun that topped the wooded ridges and blazed with a luxurious warmth upon the world of lake and forest below; loons flew skimming through the sparkling spray that the wind lifted; divers shook their dripping heads to the sun and popped smartly out of sight again; and as far as eye could reach rose the leagues of endless, crowding Bush, desolate in its lonely sweep and grandeur, untrodden by foot of man, and stretching its mighty and unbroken carpet right up to the frozen shores of Hudson Bay.

Simpson, who saw it all for the first time as he paddled hard in the bows of the dancing canoe, was enchanted by its austere beauty. His heart drank in the sense of freedom and great spaces just as his lungs drank in the cool and perfumed wind. Behind him in the stern seat, singing fragments of his native chanties, Défago steered the craft of birch bark like a thing of life, answering cheerfully all his companion's questions. Both were gay and light-hearted. On such occasions men lose the superficial, worldly distinctions; they become human beings working together for a common end. Simpson, the employer, and Défago the employed, among these primitive forces, were simply — two men, the "guider" and the "guided." Superior knowledge, of course, assumed control, and the younger man fell without a second thought into the quasi-subordinate position. He never dreamed of objecting when Défago dropped the "Mr.," and addressed him as "Say, Simpson," or "Simpson, boss," which was invariably the case before they reached the farther shore after a stiff paddle of twelve miles against a head wind. He only laughed, and liked it; then ceased to notice it at all.

For this "divinity student" was a young man of parts and character, though as yet, of course, untraveled; and on this trip — the first time he had seen any country but his own and little Switzerland — the huge scale of things somewhat bewildered him. It was one thing, he realized, to hear about primeval forests, but quite another to see them. While to dwell in them and seek acquaintance with their wild life was, again, an initiation that no intelligent man could undergo without a certain shifting of personal values hitherto held for permanent and sacred.

Simpson knew the first faint indication of this emotion when he held the new .303 rifle in his hands and looked along its pair of faultless, gleaming barrels. The three days' journey to their headquarters, by lake and portage, had carried the process a stage farther. And now that he was about to plunge beyond even the fringe of wilderness where they were camped into the virgin heart of uninhabited regions as vast as Europe itself, the true nature of the situation stole upon him with an effect of delight and awe that his imagination was fully capable of appreciating. It was himself and Défago against a multitude — at least, against a Titan!

The bleak splendors of these remote and lonely forests rather overwhelmed him with the sense of his own littleness. That stern quality of the tangled backwoods which can only be described as merciless and terrible, rose out of these far blue woods swimming upon the horizon, and revealed itself. He understood the silent warning. He realized his own utter helplessness. Only Défago, as a symbol of a distant civilization where man was master, stood between him and a pitiless death by exhaustion and starvation.

It was thrilling to him, therefore, to watch Défago turn over the canoe upon the shore, pack the paddles carefully underneath, and then proceed to "blaze" the spruce stems for some distance on either side of an almost invisible trail, with the careless remark thrown in, "Say, Simpson, if anything happens to me, you'll find the canoe all correc' by these marks; – then strike doo west into the sun to hit the home camp agin, see?"

It was the most natural thing in the world to say, and he said it without any noticeable inflexion of the voice, only it happened to express the youth's emotions at the moment with an utterance that was symbolic of the situation and of his own helplessness as a factor in it. He was alone with Défago in a primitive world: that was all. The canoe, another symbol of man's ascendancy, was now to be left behind. Those small yellow patches, made on the trees by the axe, were the only indications of its hiding place.

Meanwhile, shouldering the packs between them, each man carrying his own rifle, they followed the slender trail over rocks and fallen trunks and across half-frozen swamps; skirting numerous lakes that fairly gemmed the forest, their borders fringed with mist; and towards five o'clock found themselves suddenly on the edge of the woods, looking out across a large sheet of water in front of them, dotted with pine-clad islands of all describable shapes and sizes.

"Fifty Island Water," announced Défago wearily, "and the sun jest goin' to dip his bald old head into it!" he added, with unconscious poetry; and immediately they set about pitching camp for the night.

In a very few minutes, under those skillful hands that never made a movement too much or a movement too little, the silk tent stood taut and cozy, the beds of balsam boughs ready laid, and a brisk cooking fire burned with the minimum of smoke. While the young Scotchman cleaned the fish they had caught trolling behind the canoe, Défago "guessed" he would "jest as soon" take a turn through the Bush for indications of moose. "*May* come across a trunk where they bin and rubbed horns," he said, as he moved off, "or feedin' on the last of the maple leaves" – and he was gone.

His small figure melted away like a shadow in the dusk, while Simpson noted with a kind of admiration how easily the forest absorbed him into herself. A few steps, it seemed, and he was no longer visible.

Yet there was little underbrush hereabouts; the trees stood somewhat apart, well spaced; and in the clearings grew silver birch and maple, spearlike and slender, against the immense stems of spruce and hemlock. But for occasional prostrate monsters, and the boulders of grey rock that thrust uncouth shoulders here and there out of the ground, it might well have been a bit of park in the Old Country. Almost, one might have seen in it the hand of man. A little to the right, however, began the great burned section, miles in extent, proclaiming its real character — *brulé,* as it is called, where the fires of the previous year had raged for weeks, and the blackened stumps now rose gaunt and ugly, bereft of branches, like gigantic match heads stuck into the ground, savage and desolate beyond words. The perfume of charcoal and rain-soaked ashes still hung faintly about it.

The dusk rapidly deepened; the glades grew dark; the crackling of the fire and the wash of little waves along the rocky lake shore were the only sounds audible. The wind had dropped with the sun, and in all that vast world of branches nothing stirred. Any moment, it seemed, the woodland gods, who are to be worshipped in silence and loneliness, might stretch their mighty and terrific outlines among the trees. In front, through doorways pillared by huge straight stems, lay the stretch of Fifty Island Water, a crescent-shaped lake some fifteen miles from tip to tip, and perhaps five miles across where they were camped. A sky of rose and saffron, more clear than any atmosphere Simpson had ever known, still dropped its pale streaming fires across the waves, where the islands — a hundred, surely, rather than fifty — floated like the fairy barques of some enchanted fleet. Fringed with pines, whose crests fingered most delicately the sky, they almost seemed to move upwards as the light faded — about to weigh anchor and navigate the pathways of the heavens instead of the currents of their native and desolate lake.

And strips of colored cloud, like flaunting pennons, signaled their departure to the stars. . . .

The beauty of the scene was strangely uplifting. Simpson smoked the fish and burned his fingers into the bargain in his efforts to enjoy it and at the same time tend the frying pan and the fire. Yet, ever at the back of his thoughts, lay that other aspect of the wilderness: the indifference to human life, the merciless spirit of desolation which took no note of man. The sense of his utter loneliness, now that even Défago had gone, came close as he looked about him and listened for the sound of his companion's returning footsteps.

There was pleasure in the sensation, yet with it a perfectly comprehensible alarm. And instinctively the thought stirred in him: "What should I — *could* I, do — if anything happened and he did not come back — ?"

They enjoyed their well-earned supper, eating untold quantities of fish, and drinking unmilked tea strong enough to kill men who had not covered thirty miles of hard "going," eating little on the way. And when it was over, they smoked and told stories round the blazing fire, laughing, stretching weary limbs, and discussing plans for the morrow. Défago was in excellent spirits, though disappointed at having no signs of moose to report. But it was dark and he had not gone far. The *brulé*, too, was bad. His clothes and hands were smeared with charcoal. Simpson, watching him, realized with renewed vividness their position — alone together in the wilderness.

"Défago," he said presently, "these woods, you know, are a bit too big to feel quite at home in — to feel comfortable in, I mean. . . ! Eh?" He merely gave expression to the mood of the moment; he was hardly prepared for the earnestness, the solemnity even, with which the guide took him up.

"You've hit it right, Simpson, boss," he replied, fixing his searching brown eyes on his face, "and that's the truth, sure. There's no end to 'em — no end at all." Then he added in a lowered tone as if to himself, "There's lots found out *that*, and gone plumb to pieces!"

But the man's gravity of manner was not quite to the other's liking; it was a little too suggestive for this scenery and setting; he was sorry he had broached the subject. He remembered suddenly how his uncle had told him that men were sometimes stricken with a strange fever of the wilderness, when the seduction of the uninhabited wastes caught them so fiercely that they went forth, half fascinated, half deluded, to their death. And he had a shrewd idea that his companion held something in sympathy with that queer type. He led the conversation on to other topics, on to Hank and the doctor, for instance, and the natural rivalry as to who should get the first sight of moose.

"If they went doo west," observed Défago carelessly, "there's sixty miles between us now — with ole Punk at halfway house eatin' himself full to bustin' with fish and coffee." They laughed together over the picture. But the casual mention of those sixty miles again made Simpson realize the prodigious scale of this land where they hunted; sixty miles was a mere step; two hundred little more than a step. Stories of lost hunters rose persistently before his memory. The passion and mystery of homeless and wandering men, seduced by the beauty of great forests, swept his soul in a way too vivid to be quite pleasant. He wondered vaguely whether it was the mood of his companion that invited the unwelcome suggestion with such persistence.

"Sing us a song, Défago, if you're not too tired," he asked; "one of those old *voyageur* songs you sang the other night." He handed his tobacco pouch to the guide and then filled his own pipe, while the Canadian, nothing loath, sent his light voice across the lake in one of those plaintive, almost melancholy chanties with which lumbermen and trappers lessen the burden of their labor. There was an appealing and romantic flavor about it, something that recalled the atmosphere of the old pioneer days when Indians and wilderness were leagued together, battles frequent, and the Old Country farther off than it is today. The sound traveled pleasantly over the water, but the forest at their backs seemed to swallow it down with a single gulp that permitted neither echo nor resonance.

It was in the middle of the third verse that Simpson noticed something unusual — something that brought his thoughts back with a rush from faraway scenes. A curious change had come into the man's voice. Even before he knew what it was, uneasiness caught him, and looking up quickly, he saw that Défago, though still singing, was peering about him into the Bush, as though he heard or saw something. His voice grew fainter — dropped to a hush — then ceased altogether. The same instant, with a movement amazingly alert, he started to his feet and stood upright — *sniffing the air.* Like a dog scenting game, he drew the air into his nostrils in short, sharp breaths, turning quickly as he did so in all directions, and finally "pointing" down the lake shore, east-wards. It was a performance unpleasantly suggestive and at the same time singularly dramatic. Simpson's heart fluttered disagreeably as he watched it.

"Lord, man! How you made me jump!" he exclaimed, on his feet beside him the same instant, and peering over his shoulder into the sea of darkness. "What's up? Are you frightened — ?"

Even before the question was out of his mouth he knew it was foolish, for any man with a pair of eyes in his head could see that the Canadian had turned white down to his very gills. Not even sunburn and the glare of the fire could hide that.

The student felt himself trembling a little, weakish in the knees. "What's up?" he repeated quickly. "D'you smell moose? Or anything queer, anything — wrong?" He lowered his voice instinctively.

The forest pressed round them with its encircling wall; the nearer tree stems gleamed like bronze in the firelight; beyond that — blackness, and, so far as he could tell, a silence of death. Just behind them a passing puff of wind lifted a single leaf, looked at it, then laid it softly down again without disturbing the rest of the covey. It seemed as if a million invisible causes had combined just to produce that single visible effect.

Other life pulsed about them — and was gone.

Défago turned abruptly; the livid hue of his face had turned to a dirty grey.

"I never said I heered — or smelt — nuthin'," he said slowly and emphatically, in an oddly altered voice that conveyed somehow a touch of defiance. "I was only — takin' a look round — so to speak. It's always a mistake to be too previous with yer questions." Then he added suddenly with obvious effort, in his more natural voice, "Have you got the matches, Boss Simpson?" and proceeded to light the pipe he had half filled just before he began to sing.

Without speaking another word they sat down again by the fire. Défago changing his side so that he could face the direction the wind came from. For even a tenderfoot could tell that. Défago changed his position in order to hear and smell — all there was to be heard and smelt. And, since he now faced the lake with his back to the trees it was evidently nothing in the forest that had sent so strange and sudden a warning to his marvelously trained nerves.

"Guess now I don't feel like singing any," he explained presently of his own accord. "That song kinder brings back memories that's troublesome to me; I never oughter've begun it. It sets me on t' imagining things, see?"

Clearly the man was still fighting with some profoundly moving emotion. He wished to excuse himself in the eyes of the other. But the explanation, in that it was only a part of the truth, was a lie, and he knew perfectly well that Simpson was not deceived by it. For nothing could explain away the livid terror that had dropped over his face while he stood there sniffing the air. And nothing — no amount of blazing fire, or chatting on ordinary subjects — could make that camp exactly as it had been before. The shadow of an unknown horror, naked if unguessed, that had flashed for an instant in the face and gestures of the guide, had also communicated itself, vaguely and therefore more potently, to his companion. The guide's visible efforts to dissemble the truth only made things worse. Moreover, to add to the younger man's uneasiness, was the difficulty, nay, the impossibility he felt of asking questions, and also his complete ignorance as to the cause . . . Indians, wild animals, forest fires — all these, he knew, were wholly out of the question. His imagination searched vigorously, but in vain. . . .

*Y*et, somehow or other, after another long spell of smoking, talking and roasting themselves before the great fire, the shadow that had so suddenly invaded their peaceful camp began to shirt. Perhaps Défago's efforts, or the return of his quiet and normal attitude accomplished this; perhaps Simpson himself had exaggerated the affair out of all proportion to the truth; or possibly the vigorous air of the wilderness brought its own powers of healing. Whatever the cause, the feeling of immediate horror seemed to have passed away as mysteriously as it had come, for nothing occurred to feed it. Simpson began to feel that he had permitted himself the unreasoning terror of a child. He put it down partly to a certain subconscious excitement that this wild and immense scenery generated in his blood, partly to the spell of solitude, and partly to overfatigue. That pallor in the guide's face was, of course, uncommonly hard to explain, yet it *might* have been due in some way to an effect of firelight, or his own imagination . . . He gave it the benefit of the doubt; he was Scotch.

When a somewhat unordinary emotion has disappeared, the mind always finds a dozen ways of explaining away its causes . . . Simpson lit a last pipe and tried to laugh to himself. On getting home to Scotland it would make quite a good story. He did not realize that this laughter was a sign that terror still lurked in the recesses of his soul — that, in fact, it was merely one of the conventional signs by which a man, seriously alarmed, tries to persuade himself that he is *not* so.

Défago, however, heard that low laughter and looked up with surprise on his face. The two men stood, side by side, kicking the embers about before going to bed. It was ten o'clock — a late hour for hunters to be still awake.

"What's ticklin' yer?" he asked in his ordinary tone, yet gravely.

"I — I was thinking of our little toy woods at home, just at that moment," stammered Simpson, coming back to what really dominated his mind, and startled by the question, "and comparing them to — to all this," and he swept his arm round to indicate the Bush.

A pause followed in which neither of them said anything.

"All the same I wouldn't laugh about it, if I was you," Défago added, looking over Simpson's shoulder into the shadows. "There's places in there nobody won't never see into — nobody knows what lives in there either."

"Too big — too far off?" The suggestion in the guide's manner was immense and horrible.

Défago nodded. The expression on his face was dark. He, too, felt uneasy. The younger man understood that in a *hinterland* of this size there might well be depths of wood that would never in the life of the world be known or trodden. The thought was not exactly the sort he welcomed. In a loud voice, cheerfully, he suggested that it was time for bed. But the guide lingered, tinkering with the fire, arranging the stones needlessly, doing a dozen things that did not really need doing. Evidently there was something he wanted to say, yet found it difficult to "get at."

"Say, you, Boss Simpson," he began suddenly, as the last shower of sparks went up into the air, "you don't — smell nothing, do you — nothing pertickler, I mean?" The commonplace question, Simpson realized, veiled a dreadfully serious thought in his mind. A shiver ran down his back.

"Nothing but burning wood," he replied firmly, kicking again at the embers. The sound of his own foot made him start.

"And all the evenin' you ain't smelt — nothing?" persisted the guide, peering at him through the gloom; "nothing extrordiny, and different to anything else you ever smelt before?"

"No, no, man; nothing at all!" he replied aggressively, half angrily.

Défago's face cleared. "That's good!" he exclaimed with evident relief. "That's good to hear."

"Have *you?*" asked Simpson sharply, and the same instant regretted the question.

The Canadian came closer in the darkness. He shook his head. "I guess not," he said, though without overwhelming conviction. "It must've been jest that song of mine that did it. It's the song they sing in lumber camps and godforsaken places like that, when they're skeered the Wendigo's somewheres around, doin' a bit of swift travelin' —"

"And what's the Wendigo, pray?" Simpson asked quickly, irritated because again he could not prevent that sudden shiver of the nerves. He knew that he was close upon the man's terror and the cause of it. Yet a rushing passionate curiosity overcame his better judgment, *and* his fear.

Défago turned swiftly and looked at him as though he were suddenly about to shriek. His eyes shone, but his mouth was wide open. Yet all he said, or whispered rather, for his voice sank very low, was:

"It's nuthin' — nuthin' but what those lousy fellers believe when they've bin hittin' the bottle too long — a sort of great animal that lives up yonder," he jerked his head northwards, "quick as lightning in its tracks, an' bigger'n anything else in the Bush, an' ain't supposed to be very good to look at — that's *all!*"

"A backwoods superstition —" began Simpson, moving hastily toward the tent in order to shake off the hand of the guide that clutched his arm. "Come, come, hurry up for God's sake, and get the lantern going! It's time we were in bed and asleep if we're going to be up with the sun tomorrow. . . ."

The guide was close on his heels. "I'm coming," he answered out of the darkness, "I'm coming." And after a slight delay he appeared with the lantern and hung it from a nail in the front pole of the tent. The shadows of a hundred trees shifted their places quickly as he did so, and when he stumbled over the rope, diving swiftly inside, the whole tent trembled as though a gust of wind struck it.

The two men lay down, without undressing, upon their beds of soft balsam boughs, cunningly arranged. Inside, all was warm and cozy, but outside the world of crowding trees pressed close about them, marshaling their million shadows, and smothering the little tent that stood there like a wee white shell facing the ocean of tremendous forest.

Between the two lonely figures within, however, there pressed another shadow that was *not* a shadow from the night. It was the Shadow cast by the strange Fear, never wholly exorcised, that had leaped suddenly upon Défago in the middle of his singing. And Simpson, as he lay there, watching the darkness through the open flap of the tent, ready to plunge into the fragrant abyss of sleep, knew first that unique and profound stillness of a primeval forest when no wind stirs . . . and when the night has weight and substance that enters into the soul to bind a veil about it. . . . Then sleep took him. . . .

Thus, it seemed to him, at least. Yet it was true that the lap of the water, just beyond the tent door, still beat time with his lessening pulses when he realized that he was lying with his eyes open and that another sound had recently introduced itself with cunning softness between the splash and murmur of the little waves.

And, long before he understood what this sound was, it had stirred in him the centers of pity and alarm. He listened intently, though at first in vain, for the running blood beat all its drums too noisily in his ears. Did it come, he wondered, from the lake, or from the woods. . . ?

Then, suddenly, with a rush and a flutter of the heart, he knew that it was close beside him in the tent; and, when he turned over for a better hearing, it focused itself unmistakably not two feet away. It was a sound of weeping; Défago upon his bed of branches was sobbing in the darkness as though his heart would break, the blankets evidently stuffed against his mouth to stifle it.

And his first feeling, before he could think or reflect, was the rush of a poignant and searching tenderness. This intimate, human sound, heard amid the desolation about them, woke pity. It was so incongruous, so pitifully incongruous — and so vain! Tears — in this vast and cruel wilderness: of what avail? He thought of a little child crying in mid-Atlantic. . . . Then, of course, with fuller realization, and the memory of what had gone before, came the descent of the terror upon him, and his blood ran cold.

"Défago," he whispered quickly, "what's the matter?" He tried to make his voice very gentle. "Are you in pain — unhappy — ?" There was no reply, but the sounds ceased abruptly. He stretched his hand out and touched him. The body did not stir.

"Are you awake?" for it occurred to him that the man was crying in his sleep. "Are you cold?" He noticed that his feet, which were uncovered, projected beyond the mouth of the tent. He spread an extra fold of his own blankets over them. The guide had slipped down in his bed, and the branches seemed to have been dragged with him. He was afraid to pull the body back again, for fear of waking him.

One or two tentative questions he ventured softly, but though he waited for several minutes there came no reply, nor any sign of movement. Presently he heard his regular and quiet breathing, and putting his hand again gently on the breast, felt the steady rise and fall beneath.

"Let me know if anything's wrong," he whispered, "or if I can do anything. Wake me at once if you feel — queer."

He hardly knew what to say. He lay down again, thinking and wondering what it all meant. Défago, of course, had been crying in his sleep. Some dream or other had afflicted him. Yet never in his life would he forget that pitiful sound of sobbing, and the feeling that the whole awful wilderness of woods listened. . . .

His own mind busied itself for a long time with the recent events, of which *this* took its mysterious place as one, and though his reason successfully argued away all unwelcome suggestions, a sensation of uneasiness remained, resisting ejection, very deep-seated — peculiar beyond ordinary.

But sleep, in the long run, proves greater than all emotions. His thoughts soon wandered again; he lay there, warm as toast, exceedingly weary; the night soothed and comforted, blunting the edges of memory and alarm. Half an hour later he was oblivious of everything in the outer world about him.

Yet sleep, in this case, was his great enemy, concealing all approaches, smothering the warning of his nerves.

As, sometimes, in a nightmare events crowd upon each other's heels with a conviction of dreadfulest reality, yet some inconsistent detail accuses the whole display of incompleteness and disguise, so the events that now followed, though they actually happened, persuaded the mind somehow that the detail which could explain them had been overlooked in the confusion, and that therefore they were but partly true, the rest delusion. At the back of the sleeper's mind something remains awake, ready to let slip the judgment. "All this is not *quite* real; when you wake up you'll understand."

And thus, in a way, it was with Simpson. The events, not wholly inexplicable or incredible in themselves, yet remain for the man who saw and heard them a sequence of separate facts of cold horror, because the little piece that might have made the puzzle clear lay concealed or overlooked.

So far as he can recall, it was a violent movement, running downwards through the tent towards the door, that first woke him and made him aware that his companion was sitting bolt upright beside him – quivering. Hours must have passed, for it was the pale gleam of the dawn that revealed his outline against the canvas. This time the man was not crying; he was quaking like a leaf; the trembling he felt plainly through the blankets down the entire length of his own body. Défago had huddled down against him for protection, shrinking away from something that apparently concealed itself near the door flaps of the little tent.

Simpson thereupon called out in a loud voice some question or other – in the first bewilderment of waking he does not remember exactly what – and the man made no reply. The atmosphere and feeling of true nightmare lay horribly about him, making movement and speech both difficult. At first, indeed, he was not sure where he was – whether in one of the earlier camps, or at home in his bed at Aberdeen. The sense of confusion was very troubling.

And next – almost simultaneous with his waking, it seemed – the profound stillness of the dawn outside was shattered by a most uncommon sound. It came without warning, or audible approach; and it was unspeakably dreadful. It was a voice, Simpson declares, possibly a human voice; hoarse yet plaintive – a soft, roaring voice close outside the tent, overhead rather than upon the ground, of immense volume, while in some strange way most penetratingly and seductively sweet. It rang out, too, in three separate and distinct notes, or cries, that bore in some odd fashion a resemblance, farfetched yet recognizable, to the name of the guide: *"Dé-fa-go!"*

The student admits he is unable to describe it quite intelligently, for it was unlike any sound he had ever heard in his life, and combined a blending of such contrary qualities. "A sort of windy, crying voice," he calls it, "as of something lonely and untamed, wild and of abominable power. . . ."

And, even before it ceased, dropping back into the great gulfs of silence, the guide beside him had sprung to his feet with an answering though unintelligible cry. He blundered against the tent pole with violence, shaking the whole structure, spreading his arms out frantically for more room, and kicking his legs impetuously free of the clinging blankets. For a second, perhaps two, he stood upright by the door, his outline dark against the pallor of the dawn; then, with a furious, rushing speed, before his companion could move a hand to stop him, he shot with a plunge through the flaps of canvas — and was gone. And as he went — so astonishingly fast that the voice could actually be heard dying in the distance — he called aloud in tones of anguished terror that at the same time held something strangely like the frenzied exultation of delight —

"Oh! oh! My feet of fire! My burning feet of fire! Oh! oh! This height and fiery speed!"

And then the distance quickly buried it, and the deep silence of very early morning descended upon the forest as before.

It had all come about with such rapidity that, but for the evidence of the empty bed beside him, Simpson could almost have believed it to have been the memory of a nightmare carried over from sleep. He still felt the warm pressure of that vanished body against his side; there lay the twisted blankets in a heap; the very tent yet trembled with the vehemence of the impetuous departure. The strange words rang in his ears, as though he still heard them in the distance — wild language of a suddenly stricken mind. Moreover, it was not only the senses of sight and hearing that reported uncommon things to his brain, for even while the man cried and ran, he had become aware that a strange perfume, faint yet pungent, pervaded the interior of the tent. And it was at this point, it seems, brought to himself by the consciousness that his nostrils were taking this distressing odor down into his throat, that he found his courage, sprang quickly to his feet — and went out.

The grey light of dawn that dropped, cold and glimmering, between the trees revealed the scene tolerably well. There stood the tent behind him, soaked with dew; the dark ashes of the fire, still warm; the lake, white beneath a coating of mist, the islands rising darkly out of it like objects packed in wool; and patches of snow beyond among the clearer spaces of the Bush — everything cold, still, waiting for the sun. But nowhere a sign of the vanished guide — still, doubtless, flying at frantic speed through the frozen woods. There was not even the sound of disappearing footsteps, nor the echoes of the dying voice. He had gone — utterly.

There was nothing; nothing but the sense of his recent presence, so strongly left behind about the camp; *and* — this penetrating, all-pervading odor.

And even this was now rapidly disappearing in its turn. In spite of his exceeding mental perturbation, Simpson struggled hard to detect its nature, and define it, but the ascertaining of an elusive scent, not recognized subconsciously and at once, is a very subtle operation of the mind. And he failed. It was gone before he could properly seize or name it. Approximate description, even, seems to have been difficult, for it was unlike any smell he knew. Acrid rather, not unlike the odor of a lion, he thinks, yet softer and not wholly unpleasing, with something almost sweet in it that reminded him of the scent of decaying garden leaves, earth, and the myriad, nameless perfumes that make up the odor of a big forest. Yet the "odor of lions" is the phrase with which he usually sums it all up.

Then — it was wholly gone, and he found himself standing by the ashes of the fire in a state of amazement and stupid terror that left him the helpless prey of anything that chose to happen. Had a muskrat poked its pointed muzzle over a rock, or a squirrel scuttled in that instant down the bark of a tree, he would most likely have collapsed without more ado and fainted. For he felt about the whole affair the touch somewhere of a great Outer Horror ... and his scattered powers had not as yet had time to collect themselves into a definite attitude of fighting self-control.

Nothing did happen, however. A great kiss of wind ran softly through the awakening forest, and a few maple leaves here and there rustled tremblingly to earth. The sky seemed to grow suddenly much lighter. Simpson felt the cool air upon his cheek and uncovered head; realized that he was shivering with the cold; and, making a great effort, realized next that he was alone in the Bush — *and* that he was called upon to take immediate steps to find and succor his vanished companion.

Make an effort, accordingly, he did, though an ill-calculated and futile one. With that wilderness of trees about him, the sheet of water cutting him off behind, and the horror of that wild cry in his blood, he did what any other inexperienced man would have done in similar bewilderment: he ran about, without any sense of direction, like a frantic child, and called loudly without ceasing the name of the guide:

"Défago! Défago! Défago!" he yelled, and the trees gave him back the name as often as he shouted, only a little softened — "Défago! Défago! Défago!"

He followed the trail that lay a short distance across the patches of snow, and then lost it again where the trees grew too thickly for snow to lie. He shouted till he was hoarse, and till the sound of his own voice in all that unanswering and listening world began to frighten him. His confusion increased in direct ratio to the violence of his efforts. His distress became formidably acute, till at length his exertions defeated their own object, and from sheer exhaustion he headed back to the camp again. It remains a wonder that he ever found his way. It was with great difficulty, and only after numberless false clues, that he at last saw the white tent between the trees, and so reached safety.

Exhaustion then applied its own remedy, and he grew calmer. He made the fire and breakfasted. Hot coffee and bacon put a little sense and judgment into him again, and he realized that he had been behaving like a boy. He now made another, and more successful attempt to face the situation collectedly, and, a nature naturally plucky coming to his assistance, he decided that he must first make as thorough a search as possible, failing success in which, he must find his way into the home camp as best he could and bring help.

And this was what he did. Taking food, matches and rifle with him, and a small axe to blaze the trees against his return journey, he set forth. It was eight o'clock when he started, the sun shining over the tops of the trees in a sky without clouds. Pinned to a stake by the fire he left a note in case Défago returned while he was away.

This time, according to a careful plan, he took a new direction, intending to make a wide sweep that must sooner or later cut into indications of the guide's trail; and, before he had gone a quarter of a mile he came across the tracks of a large animal in the snow, and beside it the light and smaller tracks of what were beyond question human feet — the feet of Défago. The relief he at once experienced was natural, though brief; for at first sight he saw in these tracks a simple explanation of the whole matter: these big marks had surely been left by a bull moose that, wind against it, had blundered upon the camp, and uttered its singular cry of warning and alarm the moment its mistake was apparent. Défago, in whom the hunting instinct was developed to the point of uncanny perfection, had scented the brute coming down the wind hours before. His excitement and disappearance were due, of course, to — to his —

Then the impossible explanation at which he grasped faded, as common sense showed him mercilessly that none of this was true. No guide, much less a guide like Défago, could have acted in so irrational a way, going off even without his rifle. . . ! The whole affair demanded a far more complicated elucidation, when he remembered the details of it all — the cry of terror, the amazing language, the grey face of horror when his nostrils first caught the new odor; that muffled sobbing in the darkness, and — for this, too, now came back to him dimly — the man's original aversion for this particular bit of country. . . .

Besides, now that he examined them closer, these were not the tracks of a bull moose at all! Hank had explained to him the outline of a bull's hoofs, of a cow's or calf's, too, for that matter; he had drawn them clearly on a strip of birch bark. And these were wholly different. They were big, round, ample, and with no pointed outline as of sharp hoofs. He wondered for a moment whether bear tracks were like that. There was no other animal he could think of, for caribou did not come so far south at this season, and, even if they did, would leave hoof marks.

They were ominous signs — these mysterious writings left in the snow by the unknown creature that had lured a human being away from safety — and when he coupled them in his imagination with that haunting sound that broke the stillness of the dawn, a momentary dizziness shook his mind, distressing him again beyond belief. He felt the *threatening* aspect of it all. And, stooping down to examine the marks more closely, he caught a faint whiff of that sweet yet pungent odor that made him instantly straighten up again, fighting a sensation almost of nausea.

Then his memory played him another evil trick. He suddenly recalled those uncovered feet projecting beyond the edge of the tent, and the body's appearance of having been dragged towards the opening; the man's shrinking from something by the door when he woke later. The details now beat against his trembling mind with concerted attack. They seemed to gather in those deep spaces of the silent forest about him, where the host of trees stood waiting, listening, watching to see what he would do. The woods were closing round him.

With the persistence of true pluck, however, Simpson went forward, following the tracks as best he could, smothering these ugly emotions that sought to weaken his will. He blazed innumerable trees as he went, ever fearful of being unable to find the way back, and calling aloud at intervals of a few seconds the name of the guide. The dull tapping of the axe upon the massive trunks, and the unnatural accents of his own voice became at length sounds that he even dreaded to make, dreaded to hear. For they drew attention without ceasing to his presence and exact whereabouts, and if it were really the case that something was hunting himself down in the same way that he was hunting down another —

With a strong effort, he crushed the thought out the instant it rose. It was the beginning, he realized, of a bewilderment utterly diabolical in kind that would speedily destroy him.

*A*lthough the snow was not continuous, lying merely in shallow flurries over the more open spaces, he found no difficulty in following the tracks for the first few miles. They went straight as a ruled line wherever the trees permitted. The stride soon began to increase in length, till it finally assumed proportions that seemed absolutely impossible for any ordinary animal to have made. Like huge flying leaps they became. One of these he measured, and though he knew that "stretch" of eighteen feet must be somehow wrong, he was at a complete loss to understand why he found no signs on the snow between the extreme points. But what perplexed him even more, making him feel his vision had gone utterly awry, was that Défago's stride increased in the same manner, and finally covered the same incredible distances. It looked as if the great beast had lifted him with it and carried him across these astonishing intervals. Simpson, who was much longer in the limb, found that he could not compass even half the stretch by taking a running jump.

And the sight of these huge tracks, running side by side, silent evidence of a dreadful journey in which terror or madness had urged to impossible results, was profoundly moving. It shocked him in the secret depths of his soul. It was the most horrible thing his eyes had ever looked upon. He began to follow them mechanically, absentmindedly almost, ever peering over his shoulder to see if he, too, were being followed by something with a gigantic tread. . . . And soon it came about that he no longer quite realized what it was they signified — these impressions left upon the snow by something nameless and untamed, always accompanied by the footmarks of the little French Canadian, his guide, his comrade, the man who had shared his tent a few hours before, chatting, laughing, even singing by his side. . . .

For a man of his years and inexperience, only a canny Scot, perhaps, grounded in common sense and established in logic, could have preserved even that measure of balance that this youth somehow or other did manage to preserve through the whole adventure. Otherwise, two things he presently noticed, while forging pluckily ahead, must have sent him headlong back to the comparative safety of his tent, instead of only making his hands close more tightly upon the rifle stock, while his heart, trained for the Wee Kirk, sent a wordless prayer winging its way to heaven. Both tracks, he saw, had undergone a change, and this change, so far as it concerned the footsteps of the man, was in some undecipherable manner — appalling.

It was in the bigger tracks he first noticed this, and for a long time he could not quite believe his eyes. Was it the blown leaves that produced odd effects of light and shade, or that the dry snow, drifting like finely ground rice about the edges, cast shadows and high lights? Or was it actually the fact that the great marks had become faintly colored? For round about the deep, plunging holes of the animal there now appeared a mysterious, reddish tinge that was more like an effect of light than of anything that dyed the substance of the snow itself. Every mark had it, and had it increasingly — this indistinct fiery tinge that painted a new touch of ghastliness into the picture.

But when, wholly unable to explain or to credit it, he turned his attention to the other tracks to discover if they, too, bore similar witness, he noticed that these had meanwhile undergone a change that was infinitely worse, and charged with far more horrible suggestion. For, in the last hundred yards or so, he saw that they had grown gradually into the semblance of the parent tread. Imperceptibly the change had come about, yet unmistakably. It was hard to see where the change first began. The result, however, was beyond question. Smaller, neater, more cleanly modeled, they formed now an exact and careful duplicate of the larger tracks beside them. The feet that produced them had, therefore, also changed. And something in his mind reared up with loathing and with terror as he saw it.

Simpson, for the first time, hesitated; then, ashamed of his alarm and indecision, took a few hurried steps ahead; the next instant stopped dead in his tracks. Immediately in front of him all signs of the trail ceased; both tracks came to an abrupt end. On all sides, for a hundred yards and more, he searched in vain for the least indication of their continuance. There was — nothing.

The trees were very thick just there, big trees all of them, spruce, cedar, hemlock; there was no underbrush. He stood, looking about him, all distraught; bereft of any power of judgment. Then he set to work to search again, and again, and yet again, but always with the same result: *nothing*. The feet that printed the surface of the snow thus far had now, apparently, left the ground!

And it was in that moment of distress and confusion that the whip of terror laid its most nicely calculated lash about his heart. It dropped with deadly effect upon the sorest spot of all, completely unnerving him. He had been secretly dreading all the time that it would come — and come it did.

Far overhead, muted by great height and distance, strangely thinned and wailing, he heard the crying voice of Défago, the guide.

The sound dropped upon him out of that still, wintry sky with an effect of dismay and terror unsurpassed. The rifle fell to his feet. He stood motionless an instant, listening as it were with his whole body, then staggered back against the nearest tree for support, disorganized hopelessly in mind and spirit. To him, in that moment, it seemed the most shattering and dislocating experience he had ever known, so that his heart emptied itself of all feeling whatsoever as by a sudden draft.

"Oh! oh! This fiery height! Oh, my feet of fire! My burning feet of fire...!" ran in far, beseeching accents of indescribable appeal this voice of anguish down the sky. Once it called — then silence through all the listening wilderness of trees.

And Simpson, scarcely knowing what he did, presently found himself running wildly to and fro, searching, calling, tripping over roots and boulders, and flinging himself in a frenzy of undirected pursuit after the Caller. Behind the screen of memory and emotion with which experience veils events, he plunged, distracted and half-deranged, picking up false lights like a ship at sea, terror in his eyes and heart and soul. For the Panic of the Wilderness had called to him in that far voice — the Power of untamed Distance — the Enticement of the Desolation that destroys. He knew in that moment all the pains of someone hopelessly and irretrievably lost, suffering the lust and travail of a soul in the final Loneliness. A vision of Défago, eternally hunted, driven and pursued across the skiey vastness of those ancient forests fled like a flame across the dark ruin of his thoughts . . .

It seemed ages before he could find anything in the chaos of his disorganized sensations to which he could anchor himself steady for a moment, and think . . .

The cry was not repeated; his own hoarse calling brought no response; the inscrutable forces of the Wild had summoned their victim beyond recall — and held him fast.

*Y*et he searched and called, it seems, for hours afterwards, for it was late in the afternoon when at length he decided to abandon a useless pursuit and return to his camp on the shores of Fifty Island Water. Even then he went with reluctance, that crying voice still echoing in his ears. With difficulty he found his rifle and the homeward trail. The concentration necessary to follow the badly blazed trees, and a biting hunger that gnawed, helped to keep his mind steady. Otherwise, he admits, the temporary aberration he had suffered might have been prolonged to the point of positive disaster. Gradually the ballast shifted back again, and he regained something that approached his normal equilibrium.

But for all that the journey through the gathering dusk was miserably haunted. He heard innumerable following footsteps; voices that laughed and whispered; and saw figures crouching behind trees and boulders, making signs to one another for a concerted attack the moment he had passed. The creeping murmur of the wind made him start and listen. He went stealthily, trying to hide where possible, and making as little sound as he could. The shadows of the woods, hitherto protective or covering merely, had now become menacing, challenging; and the pageantry in his frightened mind masked a host of possibilities that were all the more ominous for being obscure. The presentiment of a nameless doom lurked ill-concealed behind every detail of what had happened.

It was really admirable how he emerged victor in the end; men of riper powers and experience might have come through the ordeal with less success. He had himself tolerably well in hand, all things considered, and his plan of action proves it. Sleep being absolutely out of the question and traveling an unknown trail in the darkness equally impracticable, he sat up the whole of that night, rifle in hand, before a fire he never for a single moment allowed to die down. The severity of the haunted vigil marked his soul for life; but it was successfully accomplished; and with the very first signs of dawn he set forth upon the long return journey to the home camp to get help. As before, he left a written note to explain his absence, and to indicate where he had left a plentiful *cache* of food and matches — though he had no expectation that any human hands would find them!

How Simpson found his way alone by the lake and forest might well make a story in itself, for to hear him tell it is to *know* the passionate loneliness of soul that a man can feel when the Wilderness holds him in the hollow of its illimitable hand — and laughs. It is also to admire his indomitable pluck.

He claims no skill, declaring that he followed the almost invisible trail mechanically, and without thinking. And this, doubtless, is the truth. He relied upon the guiding of the unconscious mind, which is instinct. Perhaps, too, some sense of orientation, known to animals and primitive men, may have helped as well, for through all that tangled region he succeeded in reaching the exact spot where Défago had hidden the canoe nearly three days before with the remark, "Strike doo west across the lake into the sun to find the camp."

There was not much sun left to guide him, but he used his compass to the best of his ability, embarking in the frail craft for the last twelve miles of his journey with a sensation of immense relief that the forest was at last behind him. And, fortunately, the water was calm; he took his line across the center of the lake instead of coasting round the shores for another twenty miles. Fortunately, too, the other hunters were back. The light of their fires furnished a steering point without which he might have searched all night long for the actual position of the camp.

It was close upon midnight all the same when his canoe grated on the sandy cove, and Hank, Punk and his uncle, disturbed in their sleep by his cries, ran quickly down and helped a very exhausted and broken specimen of Scotch humanity over the rocks toward a dying fire.

The sudden entrance of his prosaic uncle into this world of wizardry and horror that had haunted him without interruption now for two days and two nights, had the immediate effect of giving to the affair an entirely new aspect. The sound of that crisp "Hulloa, my boy! And what's up *now?*" and the grasp of that dry and vigorous hand introduced another standard of judgment. A revulsion of feeling washed through him. He realized that he had let himself "go" rather badly. He even felt vaguely ashamed of himself. The native hard-headedness of his race reclaimed him.

And this doubtless explains why he found it so hard to tell that group round the fire — everything. He told enough, however, for the immediate decision to be arrived at that a relief party must start at the earliest possible moment, and that Simpson, in order to guide it capably, must first have food and, above all, sleep. Dr. Cathcart observing the lad's condition more shrewdly than his patient knew, gave him a very slight injection of morphine. For six hours he slept like the dead.

From the description carefully written out afterwards by this student of divinity, it appears that the account he gave to the astonished group omitted sundry vital and important details. He declares that, with his uncle's wholesome, matter-of-fact countenance staring him in the face, he simply had not the courage to mention them. Thus, all the search party gathered, it would seem, was that Défago had suffered in the night an acute and inexplicable attack of mania, had imagined himself "called" by someone or something, and had plunged into the bush after it without food or rifle, where he must die a horrible and lingering death by cold and starvation unless he could be found and rescued in time. "In time," moreover, meant *at once*.

In the course of the following day, however — they were off by seven, leaving Punk in charge with instructions to have food and fire always ready — Simpson found it possible to tell his uncle a good deal more of the story's true inwardness, without divining that it was drawn out of him as a matter of fact by a very subtle form of cross examination. By the time they reached the beginning of the trail, where the canoe was laid up against the return journey, he had mentioned how Défago spoke vaguely of "something he called a 'Wendigo'"; how he cried in his sleep; how he imagined an unusual scent about the camp; and had betrayed other symptoms of mental excitement. He also admitted the bewildering effect of "that extraordinary odor" upon himself, "pungent and acrid like the odor of lions." And by the time they were within an easy hour of Fifty Island Water he had let slip the further fact — a foolish avowal of his own hysterical condition, as he felt afterwards — that he had heard the vanished guide call "for help." He omitted the singular phrases used, for he simply could not bring himself to repeat the preposterous language. Also, while describing how the man's footsteps in the snow had gradually assumed an exact miniature likeness of the animal's plunging tracks, he left out the fact that they measured a *wholly* incredible distance. It seemed a question, nicely balanced between individual pride and honesty, what he should reveal and what suppress. He mentioned the fiery tinge in the snow, for instance, yet shrank from telling that body and bed had been partly dragged out of the tent. . . .

With the net result that Dr. Cathcart, adroit psychologist that he fancied himself to be, had assured him clearly enough exactly where his mind, influenced by loneliness, bewilderment and terror, had yielded to the strain and invited delusion. While praising his conduct, he managed at the same time to point out where, when, and how his mind had gone astray. He made his nephew think himself finer than he was by judicious praise, yet more foolish than he was by minimizing the value of the evidence. Like many another materialist, that is, he lied cleverly on the basis of insufficient knowledge, *because* the knowledge supplied seemed to his own particular intelligence inadmissible.

"The spell of these terrible solitudes," he said, "cannot leave any mind untouched, any mind, that is, possessed of the higher imaginative qualities. It has worked upon yours exactly as it worked upon my own when I was your age. The animal that haunted your little camp was undoubtedly a moose, for the 'belling' of a moose may have, sometimes, a very peculiar quality of sound. The colored appearance of the big tracks was obviously a defect of vision in your own eyes produced by excitement. The size and stretch of the tracks we shall prove when we come to them. But the hallucination of an audible voice, of course, is one of the commonest forms of delusion due to mental excitement — an excitement, my dear boy, perfectly excusable, and, let me add, wonderfully controlled by you under the circumstances. For the rest, I am bound to say, you have acted with a splendid courage, for the terror of feeling oneself lost in this wilderness is nothing short of awful, and, had I been in your place, I don't for a moment believe I could have behaved with one quarter of your wisdom and decision. The only thing I find it uncommonly difficult to explain is — that — damned odor."

"It made me feel sick, I assure you," declared his nephew, "positively dizzy!" His uncle's attitude of calm omniscience, merely because he knew more psychological formulæ, made him slightly defiant. It was so easy to be wise in the explanation of an experience one has not personally witnessed. "A kind of desolate and terrible odor is the only way I can describe it," he concluded, glancing at the features of the quiet, unemotional man beside him.

"I can only marvel," was the reply, "that under the circumstances it did not seem to you even worse." The dry words, Simpson knew, hovered between the truth, and his uncle's interpretation of "the truth."

*A*nd so at last they came to the little camp and found the tent still standing, the remains of the fire, and the piece of paper pinned to a stake beside it — untouched. The *cache*, poorly contrived by inexperienced hands, however, had been discovered and opened — by musk rats, mink and squirrel. The matches lay scattered about the opening, but the food had been taken to the last crumb.

"Well, fellers, he ain't here," exclaimed Hank loudly after his fashion. "And that's as sartain as the coal supply down below! But whar he's got to by this time is 'bout as unsartain as the trade in crowns in t'other place." The presence of a divinity student was no barrier to his language at such a time, though for the reader's sake it may be severely edited. "I propose," he added, "that we start out at once an' hunt for'm like hell!"

The gloom of Défago's probable fate oppressed the whole party with a sense of dreadful gravity the moment they saw the familiar signs of recent occupancy. Especially the tent, with the bed of balsam branches still smoothed and flattened by the pressure of his body, seemed to bring his presence near to them. Simpson, feeling vaguely as if his world were somehow at stake, went about explaining particulars in a hushed tone. He was much calmer now, though overwearied with the strain of his many journeys. His uncle's method of explaining — "explaining away," rather — the details still fresh in his haunted memory helped, too, to put ice upon his emotions.

"And that's the direction he ran off in," he said to his two companions, pointing in the direction where the guide had vanished that morning in the grey dawn. "Straight down there he ran like a deer, in between the birch and the hemlock. . . ."

Hank and Dr. Cathcart exchanged glances.

"And it was about two miles down there, in a straight line," continued the other, speaking with something of the former terror in his voice, "that I followed his trail to the place where — it stopped — dead!"

"And where you heered him callin' an' caught the stench, an' all the rest of the wicked entertainment," cried Hank, with a volubility that betrayed his keen distress.

"And where your excitement overcame you to the point of producing illusions," added Dr. Cathcart under his breath, yet not so low that his nephew did not hear it.

*I*t was early in the afternoon, for they had traveled quickly, and there were still a good two hours of daylight left. Dr. Cathcart and Hank lost no time in beginning the search, but Simpson was too exhausted to accompany them. They would follow the blazed marks on the trees, and where possible, his footsteps. Meanwhile the best thing he could do was to keep a good fire going, and rest.

But after something like three hours' search, the darkness already down, the two men returned to camp with nothing to report. Fresh snow had covered all signs, and though they had followed the blazed trees to the spot where Simpson had turned back, they had not discovered the smallest indication of a human being — or for that matter, of an animal. There were no fresh tracks of any kind; the snow lay undisturbed.

It was difficult to know what was best to do, though in reality there was nothing more they *could* do. They might stay and search for weeks without much chance of success. The fresh snow destroyed their only hope, and they gathered round the fire for supper, a gloomy and despondent party. The facts, indeed, were sad enough, for Défago had a wife at Rat Portage, and his earnings were the family's sole means of support.

Now that the whole truth in all its ugliness was out, it seemed useless to deal in further disguise or pretense. They talked openly of the facts and probabilities. It was not the first time, even in the experience of Dr. Cathcart, that a man had yielded to the singular seduction of the Solitudes and gone out of his mind; Défago, moreover, was predisposed to something of the sort, for he already had a touch of melancholia in his blood, and his fiber was weakened by bouts of drinking that often lasted for weeks at a time. Something on this trip — one might never know precisely what — had sufficed to push him over the line, that was all. And he had gone, gone off into the great wilderness of trees and lakes to die by starvation and exhaustion. The chances against his finding camp again were overwhelming; the delirium that was upon him would also doubtless have increased, and it was quite likely he might do violence to himself and so hasten his cruel fate. Even while they talked, indeed, the end had probably come. On the suggestion of Hank, his old pal, however, they proposed to wait a little longer and devote the whole of the following day, from dawn to darkness, to the most systematic search they could devise. They would divide the territory between them. They discussed their plan in great detail. All that men could do they would do.

And, meanwhile, they talked about the particular form in which the singular Panic of the Wilderness had made its attack upon the mind of the unfortunate guide. Hank, though familiar with the legend in its general outline, obviously did not welcome the turn the conversation had taken. He contributed little, though that little was illuminating. For he admitted that a story ran over all this section of country to the effect that several Indians had "seen the Wendigo" along the shores of Fifty Island Water in the "fall" of last year, and that this was the true reason of Défago's disinclination to hunt there. Hank doubtless felt that he had in a sense helped his old pal to death by overpersuading him. "When an Indian goes crazy," he explained, talking to himself more than to the others, it seemed, "it's always put that he's 'seen the Wendigo.' An' pore old Défaygo was superstitious down to he very heels. . . !"

And then Simpson, feeling the atmosphere more sympathetic, told over again the full story of his astonishing tale; he left out no details this time; he mentioned his own sensations and gripping fears. He only omitted the strange language used.

"But Défago surely had already told you all these details of the Wendigo legend, my dear fellow," insisted the doctor. "I mean, he had talked about it, and thus put into your mind the ideas which your own excitement afterwards developed?"

Whereupon Simpson again repeated the facts. Défago, he declared, had barely mentioned the beast. He, Simpson, knew nothing of the story, and, so far as he remembered, had never even read about it. Even the word was unfamiliar.

Of course he was telling the truth, and Dr. Cathcart was reluctantly compelled to admit the singular character of the whole affair. He did not do this in words so much as in manner, however. He kept his back against a good, stout tree; he poked the fire into a blaze the moment it showed signs of dying down; he was quicker than any of them to notice the least sound in the night about them — a fish jumping in the lake, a twig snapping in the bush, the dropping of occasional fragments of frozen snow from the branches overhead where the heat loosened them. His voice, too, changed a little in quality, becoming a shade less confident, lower also in tone. Fear, to put it plainly, hovered close about that little camp, and though all three would have been glad to speak of other matters, the only thing they seemed able to discuss was this — the source of their fear. They tried other subjects in vain; there was nothing to say about them. Hank was the most honest of the group; he said next to nothing. He never once, however, turned his back to the darkness. His face was always to the forest, and when wood was needed he didn't go farther than was necessary to get it.

A wall of silence wrapped them in, for the snow, though not thick, was sufficient to deaden any noise, and the frost held things pretty tight besides. No sound but their voices and the soft roar of the flames made itself heard. Only, from time to time, something soft as the flutter of a pine moth's wings went past them through the air. No one seemed anxious to go to bed. The hours slipped towards midnight.

"The legend is picturesque enough," observed the doctor after one of the longer pauses, speaking to break it rather than because he had anything to say, "for the Wendigo is simply the Call of the Wild personified, which some natures hear to their own destruction."

"That's about it," Hank said presently. "An' there's no misunderstandin' when you hear it. It calls you by name right 'nough."

Another pause followed. Then Dr. Cathcart came back to the forbidden subject with a rush that made the others jump.

"The allegory *is* significant," he remarked, looking about him into the darkness, "for the Voice, they say, resembles all the minor sounds of the Bush — wind, falling water, cries of the animals, and so forth. And, once the victim hears *that* — he's off for good, of course! His most vulnerable points, moreover, are said to be the feet and the eyes; the feet, you see, for the lust of wandering, and the eyes for the lust of beauty. The poor beggar goes at such a dreadful speed that he bleeds beneath the eyes, and his feet burn."

Dr. Cathcart, as he spoke, continued to peer uneasily into the surrounding gloom. His voice sank to a hushed tone.

"The Wendigo," he added, "is said to burn his feet — owing to the friction, apparently caused by its tremendous velocity — till they drop off, and new ones form exactly like its own."

Simpson listened in horrified amazement; but it was the pallor on Hank's face that fascinated him most. He would willingly have stopped his ears and closed his eyes, had he dared.

"It don't always keep to the ground neither," came in Hank's slow, heavy drawl, "for it goes so high that he thinks the stars have set him all a-fire. An' it'll take great thumpin' jumps sometimes, an' run along the tops of the trees, carrying its partner with it, an' then droppin' him jest as a fish hawk'll drop a pickerel to kill it before eatin'. An' its food, of all the muck in the whole Bush is — moss!" And he laughed a short, unnatural laugh. "It's a moss-eater, is the Wendigo," he added, looking up excitedly into the faces of his companions. "Moss-eater," he repeated, with a string of the most outlandish oaths he could invent.

But Simpson now understood the true purpose of all this talk. What these two men, each strong and "experienced" in his own way, dreaded more than anything else was — silence. They were talking against time. They were also talking against darkness, against the invasion of panic, against the admission reflection might bring that they were in an enemy's country — against anything, in fact, rather than allow their inmost thoughts to assume control. He himself, already initiated by the awful vigil with terror, was beyond both of them in this respect. He had reached the stage where he was immune. But these two, the scoffing, analytical doctor, and the honest, dogged backwoodsman, each sat trembling in the depths of his being.

Thus the hours passed; and thus, with lowered voices and a kind of taut inner resistance of spirit, this little group of humanity sat in the jaws of the wilderness and talked foolishly of the terrible and haunting legend. It was an unequal contest, all things considered, for the wilderness had already the advantage of first attack — and of a hostage. The fate of their comrade hung over them with a steadily increasing weight of oppression that finally became insupportable.

It was Hank, after a pause longer than the preceding ones that no one seemed able to break, who first let loose all this pent-up emotion in very unexpected fashion, by springing suddenly to his feet and letting out the most ear-shattering yell imaginable into the night. He could not contain himself any longer, it seemed. To make it carry even beyond an ordinary cry he interrupted its rhythm by shaking the palm of his hand before his mouth.

"That's for Défago," he said, looking down at the other two with a queer, defiant laugh, "for it's my belief" — the sandwiched oaths may be omitted — "that my ole partner's not far from us at this very minute."

There was a vehemence and recklessness about his performance that made Simpson, too, start to his feet in amazement, and betrayed even the doctor into letting the pipe slip from between his lips. Hank's face was ghastly, but Cathcart's showed a sudden weakness — a loosening of all his faculties, as it were. Then a momentary anger blazed into his eyes, and he too, though with deliberation born of habitual self-control, got upon his feet and faced the excited guide. For this was unpermissible, foolish, dangerous, and he meant to stop it in the bud.

What might have happened in the next minute or two one may speculate about, yet never definitely know, for in the instant of profound silence that followed Hank's roaring voice, and as though in answer to it, something went past through the darkness of the sky overhead at terrific speed — something of necessity very large, for it displaced much air, while down between the trees there fell a faint and windy cry of a human voice, calling in tones of indescribable anguish and appeal —

"Oh, oh! This fiery height! Oh, oh! My feet of fire! My burning feet of fire!"

White to the very edge of his shirt, Hank looked stupidly about him like a child. Dr. Cathcart uttered some kind of unintelligible cry, turning as he did so with an instinctive movement of blind terror towards the protection of the tent, then halting in the act as though frozen. Simpson, alone of the three, retained his presence of mind a little. His own horror was too deep to allow of any immediate reaction. He had heard that cry before.

Turning to his stricken companions, he said almost calmly –

"That's exactly the cry I heard – the very words he used!"

Then, lifting his face to the sky, he cried aloud, "Défago, Défago! Come down here to us! Come down – !"

And before there was time for anybody to take definite action one way or another, there came the sound of something dropping heavily between the trees, striking the branches on the way down, and landing with a dreadful thud upon the frozen earth below. The crash and thunder of it was really terrific.

"That's him, s'help me the good Gawd!" came from Hank in a whispering cry half choked, his hand going automatically toward the hunting knife in his belt. "And he's coming! He's coming!" he added, with an irrational laugh of horror, as the sounds of heavy footsteps crunching over the snow became distinctly audible, approaching through the blackness towards the circle of light.

And while the steps, with their stumbling motion, moved nearer and nearer upon them, the three men stood round that fire, motionless and dumb. Dr. Cathcart had the appearance of a man suddenly withered; even his eyes did not move. Hank, suffering shockingly, seemed on the verge again of violent action; yet did nothing. He, too, was hewn of stone. Like stricken children they seemed. The picture was hideous. And, meanwhile, their owner still invisible, the footsteps came closer, crunching the frozen snow. It was endless – too prolonged to be quite real – this measured and pitiless approach. It was accursed.

Then at length the darkness, having thus laboriously conceived, brought forth – a figure. It drew forward into the zone of uncertain light where fire and shadows mingled, not ten feet away; then halted, staring at them fixedly. The same instant it started forward again with the spasmodic motion as of a thing moved by wires, and coming up closer to them, full into the glare of the fire, they perceived then that – it was a man; and apparently that this man was – Défago.

Something like a skin of horror almost perceptibly drew down in that moment over every face, and three pairs of eyes shone through it as though they saw across the frontiers of normal vision into the Unknown.

Défago advanced, his tread faltering and uncertain; he made his way straight up to them as a group first, then turned sharply and peered close into the face of Simpson. The sound of a voice issued from his lips —

"Here I am, Boss Simpson. I heered someone calling me." It was a faint, dried up voice, made wheezy and breathless as by immense exertion. "I'm havin' a reg'lar hellfire kind of a trip, I am." And he laughed, thrusting his head forward into the other's face.

But that laugh started the machinery of the group of waxwork figures with the wax-white skins. Hank immediately sprang forward with a stream of oaths so farfetched that Simpson did not recognize them as English at all, but thought he had lapsed into Indian or some other lingo. He only realized that Hank's presence, thrust thus between them, was welcome — uncommonly welcome. Dr. Cathcart, though more calmly and leisurely, advanced behind him, heavily stumbling.

Simpson seems hazy as to what was actually said and done in those next few seconds, for the eyes of that detestable and blasted visage peering at such close quarters into his own utterly bewildered his senses at first. He merely stood still. He said nothing. He had not the trained will of the older men that forced them into action in defiance of all emotional stress. He watched them moving as behind a glass that half destroyed their reality; it was dreamlike; perverted. Yet, through the torrent of Hank's meaningless phrases, he remembers hearing his uncle's tone of authority — hard and forced — saying several things about food and warmth, blankets, whisky and the rest . . . and, further, that whiffs of that penetrating, unaccustomed odor, vile yet sweetly bewildering, assailed his nostrils during all that followed.

It was no less a person than himself, however — less experienced and adroit than the others though he was — who gave instinctive utterance to the sentence that brought a measure of relief into the ghastly situation by expressing the doubt and thought in each one's heart.

"It *is* — YOU, isn't it, Défago?" he asked under his breath, horror breaking his speech.

And at once Cathcart burst out with the loud answer before the other had time to move his lips. "Of course it is! Of course it is! Only — can't you see — he's nearly dead with exhaustion, cold and terror! Isn't *that* enough to change a man beyond all recognition?" It was said in order to convince himself as much as to convince the others. The overemphasis alone proved that. And continually, while he spoke and acted, he held a handkerchief to his nose. That odor pervaded the whole camp.

For the "Défago" who sat huddled by the big fire, wrapped in blankets, drinking hot whisky and holding food in wasted hands, was no more like the guide they had last seen alive than the picture of a man of sixty is like a daguerreotype of his early youth in the costume of another generation. Nothing really can describe that ghastly caricature, that parody, masquerading there in the firelight as Défago. From the ruins of the dark and awful memories he still retains, Simpson declares that the face was more animal than human, the features drawn about into wrong proportions, the skin loose and hanging, as though he had been subjected to extraordinary pressures and tensions. It made him think vaguely of those bladder faces blown up by the hawkers on Ludgate Hill, that change their expression as they swell, and as they collapse emit a faint and wailing imitation of a voice. Both face and voice suggested some such abominable resemblance. But Cathcart long afterwards, seeking to describe the indescribable, asserts that thus might have looked a face and body that had been in air so rarified that, the weight of atmosphere being removed, the entire structure threatened to fly asunder and become – *incoherent. . . .*

It was Hank, though all distraught and shaking with a tearing volume of emotion he could neither handle nor understand, who brought things to a head without much ado. He went off to a little distance from the fire, apparently so that the light should not dazzle him too much, and shading his eyes for a moment with both hands, shouted in a loud voice that held anger and affection dreadfully mingled:

"You ain't Défaygo! You ain't Défaygo at all! I don't give a – damn, but that ain't you, my ole pal of twenty years!" He glared upon the huddled figure as though he would destroy him with his eyes. "An' if it is I'll swab the floor of hell with a wad of cotton wool on a toothpick, s'help me the good Gawd!" he added, with a violent fling of horror and disgust.

It was impossible to silence him. He stood there shouting like one possessed, horrible to see, horrible to hear – *because it was the truth.* He repeated himself in fifty different ways, each more outlandish than the last. The woods rang with echoes. At one time it looked as if he meant to fling himself upon "the intruder," for his hand continually jerked towards the long hunting knife in his belt.

But in the end he did nothing, and the whole tempest completed itself very shortly with tears. Hank's voice suddenly broke, he collapsed on the ground, and Cathcart somehow or other persuaded him at last to go into the tent and lie quiet. The remainder of the affair, indeed, was witnessed by him from behind the canvas, his white and terrified face peeping through the crack of the tent door flap.

Then Dr. Cathcart, closely followed by his nephew who so far had kept his courage better than all of them, went up with a determined air and stood opposite to the figure of Défago huddled over the fire. He looked him squarely in the face and spoke. At first his voice was firm.

"Défago, tell us what's happened — just a little, so that we can know how best to help you?" he asked in a tone of authority, almost of command. And at that point, it *was* command. At once afterwards, however, it changed in quality, for the figure turned up to him a face so piteous, so terrible and so little like humanity, that the doctor shrank back from him as from something spiritually unclean. Simpson, watching close behind him, says he got the impression of a mask that was on the verge of dropping off, and that underneath they would discover something black and diabolical, revealed in utter nakedness. "Out with it, man, out with it!" Cathcart cried, terror running neck and neck with entreaty. "None of us can stand this much longer. . . !" It was the cry of instinct over reason.

And then "Défago," smiling *whitely,* answered in that thin and fading voice that already seemed passing over into a sound of quite another character —

"I seen that great Wendigo thing," he whispered, sniffing the air about him exactly like an animal. "I been with it too —"

Whether the poor devil would have said more, or whether Dr. Cathcart would have continued the impossible cross examination cannot be known, for at that moment the voice of Hank was heard yelling at the top of his voice from behind the canvas that concealed all but his terrified eyes. Such a howling was never heard.

"His feet! Oh, Gawd, his feet! Look at his great changed — feet!"

Défago, shuffling where he sat, had moved in such a way that for the first time his legs were in full light and his feet were visible. Yet Simpson had no time, himself, to see properly what Hank had seen. And Hank has never seen fit to tell. That same instant, with a leap like that of a frightened tiger, Cathcart was upon him, bundling the folds of blanket about his legs with such speed that the young student caught little more than a passing glimpse of something dark and oddly massed where moccasined feet ought to have been, and saw even that but with uncertain vision.

Then, before the doctor had time to do more, or Simpson time to even think a question, much less ask it, Défago was standing upright in front of them, balancing with pain and difficulty, and upon his shapeless and twisted visage an expression so dark and so malicious that it was, in the true sense, monstrous.

"Now *you* seen it too," he wheezed, "you seen my fiery, burning feet! And now — that is, unless you kin save me an' prevent — it's 'bout time for —"

His piteous and beseeching voice was interrupted by a sound that was like the roar of wind coming across the lake. The trees overhead shook their tangled branches. The blazing fire bent its flames as before a blast. And something swept with a terrific, rushing noise about the little camp and seemed to surround it entirely in a single moment of time. Défago shook the clinging blankets from his body, turned towards the woods behind, and with the same stumbling motion that had brought him — was gone: gone, before anyone could move muscle to prevent him, gone with an amazing, blundering swiftness that left no time to act. The darkness positively swallowed him; and less than a dozen seconds later, above the roar of the swaying trees and the shout of the sudden wind, all three men, watching and listening with stricken hearts, heard a cry that seemed to drop down upon them from a great height of sky and distance —

"Oh, oh! This fiery height! Oh, oh! My feet of fire! My burning feet of fire. . . !" then died away, into untold space and silence.

Dr. Cathcart — suddenly master of himself, and therefore of the others — was just able to seize Hank violently by the arm as he tried to dash headlong into the Bush.

"But I want ter know, — you!" shrieked the guide. "I want ter see! That ain't him at all, but some — devil that's shunted into his place. . . !"

Somehow or other — he admits he never quite knew how he accomplished it — he managed to keep him in the tent and pacify him. The doctor, apparently, had reached the stage where reaction had set in and allowed his own innate force to conquer. Certainly he "managed" Hank admirably. It was his nephew, however, hitherto so wonderfully controlled, who gave him most cause for anxiety, for the cumulative strain had now produced a condition of lachrymose hysteria which made it necessary to isolate him upon a bed of boughs and blankets as far removed from Hank as was possible under the circumstances.

And there he lay, as the watches of that haunted night passed over the lonely camp, crying startled sentences, and fragments of sentences, into the folds of his blanket. A quantity of gibberish about speed and height and fire mingled oddly with biblical memories of the classroom. "People with broken faces all on fire are coming at a most awful, awful, pace towards the camp!" he would moan one minute; and the next would sit up and stare into the woods, intently listening, and whisper, "How terrible in the wilderness are — are the feet of them that —" until his uncle came across the change the direction of his thoughts and comfort him.

The hysteria, fortunately, proved but temporary. Sleep cured him, just as it cured Hank.

Till the first signs of daylight came, soon after five o'clock, Dr. Cathcart kept his vigil. His face was the color of chalk, and there were strange flushes beneath the eyes. An appalling terror of the soul battled with his will all through those silent hours. These were some of the outer signs . . .

At dawn he lit the fire himself, made breakfast, and woke the others, and by seven they were well on their way back to the home camp — three perplexed and afflicted men, but each in his own way having reduced his inner turmoil to a condition of more or less systematized order again.

They talked little, and then only of the most wholesome and common things, for their minds were charged with painful thoughts that clamored for explanation, though no one dared refer to them. Hank, being nearest to primitive conditions, was the first to find himself, for he was also less complex. In Dr. Cathcart "civilization" championed his forces against an attack singular enough. To this day, perhaps, he is not *quite* sure of certain things. Anyhow, he took longer to "find himself."

Simpson, the student of divinity, it was who arranged his conclusions probably with the best, though not most scientific, appearance of order. Out there, in the heart of unreclaimed wilderness, they had surely witnessed something crudely and essentially primitive. Something that had survived somehow the advance of humanity had emerged terrifically, betraying a scale of life still monstrous and immature. He envisaged it rather as a glimpse into prehistoric ages, when superstitions, gigantic and uncouth, still oppressed the hearts of men; when the forces of nature were still untamed, the Powers that may have haunted a primeval universe not yet withdrawn. To this day he thinks of what he termed years later in a sermon "savage and formidable Potencies lurking behind the souls of men, not evil perhaps in themselves, yet instinctively hostile to humanity as it exists."

With his uncle he never discussed the matter in detail, for the barrier between the two types of mind made it difficult. Only once, years later, something led them to the frontier of the subject — of a single detail of the subject, rather:

"Can't you even tell me what — *they* were like?" he asked; and the reply, though conceived in wisdom, was not encouraging. "It is far better you should try not to know, or to find out."

"Well — that odor — ?" persisted the nephew. "What do you make of that?"

Dr. Cathcart looked at him and raised his eyebrows.

"Odors," he replied, "are not so easy as sounds and sights of telepathic communication. I make as much, or as little, probably, as you do yourself."

He was not quite so glib as usual with his explanations. That was all.

At the fall of day, cold, exhausted, famished, the party came to the end of the long portage and dragged themselves into a camp that at first glimpse seemed empty. Fire there was none, and no Punk came forward to welcome them. The emotional capacity of all three was too overspent to recognize either surprise or annoyance; but the cry of spontaneous affection that burst from the lips of Hank, as he rushed ahead of them towards the fireplace, came probably as a warning that the end of the amazing affair was not quite yet. And both Cathcart and his nephew confessed afterwards that when they saw him kneel down in his excitement and embrace something that reclined, gently moving, beside the extinguished ashes, they felt in their very bones that this "something" would prove to be Défago — the true Défago returned.

And so, indeed, it was.

It is soon told. Exhausted to the point of emaciation, the French Canadian — what was left of him, that is — fumbled among the ashes, trying to make a fire. His body crouched there, the weak fingers obeying feebly the instinctive habit of a lifetime with twigs and matches. But there was no longer any mind to direct the simple operation. The mind had fled beyond recall. And with it, too, had fled memory. Not only recent events, but all previous life was a blank.

This time it was the real man, though incredibly and horribly shrunken. On his face was no expression of any kind whatever — fear, welcome, or recognition. He did not seem to know who it was that embraced him, or who it was that fed, warmed and spoke to him the words of comfort and relief. Forlorn and broken beyond all reach of human aid, the little man did meekly as he was bidden. The "something" that had constituted him "individual" had vanished forever.

In some ways it was more terribly moving than anything they had yet seen — that idiot smile as he drew wads of coarse moss from his swollen cheeks and told them that he was "a damned moss eater"; the continued vomiting of even the simplest food; and, worst of all, the piteous and childish voice of complaint in which he told them that his feet pained him — "burn like fire" — which was natural enough when Dr. Cathcart examined them and found that both were dreadfully frozen. Beneath the eyes there were faint indications of recent bleeding.

The details of how he survived the prolonged exposure, of where he had been, or of how he covered the great distance from one camp to the other, including an immense détour of the lake on foot since he had no canoe — all this remains unknown. His memory had vanished completely. And before the end of the winter whose beginning witnessed this strange occurrence, Défago, bereft of mind, memory and soul, had gone with it. He lingered only a few weeks.

And what Punk was able to contribute to the story throws no further light upon it. He was cleaning fish by the lake shore about five o'clock in the evening — an hour, that is, before the search party returned — when he saw this shadow of the guide picking its way weakly into camp. In advance of him, he declares, came the faint whiff of a certain singular odor.

That same instant old Punk started for home. He covered the entire journey of three days as only Indian blood could have covered it. The terror of a whole race drove him. He knew what it all meant. Défago had "seen the Wendigo."

Old Clothes

I

*I*maginative children with their odd questionings of life and their delicate nervous systems must be often a source of greater anxiety than delight to their parents, and Aileen, the child of my widowed cousin, impressed me from the beginning as being a strangely vivid specimen of her class. Moreover, the way she took to me from the first placed quasi-avuncular responsibilities upon my shoulders (in her mother's eyes), that I had no right, even as I had no inclination, to shirk. Indeed, I loved the queer, wayward, mysterious little being. Only it was not always easy to advise; and her somewhat marked peculiarities certainly called for advice of a skilled and special order.

It was not merely that her make-believe was unusually sincere and haunting, and that she would talk by the hour with invisible playmates (touching them, putting up her lips to be kissed, opening doors for them to pass in and out, and setting chairs, footstools and even flowers for them), for many children in my experience have done as much and done it with a vast sincerity; but that she also accepted what *they told her* with so steady a degree of conviction that their words influenced her life and, accordingly, her health.

They told her stories, apparently, in which she herself played a central part, stories, moreover, that were neither comforting nor wise. She would sit in a corner of the room, as both her mother and myself can vouch, face to face with some make-believe Occupant of the chair so carefully arranged; the footstool had been placed with precision, and sometimes she would move it a little this way or that; the table whereon rested the invisible elbows was beside her with a jar of flowers that changed according to the particular visitor. And there she would wait motionless, perhaps an hour at a time, staring up into the viewless features of the person who was talking with her — who was telling her a story in which she played an exceedingly poignant part. Her face altered with the run of emotions, her eyes grew large and moist, and sometimes frightened; rarely she laughed, and rarely asked a whispered question, but more often sat there, tense and eager, uncannily absorbed in the inaudible tale falling from invisible lips — the tale of her own adventures.

But it was the terror inspired by these singular recitals that affected her delicate health as early as the age of eight, and when, owing to her mother's well-meant but ill-advised ridicule, she indulged them with more secrecy, the effect upon her nerves and character became so acute that I was summoned down upon a special advisory visit I scarcely appreciated.

"Now, George, what *do* you think I had better do? Dr. Hale insists upon more exercise and more companionship, sea air and all the rest of it, but none of these things seem to do any good."

"Have you taken her into your confidence, or rather has *she* taken you into hers?" I ventured mildly.

The question seemed to give offence a little.

"Of course," was the emphatic answer. "The child has no secrets from her mother. She is perfectly devoted to me."

"But you *have* tried to laugh her out of it, haven't you now?"

"Yes. But with such success that she holds these conversations far less than she used to —"

"Or more secretly?" was my comment, that was met with a superior shrug of the shoulders.

Then, after a further pause, in which my cousins distress and my own affectionate interest in the whimsical imagination of my little niece combined to move me, I tried again —

"Make-believe," I observed, "is always a bit puzzling to us older folk, because, though we indulge in it all our lives, We no longer believe in it; whereas children like Aileen —"

She interrupted me quickly —

"You know what I feel anxious about," she said, lowering her voice. "I think there may be cause for serious alarm." Then she added frankly, looking up with grave eyes into my face, "George, I want your help — your best help, please. You've always been a true friend."

I gave it to her in calculated words.

"Theresa," I said with grave emphasis, "there is no trace of insanity on either side of the family, and my own opinion is that Aileen is perfectly well-balanced in spite of this too highly developed imagination. But, above all things, you must not drive it inwards by making fun of it. Lead it out. E — ducate it. Guide it by intelligent sympathy. Get her to tell you all about it, and so on. I think Aileen wants careful observing, perhaps — but nothing more."

For some minutes she watched my face in silence, her eyes intent, her features slightly twitching. I knew at once from her manner what she was driving at. She approached the subject with awkwardness and circumlocution, for it was something she dreaded, not feeling sure whether it was of heaven or of hell.

"You are very wonderful, George," she said at length, "and you have theories about almost everything —"

"Speculations," I admitted.

"And your hypnotic power is helpful, you know. Now — if — if you thought it safe, and that Providence would not be offended —"

"Theresa," I stopped her firmly before she had committed herself to the point where she would feel hurt by a refusal, "let me say at once that I do *not* consider a child a fit subject for hypnotic experiment, and I feel quite sure that an intelligent person like yourself will agree with me that it's unpermissible."

"I was only thinking of a little 'suggestion,'" she murmured.

"Which would come far better from the mother."

"If the mother had not already lost her power by using ridicule," she confessed meekly.

"Yes, you never should have laughed. Why did you, I wonder?"

An expression came into her eyes that I knew to be invariably with hysterical temperaments the precursor of tears. She looked round to make sure no one was listening.

"George," she whispered, and into the dusk of that September evening passed some shadow between us that left behind an atmosphere of sudden and inexplicable chill, "George, I wish — I wish it was *quite* clear to me that it really is all make-believe, I mean —"

"What do you mean?" I said, with a severity that was assumed to hide my own uneasiness. But the tears came the same instant in a flood that made any intelligent explanation out of the question.

The terror of the mother for her own blood burst forth.

"I'm frightened — horribly frightened," she said between the sobs.

"I'll go up and see the child myself," I said comfortingly at length when the storm had subsided. "I'll run up to the nursery. You mustn't be alarmed. Aileen's all right. I think I can help you in the matter a good deal."

*I*n the nursery as usual Aileen was alone. I found her sitting by the open window, an empty chair opposite to her. She was staring at it — into it, but it is not easy to describe the certainty she managed to convey that there was someone sitting in that chair, talking with her. It was her manner that did it. She rose quickly, with a start as I came in, and made a half gesture in the direction of the empty chair as though to shake hands, then corrected herself quickly, and gave a friendly little nod of farewell or dismissal — then turned towards me. Incredible as it must sound, that chair looked at once slightly otherwise. It was empty.

"Aileen, what in the world are you up to?"

"You know, uncle," she replied, without hesitation.

"Oh, rather! *I* know! " I said, trying to get into her mood so as later to get her out of it, "because I do the same thing with the people in my own stories. I talk to them too —"

She came up to my side, as though it were a matter of life and death. "But do they *answer?*"

I realized the overwhelming sincerity, even the seriousness, of the question to her mind. The shadow evoked downstairs by my cousin had followed me up here. It touched me on the shoulder.

"Unless they answer," I told her, "they are not really alive, and the story hangs fire when people read it."

She watched me very closely a moment as we leaned out of the open window where the rich perfume of the Portuguese laurels came up from the lawns below. The proximity of the child brought a distinct atmosphere of its own, an atmosphere charged with suggestions, almost with faint pictures, as of things I had once known. I had often felt this before, and did not altogether welcome it, for the pictures seemed framed in some emotional setting that invariably escaped my analysis. I understood in a vague way what it was about the child that made her mother afraid. There flashed across me a fugitive sensation, utterly elusive yet painfully real, that she knew moments of suffering by rights she ought not to have known. Bizarre and unreasonable as the conception was, it was convincing. And it touched a profound sympathy in me.

Aileen undoubtedly was aware of this sympathy.

"It's Philip that talks to me *most* of the time," she volunteered, "and he's always, always explaining — but never quite finishes."

"Explaining what, dear little Child of the Moon?" I urged gently, giving her a name she used to love when she was smaller.

"Why he couldn't come in time to save me, of course," she said. "You see, they cut off both his hands."

I shall never forget the sensation these words of a child's mental adventure caused me, nor the kind of bitter reality they forced into me that they were true, and not merely a detail of some attempted rescue of a "Princess in a Tower." A vivid rush of thought seemed to focus my consciousness upon my own two wrists, as though I felt the pain of the operation she mentioned, and with a swift instinct that slipped into action before I could control it, I had hidden both hands from her sight in my coat pockets.

"And what else does 'Philip' tell you?" I asked gently.

Her face flushed. Tears came into her eyes, then fled away again lest they should fall from their softly-colored nests.

"That he loved me *so awfully,*" she replied; "and that he loved me to the very end, and that all his life after I was gone, and after they cut his hands off, he did nothing but pray for me — from the end of the world where he went to hide —"

I shook myself free with an effort from the enveloping atmosphere of tragedy, realizing that her imagination must be driven along brighter channels and that my duty must precede my interest.

"But you must get Philip to tell you all his funny and jolly adventures, too," I said, "the ones he had, you know, when his hands grew again —"

The expression that came into her face literally froze my blood.

"That's only making-up stories," she said icily. "They never did grow again. There *were* no happy or funny adventures."

I cast about in my mind for an inspiration how to help her mind into more wholesome ways of invention. I realized more than ever before the profundity of my affection for this strange, fatherless child, and how I would give my whole soul if I could help her and teach her joy. It was a real love that swept me, rooted in things deeper than I realized.

But, before the right word was given me to speak, I felt her nestle up against my side, and heard her utter the very phrase that for some time I had been dreading in the secret places of my soul she *would* utter. The sentence seemed to shake me within. I knew a hurried, passing moment of unspeakable pain that is utterly beyond me to reason about.

"*You* know," was what she said, "because it's *you* who are Philip!"

And the way she said it — so quietly, the words touched somehow with a gentle though compassionate scorn, yet made golden by a burning love that filled her little person to the brim — robbed me momentarily of all power of speech. I could only bend down and put my arm about her and kiss her head that came up barely to the level of my chin. I swear I loved that child as I never loved any other human being.

"Then Philip is going to teach you all sorts of jolly adventures with his new hands," I remember saying, with blundering good intention, "because he's no longer sad, and is full of fun, and loves you twice as much as ever!"

And I caught her up and carried her down the long stairs of the house out into the garden, where we joined the dogs and romped together until the face of the motherly Kempster at an upper window shouted down something stupid about bedtime, supper, or the rest of it, and Aileen, flushed yet with brighter eyes, ran into the house and, turning at the door, showed me her odd little face wreathed in smiles and laughter.

*F*or a long time I paced to and fro with a cigar between the box hedges of the old-time garden, thinking of the child and her queer imaginings, and of the profoundly moving and disquieting sensations she stirred in me at the same time. Her face flitted by my side through the shadows. She was not pretty, properly speaking, but her appearance possessed an original charm that appealed to me strongly. Her head was big and in some way old-fashioned; her eyes, dark but not large, were placed close together, and she had a wide mouth that was certainly not beautiful. But the look of distressed and yearning passion that sometimes swept over these features, not otherwise prepossessing, changed her look into sudden beauty, a beauty of the soul, a soul that knew suffering and was acquainted with grief. This, at least, is the way my own mind saw the child, and therefore the only way I can hope to make others see her. Were I a painter I might put her upon canvas in some imaginary portrait and call it, perhaps, "Reincarnation" — for I have never seen anything in child-life that impressed me so vividly with that odd idea of an old soul come back to the world in a new young body — a new Suit of Clothes.

But when I talked with my cousin after dinner, and consoled her with the assurance that Aileen was gifted with an unusually vivid imagination which time and ourselves must train to some more practical end — while I said all this, and more besides, two sentences the child had made use of kept ringing in my head. One — when she told me with merciless perception that I was only "making-up" stories; and the other, when she had informed me with that quiet rush of certainty and conviction that "Philip" was — myself.

III

A big-game expedition of some months put an end temporarily to my avuncular responsibilities; at least so far as action was concerned, for there were certain memories that held curiously vivid among all the absorbing turmoil of our camp life. Often, lying awake in my tent at night, or even following the tracks of our prey through the jungle, these pictures would jump out upon me and claim attention. Aileen's little face of suffering would come between me and the sight of my rifle; or her assurance that I was the "Philip" of her imagination would attack me with an accent of reality that seemed queer enough until I analyzed it away. And more than once I found myself thinking of her dark and serious countenance when she told how "Philip" had loved her to the end, and would have saved her if they had not cut off his hands. My own Imagination, it seemed, was weaving the details of her child's invention into a story, for I never could think of this latter detail without positively experiencing a sensation of smarting pain in my wrists. . . ! When I returned to England in the spring they had moved, I found, into a house by the sea, a tumbled-down old rookery of a building my cousin s father had rarely occupied during his lifetime, nor she been able to let since it had passed into her possession. An urgent letter summoned me thither, and I traveled down the very day after my arrival to the bleak Norfolk coast with a sense of foreboding in my heart that increased almost to a presentiment when the cab entered the long drive and I recognized the grey and gloomy walls of the old mansion. The sea air swept the gardens with its salt wash, and the moan of the surf was audible even up to the windows.

"I wonder what possessed her to come here?" was the first thought in my mind. "Surely the last place in the world to bring a morbid or too-sensitive child to!" My further dread that something had happened to the little child I loved so tenderly was partly dispelled, however, when my cousin met me at the door with open arms and smiling face, though the welcome I soon found, was chiefly due to the relief she gained from my presence. Something *had* happened to little Aileen, though not the final disaster that I dreaded. She had suffered from nervous attacks of so serious a character during my absence that the doctor had insisted upon sea air, and my cousin, not with the best judgment, had seized upon the idea of making the old house serve the purpose. She had made a wing habitable for a few weeks; she hoped the entire change of scene would fill the little girl's mind with new and happier ideas. Instead — the result had been exactly the reverse. The child had wept copiously and hysterically the moment she set eyes on the old walls and smelt the odor of the sea.

But before we had been talking ten minutes there was a cry and a sound of rushing footsteps, and a scampering figure, with dark, flying hair, had dived headlong into my arms, and Aileen was sobbing —

"Oh, you've come, you've come at last! I *am* so awfully glad. I thought it would be the same as before, and you'd get caught." She ran from me next and kissed her mother, laughing with pleasure through her tears, and was gone from the room as quickly as she had come.

I caught my cousin's glance of frightened amazement.

"Now isn't *that* odd?" she exclaimed in a hushed voice. "Isn't *that* odd? Those are the tears of happiness, — the first time I've seen her smile since we came here last week."

But it rather nettled me, I think. "Why odd?" I asked. "Aileen loves me, it's delightful to —"

"Not that, not that!" she said quickly. "It's odd, I meant, she should have found you out so soon. She didn't even know you were back in England, and I'd sent her off to play on the sands with Kempster and the dogs so as to be sure of an opportunity of telling you everything before you saw her."

Our eyes met squarely, yet not with complete sympathy or comprehension.

"You see, she knew perfectly well you were here — the instant you came."

"But there's nothing in that," I asserted. "Children know things just as animals do. She scented her favorite uncle from the shore like a dog!" And I laughed in her face.

That laugh perhaps was a mistake on my part. Its well-meant cheerfulness was possibly overdone. Even to myself it did not ring quite true.

"I do believe you are in league with her — against me," was the remark that greeted it, accompanied by an increase of that expression of fear in the eyes I had divined the moment we met upon the doorstep. Finding nothing genuine to say in reply, I kissed the top of her head.

In due course, after the tea things had been removed, I learned the exact state of affairs, and even making due allowance for my cousin's excited exaggerations, there were things that seemed to me inexplicable enough on any ground of normal explanation. Slight as the details may seem when set down seriatim, their cumulative effect upon my own mind touched an impressive and disagreeable climax that I did my best to conceal from outward betrayal. As I sat in the great shadowy room, listening to my cousin's jerky description of "childish" things, it was borne in upon me that they might well have the profoundest possible

significance. I watched her eager, frightened face, lit only by the flickering flames the sharp spring evening made necessary, and thought of
the subject of our conversation flitting about the dreary halls and
corridors of the huge old building, a little figure of tragedy, laughing,
crying and dreaming in a world entirely her own — and there stirred in
me an unwelcome recognition of those mutinous and disheveled forces
that lie but thinly screened behind the commonplace details of life and
that now seemed ready to burst forth and play their mysterious *rôle*
before our very eyes.

"Tell me *exactly* what has happened," I urged, with decision but
sympathy.

"There's so little, when it's put into words, George; but — well, the
thing that first upset me was that she — knew the whole place, though
she's never been here before. She knew every passage and staircase, many
of them that I did not know myself; she showed us an underground
passage to the sea, that father himself didn't know; and she actually drew
a scrawl of the house as it used to be three hundred years ago when the
other wing was standing where the copper beeches grow now. It's
accurate, too."

It seemed impossible to explain to a person of my cousin's temperament the theories of prenatal memory and the like, or the possibility
of her own knowledge being communicated telepathically to the brain
of her own daughter. I said therefore very little, but listened with an
uneasiness that grew horribly.

"She found her way about the gardens instantly, as if she had played
in them all her life; and she keeps drawing figures of people — men and
women — in old costumes, the sort of thing our ancestors wore, you
know —"

"Well, well, well!" I interrupted impatiently; "what can be more
natural? She is old enough to have seen pictures she can remember
enough to copy — ?"

"Of course," she resumed calmly, but with a calmness due to the
terror that ate her very soul and swallowed up all minor emotions; "of
course, but one of the faces she gets is — a *portrait.*"

She rose suddenly and came closer to me across the big stone hearth,
lowering her voice to a whisper, "George," she whispered, "it's the very
image of that awful — de Lorne!

The announcement, I admit, gave me a thrill, for that particular
ancestor on my father's side had largely influenced my boyhood imagination by the accounts of his cruelty wickedness in days gone by. But
I think now the shiver that ran down my back was due to the thought
of my little Aileen practicing her memory and pencil upon so vile an

object. That, and my cousin's pale visage of alarm, combined to shake me. I said, however, what seemed wise and reasonable at the moment.

"You'll be claiming next, Theresa, that the house is haunted," I suggested.

She shrugged her shoulders with an indifference that was very eloquent of the strength of this other more substantial terror.

"That would be so easy to deal with," she said, without even looking up. "A ghost stays in one place. Aileen could hardly take it about with her."

I think we both enjoyed the pause that followed. It gave *me* time to collect my forces for what I knew was coming. It gave *her* time to get her further facts into some pretence of coherence.

"I told you about the belt?" she asked at length, weakly, and as though unutterable things she longed to disown forced the question to her unwilling lips.

The sentence shot into me like the thrust of a naked sword. . . . I shook my head.

"Well, even a year or two ago she had that strange dislike of wearing a belt with her frocks. We thought it was a whim, and did not humor her. Belts are necessary, you know, George," she tried to smile feebly. "But now it has come to such a point that I've had to give in."

"She dislikes a belt round her waist, you mean?" I asked, fighting a sudden inexplicable spasm in my heart.

"It makes her scream. The moment anything encloses her waist she sets up such a hubbub, and struggles so, and hides away, and I've been obliged to yield."

"But really, Theresa — !"

"She declares it fastens her in, and she will never get free again, and all kinds of other things. Oh, her fear is dreadful, poor child. Her face gets that sort of awful grey, don't you know? Even Kempster, who if anything is too firm, had to give in."

"And what else, pray?" I disliked hearing these details intensely. It made me ache with a kind of anger that I could not at once relieve the child's pain.

"The way she spoke to me after Dr. Hale had left — you know how awfully kind and gentle he is, and how Aileen likes him and even plays with him and sits on his knee? Well, he was talking about her diet, regulating it and so forth, teasing her that she mustn't eat this and that, and the rest of it, when she turned that horrid grey again and jumped oft his knee with her scream — that thin wailing scream she has that goes through me like a knife, George — and flew to the nursery and locked herself in with — what do you think? — with all the bread, apples, cold meat and other eatables she could find!"

"Eatables!" I exclaimed, aware of another spasm of vivid pain.

"When I coaxed her out, hours later, she was trembling like a leaf and fell into my arms utterly exhausted, and all I could get her to tell me was this — which she repeated again and again with a sort of beseeching, appealing tone that made my heart bleed —"

She hesitated an instant.

"Tell me at once."

"'I shall starve again, I shall starve again,' were the words she used. She kept repeating it over and over between her sobs. 'I shall be without anything to eat. I shall starve!' And, would you believe it, while she hid in that nursery cupboard she had crammed so much cake and stuff into her little self that she was violently sick for a couple of days. Moreover, she now hates the sight of Dr. Hale so much, poor man, that it's useless for him to see her. It does more harm than good."

I had risen and begun to walk up and down the hall while she told me this. I said very little. In my mind strange thoughts tore and raced, standing erect before me out of unbelievably immense depths of shadow. There was nothing very pregnant I found to say, however, for theories and speculations are of small avail as practical help — unless two minds see eye to eye in them.

"And the rest?" I asked gently, coming behind the chair and resting both hands upon her shoulders. She got up at once and faced me. I was afraid to show too much sympathy lest the tears should come.

"Oh, George," she exclaimed, "I *am* relieved you have come. You are really strong and comforting. To feel your great hands on my shoulders gives me courage. But, you know, truly and honestly I am frightened out of my very wits by the child —"

"You won't stay here, of course?"

"We leave at the end of this week," she replied. "You will not desert me till then, I know. And Aileen will be all right as long as you are here, for you have the most extraordinary effect on her for good."

"Bless her little suffering imagination," I said. "You can count on me. I'll send to town tonight for my things."

And then she told me about the room. It was simple enough, but it conveyed a more horrible certainty of something true than all the other details put together. For there was a room on the ground floor, intended to be used on wet days when the nursery was too far for muddy boots — and into this room Aileen could not go. Why? No one could tell. The facts were that the first moment the child ran in, her mother close behind, she stopped, swayed, and nearly fell. Then, with shrieks that were even heard outside by the gardeners sweeping the gravel path, she flung herself headlong against the wall, against a particular corner of it that is to say, and beat it with her little fists until the skin broke and left stains upon the paper. It all happened in less than a minute. The words she cried so frantically her mother was too shocked and flabbergasted to remember, or even to hear properly. Aileen nearly upset her in her bewildered efforts next to find the door and escape. And the first thing she did when escape was accomplished, was to drop in a dead faint upon the stone floor of the passage outside.

"Now, is *that* all make-believe?" whispered Theresa, unable to keep the shudder from her lips. "Is that all merely part of a story she has make up and plays a part in?"

We looked one another straight in the eyes for a space of some seconds. The dread in the mother's heart leaped out to swell a terror in my own — a terror of another kind, but greater.

"It is too late tonight," I said at length, "for it would only excite her unnecessarily; but tomorrow I will talk with Aileen. And — if it seems wise — I might — I might be able to help in other ways too," I added.

So I did talk to her — next day.

IV

I always had her confidence, this little dark-eyed maid, and there was an intimacy between us that made play and talk very delightful. Yet as a rule, without giving myself a satisfactory reason, I preferred talking with her in the sunlight. She was not eerie, bless her little heart of queerness and mystery, but she had a way of suggesting other ways of life and existence shouldering about us that made me look round in the dark and wonder what the shadows concealed or what waited round the next corner.

We were on the lawn, where the bushy yews drop thick shade, the soft air making tea possible out of doors, my cousin out driving to distant calls; and Aileen had invited herself and was messing about with my manuscripts in a way that vexed me, for I had been reading my fairy tales to her and she kept asking me questions that shamed my limited powers. I remember, too, that I was glad the collie ran to and fro past us, scampering and barking after the swallows on the lawn.

"Only *some* of your stories are true, aren't they?" she asked abruptly.

"How do you know that, young critic?" I had been waiting for an opening supplied by herself. Anything forced on my part she would have suspected.

"Oh, I can tell."

Then she came up and whispered without any hint of invitation on my part, "Uncle, it is true, isn't it, that I've been in other places with you? And isn't it only the things we did *there* that make the true stories?"

The opening was delivered all perfect and complete into my hands. I cannot conceive how it was I availed myself of it so queerly – I mean, how it was that the words and the name slipped out of their own accord as though I was saying something in a dream.

"Of course, my little Lady Aileen, because in imagination, you see, we –"

But before I had time to finish the sentence with which I hoped to coax out the true inwardness of her own distress, she was upon me in a heap.

"Oh," she cried, with a sudden passionate outburst, "then you *do* know my name? You know all the story – *our* story!

She was very excited, face flushed, eyes dancing, all the emotions of a life charged to the brim with experience playing through her little person.

"Of course, Miss Inventor, I know your name," I said quickly, puzzled, and with a sudden dismay that was hideous, clutching at my throat.

"And all that we did in this place?" she went on, pointing with increased excitement to the thick, ivy-grown walls of the old house.

My own emotion grew extraordinarily, a swift, rushing uneasiness upsetting all my calculations. For it suddenly came back to me that in calling her "Lady Aileen" I had not pronounced the name quite as usual. My tongue had played a trick with the consonants and vowels, though at the moment of utterance I had somehow failed to notice the change. "Aileen" and "Helen" are almost interchangeable sounds. . . .! And it was "Lady Helen" that I had actually said.

The discovery took my breath away for an instant – and the way she had leaped upon the name to claim it.

"No one else, you see, knows me as 'Lady Helen,'" she continued whispering, "because that's only in our story, isn't it? And now I'm just Aileen Langton. But as long as you know, it's all right. Oh, I am so awf'ly glad you knew, most awf'ly, *awf'ly* glad."

I was momentarily at a loss for words. Keenly desirous to guide the child's "pain-stories" into wiser channels, and thus help her to relief, I hesitated a moment for the right clue. I murmured something soothing

about "our story," while in my mind I searched vigorously for the best
way of leading her on to explain all her terror of the belt, the fear of
starvation, the room that made her scream, and all the rest. All *that* I
was most anxious to get out of her little tortured mind and then replace
it by some brighter dream.

But the insidious experience had shaken my confidence a little, and
these explicable emotions destroyed my elder wisdom. The little Inventor had caught me away into the reality of her own "story" with a sense
of conviction that was even beyond witchery. And the next sentence she
almost instantly let loose upon me completed my discomfiture –

"With you," she said, still half whispering, "with you I could even go
into the room. I never could – alone – !"

The spring wind whispering in the yews behind us brought in that
moment something upon me from vanished childhood days that made
me tremble. Some wave of lost passion – lost because I guessed not its
origin or nature – surged through the depths of me, sending faint
messages to the surface of my consciousness. Aileen, little mischief-
maker, changed before my very eyes as she stood there close – changed
into a tall sad figure that beckoned to me across seas of time and
distance, with the haze of ages in her eyes and gestures, . . . I was obliged
to focus my gaze upon her with a deliberate effort to see her again as
the tumble-haired girl I was accustomed to. . . .

*T*hen, sitting in the creaky garden chair, I drew her down upon my
knee, determined to win the whole story from her mind. My back was
to the house; she was perched at an angle, however, that enabled her to
command the doors and windows. I mention this because, scarcely had
I begun my attack, when I saw that her attention wandered, and that
she seemed curiously uneasy. Once or twice, as she shifted her position
to get a view of something that was going on over my shoulder, I was
aware that a slight shiver passed from her small person down to my
knees. She seemed to be expecting something – with dread.

"We'll make a special expedition, armed to the teeth," I said, with a
laugh, referring to her singular words about the room. "We'll send Pat
in first to bark at the cobwebs, and we'll take lots of provisions and –
and water in case of a siege – and a file –"

I cannot pretend to understand why I chose those precise words – or
why it was as though other thoughts than those I had intended rose up,
clamoring for expression. It seemed all I could manage not to say a lot
of other things about the room that could only have frightened instead

of relieving her.

"Will you talk *into the wall* too?" she asked, turning her eyes down suddenly upon me with a little rush and flame of passion. And though I had not the faintest conception what she meant, the question sent an agony of yearning pain through me. "Talking into the wall," I instantly grasped, referred to the core of her trouble, the very central idea that frightened her and provided the suffering and terror of all her imaginings.

But I had no time to follow up the clue thus mysteriously offered to me, for almost at the same moment her eyes fixed themselves upon something behind me with an expression of tense horror, as though she saw the approach of a danger that might — kill.

"Oh, oh!" she cried under her breath, "he's coming! He's coming to take me! Uncle George — Philip — !"

The same impulse operated upon us simultaneously, it seems, for I sprang up with my fists clenched at the very instant she shot off my knee and stood with all her muscles rigid as though to resist attack. She was shaking dreadfully. Her face went the color of linen.

"*Who's* coming — ?" I began sharply, then stopped as I saw the figure of a man moving towards us from the house. It was the butler — the new butler who had arrived only that very afternoon. It is impossible to say what there was in his swift and silent approach that was — abominable. The man was upon us, it seemed, almost as soon as I caught sight of him, and the same moment Aileen, with a bursting cry, looking wildly about her for a place to hide in, plunged headlong into my arms and buried her face in my coat.

Horribly perplexed, yet mortified that the servant should see my little friend in such a state, I did my best to pretend that it was all part of some mad game or other, and catching her up in my arms, I ran, calling the collie to follow with, "Come on, Pat! She's our prisoner!" — and only set her down when we were under the limes at the far end of the lawn. She was all white and ghostly from her terror, still looking frantically about her, trembling in such a way that I thought any minute she must collapse in a dead faint. She clung to me with very tight fingers. How I hated that man. Judging by the sudden violence of my loathing he might have been some monster who wanted to torture her. . . .

"Let's go away, oh, much farther, ever so far away!" she whispered, and I took her by the hand, comforting her as best I could with words, while realizing that the thing she wanted was my big arm about her to protect. My heart ached, oh, so fiercely, for her, but the odd thing about it was that I could not find anything of real comfort to say that I felt would be *true*. If I "made up" soothing rubbish, it would not deceive either of us and would only shake her confidence in me, so that I should lose any power I had to help. Had a tiger come upon her out of the wood I might as well have assured her it would not bite!

I did stammer something, however —

"It's only the new butler. He startled me, too; he came so softly, didn't he?" Oh! how eagerly I searched for a word that might make the thing seem as ordinary as possible — yet how vainly.

"But you know who he is — *really!*" she said in a crying whisper, running down the path and dragging me after her; "and if he gets me again . . . oh! oh!" and she shrieked aloud in the anguish of her fear.

That fear chased both of us down the winding path between the bushes.

"Aileen, darling," I cried, surrounding her with both arms and holding her very tight, "you need not be afraid. I'll always save you. I'll always be with you, dear child."

"Keep me in your big arms, always, always, won't you, Uncle — Philip?" She mixed both names. The choking stress of her voice wrung me dreadfully. "Always, always, like in our story," she pleaded, hiding her little face again in my coat.

I really was at a complete loss to know what best to do; I hardly dared to bring her back to the house; the sight of the man, I felt, might be fatal to her already too delicately balanced reason, for I dreaded a fit or seizure if she chanced to run across him when I was not with her. My mind was easily made up on one point, however.

"I'll send him away at once, Aileen," I told her. "When you wake up tomorrow he'll be gone. Of course mother won't keep him."

This assurance seemed to bring her some measure of comfort, and at last, without having dared to win the whole story from her as I had first hoped, I got her back to the house by covert ways, and saw her myself upstairs to her own quarters. Also I took it upon myself to give the necessary orders. She must set no eye upon the man. Only, why was it that in my heart of hearts I longed for him to do something outrageous that should make it possible for me to break his very life at its source and kill him. . . ?

But my cousin, alarmed to the point of taking even frantic measures, finally had a sound suggestion to offer, namely that I should take the afflicted little child away with me the very next day, run down to Harwich and carry her off for a week of absolute change across the North Sea. And I, meanwhile, had reached the point where I had persuaded myself that the experiment I had hitherto felt unable to consent to had now become a permissible, even a necessary one. Hypnotism should win the story from that haunted mind without her being aware of it, and provided I could drive her deep enough into the trance state, I could then further wipe the memory from her outer consciousness so completely that she might know at last some happiness of childhood.

V

*I*t was after ten o'clock, and I was still sitting in the big hail before the fire of logs, talking with lowered voice. My cousin sat opposite to me in a deep armchair. We had discussed the matter pretty fully, and the deep uneasiness we felt clothed not alone our minds but the very building with gloom. The fact that, instinctively, neither of us referred to the possible assistance of doctors is eloquent, I think, of the emotion that troubled us both so profoundly, the emotion, I mean, that sprang from the vivid sense of the reality of it all. No child's make-believe merely could have thus caught us away, or spread a net that entangled our minds to such a point of confusion and dismay. It was perfectly comprehensible to mc now that my cousin should have cried in very helplessness before the convincing effects of the little girl's calamitous distress. Aileen was living through a Reality, not an Invention. This was the fact that haunted the shadowy halls and corridors behind us. Already I hated the very building. It seemed charged to the roof with the memories of melancholy and ancient pain that swept my heart with shivering, cold winds.

Purposely, however, I affected some degree of cheerfulness, and concealed from my cousin any mention of the attacks that certain emotions and alarms had made upon myself: I said nothing of my replacing "Lady Aileen" with "Lady Helen," nothing of my passing for "Philip," or of my sudden dashes of quasi-memory arising from the child's inclusion of myself in her "story," and my own singular acceptance of the *rôle*. I did not consider it wise to mention *all* that the sight of the new servant with his sinister dark face and his method of stealthy approach had awakened in my thoughts. None the less these things started constantly to the surface of my mind and doubtless betrayed themselves somewhere in my "atmosphere," sufficiently at least for a woman's intuition to divine them. I spoke passingly of the "room," and of Aileen's singular aversion for it, and of her remark about "talking to the wall." Yet strange thoughts pricked their way horribly into both our minds. In the hall the stuffed heads of deer and fox and badger stared upon us like masks of things still alive beneath their fur and dead skin.

"But what disturbs me more than all the rest of her delusions put together," said my cousin, peering at me with eyes that made no pretence of hiding dark things, "is her extraordinary knowledge of this place. I assure you, George, it was the most uncanny thing I've ever known when she showed me over and asked questions as if she had actually lived here." Her voice sank to a whisper, and she looked up startled. It seemed to me for a moment that someone was coming near to listen, moving stealthily upon us along the dark approaches to the hall.

"I can understand you found it strange," I began quickly. But she interrupted me at once. Clearly it gave her a certain relief to say the things and get them out of her mind where they hid, breeding new growths of abhorrence.

"George," she cried aloud, "there's a limit to imagination. Aileen *knows*. That's the awful thing –."

Something sprang into my throat. My eyes moistened.

"The horror of the belt –" she whispered, loathing her own words.

"Leave that thought alone," I said with decision. The detail pained me inexpressibly – beyond belief.

"I wish I could," she answered, "but if you had seen the look on her face when she struggled – and the – the frenzy she got into about the food and starving – I mean when Dr. Hale spoke – oh, if you had seen all that, you would understand that I –"

She broke off with a start. Someone had entered the hall behind us and was standing in the doorway at the far end. The listener had moved upon us from the dark. Theresa, though her back was turned, had felt the presence and was instantly upon her feet.

"You need not sit up, Porter," she said, in a tone that only thinly veiled the fever of apprehension behind, "we will put the lights out," and the man withdrew like a shadow. She exchanged a quick glance with me. A sensation of darkness that seemed to have come with the servant's presence was gone. It is wholly beyond me to explain why neither myself nor my cousin found anything to say for some minutes. But it was still more a mystery, I think, why the muscles of my two hands should have contracted involuntarily with a force that drove the nails into my palms, and why the violent impulse should have leaped into my blood to fling myself upon the man and strangle the life out of his neck before he could take another breath. I have never before or since experienced this apparently causeless desire to throttle anybody. I hope I never may again.

"He hangs about rather," was all my cousin said presently. "He's always watching us –" But my own thoughts were horribly busy, and I was marveling how it was this ugly and sinister creature had ever come to be accepted in the story that Aileen lived, and that I was slowly coming to *believe* in.

*I*t was a relief to me when, towards midnight. Theresa rose to go to bed. We had skirted through the horrors of the child's possessing misery without ever quite facing it, and as we stood there lighting the candles, our voices whispering, our minds charged with the strain of thoughts neither of us had felt it wise to utter, my cousin started back against the wall and stared up into the darkness above where the staircase climbed the well of the house. She uttered a cry. At first I thought she was going to collapse. I was only just in time to catch the candle.

All the emotions of fearfulness she had repressed during our long talk came out in that brief cry, and when I looked up to discover the cause I saw a small white figure come slowly down the wide staircase and just about to step into the hall. It was Aileen, with bare feet, her dark hair tumbling down over her nightgown, her eyes wide open, an expression in them of anguished expectancy that her tender years could never possibly have known. She was walking steadily, yet somehow not quite as a child walks.

"Stop!" I whispered peremptorily to my cousin, putting my hand quickly over her mouth, and holding her back from the first movement of rescue, "don't wake her. She's walking in her sleep."

Aileen passed us like a white shadow, scarcely audible, and went straight across the hall. She was utterly unaware of our presence. Avoiding all obstructions of chairs and tables, moving with decision and purpose, the little figure dipped into the shadows at the far end and disappeared from view in the mouth of the corridor that had once — three hundred years ago — led into the wing where now the copper beeches grew upon open lawns. It was clearly a way familiar to her. And the instant I recovered from my surprise and moved after her to act, Theresa found her voice and cried aloud — a voice that broke the midnight silence with shrill discordance —

"George, oh, George! She's going to that awful room. . . !"

"Bring the candle and come after me," I replied from halfway down the hall, "but do not interrupt unless I call for you," and was after the child at a pace to which the most singular medley of emotions I have ever known urged me imperiously. A sense of tragic disaster gripped my very vitals. All that I did seemed to rise out of some subconscious region of the mind where the haunting passions of a deeply buried past stirred in their sleep and woke.

"Helen!" I cried, "Lady Helen!" I was close upon the gliding figure. Aileen turned and for the first time saw me with eyes that seemed to waver between sleep and waking. They gazed straight at me over the flickering candle flame, then hesitated. In similar fashion the gesture of her little hands towards me was arrested before it had completed itself. She saw me, knew my presence, yet was uncertain who I was. It was astonishing the way I actually surprised this momentary indecision between the two personalities in her — caught the two phases of her consciousness at grips — discerned the Aileen of Today in the act of waking to know me as her "Uncle George," and that other Aileen of her great dark story, the "Helen" of some far Yesterday, that drew her in this condition of somnambulism to the scene in the past where our two lives were linked in her imagination. For it was quite clear to me that the child was dreaming in her sleep the action of the story she lived through in the vivid moments of her waking terror.

But the choice was swift. I just had time to signal Theresa to set the candle upon a shelf and wait, when she came up, stretched her hands out in completion of the original gesture, and fell into my arms with a smothered cry of love and anguish that, coming from those childish lips, I think is the most thrilling human sound I have ever known. She knew and saw me, but not as "Uncle" George of this present life.

"Oh, Philip! "she cried, "then you have come after all —"

"Of course, dear heart," I whispered. "Of course I have come. Did I not give my promise that I would?"

Her eyes searched my face, and then settled upon my hands that held her little cold wrists so tightly.

"But — but," she stammered in comment, "they are not cut! They have made you whole again! You will save me and get me out, and we — we —"

The expressions of her face ran together into a queer confusion of perplexity, and she seemed to totter on her feet. In another instant she would probably have wakened; again she felt the touch of uncertainty and doubt as to my identity. Her hands resisted the pressure of my own; she drew back half a step; into her eyes rose the shallower consciousness of the present. Once awake it would drive out the profoundly strange passion and mystery that haunted the corridors of thought and memory and plunged so obscurely into the inmost recesses of her being. For, once awake, I realized that I should lose her, lose the opportunity of getting the complete story. The chance was unique. I heard my cousin's footsteps approaching behind us down the passage on tiptoe — and I came to an immediate decision.

In the state of deep sleep, of course, the trance condition is very close, and many experiments had taught me that the human spirit can be subjected to the influence of hypnotism far more speedily when asleep than when awake; for if hypnotism means chiefly — as I then held it to mean — the merging of the little ineffectual surface-consciousness with the deep sea of the greater subliminal consciousness below, then the process has already been partially begun in normal slumber and its completion need be no very long or difficult matter. It was Aileen's very active subconsciousness that "invented" or "remembered" the dark story which haunted her life, her subconscious region too readily within tap. . . . By deepening her sleep state I could learn the whole story. . . .

Stopping her mother's approach with a sign that I intended she should clearly understand, and which accordingly she did understand, I took immediate steps to plunge the spirit of this little sleep-walking child down again into the subconscious region that had driven her thus far, and wherein lay the potentialities of all her powers, of memory, knowledge and belief. Only the simplest passes were necessary, for she yielded quickly and easily; that first look came back into her eyes; she no longer wavered or hesitated, but drew close against me, with the name of "Philip" upon her lips, and together we moved down the long passage till we reached the door of her horrid room of terror.

And there, whether it was that Theresa's following with the candle disturbed the child — for the subconscious tie with the mother is of such unalterable power — or whether anxiety weakened my authority over her fluctuating mental state, I noticed that she again wavered and hesitated, looking up with eyes that saw partly "Uncle George," partly the "Philip" she remembered.

"We'll go in," I said firmly, "and you shall see that there is nothing to be afraid of." I opened the door, and the candle from behind threw a triangle of light into the darkness. It fell upon a bare floor, pictureless walls, and just tipped the high white ceiling overhead. I pushed the door still wider open and we went in hand in hand, Aileen shaking like a leaf in the wind.

How the scene lives in my mind, even as I write it today so many years after it took place: the little child in her nightgown facing me in that empty room of the ancient building, all the passionate emotions of a tragic history in the small young eyes, her mother like a ghost in the passage, afraid to come in, the tossing shadows thrown by the candle and the soft moan of the night wind against the outside walls.

I made further passes over the small flushed face and pressed my thumbs gently along the temples. "Sleep! " I commanded; "sleep — and remember!" My will poured over her being to control and protect. She passed still deeper into the trance condition in which the somnambulistic lucidity manifests itself and the deeper self gives up its dead. Her eyes grew wider, rounder, charged with memories as they fastened themselves upon my own. The present, which a few minutes before had threatened to claim her consciousness by waking her, faded. She saw me no longer as her familiar Uncle George, but as the faithful friend and lover of her great story, Philip, the man who had come to save her. There she stood in the atmosphere of bygone days, in the very room where she had known great suffering — this room that three centuries ago had led by a corridor into the wing of the house where now the beeches grew upon the lawns.

She came up close and put her thin bare arms about my neck and stared with peering, searching eyes into mine.

"Remember what happened here," I said resolutely. "Remember, and tell me."

Her brows contracted slightly as with the effort, and she whispered, glancing over her shoulder towards the farther end where the corridor once began, "It hurts a little, but I — I'm in your arms, Philip dear, and you will get me out, I know —"

"I hold you safe and you are in no danger, little one," I answered. "You can remember and speak without it hurting you. Tell me."

The suggestion, of course, operated instantly, for her face cleared, and she dropped a great sigh of relief. From time to time I continued the passes that held the trance condition firm.

Then she spoke in a low, silvery little tone that cut into me like a sword and searched my inmost parts. I seemed to bleed internally. I could have sworn that she spoke of things I knew as though I had lived through them.

"This was when I last saw you," she said, "this was the room where you were to fetch me and carry me away into happiness and safety from — him," and it was the voice and words of no mere child that said it; "and this was where you did come on that night of snow and wind. Through that window you entered;" she pointed to the deep, embrasured window behind us. "Can't you hear the storm? How it howls and screams! And the boom of the surf on the beach below. . . . You left the horses outside, the swift horses that were to carry us to the sea and away from all his cruelties, and then —"

She hesitated and searched for words or memories; her face darkened with pain and loathing.

"Tell me the rest," I ordered, "but forget all your own pain." And she smiled up at me with an expression of unbelievable tenderness and confidence while I drew the frail form closer.

"*You* remember, Philip," she went on, "you know just what it was, and how he and his men seized you the moment you stepped inside, and how you struggled and called for me, and heard me answer —"

"Far away — outside —" I interrupted quickly, helping her out of some flashing memory in my own deep heart that seemed to burn and leave a scar. "You answered from the lawn!"

"You thought it was the lawn, but really, you see, it was there — in there," and she pointed to the side of the room on my right. She shook dreadfully, and her voice dwindled most oddly in volume, as though coming from a distance — almost muffled.

"In there?" I asked it with a shudder that put ice and fire mingled in my blood.

"In the wall," she whispered. "You see, someone had betrayed us, and he knew you were coming. He walled me up alive in there, and only left two little holes for my eyes so that I could see. You heard my voice calling through those holes, but you never knew where I was. And then —"

Her knees gave way, and I had to hold her. She looked suddenly with torture in her eyes down the length of the room — towards the old wing of the house.

"You won't let him come," she pleaded beseechingly, and in her voice was the agony of death. "I thought I heard him. Isn't that his footsteps in the corridor?" She listened fearfully, her eyes trying to pierce the wall and see out on to the lawn.

"No one is coming, dear heart," I said, with conviction and authority. "Tell it all. Tell me everything."

"I saw the whole of it because I could not close my eyes," she continued. "There was an iron band round my waist fastening me in — an iron belt I never could escape from. The dust got into my mouth — I bit the bricks. My tongue was scraped and bleeding, but before they put in the last stones to smother me I saw them — cut both your hands off so that you could never save me — never let me out."

She dashed without warning from my side and flew up to the wall, beating it with her hands and crying aloud —

"Oh, you poor, poor thing. I know how awful it was. I remember — when I was in you and you wore and carried me, poor, poor body! That thunder of the last brick as they drove it in against the mouth, and the iron clamp that cut into the waist, and the suffocation and hunger and thirst!"

"What are you talking to in there?" I asked sternly, crushing down the tears.

"The body I was in — the one he walled up — my body — my own body!"

She flew back to my side. But even before my cousin had uttered that "mother-cry" that broke in upon the child's deeper consciousness, disturbing the memories, I had given the command with all the force of my being to "forget" the pain. And only those few who are familiar with the instantaneous changes of emotion that can be produced by suggestion under hypnosis will understand that Aileen came back to me from that moment of "talking to the wall" with laughter on her lips and in her eyes.

The small white figure with the cascade of dark hair tumbling over the nightgown ran up and jumped into my arms.

"But I saved you," I cried, "you were never properly walled-up; I got you out and took you away from him over the sea, and we were happy ever afterwards, like the people in the fairy tales." I drove the words into her with my utmost force, and inevitably she accepted them as the truth, for she clung to me with love and laughter all over her child's face of mystery, the horror fading out, the pain swept clean away. With kaleidoscopic suddenness the change came.

"So they never really cut your poor dead hands off at all," she said hesitatingly.

"Look! How could they? There they are! And I first showed them to her and then pressed them against her little cheeks, drawing her mouth up to be kissed. "They're big enough still and strong enough to carry you off to bed and stroke you into so deep a sleep that when you wake in the morning you will have forgotten everything about your dark story, about Philip, Lady Helen, the iron belt, the starvation, your cruel old husband, and all the rest of it. You'll wake up happy and jolly just like any other child —"

"If you say so, of course I shall," she answered, smiling into my eyes.

*A*nd it was just then there came in that touch of abomination that so nearly made my experiment a failure, for it came with a black force that threatened at first to discount all my "suggestion" and make it of no account. My new command that she should forget had apparently not yet fully registered itself in her being; the tract of deeper consciousness that constructed the "Story" had not sunk quite below the threshold. Thus she was still open to any detail of her former suffering that might obtrude itself with sufficient force. And such a detail *did* obtrude itself. This touch of abomination was calculated with a really superhuman ingenuity.

"Hark!" she cried — and it was that *scream in a whisper* that only utter terror can produce — "Hark! I hear his steps! He's coming! Oh, I told you he was coming! He's in *that* passage!" pointing down the room. And she first sprang from my arms as though something burned her, and then almost instantly again flew back to my protection. In that interval of a few seconds she tore into the middle of the room, put her hand to her ear to listen, and then shaded her eyes in the act of peering down through the wall at the far end. She stared at the very place where in olden days the corridor had led into the vanished wing. The window my great-uncle had built into the wall now occupied the exact spot where the opening had been.

Theresa then for the first time came forward with a rush into the room, dropping the candle-grease over the floor. She clutched me by the arm. The three of us stood there — listening — listening apparently to naught but the sighing of the sea-wind about the walls, Aileen with her eyes buried in my coat. I was standing erect trying in vain to catch the new sound. I remember my cousin's face of chalk with the fluttering eyes and the candle held aslant.

Then suddenly she raised her hand and pointed over my shoulder. I thought her jaw would drop from her face. And she and the child both spoke in the same breath the two sharp phrases that brought the climax of the vile adventure upon us in that silent room of night.

They were like two pistol-shots.

"My God! There's a face watching us. . . !" I heard her voice, all choked and dry.

And at the same second, Aileen — "Oh, oh! He's seen us. . . ! He's *here!* Look. . . . He'll get me . . . hide your hands, hide your poor hands!"

And, turning to the place my cousin stared at, I saw sure enough that a face — apparently a living human face — was pressed against the windowpane, framed between two hands as it tried to peer upon us into the semi-obscurity of the room. I saw the swift momentary rolling of the two eyes as the candle glare fell upon them, and caught a glimpse even of the hunched-up shoulders behind, as their owner, standing outside upon the lawn, stooped down a little to see better. And though the apparition instantly withdrew, I recognized it beyond question as the dark and evil countenance of the butler. His breath still stained the window.

Yet the strange thing was that Aileen, struggling violently to bury herself amid the scanty folds of my coat, could not possibly have seen what we saw, for her face was turned from the window the entire time, and from the way I held her she could never for a single instant have been in a position to know. It all took place behind her back. . . . A moment later, with her eyes still hidden against me, I was carrying her swiftly in my arms across the hall and up the main staircase to the night nursery.

My difficulty with her was, of course, while she hovered between the two states of sleep and waking, for once I got her into bed and plunged her deeply again into the trance condition, I was easily able to control her slightest thought or emotion. Within ten minutes she was sleeping peacefully, her little face smoothed of all anxiety or terror, and my imperious command ringing from end to end of her consciousness that when she woke next morning all should be forgotten. She was finally to forget . . . utterly and completely.

And, meanwhile, of course, the man, when I went with loathing and anger in my heart to his room in the servants' quarters, had a perfectly plausible explanation. He was in the act of getting ready for bed, he declared, when the noise had aroused his suspicions, and, as in duty bound, he had made a tour of the house outside, thinking to discover burglars. . . .

*W*ith a month's wages in his pocket, and a considerable degree of wonder in his soul, probably — for the man was guilty of nothing worse than innocently terrifying a child's imagination! — he went back to London the following day; and a few hours later I myself was traveling with Aileen and old Kempster over the blue waves of the North Sea, carrying her off, curiously enough, to freedom and happiness in the very way her "imagination" had pictured her escape in the "story" of long ago, when she was Lady Helen, held in bondage by a cruel husband, and I was Philip, her devoted lover.

Only this time her happiness was lasting and complete. Hypnotic suggestion had wiped from her mind the last vestige of her dreadful memories; her face was wreathed in jolly smiles; her enjoyment of the journey and our week in Antwerp was absolutely unclouded; she played and laughed with all the radiance of an unhaunted childhood, and her imagination was purged and healed.

And when we got back her mother had again moved her household gods to the original family mansion where she had first lived. Thither it was I took the restored child, and there it was my cousin and I looked up the old family records and verified certain details of the history of De Lorne, that wicked and semi-fabulous ancestor whose portrait hung in the dark corner of the stairs. That his life was evil to the brim I had always understood, but neither myself nor Theresa had known — at least had not consciously remembered — that he had married twice, and that his first wife, Lady Helen, had mysteriously disappeared, and Sir Philip Lansing, a neighboring knight, supposed to be her lover, had soon afterwards emigrated to France and left his lands and property to go to ruin.

But another discovery I made, and kept to myself, had to do with that "room of terror" in the old Norfolk house where, on the plea of necessary renovation, I had the stones removed, and in the very spot where Aileen used to beat her hands against the bricks and "talk to the wall," the workmen under my own eyes laid bare the skeleton of a woman, fastened to the granite by means of a narrow iron band that encircled the waist — the skeleton of some unfortunate who had been walled-up alive and had come to her dreadful death by the pangs of hunger, thirst and suffocation centuries ago.

Perspective

I

*T*he amount of duty and pleasure combined in Alpine summer chaplaincies of a month each just suited the Rev. Phillip Ambleside. He was still young enough to climb — carefully; and genuine enough to enjoy seeing the crowd of holiday-makers having a good time. As a rule he was on the Entertainment Committee that organized the tennis, dances, and gymkhanas. During the week one would hardly have guessed his calling. On Sundays he appeared a bronzed, lean, vigorous figure in the pulpit of the hot little wooden church, and people liked to see him. His sermons, never over ten minutes, were the same four every year: one for each Sunday of the month; and when he passed on to another month's duty in the next place he repeated them. The surroundings suggested them obviously: Beauty, Rest, Power, Majesty; and they were more like little confidential talks than sermons. Moreover, incidents from the life of the place — the escape of a tourist, the accident to a guide, and what not, usually came ready to hand to point a moral. One summer, however, there occurred a singular adventure that he has never yet been able to introduce into a sermon. Only in private conversation with souls as full of faith as himself does he ever mention it. And the short recital always begins with a sentence more or less as follows —

Talking of the wondrous ways of God, and the little understanding of the children of men, I am always struck by the huge machinery He sometimes adopts to accomplish such delicate and apparently insignificant ends. I remember once when I was doing summer 'duty' in a Swiss resort high up among the mountains of the Valais . . ."

And then follows the curious occurrence I was once privileged to hear, and have obtained permission to re-tell, duly disguised.

In the particular mountain village where he was taking a month's duty at the time, his church was full every Sunday, so full indeed that twice a week he held afternoon services for those who cared to worship more quietly. And to these little ceremonies, beloved of his own heart, came two persons regularly who attracted his attention in spite of himself. They sat together at the back; shared the same books, although there was no necessity to do so; courted the shadowy corners of the pews: in a word, they came to worship one another, not to worship God.

But the clergyman took a broad view. Courtships fostered in the holy atmosphere of the sacred building were more likely to be true than those fanned to flame in the feverish surroundings of the dance-room. And true love is ever an offering to God. He knew the couple, too. The man, quiet, earnest, well over forty; the girl, young, dashing, spirited, leader in mischief, hard to believe sincere, flirting with more than one. In spite of the careful concealment with which she covered their proceedings, choosing the deserted afternoon service rather than the glare of the garden or ballroom for their talks, the couple were marked. The difference in their ages, characters, and appearance singled them out, as much as the general knowledge that she was rich, vain, flighty, while he was poor, strenuous, living a life of practical charity in London, that precluded gaiety or pleasure, so called.

"What *can* she see in that dull man twice her age?" the elder women said to one another – the answer generally being that it probably amused the girl to turn him so easily round her little finger.

"What a chance for her fortune to be well spent," reflected one or two. While the men, when they said anything at all, contented themselves with: "Pretty hard hit, isn't he? A fine fellow though! Hope he gets her!"

It is always somewhat pathetic to see a man of real value fall before the conquering beauty of an ordinary young girl of the world. The clergyman, however, with an eye for spiritual values, even deeply hidden, divined that beneath her lightness and love for conquest's sake there lay the desire for something more real. And he guessed, though at first the wish may have been father to the thought only, that it was the elder man's fine zeal and power that attracted the butterfly in spite of herself towards a life that was more worth living. Hers, after all, he felt, was a soul worth "saving"; and this middle-aged man, perhaps, was the force God brought into her life to provide her with the opportunity of escape – could she but seize it.

So far Ambleside's story runs along ordinary lines enough. One sees his man and girl without further detail. From this point, however, it slips into a stride where the sense of proportion seems somehow lost, or else "man's little understanding " is too close to the thing to obtain the proper perspective. If anyone but this devout and clear-headed clergyman told the tale, one might say "Fancy," "Delusion," or any other description that seemed suitable. But to hear him tell it, with that air of conviction and truth, in those short, abrupt, even jerky sentences, that left so much to the imagination, and with that pallor of the skin that threw into such vivid contrast the fire burning in his far-seeing blue eyes — to sit close to him and hear the story grow in that tense low voice, was to know beyond all question that he spoke of something real and actual, in the same sense that a train or St. Paul's Cathedral are real and actual.

What he saw, he really saw: though the sight may have been of a kind unfamiliar to the majority. He was used as a real pawn in a real game. The girl's life and soul were rescued, so to speak, by the marriage brought about, and her forces of mind and spirit lifted bodily for what they were worth into the scheme that God had ordained for them from the beginning of the world. Only — the machinery brought to bear upon the end in view seemed so prodigious, so extraordinary, so unnecessary. . . . One thinks of the sentence with which Ambleside always began his tale. One wonders. But no one who heard the tale ever asked questions at its close. There was absolutely nothing to say.

Even to the smallest details the affair seemed thought out and planned, for that particular Tuesday Ambleside started without the guide-porter who usually carried his telescope, camera, and lunch. He went off at six a.m., with merely an ice-axe and a small knapsack containing food and Shetland vest for the summit.

It was one of those days towards the end of August when some quality in the atmosphere — usually sign of approaching rain — brings the mountains uncannily close, yet, at the same time, sets out every detail of pinnacle, precipice, and ridge with a terror of size and grandeur that makes one realize their true and gigantic scale. They press up close, yet at the same time stand away in the depths of the sky like unattainable masses in some dream world. This mingling of proximity and distance has a confusing effect upon the eye. When Ambleside toiled up the zigzags without actually looking beyond, he felt that the towering *massif* of the Valais Alps all about him loomed very close; but when he stopped for breath and raised his eyes steadily into their detail, he felt that their distance was too great to be conquered by any little two-legged being like himself merely taking steps. And as he rose out of the valley into the clearer strata of air this effect increased. The whole scale of the chain of Alps about him seemed raised to an immeasurably higher power than he had ever known. He felt like an insect crawling over the craters of the moon. The prodigious splendors of the scenery all round oppressed him more than ever before with his own futile littleness, yet at the same time made him conscious of the grandeur of his soul before the God who had set him and his kind above all this chaos of tumbled planet.

He thought of the mountains as part of the "garment of God," and of nature as expressing some portion of the Deity not intended to be expressed by man — all part of His purpose, alive with His informing will. This glory of the inanimate Alps linked on to some stranger glory in himself that interpreted for him, as in a mystical revelation, God's thundering message and purpose known in the great forms and moods of nature. Closely in touch with the spirit of the mountains he was; glad to be alone.

This, in a sentence, expresses his mood: that the mountains accepted him. Forces in his deepest being that were akin to the life of the planet on which he made his tiny track rose up and triumphed. Over the treacherous Pas d'Illiez, where he usually felt giddy and unsafe, he felt this morning only exhilaration. The gulf yawning at his feet touched him with its splendor, not its terror.

Thus, feeling inclined to shout and run, he eventually reached the desolate valley of rock and shale that lies, unrelieved by a single blade of grass, between the glacier-covered slopes that shut it in impassably on three sides. The bed of this valley lies some 7,000 feet above the sea. The peaks and ridges that rear about it reach 12,000 feet. Here, being a good climber, he rested for the first time at the end of two hours' steady ascent. The air nipped. The loneliness and desolation were very impressive. Beyond him hung the glaciers like immense thick blankets of blue-white upon the steep slopes, dropping from time to time lumps of ice into the shale-strewn valley below. For the sun shining in a cloudless sky was fierce. The clergyman, before attacking the long snow-field that began at his very feet, took out his blue spectacles and disentangled the cord. He ate some chocolate, and took the dried prunes from his knapsack, knowing that thirst would soon be upon him, and that ice-water was not for drinking.

"What a mite I am, to be sure, amid all this appalling wilderness!" he exclaimed; "and how splendid to be able to hold my own!"

And then it was, just as he stood up to arrange the glasses on his forehead, ready to pull down at a moment's notice, that he became aware of something that was strange — unaccustomed. Through the giant splendors of the scorching August day, across all this stupendous scenery of desolation and loneliness, something fine as a needle, delicate as a hair, had begun picking at his mind. The idea came to him that he was no longer alone. Like a man who hears his name called out of darkness he turned instinctively to find the speaker; almost as though someone had been calling to him for a considerable time, and he had only just had his attention drawn to it. He looked keenly up and down the immense, deserted valley.

In every direction, however, he saw nothing but miles of rock, dazzling snow-fields, dark precipices, and endless peaks cutting the blue sky overhead with teeth that gleamed like burnished steel. It was desolation everywhere. The gentle wind that fanned his cheek made no sound against the stones. There was neither tree nor grass for it to rustle through. No bird's wing whirred the air; and the far-off falling of a hundred cascades was of too regular and monotonous a character to have taken on the quality of a voice or the rhythm of uttered words. He examined, so far as he could, the enormous sides of mountain about him, and the great soaring ridges. It was just possible some climber in distress had spied him out, and shouted down upon him from the heights. But he searched in vain. There was no moving human figure. The sound, if sound it had been, was not repeated; only he was no longer alone, as before. That, at least, was certain. . . . He nibbled more chocolate, put a couple of sour prunes into his mouth to suck, arranged the blue snow-glass over his eyes, and started on again for a steady pull up to the next ridge.

And as he rose the scale of the surrounding mountains rose appallingly with him. The true distance of the peaks proclaimed itself; the tremendous reaches that from below appeared telescoped up into a little space opened up and stretched themselves. The hour grew into two. It was considerably after twelve before he reached the *arête* where he had promised himself lunch. And all the way, without ceasing, the idea that he was being accompanied remained insistent in his mind. It troubled and perplexed him. Perhaps it frightened him a little, too. More than once it came close enough to make him pause and consider whether he should continue or turn back.

For the curious part of it was that this idea exercised a direct and deliberate effect upon him. By a hundred little details that seemed to be spontaneous until he examined them, it kept suggesting somehow that he should change his route. Something in his consciousness grew that had not been there before. He thought of a bird bringing tiny morsels of grass and twig until a nest formed. In this way the steady stream of thoughts from somewhere outside himself came nesting in his brain until at length they acquired the consistency of an impression, next of a distinct desire, lastly, the momentum of a definite intention. They acted upon his volition, stirring softly among the roots of his will. Before he realized how it had quite come about he had *changed his mind*.

Instead of going on to the top as I intended, he said to himself, as he sat on the dizzy ledge munching hard-boiled eggs and sugar sandwiches, "I shall strike off to the left and find my way back into the valley again. That, I think, would be — nicer!"

He had no real reason; he invented none.

And the moment he said it there was a sense of pressure removed, a consciousness of relief, the knowledge, in a word, that he was following a route that it was desired he should follow.

To a man, of course, whose habit it was to seek often the will of a personal Deity he worshipped, there was nothing very out of the way in all this, although he never remembered to have felt any guidance so distinctly and forcibly indicated before. The feeling that he was being "guided" now became a certainty, and in order to follow instructions as well as possible he made his will of no account and opened himself to receive the slightest token this other Directing Agency might care to vouchsafe.

After lunch, therefore, he struck out a diagonal course across a steep snow-slope that would eventually bring him down again to the valley a little nearer its head. And before he had gone a hundred yards he ran into the track of another climber. The marks were a couple of days old, perhaps, for in their hollows lay little heaps of fine snow-dust, freshly blown. Judging by the size there had been two men. He noted the trace of the ice-axe and the occasional streak of the trailing rope. The men had made straight for the valley far below. Here and there they had glissaded. Here and there, too, they had also tumbled gloriously, for the snow was tossed about by their floundering. Yet there was no danger; no precipices intervened; the snow sloped without a break right down into the shale below.

"I'll follow their example," said the Rev. Phillip Ambleside. He strapped on the extra leather seat he carried for sliding and sat down. A moment later he was rushing at high speed over the hard surface. There were hollows of softer snow, however, which stopped him from time to time, drifts as it were into which he plunged, and from which he emerged, wet and shivering. Then he stood up and leaned on his axe, trying to glissade on his feet. For this, however, the surface was not smooth enough. The result was he tumbled, rolled, slid, sat down, and took immense gliding strides. It was very exhilarating. He reveled in it.

But all the while he kept his eyes sharply about him, for in his heart he felt that he was obeying that guiding Influence so strongly impressed upon him — the Power that had persuaded him to change his route, and was now leading him to some particular point with some particular purpose. Now, too, for the first time a vague sense of calamity touched him. Once introduced, it grew. Soon it amounted to a positive foreboding, a presentiment of disaster almost. He could not avoid the idea that he was being led by supernatural means to the scene of some catastrophe where he was to prove of use – a rescue, an arrival in the nick of time to save someone. He actually looked about him already for – yes, for the body. And through his sub-conscious mind, with the force of habit, ran the magnificent use he could make of it all in a future sermon.

Yet nothing came. The tracks of the other men stretched clear and unbroken into the valley of rocks below. He traced the wavering thin line the whole way down.

"It's nothing to do with *these* men, at any rate," he said to himself, as he sat down for the final slide that should take him to the bottom of the slope. "No accident could possibly have happened here. The snow's too soft, and there are no rocks to fall over or –"

The sentence, or the thought, remained unfinished, for the mouth of the Rev. Phillip was stopped temporarily with wet snow as he lost his balance and rushed sideways with an undignified plunge into a drifted hollow. His eyes were blinded, his feet twisted, the skin of his back drenched and icy. He rose spluttering and gasping. Luckily his axe had a leather loop, or he would have lost it; as it was, his slouch hat was already a hundred feet below, sliding and turning like a top on its way to the bottom, followed by the snow-goggles.

And in the act of brushing himself free of snow the truth came to him. It was as though a hand had struck him on the back and pointed – as though a voice had uttered the five words: *"This is the place. Look!"*

Swiftly, searchingly, keenly he looked, and saw – nothing; nothing, at least, that explained the impression of disaster that had possessed him. There was no body certainly, nor any sign of an accident; no place, indeed, where an accident could possibly have come about. He dug quickly in the loose snow with his axe, but the snow was barely two feet deep in this particular hollow, and all round it was a hard surface of smoothly and tightly-packed stuff that was almost ice. Nothing bigger than a cat could have lain buried there!

"This is the place! Look well!" the words seemed to ring in his ears.

Yet the more he looked and saw nothing, the more strongly beat this message upon his brain. This was the place where he was to come, where he was to fulfill some purpose, to find something, do something, accomplish the end intended by the Will that had so carefully guided him all day. The feeling was positive; not to be denied. It was, at the same time, distressingly vast – mighty.

Fixing himself securely against his axe, he stood and stared. The sun beat back into his face from the glittering snow on all sides. Tremendous black precipices towered not far behind him; to his left rolled the frozen mass of the huge glacier, its pinnacles of tottering ice catching the afternoon sun; to his right stretched into bewildering distance the interminable and desolate reaches of shale and moraine till the eye rested upon summits of a dozen peaks that literally swam in the sky where white clouds streamed westwards. There was no sound but falling water, no sign of humanity except the single track of those other climbers, no indication of any disturbance upon the vast face of nature that spread all about him, immense, still, terrific.

Then, piercing the monotony of the falling water, a faint sound of fluttering, heard for the first time, reached his ear. He turned as at the sound of a pistol-shot in the direction whence it came — but again saw nothing. The sound ceased. From the slope below came a breath of icy wind that made him shiver, and with it, he fancied, came the faint hissing noise of his sliding hat and spectacles. This, perhaps, was the sound he had heard as "fluttering."

At length after prolonged and vain searching, the clergyman decided there was nothing for him to do but continue his journey, for the sun was getting low, and he had a long way to go before dusk could be regarded with equanimity. He felt exhausted, wearied, impatient too if the truth were told, yet ashamed of his impatience.

"If this is all *real*," he argued under his breath, "why isn't it made clear what I'm to do?"

And immediately upon the heels of the thought came again that faint and curious sound of something fluttering.

Now, there can be no question that he understood perfectly well that this sound of fluttering had a direct connection with the whole purpose of the day — that it was the clue to his presence in this particular spot, and that he had been forced to halt here by means of his fall in order that he might investigate something or other on this very spot. He knew it; he felt it. But he was too impatient, too cold, too weary to spend any further time over it all. Alarm, too, was plucking uneasily at his reins.

So this time he affected to ignore the sound. Leaning back on his axe he threw his body into position for sliding down to the bottom of the slope. In another second he would have started — when something that froze him into the immobility of a terror worse than death arrested him with a power beyond anything he had ever known before in his life — a Power that seemed to carry behind it the pressure of the entire universe.

There, close beside him in this mountain wilderness, had risen up suddenly a Face — close as the handle of the ice-axe he so tightly grasped, yet at the same time so far away, so immense, so stupendous in scale that he has never understood to this day how it was he could have perceived that it was — a Face. Yet a face it undoubtedly was, a living face; and its eyes — its regard, at any rate, for eyes he divined rather than saw — were focused upon some object that lay at his very feet.

Clammy with fear, his heart thumping dreadfully, he dropped back upon the snow. Without looking at any particular detail he became aware that the entire world of giant scenery about him was involved in the building up of this appalling Countenance, whose gaze was directed upon a tiny point immediately before him — the point, he now perceived, whence proceeded that familiar little sound of fluttering.

Words obviously fail him when he attempts to describe the terror of this Visage that rose about him through the day. Pallid and immense, it seemed to stretch itself against the wastes of grey rock, with entire slopes of snow upon the cheeks, ridged and furrowed by precipice and cliff, with torn clouds of flying hair that streaked the blue, and the expanse of glaciers for the splendid brows. Across it the dark line of two moraines tilted for eyebrows, and the massive columns of compressed strata embedded in the whole structure of the mountain chain bulged for the muscles of the awful neck. . . . Moreover, the shoulders upon which it all rested — the vast framework of body that he divined below — the dizzy drop in space where such fearful limbs must seek their resting-place —

His mind went reeling. The titanic proportions of this Countenance of splendor threatened in some horrible way to overwhelm his life. Its calmness, its iron immobility, its remorseless fixity of mien petrified him. The thought that he had dared to question it, to put himself in opposition to its purpose, even to be impatient with it — this turned all his soul within him soft and dead with a kind of ultimate terror that bereft him of any clear memory, perhaps momentarily, too, of consciousness.

The clergyman *thinks* he fainted. Exactly what happened, probably, he never knew nor realized. All that he can say in attempting to describe it is that he found his own eyes caught up and carried away in the gigantic stream of vision that this Face of Mountains poured upon the ground — caught up and directed upon a tiny little white object that fluttered in the wind at his very feet.

He saw what the Face was looking at and wished him to look at. It made him see what it saw.

For there, in front of him, unnoticed hitherto, lay a scrap of paper half embedded in the snow. Automatically he stooped and picked it up. It was an envelope bearing the printed inscription of an hotel in the village. It was sealed. On the outside in a fine handwriting, he read the Christian name of a man. Opening the corner he saw inside a small lock of dark-colored hair. And this was all. . . !

Then it was just at this moment that the snow where his feet rested gave way, and he started off at full speed to slide to the bottom of the slope, where he only just stopped himself in time to prevent shooting with a violent collision into a mass of shale and loose stones.

In less than thirty seconds it had all happened . . . and the swift descent and tumble had shaken him back as it were into a normal state of mind. But the oppression that had burdened him all day was gone. The mountains looked as usual. An indescribable sense of relief came over him. He felt a free agent once more — no longer guided, pushed, directed. He had fulfilled the purpose.

Putting the little envelope in his inside pocket he picked up his slouch hat and snow-goggles, ate some chocolate and dried prunes, and started off at a brisk pace for his return journey of three hours to the village and — dinner. And the whole way home the grandeur of that face, with its splendid pallor, and its expression of majesty, haunted him with indescribable sensations. With it, however, all the time ran the accompanying thought: "What a tremendous business for so small a result! All that vast maneuvering, all that terror of the imagination, and all that complex pressure upon my insignificant spirit merely in the end to find a wisp of girl's hair in an envelope evidently fallen from the pocket of some careless climber!"

The more the Rev. Phihlip Ambleside thought about it, the more bewildered he felt. He was uncommonly glad, however, to get in before dark. The memory of that Mountain Countenance was no agreeable companion for the forest paths and lonely slopes through which his way led in the dusk.

II

*T*hat same night it so happened, before he was able to take any steps to trace the owner of the little envelope, there was a Bal de Têtes at the principal hotel. Although the clergyman was on the Entertainment Committee which organized the simple gaieties of the place, he held that honorary position only as a personal compliment to himself; he did not at a rule take an active part in the detail, nor did he as a general rule attend the balls.

This particular night, however, he strolled down to the hotel, and after a little conversation with one or two friends in the hail he made his way to a secluded corner of the glass gallery where the dancers sat out between times, and lit his pipe for a quiet smoke. From behind the shelter of a large sham palm he was able to see all he wanted of the ballroom, to hear the music, and to take in the pleasant sight of all the people enjoying themselves. And the sight did him good. He liked to see it. A number were in costume, which added to the picturesqueness of the scene. Perhaps he sat more in the shadows than he knew, or perhaps the dancers who came to "sit out" near him in the gallery did not realize how their voices carried. Several couples, as the evening advanced, came so close to him that, had he wished, he could have overheard easily every word they uttered. He did not wish, however. His mind was busy with thoughts of its own. That haunting scene of desolation in the mountains obsessed him still; and about ten o'clock, his pipe being finished, he was on the point of getting up to leave, when two dancers came and sat down immediately behind him and began to talk in such very distinct tones that it was impossible to avoid hearing every single word they uttered.

The clergyman pushed his chair aside to make room to go, when, in doing so, he threw a passing glance at the couple — and instantly recognized them. The girl, a Carmen, and a very becoming Carmen, was the one who frequented his afternoon services, and the man, who wore simple evening dress and was not in costume at all, was the middle-aged Englishman who had been at her heels like a slave all the summer. They were absorbed in one another, and evidently unaware of his presence.

To say that he hesitated would not be true. Some force beyond himself simply took him by the shoulders and pushed him back into the chair. Against his own will — for Mr. Ambleside was no eavesdropper — he remained there deliberately to listen.

In telling the story he tells it just like this, making no excuses for conduct that was certainly dishonorable. He declares he could not help himself; the instinct was too imperious to be disobeyed. Again, as in the afternoon, he understood that he was merely being used as a pawn in the game, a game of great importance to some Intelligence that saw through to the distant end.

The man was quiet, but tremendously in earnest, with the kind of steady manner that no woman likes unless she finds it in her to respond with a similar sincerity. Under the bronze his skin showed pale a little. He began to speak the instant they sat down; and in his voice was passion.

"I want you, and I want your money, and I want your life and soul — everything," he said, evidently continuing a conversation; "your youth and energy, your talents, your will, all that is you and yours — *all.*" His voice was pitched very low, yet without tremor. He was playing the whole stake, as a strong man of middle age plays it when he is utterly in earnest. "For my scheme, for *our* scheme, for God's scheme I want you; and no one else but you will do. I want you to awake, and change your life, and be your true, fine self. We can make a success, you and I, a success for ourselves and for others. I shall never give you up until — until you give yourself to the world, or" — his voice dropped very low — "to another."

The clergyman waited breathlessly for the answer. The man's words vibrated with such suppressed fire that only a serious reply could be forthcoming. But for a space Carmen merely toyed with her fan, the little red spangled fan that swung from a single finger. Behind the black domino her eyes sparkled, but the expression of her face was hidden.

"The difference in age is nothing," he continued almost sternly. "For me, you are *the* woman, and for you I will prove that I am *the* man. I see clean through to the great soul hidden in you. I can bring it out. I can make you *real* — a soul of value in the big order of God's purposes. What can these boys ever be, or do, for you? I've got a big, useful, practical scheme that can use you, just as it can use me. And my great unselfish love has picked you out of the whole world as the one woman necessary. Will you come to me?"

Still the girl was silent. She tapped him on the knee two or three times, would-be playfully, with the tip of her fan. Her head was bent down a little.

"And I'm strong," he went on earnestly; "I'm a man. The power in me recognizes and calls to the power in you. Let me hold you and mold you, and let's take the fine, high life together. Drop this life of child's play you've been leading. Come to me; my arms are hungry for you! But I want you for a higher purpose than my own happiness — though I swear I can make you happy as no woman in this world has ever before been happy. And without you," he added more softly after a slight pause, "this splendid scheme of mine, of ours, can come to nothing. For I cannot do it alone — and there is only one *You* in the world. Answer me now. It was tonight, remember, you promised. I leave tomorrow, and London days lie far ahead. Give me your answer to go back with."

It was a curious way to make love. The reverend gentleman thought he had never heard anything quite like it. An ordinarily frivolous girl, of course, would have been impatient long ago. But the fine passion of the man broke everywhere through his rather lame words, and set something in the air about them aflame. The violins sounded thin and trashy compared to the rhythm of this earnest voice; all the glitter of the ballroom seemed cheap — the costume of Carmen absurdly incongruous. Mr. Ambleside slipped back somehow into the key of the afternoon when Cosmic Powers had held direct communion with his soul. He understood that he was meant to listen. Something big was in progress, something important in a high sense. He did listen – to every word. It was Carmen speaking now; but her voice marred the picture. It was thin, trifling, even affected.

"It's very flattering," she simpered, "but – don't you see – it means the end of all my fun and enjoyment in life. You're so fearfully in earnest. You'd exhaust me in the first week!" She cocked her pretty head on one side, holding the fan against her cheek. Something, nevertheless, belied the lightness of her words, the listener felt.

"But I'll teach you a different kind of happiness," replied the man eagerly, "so that you'll never again want this passing excitement, this 'unrest which men miscall delight.' Give me your answer – now. I see it in your eyes. Let me go away tomorrow with this great new happiness in my heart." He leaned forward. "Let your real self speak out once for all!" He took her fan away and she made no resistance. She clasped her hands in her lap, still looking at him mischievously through her mask.

"Let's wait till we meet later in town," she sighed at length prettily, coaxingly. "I shall be able to enjoy myself here then for the rest of the summer first – I feel so young for such a program."

But the man cut her short.

"Now," he said, holding her steadily with his eyes. "You said that to me a year ago, remember. I have waited ever since. It is your youth I want."

The girl played with him for another ten minutes, while the clergyman listened, wondering greatly at the other's patience. Clearly, she delighted to feel his great love beating up against the citadel she meant in the end to yield. The lighter side of her was vastly interested and amused by it; but all the time the deeper part was ready with its answer. It was only that the "child" in her wanted to enjoy itself a little longer before it capitulated forever to the strength that should take her captive, and lead her by sharp ways of sacrifice to the high *rôle* she was meant to fill.

It would all have vexed and wearied Mr. Ambleside exceedingly, but for this singular feeling that it was part of some much larger scheme of which he might never know the whole perhaps, but in which he was playing his little part with a secret thrill. Through the tawdry glitter of that scented ballroom he saw again that terrible white-lipped Face, and felt the measure of this great purpose rolling past him – immense, remorseless – which, for all its splendor, could include even so small a thing as this vain and silly girl. The tide of it rose about him with a flood of power. He glanced at the small black domino of the Carmen opposite him . . . he saw the little flashing eyes, the pert lips and mouth

— thinking with something like a shudder of that other Countenance in the hollow of whose eyes hid tempests, yet which could look down upon a tiny fluttering paper, because that paper was an item of importance in its great scheme of which both beginning and end were nevertheless veiled. . . .

His thoughts must have wandered for a time. The conversation, at any rate, had meanwhile taken a singular turn. The girl was on her feet, the man facing her.

"Then what is this test of yours?" he was saying, half serious, half laughing — "this test which you say will prove how much I care?"

The girl put back between her lips the small red rose that was part of the Carmen costume. Either it was that the stalk made her lisp a little, or else that a sudden rush of the violins in the waltz drowned her words. The Reverend Phillip, standing there trembling — he never quite understood why he should have awaited her answer so nervously — only caught the second half of her phrase.

". . . that I gave you in this very room six weeks ago, and that you promised to carry about with you always?" he heard the end of her sentence, in a voice that for the first time that evening was serious; "because, if you've kept your word in a small thing like that I can trust you to keep it in bigger things. It was a part of myself, you know, that little bit of hair!" She laughed deliciously in his face, raising herself on tiptoe with her hands behind her back. "You said so yourself, didn't you? You promised it should never, *never* leave you."

The man made a curiously sudden gesture as though a pain beyond his control passed through him. His hands were on the back of a chair. The chair squeaked audibly along the polished floor beneath a violent momentary pressure. He looked straight into his companion's eyes, but made no immediate reply.

Carmen's gaze behind the black mask became hard. With a truly feminine idiocy she was obviously playing this whim as a serious move in the game.

"For if you have lost *that,*" she continued, her face flushing beneath the paint, "how can you expect to keep the rest of me, the important part of me?" She spoke as though she believed that he, too, was half-playing — that the next minute he would put his hand into his pocket and produce it. His delay, his awkwardness, above all his silence, angered her. For the surface of her self-contradictory character was obviously — minx.

After a pause that seemed interminable the man spoke, and for the first time his deep voice shook a little.

"This time tomorrow night you shall have it," he said.

"But you're leaving, you said, in the morning!" The tone was piqued and shrill.

"I shall stay another day — on purpose." A pause followed.

"Then you really have lost it — envelope and all — with your name in *my* writing on the outside, and *my* hair for all to recognize who find it — and to sneer."

Her eyes flashed as she said it. The girl was disappointed, incensed, furious. It was all silly enough, of course, and utterly out of proportion. But how silly and childish real life is apt to be at such moments, only those who have reached middle age and have observed closely can know. At the time, to the clergyman who stood there listening and observing, it seemed genuinely poignant, even tragic.

"Until the day before yesterday it had never left me for a single instant," he said at length. "I was in the mountains — glissading with your brother. It fell out of my pocket with a lot of other papers. I lost it on the upper snow slopes of the Dents Blenches —"

The rest of his words were drowned by an inrush of people, for the band was beginning a two-step and couples were sorting themselves and seeking their partners. A Frenchman, dressed as Napoleon, came up to claim his dance. Carmen was swept away. Scornfully, angrily, with concentrated resentment in her voice and manner, she turned upon her heel and from the lips that bit the stalk of the small red rose came the significant words —

"And with it you have also lost — me!"

She was gone. Perhaps the Reverend Phillip Ambleside only imagined the tears in her voice. He never knew, and had no time to think, for he found himself looking straight into the eyes of the lover, thus absurdly rejected, and who now became aware of his close presence for the first time. Even then the absurdity of the whole situation did not wholly reveal itself. It came later with reflection. At the moment he felt that it was all like a vivid and singular dream in which the values and proportions were oddly exaggerated, yet in which the sense of tragedy was distressingly real. His heart went out to the faithful and patient man who was being so trifled with, yet who might be in danger of losing by virtue of his very simplicity what was to be of real value in his life — and scheme.

"It's *my* move now," was the thought in his mind as he took a step forward.

The other, embarrassed and annoyed to discover that the whole scene had probably been overheard, made an awkward movement to withdraw, but before he could do so, the clergyman approached him. Only one step was necessary. He moved up from behind a palm, and drawing his hand from an inner pocket, he handed across to him a white envelope bearing the printed name of the hotel and a neat inscription in feminine writing just below it.

"I found this on the snow slopes of the Dents Blanches this afternoon," he said courteously. The other stared him steadily in the face — his color coming and going quickly. "Take it to her and say that after all it was you — you, who were applying the test — that you wished to see if for so small a thing she was ready to reject so true a love. And, pray, pardon this interference which — er — chance has placed in my power. The matter, I need hardly say, is entirely between yourself and me."

The man took the paper awkwardly, a soft smile of gratitude and comprehension dawning in his eyes. He began to stammer a few words, but the clergyman did not stay to listen. He bowed politely and left him.

He went out of the hotel into the night, and a wind from the surrounding snow slopes brushed his face with its touch of great spaces. He looked up and saw the crowding stars, brilliant as in winter. The mountains in this faint light seemed incredibly close. Slowly he walked up the village street to his rooms in the chalet by the church.

And suddenly the true, proportion of normal things in this little life returned to him, and with it a sharp realization of the triviality of the scene he had been forced to witness — and of the horrible grandeur of the means by which he had been dragged, by the scruff of his priestly neck as it were, so awkwardly into the middle of it all: merely to provide a scrap of evidence the loss of which threatened to bring about a foolish estrangement, and might conceivably have prevented a marriage of apparently insignificant importance.

He felt as though the machinery of the entire solar system had been employed to help a pair of ants carry a pine-needle too heavy for them to the top of the nest.

And then a moment's reflection brought to him another thought. For who could say what the result of this marriage might be? Who could say that from just the exact combination of those two forces — the earnest man, and the lighter girl — a son might not be born who should shake the world and lead some cherished purpose of Deity to completion? For, truly, of the threads which weave into the pattern of life and out again, men see but the tiny section immediately beneath their eyes. The majority focus their gaze upon some detail — thus losing the view of the whole. The beginning and the end are forever hidden; and what appears insignificant and out of proportion when caught alone at close quarters, may reveal all the splendor of the Eternal Purpose when surveyed with the proper perspective — of the Infinite. The Reverend

Philhip Ambleside felt as if for a moment he had been lifted to a height whence he had caught perhaps a glimpse of these larger horizons.

With his faith vastly strengthened, but his nerves considerably shaken, the clergyman went to bed and slept the sleep of a just man who has done his duty by chance as it were, He had helped forward a purpose of which he really understood nothing, but which, he somehow felt, was bigger than anything with which he had so far been connected in his life. Some day — his faith whispered it next morning while he was preparing his sermon — he would see the matter with proper perspective, and would understand.

The Terror of the Twins

That the man's hopes had built upon a son to inherit his name and estates — a single son, that is — was to be expected; but no one could have foreseen the depth and bitterness of his disappointment, the cold, implacable fury, when there arrived instead — twins. For, though the elder legally must inherit, that other ran him so deadly close. A daughter would have been a more reasonable defeat. But twins — ! To miss his dream by so feeble a device — !

The complete frustration of a hope deeply cherished for years may easily result in strange fevers of the soul, but the violence of the father's hatred, existing as it did side by side with a love he could not deny, was something to set psychologists thinking. More than unnatural, it was positively uncanny. Being a man of rigid self-control, however, it operated inwardly, and doubtless along some morbid line of weakness little suspected even by those nearest to him, preying upon his thought to such dreadful extent that finally the mind gave way. The suppressed rage and bitterness deprived him, so the family decided, of his reason, and he spent the last years of his life under restraint. He was possessed naturally of immense forces — of will, feeling, desire; his dynamic value truly tremendous, driving through life like a great engine; and the intensity of this concentrated and buried hatred was guessed by few. The twins themselves, however, knew it. They divined it, at least, for it operated ceaselessly against them side by side with the genuine soft love that occasionally sweetened it, to their great perplexity. They spoke of it only to each other, though.

"At twenty-one," Edward, the elder, would remark sometimes, unhappily, "we shall know more." "Too much," Ernest would reply, with a rush of unreasoning terror the thought never failed to evoke — *in him.* "Things father said always happened — in life." And they paled perceptibly. For the hatred, thus compressed into a veritable bomb of psychic energy, had found at the last a singular expression in the cry of the father's distraught mind. On the occasion of their final visit to the asylum, preceding his death by a few hours only, very calmly, but with an intensity that drove the words into their hearts like points of burning metal, he had spoken. In the presence of the attendant, at the door of the dreadful padded cell, he said it: "You are not two, but *one*. I still regard you as one. And at the coming of age, by h———, you shall find it out!"

The lads perhaps had never fully divined that icy hatred which lay so well concealed against them, but that this final sentence was a curse, backed by all the man's terrific force, they quite well realized; and accordingly, almost unknown to each other, they had come to dread the day inexpressibly. On the morning of that twenty-first birthday — their father gone these five years into the Unknown, yet still sometimes so strangely close to them — they shared the same biting, inner terror, just as they shared all other emotions of their life — intimately, without speech. During the daytime they managed to keep it at a distance; but when the dusk fell about the old house they knew the stealthy approach of a kind of panic sense. Their self-respect weakened swiftly . . . and they persuaded their old friend, and once tutor, the vicar, to sit up with them till midnight . . . He had humored them to that extent, willing to forgo his sleep, and at the same time more than a little interested in their singular belief — that before the day was out, before midnight struck, that is, the curse of that terrible man would somehow come into operation against them.

Festivities over and the guests departed, they sat up in the library, the room usually occupied by their father, and little used since. Mr. Curtice, a robust man of fifty-five, and a firm believer in spiritual principalities and powers, dark as well as good, affected (for their own good) to regard the youths' obsession with a kindly cynicism. "I do not think it likely for one moment," he said gravely, "that such a thing would be permitted. All spirits are in the hands of God, and the violent ones more especially." To which Edward made the extraordinary reply: "Even if father does not come himself he will — *send!*" And Ernest agreed: "All this time he's been making preparations for this very day. We've both known it for a long time — by odd things that have happened, by our dreams, by nasty little dark hints of various kinds, and by these persistent attacks of terror that come from nowhere, especially of late. Haven't we, Edward?" Edward assenting with a shudder. "Father has been at us of late with renewed violence. Tonight it will be a regular assault upon our lives, or minds, or souls!"

"Strong personalities *may* possibly leave behind them forces that continue to act," observed Mr. Curtice with caution, while the brothers replied almost in the same breath: "That's exactly what we feel so curiously. Though — nothing has actually happened yet, you know, and it's a good many years now since —"

This was the way the twins spoke of it all. And it was their profound conviction that had touched their old friend's sense of duty. The experiment should justify itself — and cure them. Meanwhile none of the family knew. Everything was planned secretly.

The library was the quietest room in the house. It had shuttered bow-windows, thick carpets, heavy doors. Books lined the walls, and there was a capacious open fireplace of brick in which the wood logs blazed and roared, for the autumn night was chilly. Round this the three of them were grouped, the clergyman reading aloud from the Book of Job in low tones; Edward and Ernest, in dinner-jackets, occupying deep leather armchairs, listening. They looked exactly what they were — Cambridge "undergrads," their faces pale against their dark hair, and alike as two peas. A shaded lamp behind the clergyman threw the rest of the room into shadow. The reading voice was steady, even monotonous, but something in it betrayed an underlying anxiety, and although the eyes rarely left the printed page, they took in every movement of the young men opposite, and noted every change upon their faces. It was his aim to produce an unexciting atmosphere, yet to miss nothing; if anything did occur to see it from the very beginning. Not to be taken by surprise was his main idea. . . . And thus, upon this falsely peaceful scene, the minutes passed the hour of eleven and slipped rapidly along towards midnight.

The novel element in his account of this distressing and dreadful occurrence seems to be that what happened — happened without the slightest warning or preparation. There was no gradual presentiment of any horror; no strange blast of cold air; no dwindling of heat or light; no shaking of windows or mysterious tapping upon furniture. Without preliminaries it fell with its black trappings of terror upon the scene.

The clergyman had been reading aloud for some considerable time, one or other of the twins — Ernest usually — making occasional remarks, which proved that his sense of dread was disappearing. As the time grew short and nothing happened they grew more at their ease. Edward, indeed, actually nodded, dozed, and finally fell asleep. It was a few minutes before midnight. Ernest, slightly yawning, was stretching himself in the big chair. "Nothing's going to happen," he said aloud, in a pause. "Your good influence has prevented it." He even laughed now. "What superstitious asses we've been, sir; haven't we — ?"

Curtice, then, dropping his Bible, looked hard at him under the lamp. For in that second, even while the words sounded, there had come about a most abrupt and dreadful change; and so swiftly that the clergyman, in spite of himself, was taken utterly by surprise and had no time to think. There had swooped down upon the quiet library — so he puts it — an immense hushing silence, so profound that the peace already reigning there seemed clamor by comparison; and out of this enveloping, stillness there rose through the space about them a living and abominable Invasion — soft, motionless, terrific. It was as though vast engines, working at full speed and pressure, yet too swift and delicate to be appreciable to any definite sense, had suddenly dropped down upon them — from nowhere. "It made me think," the vicar used to say afterwards, "of the *Mauretania* machinery compressed into a nutshell, yet losing none of its awful power."

". . . haven't we?" repeated Ernest, still laughing. And Curtice, making no audible reply, heard the true answer in his heart: "Because everything has *already happened* — even as you feared."

Yet, to the vicar's supreme astonishment, Ernest still noticed — nothing!

"Look," the boy added, "Eddy's sound asleep — sleeping like a pig. Doesn't say much for your reading, you know, sir!" And he laughed again — lightly, even foolishly. But that laughter jarred, for the clergyman understood now that the sleep of the elder twin was either feigned — or *unnatural.*

And while the easy words fell so lightly from his lips, the monstrous engines worked and pulsed against him and against his sleeping brother, all their huge energy concentrated down into points fine as Suggestion, delicate as Thought. The Invasion affected everything. The very objects in the room altered incredibly, revealing suddenly behind their normal exteriors horrid little hearts of darkness. It was truly amazing, this vile metamorphosis. Books, chairs, pictures, all yielded up their pleasant aspect, and betrayed, as with silent mocking laughter, their inner soul of blackness — their *decay.* This is how Curtice tries to body forth in words what he actually witnessed. . . . And Ernest, yawning, talking lightly, half foolishly — still noticed nothing!

For all this, as described, came about in something like ten seconds; and with it swept into the clergyman's mind, like a blow, the memory of that sinister phrase used more than once by Edward: "If father doesn't come, he will certainly — *send.*" And Curtice understood that he had done both — both sent and come himself. . . . That violent mind, released from its spell of madness in the body, yet still retaining the old implacable hatred, was now directing the terrible, unseen assault. This silent room, so hushed and still, was charged to the brim. The horror of it, as he said later, "seemed to peel the very skin from my back." . . . And, while Ernest noticed nothing, Edward slept. . . ! The soul of the clergyman, strong with the desire to help or save, yet realizing that he was alone against a Legion, poured out in wordless prayer to his Deity. The clock just then, whirring before it struck, made itself audible.

"By Jove! It's all right, you see!" exclaimed Ernest, his voice oddly fainter and lower than before. "There's midnight — and nothing's happened. Bally nonsense, all of it!" His voice had dwindled curiously in volume. "I'll get the whisky and soda from the hall." His relief was great and his manner showed it. But in him somewhere was a singular change. His voice, manner, gestures, his very tread as he moved over the thick carpet toward the door, all showed it. He seemed less *real*, less alive, reduced somehow to littleness, the voice without timbre or quality, the appearance of him diminished in some fashion quite ghastly. His presence, if not actually shriveled, was at least impaired. Ernest had suffered a singular and horrible *decrease.* . . .

The clock was still whirring before the strike. One heard the chain running up softly. Then the hammer fell upon the first stroke of midnight.

"I'm off," he laughed faintly from the door; "it's all been pure funk — on my part, at least. . . !" He passed out of sight into the hall. *The Power that throbbed so mightily about the room followed him out.* Almost at the same moment Edward woke up. But he woke with a tearing and indescribable cry of pain and anguish on his lips: "Oh, oh, oh! But it hurts! It hurts! I can't hold you; leave me. It's breaking me asunder —"

The clergyman had sprung to his feet, but in the same instant everything had become normal once more — the room as it was before, the horror gone. There was nothing he could do or say, for there was no longer anything to put right, to defend, or to attack. Edward was speaking; his voice, deep and full as it never had been before: "By Jove, how that sleep has refreshed me! I feel twice the chap I was before — twice the chap. I feel quite splendid. Your voice, sir, must have hypnotized me to sleep. . . ." He crossed the room with great vigor. "Where's — er — where's — Ernie, by the bye?" he asked casually, hesitating — almost searching — for the name. And a shadow as of a vanished memory crossed his face and was gone. The tone conveyed the most complete indifference where once the least word or movement of his twin had wakened solicitude, love. "Gone away, I suppose — gone to bed, I mean, of course."

Curtice has never been able to describe the dreadful conviction that overwhelmed him as he stood there staring, his heart in his mouth — the conviction, the positive certainty, that Edward had changed interiorly, had suffered an incredible accession to his existing personality. But he *knew* it as he watched. His mind, spirit, soul had most wonderfully increased. Something that hitherto the lad had known from the outside only, or by the magic of loving sympathy, had now passed, to be incorporated with his own being. And, being himself, it required no expression. Yet this visible increase was somehow terrible. Curtice shrank back from him. The instinct — he has never grasped the profound psychology of *that*, nor why it turned his soul dizzy with a kind of nausea — the instinct to strike him where he stood, passed, and a plaintive sound from the hall, stealing softly into the room between them, sent all that was left to him of self-possession into his feet. He turned and ran. Edward followed him — very leisurely.

They found Ernest, or what had been Ernest, crouching behind the table in the hail, weeping foolishly to himself. On his face lay blackness. The mouth was open, the jaw dropped; he dribbled hopelessly; and from the face had passed all signs of intelligence — of spirit.

For a few weeks he lingered on, regaining no sign of spiritual or mental life before the poor body, hopelessly disorganized, released what was left of him, from pure inertia — from complete and utter loss of vitality.

And the horrible thing — so the distressed family thought, at least — was that all those weeks Edward showed an indifference that was singularly brutal and complete. He rarely even went to visit him. I believe, too, it is true that he only once spoke of him by name; and that was when he said — "Ernie? Oh, but Ernie is much better and happier where he is — !"

The Man from the 'Gods'

*T*hat there was something wrong with all his work Le Maistre well knew. Words and music, as the critics never failed to remind him, "just missed" that nameless "something" which would have made them good – perhaps great. Moreover, he was sane enough to realize that the blame lay not with an uncomprehending public, but simply with himself. The spark of inspiration that was beyond question in all his work never gathered to the flame stage. Thus his productions warmed people, but did not light them. He understood well enough what was lacking – and that no amount of mere painstaking "work" could put it right.

But on one occasion Le Maistre achieved a singular and startling success. As a sober record of fact, concealed by initials, it was reported in the Proceedings of the French Psychological Society for that year; and people who believed in the Subliminal Self, the Higher Ego, and all that consoling teaching about an attainable God within, made great havoc with the facts.

The way it came about, moreover, probably has a profound psychical significance. In any case, the result remains as the very best kind of tangible proof; for it was the only great thing he ever really achieved – this Fairy Play (so called); and its beauty was absolutely arresting.

He was something over fifty when he wrote it in its original form. The central idea came to him with the quick flash of a genuine inspiration; so did most of the music; but, in the working out of both, the fire had become smothered. The spark had never gathered into flame. The result was mediocrity. Yet, like so many artists, he confused what was in his mind and imagination with what he had actually set down upon paper; for, when he went over the score to himself, he heard the original beauty in his thoughts and believed he had transferred into his work his own memory of that beauty. The music and words themselves, however, had *not* caught it. Thus, those who heard the preliminary recital in his rooms were more or less bored according to their powers of divination.

"It's fine; it's original," they remarked, shaking their heads as they went home after the performance; "but just misses it!"

The transformation that changed the common lead into gold as by some mysterious process of spiritual alchemy came about as follows: —

The little play was finished, and Le Maistre, having his eye upon a certain manager, went to that particular theater one night in order to study the "feel" of it — to catch the flavor of the house, the size of the stage, and any other details he could. The management had given him a dress circle box, and he saw admirably. It was characteristic of the man, rather, that he put himself to this far-fetched kind of trouble. During the performance his mind was keenly at work. Yet he saw nothing of what was going on before his eyes; he had come with a definite purpose; he saw his own play all the time, heard his own music; watched his own creatures come on and go off among his own scenery.

At the same time the music, light and color provided a stimulus that acted upon his own imagination, and set all the finer machinery of his own creative genius working. Sub-consciously he revised his own work, with the illuminating result 'that a white light shone through his mind and showed up all the flaws, all the places where he had "missed it"; all the passages where he had trailed off into banality. And a tremendous desire went crashing through his being to revise his work in the light of this knowledge. "I felt," he said, "as though a great prayer had gone out of me — a cry, as it were, to my higher self to come to my assistance. Never in my life have I wished anything so intensely before."

Then, in that curious fashion with which many artists must be familiar, it all faded again, and the reaction set in. The effort had no doubt exhausted him. He turned his attention to the actual performances on the stage before him, and lost the power to visualize his own piece. But the play — trivial, vulgar and untrue to life — wearied him; and he withdrew into the back of the box, and incontinently — fell asleep upon the little plush sofa!

When a considerable time later he woke up, the entire theater was dark and empty; the piece was over; the audience had gone home to a man; and the building was deserted.

Le Maistre at once realized what had happened, though he could not understand why the final applause had not waked him, and hurried into his overcoat. A faint glimmer pervaded the vast auditorium, for as he leaned over the edge he could just make out the rows of empty stalls, the scattered white patches where the discarded programs lay, the music-stands of the orchestra, and the exit doors of glass where the pit began. The air still smelt unpleasantly of a crowd — wraps, furs, stale scent and cigarettes.

Then he struck a match and saw by his watch that it was two o'clock in the morning. He had slept three hours!

He pushed open the door and passed out into the passage, his one idea being how he could get out into the street, or how he would spend the time if he did not get out. He felt hungry, stiff and a trifle chilly. Feeling his way along by the backs of the upper circle seats, he advanced slowly and carefully, his footsteps making no sound upon the soft carpet, and so came at last to the first exit door. It was locked and barred. He tried the next door with the same result. There was no other exit — nothing but that narrow semi-circular gangway between the wall and the seats, a box at either end, and pillars at intervals to mark the distance. "Like the exercise-walk in a prisonyard," he thought to himself, laughing. No single light was left burning anywhere in the building. Even the hall was in darkness. He saw the gilt-framed pictures of actors and actresses on the walls; a faint rumble from the streets reached him too — voices, traffic, footsteps, wind. Then he turned back into the theater and carefully made his way down the aisle to the front, feeling the steps first with his toe, and peered over into the body of the house. A sea of shadows swam to and fro below him. Here and there certain stalls picked themselves out of the general gloom almost as though they were occupied; he could easily imagine he saw figures still sitting in them. . . .

And it was here, just at this point, he said, that he began for the first time to feel a little uneasy. A slight tremor of the nerves passed over him, and sitting down in one of the front-row seats he considered the situation carefully and deliberately. There was not much to consider. He was shut in for the rest of the night; the dress circle seemed to be the limits of his prison; he could get neither up nor down; there was no escape till the morning. The prospect was not pleasant; still, it was not very terrible, and his sense of humor would easily have carried him through with credit, but for one thing — this curiously disturbing sense of something he could not quite define: of something that was *going to happen*, it seemed. . . .

It was too vague, too remote for him to deal with squarely. His mind, always keenly imaginative and pictorial, preferred to see it in the terms of a picture. He thought of the Thames as he had sometimes seen it from the Chelsea Embankment in the dusk when dark barges, too far for their outline to be defined, come looming up through the mist. In this way thoughts lie in the depths of the mind; in this way they rise gradually before the consciousness; in this way the cause of his present discomfort would presently reach the point where he would recognize it and understand. In similar fashion, he felt this "something" that moved at the back of his mind, coming slowly forward.

A sudden idea came to him —

"If I could climb down to the auditorium floor I might find a door open somewhere, or escape by way of the orchestra, perhaps!"

And the idea of action was pleasant; though how he climbed over the edge of the box in the dark and swarmed down the slippery pillar, landing with a crash upon the rim of the stage box below, he never quite understood. With a plunge he dropped backwards into the dark space, kicking over as he did so a couple of chairs, which fell with a loud clatter and woke resounding echoes all through the empty building. That clatter seemed prodigious. He held his breath for several seconds to listen, standing motionless against the wall with the distinct idea that all this noise would attract attention to himself, and that if, after all, there was anyone watching him — that if among those shadows some-one —

"Ah!" he exclaimed quickly. "Now I've got it! There *is* someone watching me in another part of the building. That's why I felt uneasy —"

That tumble into the box had shaken the thought up to the surface of his mind. The picture had emerged from the mist, and he recognized the cause of his uneasiness. All this time, though none of his senses had yet proved it to him, the mind of another person, perhaps the eyes too, had been focused upon him. He was not alone.

Le Maistre felt no alarm, he said, but rather a definite thrill of exhilaration, as though the idea of this other person came to him with a sense of pleasurable excitement. His first instinct to sit concealed in the corner of the box and await events he dismissed almost at once in favor of some kind of prompt action. Stumbling in the gloom, he made his way down to the orchestra, and while groping cautiously among the crowded easels, his hand touched a tiny knob, and a dozen lights that bent over the music folios, like little heads screened under black bonnets, sprang into brilliance. The first thing he noticed was that the fire curtain was down, closing the cavernous mouth of the stage.

The shaded lights, however, were so carefully arranged that they fell only upon the music, and the main body of the theater still yawned in comparative darkness behind him. Vast and unfriendly it seemed; charged to the brim with faint shufflings and whispers as though an audience sat there stealthily turning over programs. The stalls faced him like fixed but living beings; the balconies frowned down upon him; the boxes — especially the upper ones — had an air of concealing people behind their curtains. Far overhead, glimmered a huge skylight; he heard the wind sighing across it like wind in the rigging of a ship. And, more than once, he fancied he caught the faint tread of footsteps moving about among the stalls and gangways.

Regretting that he had turned the lights up (they made himself so conspicuous, so easily visible!), he made an instinctive movement to turn them out again; but he touched the wrong knob, so that a row of lights flashed out up under the roof. In that topmost gallery of all, known as "the gods," a little line of starry lights leaped into being, and the first thing he noticed as he looked up was the figure of a man leaning over the edge of the railing — watching him.

The same moment he saw that this figure was making a movement of some kind — a gesture. It beckoned to him. So his feeling that someone was in the theater with him was justified. There had been a man in the gods all the time.

Le Maistre admitted frankly that, in his first surprise, he collapsed backwards upon the stool usually occupied by the second 'cello. But his alarm passed with a strange swiftness, and gave place almost immediately to a peculiar and deep-seated thrill. The instant he perceived this dim figure of a man up there under the roof his heart leaped with an emotion that was partly delight, partly pleasurable anticipation, and partly — most curious of all — awe. And in a voice that was unlike his own, and that carried across the intervening space, for all its faintness, with perfect ease, he heard the words driven out of him as if by command of some deeper instinct than he understood yet the very last words that he could have imagined as appropriate —

"You're up there in the gods!" he called out. "Won't you come down to me here?"

And then the figure withdrew, and he heard the sound of the footsteps descending the winding passages and stairs behind, as their owner obeyed him and came.

Alarmed, yet curiously exultant, Le Maistre stood up among the music-easels to await his coming. He was extraordinarily alert, prepared. He fumbled again with the little switch-board under the conductor's desk, for he wished to see the man face to face in full light — not to be gradually approached in darkness. But the only thing that came of the button he pressed was a creaking noise behind him, and when he turned quickly to examine, lo and behold, he saw the huge fire-curtain rising slowly and majestically into the air. And, as it rose, revealing the stage beyond, he got the distinct impression that this very stage, now empty, had a moment before been crowded with a throng of living people, and that even now they were there concealed among the wings within a few feet of where he stood, waiting the summons to appear.

Moreover, this discovery, far from causing him the kind of amazement that might have been expected, only communicated, for the second time within the space of a few minutes, another thrill of delight.

Again this lightning sense of exhilaration swept him from head to foot.

The footsteps, meanwhile, came nearer; sometimes disappearing behind a thickness of walls that rendered them inaudible, and at other times starting suddenly into greater clearness as they came down from floor to floor. Le Maistre, unable to endure the suspense any longer, felt impelled to go forward and meet them halfway. An intense desire to see this stranger face to face came upon him. He climbed awkwardly over the orchestra railing and made his way past the first rows of the stalls. Already the steps sounded upon the same floor as himself. Hardly a dozen yards, to judge by the fall of these oddly cushioned footsteps, could now separate them. He moved more slowly, and the stranger moved more slowly too – entering at last the gangway in which he stood.

"And it is from this point," to use the words of the report he afterwards wrote for the society, "that my memory begins to fade somewhat, or rather, that the sense of bewilderment grew so astonishingly disturbing that I find it difficult to look back and recall with accuracy the true sequence of what followed. My normal measurement of the passage of time changed too, I think; all went so swiftly, almost as in a dream, though at the time it did not appear to me to be short or hurried. But – describe the sense of glory, wonder and happiness that enveloped me as in a cloud, I simply cannot. As well might a hashish-eater attempt during the dullness of next morning to reconstruct the phantasmal wonder of all he experienced the night before. Only, this was no phantasy; it was real and actual, and more palpitatingly vivid than any other experience of my life.

"I stood waiting in the gangway while this other person – the stranger – came towards me along the narrow space between the wall and the main body of seats. The footsteps were unhurried and regular. It was very dark; all I could see were two faint patches of light where the exit doors of the pit glimmered beyond. First one patch of light, then the other, was temporarily obscured as he passed in front of these doors. Down he moved steadily towards me through the gloom, and at the barrier of velvet rope that separated the stalls from the pit, he stopped – just near enough for me to distinguish the head and shoulders of a man about my own height and about my own size. He stood facing me there, some ten or twelve feet away.

"For a few seconds there was complete silence – like the silence in a mine, I remember thinking – and I instinctively clenched my fists, almost expecting something violent to happen. But the next instant the man spoke; and the moment I heard his voice all traces of fear left me, and I felt nothing but this peculiarly delightful sense of exhilaration I have already mentioned. It ran through me like the flush of a generous wine, rousing all my faculties, critical and imaginative, to their highest possible power, yet at the same time so bewildering me for the moment that I scarcely realized what I was saying, doing, or thinking. From this point I went through the whole scene without hesitation or dismay — certainly without a thought of disobeying. I mean, it was a pleasure to me to help it all forward, rather than to seek to prevent.

"'Here I am,' said the man in a voice wholly wonderful. 'You called me down, and I have come!'

"'You have come from up there — from the gods,' I heard myself reply.

"'I have come from up there — from the gods,' he answered; and his sentence seemed to mean so much more than mine did, although we used identical words.

"I held on to the back of the stall nearest to me. I could think for the moment of nothing further to say. The idea of what was coming thrilled me inexpressibly, though I could only hazard wild guesses as to its character.

"'Are you ready then?' he asked.

"'Ready! Ready for what?'

"'For the rehearsal,' he said, 'the secret rehearsal.'

"'The secret rehearsal?' I stammered, pretending, as a child pretends in order to heighten its joy, that I did not understand.

"' — of your play, you know; your fairy play,' he finished the sentence.

"Then he moved towards me a few steps, and, hardly knowing why, I retreated. It was still impossible to see his face. The curious idea came to me that there was something odd about the man that prevented, and that would always prevent, me getting closer to him, and that perhaps I should never see his face completely at all. I cannot point to anything definite that caused this impression; I can merely report that it was so.

"'Look!' he went on, 'everyone is ready and waiting. The moment the music starts we can begin. You will find a violin down there; the rehearsal can go on at once.'

"And although it struck me at the time as most curious he should be aware of the fact, it seemed quite natural, because I do play the violin, and in fact compose all my melodies first on that instrument before I put a pen to paper. At the same time I can remember faintly protesting —

"'I?' I remember asking; 'I'm to play?'

"'Certainly,' replied this soft-spoken figure among the shadows. 'You're to play. Who else, pray? And see! Everyone is ready and waiting.'

"I was far too happily bewildered to object further; there seemed, indeed, no time for reflection at all; I felt impelled, driven forward as it were, to go through with the adventure and to ask no questions. Besides, I wanted to go through with it. I felt the old power of the first inspiration upon me — only heightened; I felt in me the supreme and splendid confidence that I could do it all better than I had ever dreamed — do it perfectly as it should be done. I was borne forwards upon a wave of inspiration that nothing in the whole world could interfere with.

"And, as I turned to obey, I saw for the first time that the stage was brilliantly lighted; that the scenery was the scenery already chosen by my mind; that the performers thronged the wings, and the opening characters were actually standing in their places waiting for the signal of the music to begin. The performers, moreover, I perceived, were identical in figure, feature and bearing with those ideal performers who had already enacted the play upon the inner stage of my imagination. It was all, in fact, precisely as the original inspiration had come to me weeks ago before the fires of beauty had faded during the wearisome toil of working it all out in limited terms upon the paper.

"The power that drove me forward, and at the same time filled me with this splendor of untrammeled creation, refused me, however, the least moment for consideration. I could only make my way into the orchestra and pick up the first violin-case that came to hand, belonging, doubtless, to some member of the band I had listened to earlier in the evening; and all eyes were fixed upon me from the stage as I clambered into the conductor's seat and drew the bow across the strings to tune the instrument. At the first sound I realized that my fingers, accustomed to the harsh tones of my own cheaper fiddle, were now feeling their way over the exquisite nervous system of a genuine Guarnierius that responded instantly to the lightest touch; and that the bow in my right hand was so perfectly balanced that even the best Tourte ever made could only seem like a strip of raw, unfinished wood by comparison. For the bow 'swam' over the strings, the sound streamed, smooth as honey, past my ears, and my fingers found the new intervals as easily as if they had never known any other key-board. Harmonics, double-stopping and arpeggios issued from my efforts as perfectly as trills from the throat of a bird.

"In that moment I *lived;* I understood much; I heard my soul singing within me. . . . I finished tuning, and tapped sharply on the back of the violin to indicate that I was ready, and in the slight pause that ensued before I actually played the opening bars, I became aware that the stalls behind me, the boxes, the dress circle, and the whole house in fact right up to the 'gods,' were crowded with eager listeners; and, further, that the stranger — that man among the shadows in the background — standing ever beyond the reach of the light, still remained in some mysterious and potent fashion intimately in touch with my inner self, directing, helping, inspiring the performance from beginning to end.

"And, in front of me, upon the conductor's desk, lay the score of my own music in clearest manuscript, no longer crossed out and corrected as it lay in my rooms after all the first passion of beauty had been ground out of it, but lovely and perfect as the original inspiration had rushed flamelike into my soul months before.

"The whole performance from that moment – 'rehearsal' seems no adequate word to describe it – went with the smoothness of a dream from beginning to end. Just as the music was my own music made perfect, so the words and songs were the mature expression of the original conception before my blundering efforts had confined them, stammering and incomplete, in broken form. Moreover – more wonderful still – I noticed the very places in my score where I had floundered, and where, in the laborious process of composition, the first inspiration had failed me and I had filled in with what was mediocre and banal. It was as if a master pointed out to me with the simplicity of true power the passages where the commonplace might pass – could – did pass – by deft, inspired touches into what was fine, moving, noble.

The lesson was a sublime one; at the time, however, it all seemed so ridiculously simple and easy that I felt I could never again write anything that was not great and splendid.

"Moreover, the acting, speaking and dancing provided the perfect medium for my ideas; and the whole performance was the consummate representation of my first conception; even the scenery shifted swiftly and noiselessly, and the intervals between the acts were hardly noticeable.

"And the end came with a curious abruptness, bringing me to myself – my limited, stammering, caged little self, as, it seemed, after these moments of intoxicating expression – with a sharp sense of pain that all was over; and I became aware that, without hurry, without noise, the entire audience that filled the huge building had risen to their feet like one man, and that thousands of hands were clapping *silently* the measure of their intense appreciation. From floor to ceiling, and from wall to wall, flew a great wave of emotion that swept their praise into me, gathered and focused into a single mighty draft of applause. It was, I remember thinking, all their thoughts of joy, their feelings of gratitude, beating in upon my soul in that form of praise which is the artist's only adequate reward; and it reminded me of nothing so much as the whirring of innumerable soft wings all rising through the air at the same moment. Pictorially, in this fashion, it came before my mind.

"Violin in hand, I rose too, and turned to face the auditorium, for I realized that they were calling for the author – for him who had ministered so adequately to their pleasure – and that I must be prepared to say something in reply. I had, indeed, made my first bow, and was already casting about in my mind for suitable words, when, for the first time during the whole adventure – something in me *hesitated.* Either it was that the sea of glimmering faces frightened me, or that I was obeying instinctively some faint warning that it was not myself, but some other, who was the true author of the play, and that it was for him these thousands before me clamored and called.

"But when, still hesitating in confusion, I turned again towards the stage, I saw that the great fire curtain had meanwhile descended and that a footstep, regular and unhurried, was at that very moment coming forward towards the footlights. I heard the tread. I knew at once who it was. The stranger from the shadows behind me who had directed the entire performance was now moving to the front. It was he for whom the audience clamored; it was he who was the true author of the play!

"And instantly I clamored with them, forgetting my own small pain in a kind of delightful exultation that I, too, owed this man everything, and that I should at last see him face to face and join my thanks and gratitude to theirs.

"Almost that same instant he appeared and stood before the center of the curtains, the glare of the footlights casting upwards into his face. And he looked, not at the great throng behind and beyond me, but down into *my own* face, into *my own* eyes, smiling, approving, his expression radiant with a glory I have never seen before or since upon any human countenance.

"And the stranger, I then realized – was *myself!*

"What happened next is so difficult to describe – though I scarcely know why it should be so – that I cannot hope to convey the reality of it properly, or paint the instantaneous manner in which he vanished and was gone. He neither faded nor moved. But in a second that seemed to have no perceptible duration he was beside me – with me – in me; and this swift way he became suddenly merged into myself has always seemed to me the most amazing thing I have ever witnessed. The wave of delight and exultation swept into me anew. I felt for one brief moment that I was as a god – with a god's power of perfect expression.

"But for one second only; for, at once, a new sound, terrible and overwhelming, rose in a flood and tore me away from all that I had ever known. And the sound was ugly and distressing . . . and darkness followed it. . . .

"It was real clapping this time, the clapping of human hands . . . and an indifferent orchestra was playing a noisy march just below me with a great blare of brass out of tune. The lights were up all over the theater; the audience, busy with wraps and overcoats and applause, were hurrying out. I saw the actors and actresses of the play bowing and scraping before the curtain; and the sight of the perspiration trickling down over the grease-paint of the leading man directly beneath my box struck me like a blow in the face. Then came the frantic whistling for broughams and taxicabs and the hoarse shouting from the street where men cried the evening papers in the roar of the outer world. I picked up my opera-hat, which had rolled into the middle of the floor while I had slept upon the sofa, scrambled into my overcoat, rushed out into the street, and told the driver of the first taxicab I found to drive for his life at double rates. . . .

"And all that night, before the memory of the wonder and the glory faded, I worked upon my score of words and music, striving to get down on the paper something at least of what had been shown to me. How much, or how little I succeeded it is now impossible to say. As I have already explained in this report, the memory faded with distressing swiftness. But I did my best. I hope — I believe — I am told, at least — that there is something in the work that people like. . . .

The Man Who Played upon the Leaf

*W*here the Jura pine-woods push the fringe of their purple cloak down the slopes till the vineyards stop them lest they should troop into the lake of Neuchâtel, you may find the village where lived the Man Who Played upon the Leaf.

My first sight of him was genuinely prophetic — that spring evening in the garden *café* of the little mountain auberge. But before I saw him I heard him, and ever afterwards the sound and the sight have remained inseparable in my mind.

Jean Grospierre and Louis Favre were giving me confused instructions — the *vin rouge* of Neuchâtel is heady, you know — as to the best route up the Tête-de-Rang, when a thin, wailing music, that at first I took to be rising wind, made itself heard suddenly among the apple trees at the end of the garden, and riveted my attention with a thrill of I know not what.

Favre's description of the bridle path over Mont Racine died away; then Grospierre's eyes wandered as he, too, stopped to listen; and at the same moment a mongrel dog of indescribably forlorn appearance came whining about our table under the walnut tree.

"It's Perret 'Comment-va,' the man who plays on the leaf," said Favre.

"And his cursed dog," added Grospierre, with a shrug of disgust. And, after a pause, they fell again to quarreling about my complicated path up the Tête-de-Rang.

I turned from them in the direction of the sound.

The dusk was falling. Through the trees I saw the vineyards sloping down a mile or two to the dark blue lake with its distant-shadowed shore and the white line of misty Alps in the sky beyond. Behind us the forests rose in folded purple ridges to the heights of Boudry and La Tourne, soft and thick like carpets of cloud. There was no one about in the cabaret. I heard a horse's hoofs in the village street, a rattle of pans from the kitchen, and the soft roar of a train climbing the mountain railway through gathering darkness towards France — and, singing through it all, like a thread of silver through a dream, this sweet and windy music.

But at first there was nothing to be seen. The Man Who Played on the Leaf was not visible, though I stared hard at the place whence the sound apparently proceeded. The effect, for a moment, was almost ghostly.

Then, down there among the shadows of fruit trees and small pines, something moved, and I became aware with a start that the little *sapin* I had been looking at all the time was really not a tree, but a man — hatless, with dark face, loose hair, and wearing a *pélerine* over his shoulders. How he had produced this singularly vivid impression and taken upon himself the outline and image of a tree is utterly beyond me to describe. It was, doubtless, some swift suggestion in my own imagination that deceived me. . . . Yet he was thin, small, straight, and his flying hair and spreading *pélerine* somehow pictured themselves in the network of dusk and background into the semblance, I suppose, of branches.

I merely record my impression with the truest available words — also my instant persuasion that this first view of the man was, after all, significant and prophetic: his dominant characteristics presented themselves to me symbolically. I saw the man first as a tree; I heard his music first as wind.

Then, as he came slowly towards us, it was clear that he produced the sound by blowing upon a leaf held to his lips between tightly closed hands. And at his heel followed the mongrel dog.

"The inseparables!" sneered Grospierre, who did not appreciate the interruption. He glanced contemptuously at the man and the dog, his face and manner, it seemed to me, conveying a merest trace, however, of superstitious fear. "The tune your father taught you, *hein?*" he added, with a cruel allusion I did not at the moment understand.

"Hush!" Favre said; "he plays thunderingly well all the same!" His glass had not been emptied quite so often, and in his eyes as he listened there was a touch of something that was between respect and wonder.

"The music of the devil," Grospierre muttered as he turned with the gesture of surly impatience to the wine and the rye bread. "It makes me dream at night. Ooua!"

The man, paying no attention to the gibes, came closer, continuing his leaf-music, and as I watched and listened the thrill that had first stirred in me grew curiously. To look at, he was perhaps forty, perhaps fifty; worn, thin, broken; and something seizingly pathetic in his appearance told its little wordless story into the air. The stamp of the outcast was mercilessly upon him. But the eyes were dark and fine. They proclaimed the possession of something that was neither worn nor broken, something that was proud to be outcast, and welcomed it.

"He's cracky, you know," explained Favre, "and half blind. He lives in that hut on the edge of the forest" — pointing with his thumb toward Côtendard — "and plays on the leaf for what he can earn."

We listened for five minutes perhaps while this singular being stood there in the dusk and piped his weird tunes; and if imagination had influenced my first sight of him it certainly had nothing to do with what I now heard. For it was unmistakable; the man played, not mere tunes and melodies, but the clean, strong, elemental sounds of Nature — especially the crying voices of wind. It was the raw material, if you like, of what the masters have used here and there — Wagner, and so forth — but by him heard closely and wonderfully, and produced with marvelous accuracy. It was now the notes of birds or the tinkle and rustle of sounds heard in groves and copses, and now the murmur of those airs that lose their way on summer noons among the tree tops; and then, quite incredibly, just as the man came closer and the volume increased, it grew to the crying of bigger winds and the whispering rush of rain among tossed branches. . . .

How he produced it passed my comprehension, but I think he somehow mingled his own voice with the actual notes of the vibrating edge of the leaf; perhaps, too, that the strange passion shaking behind it all in the depths of the bewildered spirit poured out and reached my mind by ways unknown and incalculable.

I must have momentarily lost myself in the soft magic of it, for I remember coming back with a start to notice that the man had stopped, and that his melancholy face was turned to me with a smile of comprehension and sympathy that passed again almost before I had time to recognize it, and certainly before I had time to reply. And this time I am ready to admit that it was my own imagination, singularly stirred, that translated his smile into the words that no one else heard —

"I was playing for you — because you understand."

Favre was standing up and I saw him give the man the half loaf of coarse bread that was on the table, offering also his own partly-emptied wine-glass. "I haven't the sou today," he was saying, "but if you're hungry, mon brave —" And the man, refusing the wine, took the bread with an air of dignity that precluded all suggestion of patronage or favor, and ought to have made Favre feel proud that he had offered it.

"And that for his son!" laughed the stupid Grospierre, tossing a cheese-rind to the dog, "or for his forest god!"

The music was about me like a net that still held my words and thoughts in a delicate bondage — which is my only explanation for not silencing the coarse guide in the way he deserved; but a few minutes later, when the men had gone into the inn, I crossed to the end of the garden, and there, where the perfumes of orchard and forest deliciously mingled, I came upon the man sitting on the grass beneath an apple tree. The dog, wagging its tail, was at his feet, as he fed it with the best and largest portions of the bread. For himself, it seemed, he kept nothing but the crust, and — what I could hardly believe, had I not actually witnessed it — the cur, though clearly hungry, had to be coaxed with smiles and kind words to eat what it realized in some dear dog-fashion was needed even more by its master. A pair of outcasts they looked indeed, sharing dry bread in the back garden of the village inn; but in the soft, discerning eyes of that mangy creature there was an expression that raised it, for me at least, far beyond the ranks of common curdom; and in the eyes of the man, half-witted and pariah as he undoubtedly was, a look that set him somewhere in a lonely place where he heard the still, small voices of the world and moved with the elemental tides of life that are never outcast and that include the farthest suns.

He took the franc I offered; and, closer, I perceived that his eyes, for all their moments of fugitive brilliance, were indeed half sightless, and that perhaps he saw only well enough to know men as trees walking. In the village some said he saw better than most, that he saw in the dark, possibly even into the peopled regions beyond this world, and there were reasons — uncanny reasons — to explain the belief. I only know, at any rate, that from this first moment of our meeting he never failed to recognize me at a considerable distance, and to be aware of my where-abouts even in the woods at night; and the best explanation I ever heard, though of course unscientific, was Louis Favre's whispered communication that "he sees with the whole surface of his skin!"

He took the franc with the same air of grandeur that he took the bread, as though he conferred a favor, yet was grateful. The beauty of that gesture has often come back to me since with a sense of wonder for the sweet nobility that I afterwards understood inspired it. At the time, however, he merely looked up at me with the remark, *"C'est ponr le Dieu — merci!"*

He did not say "le *bon* Dieu," as everyone else did.

And though I had meant to get into conversation with him, I found no words quickly enough, for he at once stood up and began to play again on his leaf; and while he played his thanks and gratitude, or the thanks and gratitude of his God, that shaggy mongrel dog stopped eating and sat up beside him to listen.

Both fixed their eyes upon me as the sounds of wind and birds and forest poured softly and wonderfully about my ears . . . so that, when it was over and I went down the quiet street to my *pension*, I was aware that some tiny sense of bewilderment had crept into the profounder regions of my consciousness and faintly disturbed my normal conviction that I belonged to the common world of men as of old. Some aspect of the village, especially of the human occupants in it, had secretly changed for me.

Those pearly spaces of sky, where the bats flew over the red roofs, seemed more alive, more exquisite than before; the smells of the open stables where the cows stood munching, more fragrant than usual of sweet animal life that included myself delightfully, keenly; the last chatterings of the sparrows under the eaves of my own *pension* more intimate and personal. . . .

Almost as if those strands of elemental music the man played on his leaf had for the moment made me free of the life of the earth, as distinct from the life of men. . . .

I can only suggest this, and leave the rest to the care of the imaginative reader; for it is impossible to say along what inner byways of fancy I reached the conclusion that when the man spoke of "the God," and not "the *good* God," he intended to convey his sense of some great woodland personality — some Spirit of the Forests whom he knew and loved and worshipped, and whom, he was intuitively aware, I also knew and loved and worshipped.

*D*uring the next few weeks I came to learn more about this poor, half-witted man. In the village he was known as Perret "Comment-va," the Man Who Plays on the Leaf; but when the people wished to be more explicit they described him as the man "without parents and without God." The origin of "Comment-va" I never discovered, but the other titles were easily explained — he was illegitimate and outcast. The mother had been a wandering Italian girl and the father a loose-living *bûcheron*, who was, it seems, a standing disgrace to the community. I think the villagers were not conscious of their severity; the older generation of farmers and *vignerons* had pity, but the younger ones and those of his own age were certainly guilty, if not of deliberate cruelty, at least of a harsh neglect and the utter withholding of sympathy. It was like the thoughtless cruelty of children, due to small unwisdom, and to that absence of charity which is based on ignorance. They could not in the least understand this crazy, picturesque being who wandered day and night in the forests and spoke openly, though never quite intelligibly, of worshipping another God than their own anthropomorphic deity.

People looked askance at him because he was queer; a few feared him; one or two I found later – all women – felt vaguely that there was something in him rather wonderful, they hardly knew what, that lifted him beyond the reach of village taunts and sneers. But from all he was remote, alien, solitary – an outcast and a pariah.

It so happened that I was very busy at the time, seeking the seclusion of the place for my work, and rarely going out until the day was failing; and so it was, I suppose, that my sight of the man was always associated with a gentle dusk, long shadows and slanting rays of sunlight. Every time I saw that thin, straight, yet broken figure, every time the music of the leaf reached me, there came too, the inexplicable thrill of secret wonder and delight that had first accompanied his presence, and with it the subtle suggestion of a haunted woodland life, beautiful with new values. To this day I see that sad, dark face moving about the street, touched with melancholy, yet with the singular light of an inner glory that sometimes lit flames in the poor eyes. Perhaps – the fancy entered my thoughts sometimes when I passed him – those who are half out of their minds, as the saying goes, are at the same time half in another region whose penetrating loveliness has so bewildered and amazed them that they no longer can play their dull part in our commonplace world; and certainly for me this man's presence never failed to convey an awareness of some hidden and secret beauty that he knew apart from the ordinary haunts and pursuits of men.

Often I followed him up into the woods – in spite of the menacing growls of the dog, who invariably showed his teeth lest I should approach too close – with a great longing to know what he did there and how he spent his time wandering in the great forests, sometimes, I was assured, staying out entire nights or remaining away for days together. For in these Jura forests that cover the mountains from Neuchâtel to Yverdon, and stretch thickly up to the very frontiers of France, you may walk for days without finding a farm or meeting more than an occasional *bûcheron*. And at length, after weeks of failure, and by some process of sympathy he apparently communicated in turn to the dog, it came about that I was – *accepted*. I was allowed to follow at a distance, to listen and, if I could, to watch.

I make use of the conditional, because once in the forest this man had the power of concealing himself in the same way that certain animals and insects conceal themselves by choosing places instinctively where the color of their surroundings merge into their outlines and obliterate them. So long as he moved all was well; but the moment he stopped and a chance dell or cluster of trees intervened I lost sight of him, and more than once passed within a foot of his presence without knowing it, though the dog was plainly there at his feet. And the instant I turned at the sound of the leaf, there he was, leaning against some dark tree-stem, part of a shadow perhaps, growing like a forest-thing out of the thick moss that hid his feet, or merging with extraordinary intimacy into the fronds of some drooping pine bough! Moreover, this concealment was never intentional, it seems, but instinctive. The life to which he belonged took him close to its heart, draping about the starved and wasted shoulders the cloak of kindly sympathy which the world of men denied him.

And, while I took my place some little way off upon a fallen stem, and the dog sat looking up into his face with its eyes of yearning and affection, Perret "Comment-va" would take a leaf from the nearest ivy, raise it between tightly pressed palms to his lips and begin that magic sound that seemed to rise out of the forest-voices themselves rather than to be a thing apart.

*I*t was a late evening towards the end of May when I first secured this privilege at close quarters, and the memory of it lives in me still with the fragrance and wonder of some incredible dream. The forest just there was scented with wild lilies of the valley which carpeted the more open spaces with their white bells and big, green leaves; patches of violets and pale anemone twinkled down the mossy stairways of every glade; and through slim openings among the pine-stems I saw the shadowed blues of the lake beyond and the far line of the high Alps, soft and cloudlike in the sky. Already the woods were drawing the dusk out of the earth to cloak themselves for sleep, and in the east a rising moon stared close over the ground between the big trees, dropping trails of faint and yellowish silver along the moss. Distant cowbells, and an occasional murmur of village voices, reached the ear. But a deep hush lay over all that mighty slope of mountain forest, and even the footsteps of ourselves and the dog had come to rest.

Then, as sounds heard in a dream, a breeze stirred the topmost branches of the pines, filtering down to us as from the wings of birds. It brought new odors of sky and sun-kissed branches with it. A moment later it lost itself in the darkening aisles of forest beyond; and out of the stillness that followed, I heard the strange music of the leaf rising about us with its extraordinary power of suggestion.

And, turning to see the face of the player more closely, I saw that it had marvelously changed, had become young, unlined, soft with joy. The spirit of the immense woods possessed him, and he was at peace....

While he played, too, he swayed a little to and fro, just as a slender *sapin* sways in wind, and a revelation came to me of that strange beauty of combined sound and movement — trees bending while they sing, branches trembling and a-whisper, children that laugh while they dance. And, oh, the crying, plaintive notes of that leaf, and the profound sense of elemental primitive sound that they woke in the penetralia of the imagination, subtly linking simplicity to grandeur! Terribly yet sweetly penetrating, how they searched the heart through, and troubled the very sources of life! Often and often since have I wondered what it was in that singular music that made me *know* the distant Alps listened in their sky-spaces, and that the purple slopes of Boudry and Mont Racine bore it along the spires of their woods as though giant harp strings stretched to the far summits of Chasseral and the arid wastes of Tête de Rang.

In the music this outcast played upon the leaf there was something of a wild, mad beauty that plunged like a knife to the home of tears, and at the same time sang out beyond them — something coldly elemental, close to the naked heart of life. The truth, doubtless, was that his strains, making articulate the sounds of Nature, touched deep, primitive yearnings that for many are buried beyond recall. And between the airs, even between the bars, there fell deep weeping silences when the sounds merged themselves into the sigh of wind or the murmur of falling water, just as the strange player merged his body into the form and color of the trees about him.

And when at last he ceased, I went close to him, hardly knowing what it was I wanted so much to ask or say. He straightened up at my approach. The melancholy dropped its veil upon his face instantly.

"But that was beautiful — unearthly!" I faltered. "You never have played like that in the village —"

And for a second his eyes lit up as he pointed to the dark spaces of forest behind us:

"In there," he said softly, "there is light!"

"You hear true music in these woods," I ventured, hoping to draw him out; "this music you play — this exquisite singing of winds and trees?"

He looked at me with a puzzled expression and I knew, of course, that I had blundered with my banal words. Then, before I could explain or alter, there floated to us through the trees a sound of church bells from villages far away; and instantly, as he heard, his face grew dark, as though he understood in some vague fashion that it was a symbol of the faith of those parents who had wronged him, and of the people who continually made him suffer. Something of this, I feel sure, passed through his tortured mind, for he looked menacingly about him, and the dog, who caught the shadow of all his moods, began to growl angrily.

"My music," he said, with a sudden abruptness that was almost fierce, "is for my God."

"Your God of the Forests?" I said, with a real sympathy that I believe reached him.

"Pour sûr! Pour sûr! I play it all over the world" – he looked about him down the slopes of villages and vineyards – "and for those who understand – those who belong – to come."

He was, I felt sure, going to say more, perhaps to unbosom himself to me a little; and I might have learned something of the ritual this self-appointed priest of Pan followed in his forest temples – when, the sound of the bells swelled suddenly on the wind, and he turned with an angry gesture and made to go. Their insolence, penetrating even to the privacy of his secret woods, was too much for him.

"And you find many?" I asked.

Perret "Comment-va" shrugged his shoulders and smiled pityingly.

"Moi. Puis le chien – puis maintenant – *vous!*"

He was gone the same minute, as if the branches stretched out dark arms to draw him away among them, . . . and on my way back to the village, by the growing light of the moon, I heard far away in that deep world of a million trees the echoes of a weird, sweet music, as this unwitting votary of Pan piped and fluted to his mighty God upon an ivy leaf.

And the last thing I actually saw was the mongrel cur turning back from the edge of the forest to look at me for a moment of hesitation. He thought it was time now that I should join the little band of worshippers and follow them to the haunted spots of worship.

"Moi – puis le chien – puis maintenant – *vous!*"

*F*rom that moment of speech a kind of unexpressed intimacy between us came into being, and whenever we passed one another in the street he would give me a swift, happy look, and jerk his head significantly towards the forests. The feeling that, perhaps, in his curious lonely existence I counted for something important made me very careful with him. From time to time I gave him a few francs, and regularly twice a week when I knew he was away, I used to steal unobserved to his hut on the edge of the forest and put parcels of food inside the door – *salamé,* cheese, bread; and on one or two occasions when I had been extravagant with my own tea, pieces of plumcake – what the Colombier baker called *plume-cak'!*

He never acknowledged these little gifts, and I sometimes wondered to what use he put them, for though the dog remained well favored, so far as any cur can be so, he himself seemed to waste away more rapidly than ever. I found, too, that he did receive help from the village — official help — but that after the night when he was caught on the church steps with an oil can, kindling-wood and a box of matches, this help was reduced by half, and the threat made to discontinue it altogether. Yet I feel sure there was no inherent maliciousness in the Man who Played upon the Leaf, and that his hatred of an "alien" faith was akin to the mistaken zeal that in other days could send poor sinners to the stake for the ultimate safety of their souls.

Two things, moreover, helped to foster the tender belief I had in his innate goodness: first, that all the children of the village loved him and were unafraid, to the point of playing with him and pulling him about as though he were a big dog; and, secondly, that his devotion for the mongrel hound, his equal and fellow-worshipper, went to the length of genuine self-sacrifice. I could never forget how he fed it with the best of the bread, when his own face was pinched and drawn with hunger; and on other occasions I saw many similar proofs of his unselfish affection. His love for that mongrel, never uttered, in my presence at least, perhaps unrecognized as love even by himself, must surely have risen in some form of music or incense to sweeten the very halls of heaven.

In the woods I came across him anywhere and everywhere, sometimes so unexpectedly that it occurred to me he must have followed me stealthily for long distances. And once, in that very lonely stretch above the mountain railway, towards Mont-mollin, where the trees are spaced apart with an effect of cathedral aisles and Gothic arches, he caught me suddenly and did something that for a moment caused me a thrill of genuine alarm.

Wild lilies of the valley grow very thickly thereabouts, and the ground falls into a natural hollow that shuts it off from the rest of the forest with a peculiar and delightful sense of privacy; and when I came across it for the first time I stopped with a sudden feeling of quite bewildering enchantment — with a kind of childish awe that caught my breath as though I had slipped through some fairy door or blundered out of the ordinary world into a place of holy ground where solemn and beautiful things were the order of the day.

I waited a moment and looked about me. It was utterly still. The haze of the day had given place to an evening clarity of atmosphere that gave the world an appearance of having just received its finishing touches of pristine beauty. The scent of the lilies was overpoweringly sweet. But the whole first impression – before I had time to argue it away – was that I stood before some mighty chancel steps on the eve of a secret festival of importance, and that all was prepared and decorated with a view to the coming ceremony. The hush was the most delicate and profound imaginable – almost forbidding. I was a rude disturber.

Then, without any sound of approaching footsteps, my hat was lifted from my head, and when I turned with a sudden start of alarm, there before me stood Perret "Comment-va," the Man Who Played upon the Leaf.

An extraordinary air of dignity hung about him. His face was stern, yet rapt; something in his eyes genuinely impressive; and his whole appearance produced the instant impression – it touched me with a fleeting sense of awe – that here I had come upon him in the very act – had surprised this poor, broken being in some dramatic moment when his soul sought to find its own peculiar region, and to transform itself into loveliness through some process of outward worship.

He handed the hat back to me without a word, and I understood that I had unwittingly blundered into the secret place of his strange cult, some shrine, as it were, haunted doubly by his faith and imagination, perhaps even into his very Holy of Hoies. His own head, as usual, was bared. I could no more have covered myself again than I could have put my hat on in Communion service of my own church.

"But – this wonderful place – this peace, this silence!" I murmured, with the best manner of apology for the intrusion I could muster on the instant. "May I stay a little with you, perhaps – and see?"

And his face passed almost immediately, when he realized that I understood, into that soft and happy expression the woods invariably drew out upon it – the look of the soul, complete and healed.

"Hush!" he whispered, his face solemn with the mystery of the listening trees; *"Vous êtes un pen en retard – mais pourtant. . . ."*

And lifting the leaf to his lips he played a soft and whirring music that had for its undercurrent the sotinds of running water and singing wind mingled exquisitely together. It was half chant, half song, solemn enough for the dead, yet with a strain of soaring joy in it that made me think of children and a perfect faith. The music *blessed* me, and the leagues of forest, listening, poured about us all their healing forces.

I swear it would not have greatly surprised me to see the shaggy flanks of Pan himself disappearing behind the moss-grown boulders that lay about the hollows, or to have caught the flutter of white limbs as the nymphs stepped to the measure of his tune through the mosaic of slanting sunshine and shadow beyond.

Instead, I saw only that picturesque madman playing upon his ivy leaf, and at his feet the faithful dog staring up without blinking into his face, from time to time turning to make sure that I listened and understood.

*B*ut the desolate places drew him most, and no distance seemed too great either for himself or his dog.

In this part of the Jura there is scenery of a somber and impressive grandeur that, in its way, is quite as majestic as the revelation of far bigger mountains. The general appearance of soft blue pine woods is deceptive. The Boudry cliffs, slashed here and there with inaccessible couloirs, are undeniably grand, and in the sweep of the Creux du Van precipices there is a splendid terror quite as solemn as that of the Matter-horn itself. The shadows of its smooth, circular walls deny the sun all day, and the winds, caught within the 700 ft. sides of its huge amphitheater, as in the hollow of some awful cup, boom and roar with the crying of lost thunders.

I often met him in these lonely fastnesses, wearing that half-bewildered, half-happy look of the wandering child; and one day in particular, when I risked my neck scrambling up the most easterly of the Boudry couloirs, I learned afterwards that he had spent the whole time — four hours and more — on the little Champ de Trémont at the bottom, watching me with his dog till I arrived in safety at the top. His fellow-worshippers were few, he explained, and worth keeping; though it was ever inexplicable to me how his poor damaged eyes performed the marvels of sight they did.

And another time, at night, when, I admit, no sane man should have been abroad, and I had lost my way coming home from a climb along the torn and precipitous ledges of La Tourne, I heard his leaf thinly piercing the storm, always in front of me yet never overtaken, a sure though invisible guide. The cliffs on that descent are sudden and treacherous. The torrent of the Areuse, swollen with the melting snows, thundered ominously far below; and the forests swung their vast wet cloaks about them with torrents of blinding rain and clouds of darkness — yet all fragrant with warm wind as a virgin world answering to its first spring tempest. There he was, the outcast with his leaf, playing to his God amid all these crashings and bellowings. . . .

In the night, too, when skies were quiet and stars a-gleam, or in the still watches before the dawn, I would sometimes wake with the sound of clustered branches combing faint music from the gently-rising wind, and figure to myself that strange, lost creature wandering with his dog and leaf, his *pelerine*, his flying hair, his sweet, rapt expression of an inner glory, out there among the world of swaying trees he loved so well. And then my first soft view of the man would come back to me when I had seen him in the dusk as a tree; as though by some queer optical freak my outer and my inner vision had mingled so that I perceived both his broken body and his soul of magic. For the mysterious singing of the leaf, heard in such moments from my window while the world slept, expressed absolutely the inmost cry of that lonely and singular spirit, damaged in the eyes of the village beyond repair, but in the sight of the wood-gods he so devoutly worshipped, made whole with their own peculiar loveliness and fashioned after the image of elemental things.

The spring wonder was melting into the peace of the long summer days when the end came. The vineyards had begun to dress themselves in green, and the forest in those soft blues when individual trees lose their outline in the general body of the mountain. The lake was indistinguishable from the sky; the Jura peaks and ridges gone a-soaring into misty distances; the white Alps withdrawn into inaccessible and remote solitudes of heaven. I was making reluctant preparations for leaving — dark London already in my thoughts — when the news came. I forget who first put it into actual words. It had been about the village all the morning, and something of it was in every face as I went down the street. But the moment I came out and saw the dog on my doorstep, looking up at me with puzzled and beseeching eyes, I knew that something untoward had happened; and when he bit at my boots and caught my trousers in his teeth, pulling me in the direction of the forest, a sudden sense of poignant bereavement shot through my heart that I found it hard to explain, and that must seem incredible to those who have never known how potent may be the conviction of a sudden intuition.

I followed the forlorn creature whither it led, but before a hundred yards lay behind us I had learned the facts from half-a-dozen mouths. That morning, very early, before the countryside was awake, the first mountain train, swiftly descending the steep incline below Chambrelien, had caught Perret "Comment-va" just where the Mont Racine *sentier* crosses the line on the way to his best-beloved woods, and in one swift second had swept him into eternity. The spot was in the direct line he always took to that special woodland shrine — his Holy Place.

And the manner of his death was characteristic of what I had divined in the man from the beginning; for he had given up his life to save his dog — this mongrel and faithful creature that now tugged so piteously at my trousers. Details, too, were not lacking; the engine-driver had not failed to tell the story at the next station, and the news had traveled up the mountainside in the way that all such news travels — swiftly.

Moreover, the woman who lived at the hut beside the crossing, and lowered the wooden barriers at the approach of all trains, had witnessed the whole sad scene from the beginning.

And it is soon told. Neither she nor the engine-driver knew exactly how the dog got caught in the rails, but both saw that it *was* caught, and both saw plainly how the figure of the half-witted wanderer, hatless as usual and with cape flying, moved deliberately across the line to release it. It all happened in a moment. The man could only have saved himself by leaving the dog to its fate. The shrieking whistle had as little effect upon him as the powerful breaks had upon the engine in those few available moments. Yet, in the fraction of a second before the engine caught them, the dog somehow leapt free, and the soul of the Man Who Played upon the Leaf passed into the presence of his God — singing.

As soon as it realized that I followed willingly, the beastie left me and trotted on ahead, turning every few minutes to make sure that I was coming. But I guessed our destination without difficulty. We passed the Pontarlier railway first, then climbed for half-an-hour and crossed the mountain line about a mile above the scene of the disaster, and so eventually entered the region of the forest, still quivering with innumerable flowers, where in the shaded heart of trees we approached the spot of lilies that I knew — the place where a few weeks before the devout worshipper had lifted the hat from my head because the earth whereon I stood was holy ground. We stood in the pillared gateway of his Holy of Holies. The cool airs, perfumed beyond belief, stole out of the forest to meet us on the very threshold, for the trees here grew so thickly that only patches of the summer blaze found an entrance. And this time I did not wait on the outskirts, but followed my four-footed guide to a group of mossy boulders that stood in the very center of the hollow.

And there, as the dog raised its eyes to mine, soft with the pain of its great unanswerable question, I saw in a cleft of the grey rock the ashes of many hundred fires; and, placed about them in careful array, an assortment of the sacrifices he had offered, doubtless in sharp personal deprivation, to his deity: — bits of moldy bread, half-loaves, untouched portions of cheese, *salamé* with the skin uncut — most of it exactly as I had left it in his hut; and last of all, wrapped in the original white paper, the piece of Colombier *plume-cak'*, and a row of ten silver francs round the edge. . . .

I learned afterwards, too, that among the almost unrecognizable remains on the railway, untouched by the devouring terror of the iron, they had found a hand — tightly clasping in its dead fingers a crumpled ivy leaf. . . .

My efforts to find a home for the dog delayed my departure, I remember, several days; but in the autumn when I returned it was only to hear that the creature had refused to stay with anyone, and finally had escaped into the forest and deliberately starved itself to death. They found its skeleton, Louis Favre told me, in a rocky hollow on the lower slopes of Mont Racine in the direction of Montmollin. But Louis Favre did not know, as I knew, that this hollow had received other sacrifices as well, and was consecrated ground.

And somewhere, if you search well the Jura slopes between Champ du Moulin, where Jean-Jacques Rousseau had his temporary house, and Côtendard where he visited Lord Wemyss when "Milord Maréchal Keith" was Governor of the Principality of Neuchâtel under Frederic II, King of Prussia — if you look well these haunted slopes, somewhere between the vineyards and the gleaming limestone heights, you shall find the forest glade where lie the bleached bones of the mongrel dog, and the little village cemetery that holds the remains of the Man Who Played upon the Leaf to the honor of the Great God Pan.

The Price of Wiggins's Orgy

I

*I*t happened to be a Saturday when Samuel Wiggins drew the first cash
sum on account of his small legacy — some twenty pounds, ten in gold
and ten in notes. It felt in his pocket like a bottled-up prolongation of
life. Never before had he seen so many dreams within practical reach.
It produced in him a kind of high and elusive exaltation of the spirit.
From time to time he put his hand down to make the notes crackle and
let his fingers play through the running sovereigns as children play
through sand.

For twenty years he had been secretary to a philanthropist interested
in feeding — feeding the poor. Soup kitchens had been the keynote of
those twenty years, the distribution of victuals his sole objective. And
now he had his reward — a legacy of £100 a year for the balance of his
days.

To him it was riches. He wore a shortish frock-coat, a low, spreading
collar, a black made-up tie, and boots with elastic sides. On this particular day he wore also a new pair of rather bright yellow leather gloves.
He was unmarried, over forty, bald, plump in the body, and possessed
of a simple and emotional heart almost childlike. His brown eyes shone
in a face that was wrinkled and dusty — all his dreams driven inwards
by the long years of uninspired toil for another.

For the first time in his life, released from the dingy purlieus of soup
kitchens and the like, he wandered towards evening among the gay and
lighted streets of the "West End" — Piccadilly Circus where the flaming
lamps positively hurt the eyes, and Leicester Square. It was bewildering
and delightful, this freedom. It went to his head. Yet he ought to have
known better.

"I'm going to dine at a restaurant tonight, by Jove," he said to himself,
thinking of the gloomy boarding-house where he usually sat between a

missionary and a typewriter. He fingered his money. "I'm going to celebrate my legacy. I've earned it." The thought of a motorcar flashed absurdly through his mind; it was followed by another: a holiday in Spain, Italy, Hungary — one of those sunny countries where music was cheap, in the open air, and of the romantic kind he loved. These thoughts show the kind of exaltation that possessed him.

"It's nearly, though not quite, £2 a week," he repeated to himself for the fiftieth time, reflecting upon his legacy. "I simply can't believe it!"

After indecision that threatened to be endless, he turned at length through the swinging glass doors of a big and rather gorgeous restaurant. Only once before in his life had he dined at a big London restaurant — a Railway Hotel! Passing with some hesitation through the gaudy *café* where a number of foreigners sat drinking at little marble tables, he entered the main dining room, long, lofty, and already thronged. Here the light and noise and movement dazed him considerably, and for the life of him he could not decide upon a table. The people all looked so prosperous and important; the waiters so like gentlemen in evening dress — the kind that came to the philanthropist's table. The roar of voices, eating, knives and forks, rose about him and filled him with a certain dismay. It was all rather overwhelming.

"I should have liked a smaller place better," he murmured, "but still —" And again he fingered his money to gain confidence.

The choice of a table *was* intimidating, for he was absurdly retiring, was Wiggins; more at home with papers and the reports of philanthropic societies; his holidays spent in a boarding-house at Worthing with his sister and her invalid husband. Then relief came in the form of a subhead waiter who, spying his helplessness, inquired with a bland grandeur of manner if he "looked perhaps for someone?"

"Oh, a table, thanks, only a table —"

The man, washing his hands in mid-air, swept down the crowded aisles and found one without the least difficulty. It emerged from nowhere so easily that Wiggins felt he had been a fool not to discover it alone. He wondered if he ought to tip the man half-a-crown now or later, but, before he could decide, another occupied his place, bland and smiling, with black eyes and plushlike hair, bending low before him and holding out a large pink program.

He examined it, feeling that he ought to order dishes with outlandish names just to show that he knew his way about. Before he could steady his eye upon a single line, however, a third waiter, very youthful, suggested in broken English that Wiggins should leave his hat, coat and umbrella elsewhere. This he did willingly, though without grace or dispatch, for the yellow gloves stuck ridiculously to his hands. Then he sat down and turned to the menu again.

It was a very ordinary restaurant really, in spite of the vast height of the gilded ceiling, the scale of its sham magnificence and the excessive glitter of its hundred lights. The menu, disguised by various expensive and *recherché* dishes (which when ordered were invariably found to be "off "), was even more ordinary than the hall. But to the dazed Wiggins the words looked like a series of death-sentences printed in different languages, but all meaning the same thing: *order me – or die!* That waiter standing over him was the executioner. Unless he speedily ordered something really worth the proprietor's while to provide, the head waiter would be summoned and he, Wiggins, would be beheaded. Those stars against certain cheap dishes meant that they could only be ordered by privileged persons, and those crosses –

"This is *vairy* nice this *sevening*, sir," said the waiter, suddenly bending and pointing with a dirty finger to a dish that Wiggins found buried in a list uncommonly like "Voluntary Subscriptions" in his reports. It was entitled "Lancashire Hot-Pot . . . 2/0" – two shillings, not two pounds, as he first imagined! He leaped at it.

"Yes, thanks; that'll do, then – for tonight," he said, and the waiter ambled away indifferently, looking all round the room in search of sympathy.

By degrees, however, the other recovered his self-possession, and realized that to spend his legacy on mere Hot-Pot was to admit he knew not the values of life. He called the plush-headed waiter back and with a rush of words ordered some oysters, soup, a fried sole, and half a partridge to follow.

"Then ze 'Ot-Pot, sir?" queried the man, with respect.

"I'll see about that later."

For he was already wondering what he should drink, knowing nothing of wines and vintages. At luncheon with the philanthropist he sometimes had a glass of sherry; at Worthing with his sister he drank beer. But now he wanted something really good, something generous that would help him to celebrate. He would have ordered champagne as a conciliation to the waiter, now positively obsequious, but someone had told him once that there was not enough champagne in the world to go round, and that hotels and restaurants were supplied with "something rather bad." Burgundy, he felt, would be more the thing – rich, sunny, full-bodied.

He studied the wine-card till his head swam. A waiter, while he was thus engaged, sidled up and watched him from an angle. Wiggins, looking up distractedly at the same moment, caught his eye. Whew! It was the Head Waiter himself, a man of quite infinite presence, who at

once bowed himself forward, and with a gentle but commanding manner drew his attention to the wines he could "especially recommend."
Something in the man's face struck him momentarily as familiar —
vaguely familiar — then passed.

Now Wiggins, as has been said, did not know one wine from another;
but the spirit of his foolish pose fairly had him by the throat at last,
and each time this condescending individual indicated a new vintage
he shook his head knowingly and shrugged his shoulders with the air
of a connoisseur. This pantomime continued for several minutes.

"Something *really* good, you know," he mumbled after a while,
determined to justify himself in the eyes of this high official who was
taking such pains. "A rare wine — er — with body in it." Then he added,
with a sudden impulse of confidence, "It's Saturday night, remember!"
And he smiled knowingly, making a gesture that a man of the world
was meant to understand.

Why he should have said this remains a mystery. Perhaps it was a
semi-apologetic reference to the supposed habit of men to indulge
themselves on a Saturday because they need not rise early to work next
day. Perhaps it was meant in some way to excuse all the trouble he was
giving. In any case, there can be no question that the manner of the
Head Waiter instantly changed in a subtle way difficult to describe, and
from mere official politeness passed into deferential attention. He
bowed slightly. He increased his distance by an inch or two. Wiggins,
noticing it and slightly bewildered, repeated his remark, for want of
something to say more than anything else. "It's Saturday night, of
course," he repeated, murmuring, yet putting more meaning into the
words than they could reasonably hold.

"As Monsieur says," the man replied, with a marked respect in his
tone not there before; "and we — close early."

"Of course," said the other, gaining confidence pleasantly, "you close
early."

He had quite forgotten the fact, even if he ever knew it, but he spoke
with decision. Glancing up from the wine-list, he caught the man's eye;
then instantly lowered his gaze, for the Head Waiter was staring at him
in a fixed and curious manner that seemed unnecessary. And once again
that passing touch of familiarity appeared upon the features and was
gone.

"Monsieur is here for the first time, if I may ask?" came next.

"Er — yes, I am," he replied, thinking all this attention a trifle
excessive.

"Ah, *pardon*, of course, I understand," the Head Waiter added softly.
"A new — a recent member, then — ?"

A little nonplussed, a little puzzled, Wiggins agreed with a nod of the head. He did not know that head waiters referred to customers as "members." For an instant it occurred to him that possibly he was being mistaken for somebody else. It was really — but at that moment the oysters arrived. The Head Waiter said something in rapid Italian to his subordinate — something that obviously increased that plush-headed person's desire to please — bent over with his best manner to murmur, "And I will get monsieur the wine he will like, the right kind of wine!" and was gone.

It was a new and delightful sensation. Wiggins, feeling proud, pleased and important under the effect of this excellent service and attention, turned to his oysters. The wine would come presently. And, meanwhile, the music had begun. . . .

II

*H*e began to enjoy himself thoroughly, and the wine — still, fragrant, soft — soon ran in his veins and drove out the last vestige of his absurd shyness. Behind the palm trees, somewhere out of sight, the orchestra played soothingly, and if the selections were somewhat bizarre it made no difference to him. He drank in the sound just as he drank in the wine — eagerly. Both fed the consciousness that he was enjoying himself, and the Danse Macabre gave him as much pleasure as did the Bohème, the Strauss Waltz, or Donizetti. Everything — wine, music, food, people — served to intensify his interest *in himself.* He examined his face in the big mirrors and realized what a dog he was and what a good time he was having. He watched the other customers, finding them splendid and distinguished. The whole place was really fine — he would come again and again, always ordering the same wine, for it was certainly an unusual wine, as the Head Waiter had called it, "the right kind." The price of it he never asked, for in his pocket lay the price of a whole case. His hand slipped down to finger the sovereigns — hot and slippery now — and the notes, somewhat moist and crumpled. . . . The needles of the big staring clock meanwhile swung onwards. . . .

Thus, aided by the tactful and occasional superintendence of the Head Waiter from a distance, the evening passed along in a happy rush of pleasurable emotion. The half-partridge had vanished, and Wiggins toyed now with a wonderful-looking "sweet" — the most expensive he could find. He did not eat much of it, but liked to see it on his plate. The wine helped things enormously. He had ordered another half-bottle some time ago, delighted to find that it exhilarated without confusing him. And everyone else in the place was enjoying himself in the same way. He was thrilled to discover this.

Only one thing jarred a little. A very big man, with a round, clean-shaven face inclined to fatness, stared at him more than he cared about from a table in the corner diagonally across the room. He had only come in half-an-hour ago. His face was somehow or other doglike — something between a boar-hound and a pup, Wiggins thought. Each time he looked up the fellow's large and rather fierce eyes were fixed upon him, then lingeringly withdrawn. It was unpleasant to be stared at in this way by an offensive physiognomy.

But most of the time he was too full of personal visions conjured up by the wine to trouble long about external matters. His head was simply brimming over with thoughts and ideas — about himself, about soup-kitchens, feeding the poor, the change of life effected by the legacy, and a thousand other details. Once or twice, however, in sharp, clear moments when the tide of alcohol ebbed a little, other questions assailed him: Why should the Head Waiter have become so obsequious and attentive? What was it in his face that seemed familiar? What was there about the remark "It's Saturday evening" to change his manner? And — what was it about the dinner, the restaurant and the music that seemed just a little out of the ordinary?

Or was he merely thinking nonsense? And was it his imagination that this man stared so oddly? The alcohol rushed deliciously in his veins.

The vague uneasiness, however, was a passing matter, for the orchestra was tearing madly through a Csardas, and his thoughts and feelings were swept away in the wild rhythm. He drank his bottle out and ordered another. Was it the second or the third? He could not remember. Counting always made his head ache. He did not care anyhow. "Let 'er go! I'm enjoying myself! I've got a fat legacy — money lying in the bank — money I haven't earned!" The carefulness of years was destroyed in as many minutes. "That music's simply spiffing!"

Then he glanced up and caught the clean-shaven face bearing down upon him across the shimmering room like the muzzle of a moving gun. He tried to meet it, but found he could not focus it properly. The same moment he saw that he was mistaken; the man was merely staring at him. Two faces swam and wobbled into one. This movement, and the appearance of coming towards him, were both illusions produced by the alcohol. He drank another glass quickly to steady his vision — and then another. . . .

"I'll call for my bill. Itsh time to go. . . !" he murmured aloud later, with a very deep sigh. He looked about him for the waiter, who instantly appeared — with coffee and liqueurs, however.

"Dear me, yes. Qui' forgot I or'ered those," he observed offhand, smiling in the man's face, willing and anxious to say a lot of things, but not quite certain what.

"My bill," was what he said finally, "mush b'off!"

The waiter laughed pleasantly, but very politely, in reply. Wiggins repeated his remark about his bill.

"Oh, that will be all right, sir," returned the man, as though no such thing as payment was ever heard of in *this* restaurant. It was rather confusing. Wiggins laughed to himself, drank his liqueur and forgot about everything except the ballet music of Délibes the strings were sprinkling in a silver shower about the hall. His mind ran after them through the glittering air.

"Just fancy if I could catch 'em and take 'em home in a bunch," he said to himself, immensely pleased. He was enjoying himself hugely by now.

And then, suddenly, he became aware that the place was rapidly thinning, lights being lowered, good-nights being said, and that everybody seemed — drunk.

"P'rapsh they've all got legacies!" he thought, flushing with excitement.

He rose unsteadily to his feet and was delighted to find that *he* was not in the least — drunk. He at once respected himself.

"Itsh really 'sgusting that fellows can't stop when they've had 'nough!" he murmured, making his way with steps that required great determination towards the door, and remembering before he got halfway that he had not paid his bill. Turning in a half-circle that brought an unnecessary quantity of the room round with him, he made his way back, lost his way, fumbled about in the increasing gloom, and found himself face to face with the — Head Waiter. The unexpected meeting braced him astonishingly. The dignity of the man had curiously increased.

"I'm looking for my bill," observed Wiggins thickly, wondering for the twentieth time of whom the man's face reminded him; "you haven't seen it about anywhere, I shuppose?" He sat down with more dignity than he could have supposed possible and produced a £5 note from his pocket, the lining of the pocket coming out with it like a dirty glove.

Most of the guests had gone out by this time, and the big hall was very dark. Two lights only remained, and these, reflected from mirror to mirror, made its proportions seem vast and unreal. They flew from place to place, too, distressingly — these lights.

"Half-a-crown will settle that, sir," replied the man, with a respectful bow.

"Nonshense!" replied the other. "Why, I ordered Lancashire hotch-potch, grilled shole, a — a bird or something of the kind, and the wine —"

"I beg your pardon, sir, but — if you will permit me to say so — the others will soon be here now, and — as there will be a specially large attendance, perhaps you would like to make sure of your place." He pocketed the half-crown with a bow, pointed to the far, dim corner of the room, and stepped aside a little to make space for Wiggins to pass.

And Wiggins did pass — though it is not quite clear how he managed to dodge the flying tables. With deep sighs, hot, confused and puzzled, but too obfuscated to understand what it was all about, he obeyed the directions, at the same time wondering uneasily how it was he had forgotten what was a-foot. He wandered towards the end of the hall with the uncertainty of a butterfly that makes many feints before it settles. . . . At a vast distance off the Head Waiter was moving to close the main doors, utterly oblivious now of his existence. He felt glad of that. Something about that fellow was disagreeable — downright nasty. This suddenly came over him with a flood of conviction. The man was more than peculiar: he was sinister. . . . The air smelt horribly of cooked food, tobacco smoke, breathing crowds, scented women and the rest. Whiffs of it, hot and fœtid, brought him a little to his senses. . . . Then suddenly he noticed that the big man with the face that was dark and smooth like the muzzle of a cannon, was watching him keenly from a table on the other side where an electric light still burned.

"By George! There he is again, that feller! Wonder whatsh he's smiling at me for. Looking for'sh bill too, p'raps — Now, in a Soup Kishen nothing of the kind —" He bowed in return, smiling insolently, holding himself steady by a chair to do so. He shoved and stumbled his way on into the shadows, half-mingling with the throng passing out into the street. Then, making a sharp turn back into the room unobserved, he took a few uncertain steps and collapsed silently and helplessly upon a chair that was hidden behind a big palm tree in a dark corner.

And the last thing he remembered as he sank, boneless, like soft hay, into that corner was that the sham palm tree bowed towards him, then ran off into the ceiling, and from that elevation, which in no way diminished its size, bowed to him yet again. . . .

It was just after his eyes closed that the door in the gilt paneling at the end of the room softly opened and a woman entered on tiptoe. She was followed by other women and several girls; these, again, from time to time, by men, all dressed in black, all silent, and all ushered by the majestic Head Waiter to their places. The big man with the face like a gun-muzzle superintended. And each individual, on entering, was held there at the secret doorway until a certain sentence had passed his lips. Evidently a password: "It is Saturday night," said the one being admitted, "and we close early," replied the Head Waiter and the big man. And then the door was closed until the next soft tapping came.

But Wiggins, plunged in the stupor of the first sleep, knew none of all this. His frock-coat was bunched about his neck, his black tie under his ear, his feet resting higher than his head. He looked like a collapsed air-ship in a hedge, and he snored heavily.

III

*I*t was about an hour later when he opened his eyes, climbed painfully and heavily to his feet, staggered back against the wall utterly bewildered — and stared. At the far end of the great hall, its loftiness now dim, was a group of people. The big mirrors on all sides reflected them with the effect of increasing their numbers indefinitely. They stood and sat upon an improvised platform. The electric lights, shaded with black, dropped a pale glitter upon their faces. They were systematically grouped, the big man in the center, the Head Waiter at a small table just behind him. The former was speaking in low, measured tones.

In his dark and distant corner Wiggins first of all seized the carafe and quenched his feverish thirst. Next he advanced slowly and with the utmost caution to a point nearer the group where he could hear what was being said. He was still a good deal confused in mind, and had no idea what the hour was or what he had been doing in the meantime. There were some twenty or thirty people, he saw, of both sexes, well dressed, many of them distinguished in appearance, and all wearing black; even their gloves were black; some of the women, too, wore black veils — very thick. But in all the faces without exception there was something — was it about the lips and mouths? — that was peculiar and — repellent.

Obviously this was a meeting of some kind. Some society had hired the hall for a private gathering. Wiggins, understanding this, began to feel awkward. He did not wish to intrude; he had no right to listen; yet to make himself known was to betray that he was still very considerably intoxicated. The problem presented itself in these simple terms to his dazed intelligence. He was also aware of another fact: about these black-robed people there was something which made him secretly and horribly — afraid.

The big man with the smooth face like a gun-muzzle sat down after a softly-uttered speech, and the group, instead of applauding with their hands, waved black handkerchiefs. The fluttering sound of them trickled along the wastes of hall towards the concealed eavesdropper. Then the Head Waiter rose to introduce the next speaker, and the instant Wiggins saw him he understood what it was in his face that was familiar. For the false beard no longer adorned his lips, the wig that altered the shape of his forehead and the appearance of his eyes had been removed, and the likeness he bore to the philanthropist, Wiggins's late employer, was too remarkable to be ignored. Wiggins just repressed a cry, but a low gasp apparently did escape him, for several members of the group turned their heads in his direction and stared.

The Head Waiter, meanwhile, saved him from immediate discovery by beginning to speak. The words were plainly audible, and the resemblance of the voice to that other voice he knew now to be stopped with dust, was one of the most dreadful experiences he had ever known. Each word, each trick of expression came as a new and separate shock.

". . . and the learned Doctor will say a few words upon the *rationale* of our subject," he concluded, turning with a graceful bow to make room for a distinguished-looking old gentleman who advanced shambling from the back of the improvised platform.

What Wiggins then heard — in somewhat disjointed sentences owing to the buzzing in his ears — was at first apparently meaningless. Yet it was freighted, he knew, with a creeping and sensational horror that would fully reveal itself the instant he discovered the clue. The old clever-faced scoundrel was saying vile things. He knew it. But the key to the puzzle being missing, he could not quite guess what it was all about. The Doctor, gravely and with balanced phrases, seemed to be speaking of the fads of the day with regard to food and feeding. He ridiculed vegetarianism, and all the other *isms*. He said that one and all were based upon ignorance and fallacy, declaring that the time had at last come in the history of the race when a rational system of feeding was a paramount necessity. The physical and psychical conditions of the times demanded it, and the soul of man could never be emancipated until it was adopted. He himself was proud to be one of the founders of their audacious and secret Society, revolutionary and pioneer in the best sense, to which so many of the medical fraternity now belonged, and so many of the brave women too, who were in the van of the feminist movements of the times. He said a great deal in this vein. Wiggins, listening in growing amazement and uneasiness, waited for the clue to it all.

In conclusion, the speaker referred solemnly to the fact that there was a stream of force in their Society which laid them open to the melancholy charge of being called "hysterical." "But after all," he cried, with rising enthusiasm and in accents that rang down the hall, "a Society without hysteria is a dull Society, just as a woman without hysteria is a dull woman. Neither the Society nor the woman need yield to the tendency; but that it is present potentially infers the faculty, so delicious in the eyes of all sane men — the faculty of running to extremes. It is a sign of life, and of very vivid life. It is not for nothing, dear friends, that we are named the —" But the buzzing in Wiggins's ears was so loud at this moment that he missed the name. It sounded to him something between "Can-I-believes" and "Camels," but for the life of him he could not overtake the actual word. The Doctor had uttered it, moreover, in a lowered voice — a suddenly lowered voice. . . . When the noise in his ears had passed he heard the speaker bring his address to an end in these words: ". . . and I will now ask the secretaries to make their reports from their various sections, after which, I understand" — his tone grew suddenly thick and clouded — "we are to be regaled with a collation — a sacramental collation — of the usual kind. . . ." His voice hushed away to nothing. His mouth was working most curiously. A wave of excitement unquestionably ran over the faces of the others. Their mouths also worked oddly. Dark and somber things were afoot in that hall.

Wiggins crouched a little lower behind the edge of the overhanging tablecloth and listened. He was perspiring now, but there were touches of icy horror fingering about in the neighborhood of his heart. His mental and physical discomfort were very great, for the conviction that he was about to witness some dreadful scene — black as the garments of the participants in it — grew rapidly within him. He devised endless plans for escape, only to reject them the instant they were formed. There was no escape possible. He had to wait till the end.

A charming young woman was on her feet, addressing the audience in silvery tones; sweet and comely she was, her beauty only marred by that singular leer that visited the lips and mouths of all of them. The flesh of his back began to crawl as he listened. He would have given his whole year's legacy to be out of it, for behind that voice of silver and sweetness there crowded even to her lips the rush of something that was unutterable — loathsome. Wiggins felt it. The uncertainty as to its exact nature only added to his horror and distress.

". . . so this question of supply, my friends," she was saying, "is becoming more and more difficult. It resolves itself into a question of ways and means." She looked round upon her audience with a touch of nervous apprehension before she continued. "In my particular sphere of operations — West Kensington — I have regretfully to report that the suspicions and activity of the police, the foolish, old-fashioned police, have now rendered my monthly contributions no longer possible. There have been too many disappearances of late —" She paused, casting her eyes down. Wiggins felt his hair rise, drawn by a shivery wind. The words "contributions" and "disappearances" brought with them something quite freezing.

". . . .As you know," the girl resumed, "it is to the doctors that we must look chiefly for our steadier supplies, and unfortunately in my sphere of operations we have but one doctor who is a member. . . . I do not like to — to resign my position, but I must ask for lenient consideration of my failure" — her voice sank lower still — ". . . my failure to furnish tonight the materials —" She began to stammer and hesitate dreadfully; her voice shook; an ashen pallor spread to her very lips. ". . . the elements for our customary feast —"

A movement of disapproval ran over the audience like a wave; murmurs of dissent and resentment were heard. As the girl paled more perceptibly the singular beauty of her face stood out with an effect of almost shining against that dark background of shadows and black garments. In spite of himself, and forgetting caution for the moment, Wiggins peeped over the edge of the table to see her better. She was a lady, he saw, highbred and spirited. That pallor, and the timidity it bespoke, was but evidence of a highly sensitive nature facing a situation of peculiar difficulty — and danger. He read in her attitude, in the poise of that slim figure standing there before disapproval and possible disaster, the bearing and proud courage of a type that would face execution with calmness and dignity. Wiggins was amazed that this thought should flash through him so vividly — from nowhere. Born of the feverish aftermath of alcohol, perhaps — yet born inevitably, too, of this situation before his eyes.

With a thrill he realized that the girl was speaking again, her voice steady, but faint with the gravity of her awful position.

". . . .and I ask for that justice in consideration of my failure which — the difficulties of the position demand. I have had to choose between that bold and ill-considered action which might have betrayed us all to the authorities, and — the risk of providing nothing for tonight."

She sat down. Wiggins understood that it was a question of life and death. The air about him turned icy. He felt the perspiration trickling on several different parts of his body at once.

An old lady rose instantly to reply; her face was stern and dreadful, although the signature of breeding and culture was plainly there in the delicate lines about the nostrils and forehead. Her mien held something implacable. She was dressed in black silk that rustled, and she was certainly well over sixty; but what made Wiggins squirm there in his narrow hiding place was the extraordinary resemblance she bore to Mrs. Sturgis, the superintendent of one of his late employer's soup kitchens. It was all diabolically grotesque. She glanced round upon the group of members, who clearly regarded her as a leader. The machinery of the whole dreadful scene then moved quicker.

"Then are we to understand from the West Kensington secretary," she began in firm, even tones, "that for tonight there is — nothing?" The young girl bowed her head without rising from her chair.

"I beg to move, then, Mr. Chairman," continued the terrible old lady in iron accents, "that the customary procedure be followed, and that a Committee of Three be appointed to carry it into immediate effect." The words fell like bomb-shells into the deserted spaces of the hall.

"I second the motion," was heard in a man's voice.

"Those in favor of the motion will show their hands," announced the big chairman with the clean-shaven face.

Several score of black-gloved hands waved in the air, with the effect of plumes upon a jolting hearse.

"And those who oppose it?"

No single hand was raised. An appalling hush fell upon the group.

"I appoint Signor Carnamorte as chairman of the sub-committee, with power to choose his associates," said the big man. And the "Head Waiter" bowed his acceptance of the duty imposed upon him. There was at once then a sign of hurried movement, and the figure of the young girl was lost momentarily to view as several members surged round her. The next instant they fell away and she stood clear, her hands bound. Her voice, soft as before but very faint, was audible through the hush.

"I claim the privilege belonging to the female members of the Society," she said calmly; "the right to find, if possible, a substitute."

"Granted," answered the chairman gravely. "The customary ten minutes will be allowed you in which to do so. Meanwhile, the preparations must proceed in the usual way."

With a dread that ate all other emotions, Wiggins watched keenly from his concealment, and the preparations that he saw in progress, though simple enough in themselves, filled him with a sense of ultimate horror that was freezing. The Committee of Three were very busy with something at the back of the improvised platform, something that was heavy and, on being touched, emitted a metallic and sonorous ring. As in the strangling terror and heat of nightmare the full meaning of events is often kept concealed until the climax, so Wiggins knew that this simple sound portended something that would only be revealed to him later — something appalling as Satan — sinister as the grave. That ring of metal was the Gong of Death. He heard it in his own heart, and the shock was so great that he could not prevent an actual physical movement. His jerking leg drove sharply against a chair. The chair — squeaked.

The sound pierced the deep silence of the big hall with so shrill a note that of course everybody heard it. Wiggins, expecting to have the whole crew of these black-robed people about his ears, held his breath in an agony of suspense. All those pairs of eyes, he felt, were searching the spot where he lay so thinly hidden by the tablecloth. But no steps came towards him. A voice, however, spoke: the voice of the girl: she had heard the sound and had divined its cause.

"Loosen my bonds," she cried, "for there is someone yonder among the shadows. I have found a substitute! And — I swear to Heaven — *he is plump!*"

The sentence was so extraordinary, that Wiggins felt a spring of secret merriment touched somewhere deep within him, and a gush of uncontrollable laughter came up in his throat so suddenly that before he could get his hand to his mouth, it rang down the long dim hall and betrayed him beyond all question of escape. Behind it lay the strange need of violent expression. He had to do something. The life of this slender and exquisite girl was in danger. And the nightmare strain of the whole scene, the hints and innuendoes of a dark purpose, the implacable nature of the decree that threatened so fair a life — all resulted in a pressure that was too much for him. Had he not laughed, he would certainly have shrieked aloud. And the next minute he did shriek aloud. The screams followed his laughter with a dreadful clamor, and at the same instant he staggered noisily to his feet and rose into full view from behind the table. Everybody then saw him.

Across the length of that dimly-lighted hall he faced the group of people in all their hideous reality, and what he saw cleared from his fuddled brain the last fumes of the alcohol. The white visage of each member seemed already close upon him. He saw the glimmering pallor of their skins against the black clothes, the eyes ashine, the mouths working, fingers pointing at him. There was the Head Waiter, more than ever like the dead philanthropist whose life had been spent in feeding others; there the odious smooth face of the big chairman; there the stern-lipped old lady who demanded the sentence of death. The whole silent crew of them stared darkly at him, and in front of them, like some fair lily growing amid decay, stood the girl with the proud and pallid face, calm and self-controlled. Immediately beyond her, a little to one side, Wiggins next perceived the huge iron cauldron, already swinging from its mighty tripod, waiting to receive her into its capacious jaws. Beneath it gleamed and flickered the flames from a dozen spirit-lamps.

"My substitute!" rang out her clear voice. "My substitute! Unloose my hands! And seize him before he can escape!"

"He cannot escape!" cried a dozen angry voices.

"In darkness!" thundered the chairman, and at the same moment every light was extinguished from the switch-board — every light but one. The bulb immediately behind him in the wall was left burning.

And the crew were upon him, coming swiftly and stealthily down the empty aisles between the tables. He saw their forms advance and shift by the gleam of the lamps beneath the awful cauldron. With the advance came, too, the sound of rushing, eager breathing. He imagined, though he could not see, those evil mouths a-working. And at this moment the subconscious part of him that had kept the secret all this time, suddenly revealed in letters of flame the name of the Society which fifteen minutes before he had failed to catch. The subconscious self, that supreme stage manager, that arch conspirator, rose and struck him in the face as it were out of the darkness, so that he understood, with a shock of nauseous terror, the terrible nature of the net in which he was caught.

For this Secret Society, meeting for their awful rites in a great public restaurant of mid-London, were maniacs of a rare and singular description — vilely mad on one point but sane on all the rest. They were Cannibals!

*N*ever before had he run with such speed, agility and recklessness; never before had he guessed that he could leap tables, clear chairs with the flying manner of a hurdle race, and dodge palms and flower-pots as an athlete of twenty dodges collisions in the football field. But in each dark corner where he sought a temporary refuge, the electric light on the wall above immediately sprang into brilliance, one of the crew having remained by the switchboard to control this diabolically ingenious method of keeping him ever in sight.

For a long time, however, he evaded his crowding and clumsy pursuers. It was a vile and ghastly chase. His flying frock-coat streamed out behind him, and he felt the elastic side of his worn boots split under the unusual strain of the twisting, turning ankles as he leaped and ran. His pursuers, it seemed, sought to prolong the hunt on purpose. The passion of the chase was in their blood. Round and round that hall, up and down, over tables and under chairs, behind screens, shaking the handles of doors — all immovable, past gleaming dish-covers on the wheeled jointtables, taking cover by swing doors, curtains, palms, everything and anything, Wiggins flew for his life from the pursuing forces of a horrible death.

And at last they caught him. Breathless and exhausted, he collapsed backwards against the wall in a dark corner. But the light instantly flashed out above him. He lay in full view, and in another second the advancing horde — he saw their eyes and mouths so close — would be upon him, when something utterly unexpected happened: his head in falling struck against a hard projecting substance and — a bell rang sharply out. It was a telephone!

How he ever managed to get the receiver to his lips, or why the answering exchange came so swiftly he does not pretend to know. He had just time to shout, "Help! help! Send police X. . . . Restaurant! Murder! Cannibals!" when he was seized violently by the collar, his arms and legs grasped by a dozen pairs of hands, and a struggle began that he knew from the start must prove hopeless.

The fact that help might be on the way, however, gave him courage. Wiggins smashed right and left, screamed, kicked, bit and butted. His frock coat was ripped from his back with a whistling tear of cloth and lining, and he found himself free at the edge of a group that clawed and beat everywhere about him. The dim light was now in his favor. He shot down the hall again like a hare, leaping tables on the way, and flinging dish-covers, carafes, menus at the pursuing crowd as fast as he could lay hands upon them.

Then came a veritable pandemonium of smashed glass and crockery, while a grip of iron caught his arms behind and pinioned them beyond all possibility of moving. Turning quickly, he found himself looking straight into the eyes of a big blue policeman, the door into the street open beside him. The crowd became at once inextricably mixed up and jumbled together. The chairman, and the girl who was to have been eaten, melted into a single person. The philanthropist and the old lady slid into each other. It was a horrible bit of confusion. He felt deadly sick and dizzy. Everything dropped away from his sight then, and darkness tore up round him from the carpet. He remembered nothing more for a long time.

*P*erhaps the most vivid recollection of what occurred afterwards —

he remembers it to this day, and his memory may be trusted, for he never touched wine again — was the weary smile of the magistrate, and the still more weary voice as he said in the court two days later —

"Forty shillings, and be bound over to keep the peace in two sureties for six months. And £5 to the proprietor of the restaurant to pay damages for the broken windows and crockery. Next case. . . !"

Carlton's Drive

It is difficult, of course, to estimate the effect of such a thing upon another's temperament. The change seemed bewilderingly sudden; yet spiritual chemistry is a process incalculable, past finding out, and the results in this case were undeniable. Carlton had changed in the course of a brief year or two. And he dates it from that drive. He knows.

He told it to a few intimates only. Those who know his face as it is today, serene and strong, yet recall how it was scored and beaten with the ravages of dissipation a few years before (so that the human seemed almost to have dropped back into the beast), can scarcely credit his identity. Now — its calm austerity, softened by the greatest yearning known to men, the yearning to save, proclaim at a glance the splendid revolution; whereas *then!* The memory is unpleasant; exceedingly wonderful the contrast. His life was inoffensive enough, negatively, at least, till the money came; then, with the inheritance, his innate sensuality broke out. Yet it seemed a prodigious step for a man to make in so brief a time: from that life of depravity that stained his face and smothered his soul, to the Brotherhood of Devotion he founded, and himself led full charge against the vice of the world! But not incomprehensible, perhaps. He did nothing by halves. It was the swing of the pendulum.

He was somewhere about thirty, his nerves shattered by the savagery of concentrated fast living, his system too exhausted to respond even to unusual stimulant, when he found himself one early spring morning on the pavement beside St. George's Hospital. He had been up all night, and was making his way homewards on foot, his pockets stuffed with the proceeds of lucky gambling; and how he happened to be standing at that particular spot, watching the traffic, at eight in the morning, is not clear. Probably, seduced by the sweetness of the air, he had wandered, driven by gusts of mood as by gusts of wind. Though he had drunk steadily since midnight he was not so much intoxicated as fuddled — stupid. He was on the south corner, where the 'buses stop in their journey westwards. The sun poured a flood of light down Piccadilly; the street was brisk with pedestrians going to work; the hospital side-entrance behind him already astir. Across the road the trees in the park shimmered in a wave of fluttering green. The pride of life was in the June air. In his own heart, however, was a loathsome satiety — sign of the first death.

In a line with the trees opposite stood a solitary hansom. A faint surprise that it should be there at such an hour jostled in his sodden brain with the idea that he might as well drive home — when, suddenly, he became aware that the man perched on the box was looking at him across the street with a fixity of manner that was both singular and offensive. Carlton felt his own gaze, blear-eyed and troubled, somehow caught and held — uncomfortably. The other's eyes were fastened upon his own — had been fastened for some time — sinisterly, and with a purpose. Just at this moment, however, a sharp spasm of pain and faintness, due to exhaustion and debauch, shot through him, so that he reeled, half staggering, and, before he quite knew what he was doing, he had nodded to the driver, and saw that the horse was already turning with clattering hoofs to cross the slippery street. A minute later he had climbed heavily in, noticing vaguely that the driver wore all black, the horse was black, and on the whip was a strip of crêpe that fluttered in the breeze. As he got in, too, the effort strained him. But, more than that, something that was cold and terrible — "like a hand of ragged steel," he described it afterwards — clutched at his heart. It puzzled him; but he was too "done" to think; and he lurched back wearily on the cushions as the horse started forward with the jerkiness of long habit.

"Same address, sir?" the man called down through the trap. His voice was harsh "like iron"; and Carlton, supposing that he recognized a fare, replied testily, "Of course, you fool! And let her rip — to the devil!" The spasm of strange pain had passed. He only felt tired to brokenness, sick with his corrupt and unsatisfying life, a dull, incomprehensible anger burning in him against the world, the driver — and himself.

The hansom swung forwards over the smooth, uncrowded streets like a ship with a breeze behind her, for the horse was fresh, and the man drove well. He took off his opera hat and let the cool wind fan his face. That drive of a mile to his rooms was the most soothing and restful he had ever known. But, after a while, braced, perhaps, by the morning wind, he began to notice that they were following a strange route through streets he did not recognize. He had been lolling in the corner with half-closed eyes; now he sat up and looked about him. Time had passed. He ought to have reached home long ago. They were going at a tremendous and unholy pace, too. He poked open the trap sharply.

"Hi, hi!" he called out angrily; "are you drunk? Where, in the name of – are you driving to?"

"It's all right, sir; it's the shortest way. The usual roads are closed."

The man's voice – deep, with a curious rumbling note – had such conviction and authority in it that Carlton accepted the explanation with a growl and flung himself back into his soft corner. Again, however, for a single second, that cold thing of steel moved horribly in his heart. He felt as if the "ragged hand " had given it another twist. Then it passed, and he gave himself up to the swinging motion of the drive. The hansom tore along now; it was delightful. Curious, though, that *all* the known streets should be "up!" Positively the houses were getting less, as though he was driving out into the country. Perhaps, too, the feeling of *laisser aller* that came over him was caused by some inhibition of the will due to prolonged excesses. Canton admits it was unlike his normal self not to *force* the man to drive where he wanted; but he felt lulled, lazy, indifferent. "Let the fool take his own way!" his thought ran; "I shan't pay him anymore for it!"

Somebody was waving to him from the pavement with a colored parasol – a girl he knew, one of his sort; gay and smiling, tripping along quickly. With a momentary surprise that she should be thus early astir, he smiled through the window and waved his hand. It gave him pleasure to see she was going in the same direction as himself. The instant he passed her the horse leaped forward with increased speed, so that the hansom rattled, shaking him a little as it lurched from side to side.

"Steady on, idiot!" he shouted, "or you'll smash me up before I get to the end!" And he was just going to bang open the trap and swear, when his attention was caught by another salutation from the pavement. It was a man this time – running hard; a man who played, drank, and the rest of it even harder than himself, a man who shared his trips to Paris. He was radiant and gesticulating. "Good journey, old man!" he heard him cry as the hansom shot past; "Hurry up! We're coming, too! We shall be there together!" Canton did not quite like this greeting. It reminded him for a second that he was a bit uncertain where the mad driver was heading for. It gave him a passing uneasiness – almost immediately forgotten, however. The pace was too delicious to bring to an end just yet. Presently he would call the fellow to order with a vengeance, but meanwhile – "let her rip!" His friends were all going the same way; it must be all right. His thoughts, he admits, were somewhat mixed; for great speed destroys calm judgment; it exhilarated, but it also bewildered. The pace, assuredly, had something to do with his mental confusion, for it was terrific. Yet he saw on the pavement, from time to time, more friends and acquaintances, and somehow at the moment it did not strike him as *too* peculiar that they should be there, all moving hurriedly in the same direction. He had an odd feeling that they all knew of some destination agreed upon; that he, too, knew it; but that it was not "playing the game" to admit that he knew. Yet about some of them — their hurried steps, their gay faces, their waving hands — there was a queer fugitive suggestion of sadness, even of fear. One or two touched the source of horror in him even. It hardly surprised him that the horse, steaming and sweating, should start forward with a frightened leap as each figure in turn was sighted and left behind. Probably he was himself too much a part of the wild, exhilarating rush to realize how singular it was. Certainly, it seemed as though some faculty of his mind was suspended during that drive.

But at last, after passing another friend, the horse gave a leap that really frightened him, flinging him against the boards. It was a man, twice his own age, who more than any other had helped him in his evil living, not by doing likewise, but by smothering his first remorse with a smile and a sentence: "Of course, my boy, sow your wild oats! You'll settle down later. No man is worth his salt who hasn't sown his wild oats!" He was sliding along — a kind of crawl, with something loathsome in his motion that suggested the reptile. Carlton nodded to him. The same second the horse gave its terrible bound. The whip for the first time slashed down across its flanks. He saw the strip of crêpe, black against the green and sunny landscape. For by now all houses were left behind, and they were rushing at a mad pace along a broad country road, growing momentarily steeper, and — downhill.

At the same moment he caught his own face in the glass. To his utter horror he saw that a black veil, crêpelike, hung over the upper part, already hiding the eyes, and that it was moving downwards, slowly creeping. The hand of steel turned again within him. He knew that it was Death.

Yet, most singular of all, he instantly found in himself the power to believe it was not there. His hand brushed it off. His face was young, clean, and smiling once more. . . . And now the hansom flew. The horse was running away; he heard the driver shouting to it, and the shouting sounded like a song. The man *was* drunk after all. Mingled with his song, too, came a confused murmur of voices behind — far away. What in the world did it all mean? Dashing aside the little curtain he looked back out of the window, and the first thing he saw was a face pressed close against the glass, staring straight into his eyes with a beseeching, pitiful expression. Good God! It was the face of his mother. He swore; the face melted away — and he then saw that the whole country behind him was black, and through it, down the darkened road, ran the figures he had passed. But how changed! The girl was no longer gay and smiling;

her face was old, streaked with evil, and with one hand she clutched her heart as she ran — trying in vain to stop. Behind her were the others — worn and broken, with bloodshot eyes and toothless gums, all grinning dreadfully, all racing down the ever-steepening descent, yet all trying frantically to stop. One or two, however, still ran with a brave show as if they wished to; debonair, holding themselves with a certain appearance of dignity and pleasure. And some — the old man of the "wild oats" sentence at their head — were close upon the hansom, *pushing it* ... The face of his mother slid once again upon the glass, between their evil, outstretched hands and himself, but less close, less visible than before. ...

Carlton knew a spasm of pain that was terrible. He sat up. He flung open the doors, and his eyes measured the leap. But the faculty of mind that had all the time been in suspension returned a little, and he saw that to jump was — impossible. He smashed the trap open with his fist and cried out, "Stop! I tell you, stop!"

"Can't stop here, sir," the driver answered, peering down at him out of the square opening that let in — darkness. "It's not allowed. It's not usual, either."

"Stop, I say," thundered Canton, trying to rise and strike him.

But the driver laughed through that square of blackness.

"Can't be done, sir. You told me 'same address.' There's no stopping now!"

Canton's clenched fist was close to the man's eyes when the fingers grew limp and opened. He sank back upon the seat again. The face peering down upon him was — his own.

And in this supreme moment it was that some secret reserve of soul, hitherto untainted — stirred into life, he declares, by the sight of his mother's face at the window — rose and offered itself to him. He accepted it. *His will moved in its sleep and woke.*

"But I say you *shall* stop! " he cried, catching the reins in both hands, and, when they snapped, seizing the rims, and even the spokes, of the wheels. His great strength acted like a brake. The hansom reeled, shook, then slackened. It was a most curious thing, but the force that twisted his heart with its hand of "ragged steel" seemed to lend him its power. His will moved and gripped; the machinery groaned, but worked. Canton did nothing by halves; he put his life into his efforts; the skin was torn like paper from his hands. The hansom stopped with a trembling jerk and flung him out upon his face in the mud. And the same second he saw the horse and driver, both torn from their fastenings, whirled past him overhead to disappear into a gulf that yawned dreadfully under his very eyes, blacker than night, deeper than all things. . . .

And when, at length, he rose to his feet, he found that he was tied with bands of iron to the shafts. Slowly, with vast efforts, groaning and sweating, he turned and began painfully to reclimb the huge and toilsome ascent, dragging the awful weight behind him . . . towards the Light.

For the glare that suddenly broke through the sky was the sunshine coming through the windows of the hospital room — St. George's Hospital — where they had carried him when he fainted on the pavement half-an-hour before.

The Eccentricity of Simon Parnacute

I

*I*t was one of those mornings in early spring when even the London streets run beauty. The day, passing through the sky with clouds of flying hair, touched everyone with the magic of its own irresponsible gaiety, as it alternated between laughter and the tears of sudden showers.

In the parks the trees, faintly clothed with gauze, were busying themselves shyly with the thoughts of coming leaves. The air held a certain sharpness, but the sun swam through the dazzling blue spaces with bursts of almost summer heat; and a wind, straight from the haunted south, laid its soft persuasion upon all, bringing visions too fair to last — long thoughts of youth, of cowslip-meadows, white sails, waves on yellow sand, and other pictures innumerable and enchanting.

So potent, indeed, was this spell of awakening spring that even Simon Parnacute, retired Professor of Political Economy — elderly, thin-faced, and ruminating in his big skull those large questions that concern the polity of nations — formed no exception to the general rule. For, as he slowly made his way down the street that led from his apartment to the Little Park, he was fully aware that this magic of the spring was in his own blood too, and that the dust which had accumulated with the years upon the surface of his soul was being stirred by one of the softest breezes he had ever felt in the whole course of his arduous and tutorial career.

And — it so happened — just as he reached the foot of the street where the houses fell away towards the open park, the sun rushed out into one of the sudden blue spaces of the sky, and drenched him in a wave of delicious heat that for all the world was like the heat of July.

Professor Parnacute, once lecturer, now merely ponderer, was an exact thinker, dealing carefully with the facts of life as he saw them. He was a good man and a true. He dealt in large emotions, becoming for one who studied nations rather than individuals, and of all diplomacies of the heart he was rudely ignorant. He lived always at the center of the circle — his own circle — and eccentricity was a thing to him utterly abhorrent. Convention ruled him, body, soul and mind. To know a disordered thought, or an unwonted emotion, troubled him as much as to see a picture crooked on a wall, or a man's collar projecting beyond his overcoat. Eccentricity was the symptom of a disease.

Thus, as he reached the foot of the street and felt the sun and wind upon his withered cheeks, this unexpected call of the spring came to him sharply as something altogether out of place and illegitimate — symptom of an irregular condition of mind that must be instantly repressed. And it was just here, while the crowd jostled and delayed him, that there smote upon his ear the song incarnate of the very spring whose spell he was in the ad of relegating to its proper place in his personal economy: he heard the entrancing *singing of a bird!*

Transfixed with wonder and delight, he stood for a whole minute and listened. Then, slowly turning, he found himself staring straight into the small beseeching eyes of a — thrush; a thrush in a cage that hung upon the outside wall of a bird-fancier's shop behind him.

Perhaps he would not have lingered more than these few seconds, however, had not the crowd held him momentarily prisoner in a spot immediately opposite the shop, where his head, too, was exactly on a level with the hanging cage. Thus he was perforce obliged to stand, and watch, and listen; and, as he did so, the bird's rapturous and appealing song played upon the feelings already awakened by the spring, urging them upwards and outwards to a point that grew perilously moving.

Both sound and sight caught and held him spellbound.

The bird, once well-favored perhaps, he perceived was now thin and bedraggled, its feathers disarrayed by continual flitting along its perch, and by endless fluttering of wings and body against the bars of its narrow cage. There was not room to open both wings properly; it frequently dashed itself against the sides of its wooden prison; and all the force of its vain and passionate desire for freedom shone in the two small and glittering eyes which gazed beseechingly through the bars at the passers-by. It looked broken and worn with the ceaseless renewal of the futile struggle. Hopping along the bar, cocking its dainty little head on one side, and looking straight into the Professor's eyes, it managed (by some inarticulate magic known only to the eyes of creatures in prison) to spell out the message of its pain — the poignant longing for the freedom of the open sky, the lift of the great winds, the glory of the sun upon its lusterless feathers.

Now it so chanced that this combined onslaught of sight and sound caught the elderly Professor along the line of least resistance — the line of an untried, and therefore unexhausted, sensation. Here, apparently, was an emotion hitherto unrealized, and so not yet regulated away into atrophy.

For, with an intuition as singular as it was searching, he suddenly understood something of the passion of the wild Caged Things of the world, and realized in a flash of passing vision something of their unutterable pain.

In one swift moment of genuine mystical sympathy he *felt with* their peculiar quality of unsatisfied longing exactly as though it were his own; the longing, not only of captive birds and animals, but of anguished men and women, trapped by circumstance, confined by weakness, cabined by character and temperament, all yearning for a freedom they knew not how to reach — caged by the smallness of their desires, by the impotence of their wills, by the pettiness of their souls — caged in bodies from which death alone could finally bring release.

Something of all this found its way into the elderly Professor's heart as he stood watching the pantomime of the captive thrush — the Caged Thing; — and, after a moment's hesitation that represented a vast amount of condensed feeling, he deliberately entered the low doorway of the shop and inquired the price of the bird.

"The thrush — er — singing in the small cage," he stammered.

"One *and* six only, sir," replied the coarse, red-faced man who owned the shop, looking up from a rabbit that he was pushing with clumsy fingers into a box; "only one shilling *and* sixpence," — and then went on with copious remarks upon thrushes in general and the superior qualities of this one in particular. "Been 'ere four months and sings just lovely," he added, by way of climax.

"Thank you," said Parnacute quietly, trying to persuade himself that he did not feel mortified by his impulsive and eccentric action; "then I will purchase the bird — at once — er — if you please."

"Couldn't go far wrong, sir," said the man, shoving the rabbit to one side, and going outside to fetch the thrush.

"No, I shall not require the cage, but — er — you may put him in a cardboard box perhaps, so that I can carry him easily."

He referred to the bird as "him," though at any other time he would have said "it," and the change, noted surreptitiously as it were, added to his general sense of confusion. It was too late, however, to alter his mind, and after watching the man force the bird with gross hands into a cardboard box, he gathered up the noose of string with which it was tied and walked with as much dignity and self-respect as he could muster out of the shop.

But the moment he got into the street with this living parcel under his arm — he both heard and felt the scuttling of the bird's feet — the realization that he had been guilty of what he considered an outrageous act of eccentricity almost overwhelmed him. For he had succumbed in most regrettable fashion to a momentary impulse, and had bought the bird in order to release it.

"Dear me!" he thought, "how ever could I have allowed myself to do so eccentric and impulsive a thing!"

And, but for the fact that it would merely have accentuated his eccentricity, he would then and there have returned to the shop and given back the bird.

That, however, being now clearly impossible, he crossed the road and entered the Little Park by the first iron gateway he could find. He walked down the gravel path, fumbling with the string. In another minute the bird would have been out, when he chanced to glance round in order to make sure he was unobserved and saw against the shrubbery on his left — a policeman.

This, he felt, was most vexatious, for he had hoped to complete the transaction unseen. Straightening himself up, he nervously fastened the string again, and walked on slowly as though nothing had happened, searching for a more secluded spot where he should be entirely free from observation.

Professor Parnacute now became aware that his vexation — primarily caused by his act of impulse, and increased by the fact that he was observed — had become somewhat acute. It was extraordinary, he reflected, how policemen had this way of suddenly outlining themselves in the least appropriate — the least necessary — places. There was no reason why a policeman should have been standing against that innocent shrubbery, where there was nothing to do, no one to watch. At almost any other point in the Little Park he might have served some possibly useful purpose, and yet, forsooth, he must select the one spot where he was not wanted — where his presence, indeed, was positively objectionable.

The policeman, meanwhile, watched him steadily as he retreated with the obnoxious parcel. He carried it upside down now without knowing it. He felt as though he had been detected in a crime. He watched the policeman, too, out of the corner of his eye, longing to be done with the whole business.

"That policeman is a tremendous fellow," he thought to himself. "I have never seen a constable so large, so stalwart. He must be *the* policeman of the district" — whatever that might mean — "a veritable wall and tower of defense." The helmet made him think of a battering ram, and the buttons on his overcoat of the muzzles of guns.

He moved away round the corner with as much innocence as he could assume, as though he were carrying a package of books or some new article of apparel.

It is, no doubt, the duty of every alert constable to observe as acutely as possible the course of events passing before his eyes, yet this particular Bobby seemed far more interested than the circumstances warranted in Parnacute's cardboard box. He kept his gaze remorselessly upon it. Perhaps, thought the Professor, he heard the scutterings of the frightened bird within. Perhaps he thought it was a cat going to be drowned in the ornamental water. Perhaps — oh, dreadful idea! — he thought it was a baby!

The suspicions of an intelligent policeman, however, being past finding out, Simon Parnacute wisely ignored them, and just then passed round a corner where he was screened from this persistent observer by a dense growth of rhododendron bushes.

Seizing the opportune moment, and acting with a prompt decision born of the dread of the reappearing policeman, he cut the string, opened the lid of the box, and an instant later had the intense satisfaction of seeing the imprisoned thrush hop upon the cardboard edge and then fly with a beautiful curving dip and a whirr of wings off into the open sky. It turned once as it flew, and its bright brown eye looked at him. Then it was gone, lost in the sunshine that blazed over the shrubberies and beckoned it out over their waving tops across the river.

The prisoner was free. For the space of a whole minute, the Professor stood still, conscious of a sense of genuine relief. That sound of wings, that racing sweep of the little quivering body escaping into limitless freedom, that penetrating look of gratitude from the wee brown eyes — these stirred in him again the same prodigious emotion he had experienced for the first time that afternoon outside the bird-fanciers s shop. The release of the "caged creature" provided him with a kind of vicarious experience of freedom and delight such as he had never before known in his whole life. It almost seemed as though he had escaped himself — out of his "circle."

Then, as he faced about, with the empty box dangling in his hand, the first thing he saw, coming slowly down the path towards him with measured tread, was — the big policeman.

Something very stern, something very forbidding, hung like an atmosphere of warning about this guardian of the law in a blue uniform. It brought him back sharply to the rigid facts of life, and the soft beauty of the spring day vanished and left him untouched. He accepted the reminder that life is earnest, and that eccentricities are invitations to disaster. Sooner or later the Policeman is bound to make his appearance.

However, this particular constable, of course, passed him without word or gesture, and as soon as he came to one of the little wire baskets provided for the purpose, the Professor dropped his box into it, and then made his way slowly and thoughtfully back to his apartment and his luncheon.

But the eccentricity of which he had been guilty circled and circled in his mind, reminding him with merciless insistence of a foolish act he should not have committed, and plaguing him with remorseless little stabs for having indulged in an impulsive and irregular proceeding.

For, to him, the inevitableness of life came as a fact to which he was resigned, rather than as a force to be appropriated for the ends of his own soul; and the sight of the happy bird escaping into sky and sunshine, with the figure of the inflexible and stern-lipped policeman in the background, made a deep impression upon him that would sooner or later be certain to bear fruit.

"Dear me," thought the Professor of Political Economy, giving mental expression to this sentiment, "I shall pay for this in the long run! Without question I shall pay for it!"

II

*I*f it may be taken that there is no Chance, playing tricksy-wise behind the scenes of existence, but that all events falling into the lives of men are the calculated results of adequate causes, then Mr. Simon Parnacute, late Professor of Political Economy in C——— College, certainly did pay for his spring aberration, in the sense that he caught a violent chill which brought him to bed and speedily developed into pneumonia.

It was the evening of the sixth day, and he lay weary and feverish in his bedroom on the top floor of the building which held his little self-contained apartment. The nurse was downstairs having her tea. A shaded lamp stood beside the bed, and through the window — the blinds being not yet drawn — he saw the sea of roofs and chimney-pots, and the stream of wires, sharply outlined against a sunset sky of gold and pink. High and thin above the dusk floated long strips of colored cloud, and the first stars twinkled through the April vapors that gathered with the approach of night.

Presently the door opened and someone came in softly halfway across the room, and then stopped. The Professor turned wearily and saw that the maid stood there and was trying to speak. She seemed flustered, he noticed, and her face was rather white.

"What's the matter *now,* Emily?" he asked feebly, yet irritably.

"Please, Professor — there's a gentleman —" and there she stuck.

"Someone to see me? The doctor again already?" queried the patient, wondering in a vague, absent way why the girl should seem so startled.

As he spoke there was a sound of footsteps on the landing outside — heavy footsteps.

"But please, Professor, sir, it's *not* the doctor," the maid faltered, "only I couldn't get his name, and I couldn't stop him, an' he said you expected him — and I think he looks like —"

The approaching footsteps frightened the girl so much that she could not find words to complete her description. They were just outside the door now.

"— like a perliceman! " she finished with a rush, backing towards the door as though she feared the Professor would leap from his bed to demolish her.

"A *policeman!*" gasped Mr. Parnacute, unable to believe his ears. "A policeman, Emily! In my apartment?"

And before the sick man could find words to express his particular annoyance that any stranger (above all a constable) should intrude at such a time, the door was pushed wide open, the girl had vanished with a flutter of skirts, and the tall figure of a man stood in full view upon the threshold, and stared steadily across the room at the occupant of the bed on the other side.

It was indeed a policeman, and a very large policeman. Moreover, it was *the* policeman.

The instant the Professor recognized the familiar form of the man from the park his anger, for some quite unaccountable reason, vanished almost entirely; the sharp vexation he had felt a moment before died away; and, sinking back exhausted among the pillows, he only found breath to ask him to close the door and come in. The fact was, astonishment had used up the small store of energy at his disposal, and for the moment he could think of nothing else to do.

The policeman closed the door quietly and moved forward towards the center of the room, so that the circle of light from the shaded lamp at the head of the bed reached his figure but fell just short of his face.

The invalid sat up in bed again and stared. As nothing seemed to happen he recovered his scattered wits a little.

"You are the policeman from the park, unless I mistake?" he asked feebly, with mingled pomposity and resentment.

The big man bowed in acknowledgment and removed his helmet, holding it before him in his hand. His face was peculiarly bright, almost as though it reflected the glow of a bull's-eye lantern concealed somewhere about his huge person.

"I thought I recognized you," went on the Professor, exasperated a little by the other's self-possession. "Are you perhaps aware that I am ill — too ill to see strangers, and that to force your way up in this fashion — !" He left the sentence unfinished for lack of suitable expletives.

"You are certainly ill," replied the constable, speaking for the first time; "but then — I am *not* a stranger." His voice was wonderfully pitched and modulated for a policeman.

"Then, by what right, pray, do you dare to intrude upon me at such a time?" snapped the other, ignoring the latter statement.

"My duty, sir," the man replied, with a rather wonderful dignity, "knows nothing of time or place."

Professor Parnacute looked at him a little more closely as he stood there helmet in hand. He was something more, he gathered, than an ordinary constable; an inspector perhaps. He examined him carefully; but he understood nothing about differences in uniform, of bands or stars upon sleeve and collar.

"If you are here in the prosecution of your duty, then," exclaimed the man of careful mind, searching feverishly for some possible delinquency on the part of his small staff of servants, "pray be seated and state your business; but as briefly as possible. My throat pains me, and my strength is low." He spoke with less acerbity. The dignity of the visitor began to impress him in some vague fashion he did not understand.

The big figure in blue bowed again, but made no sign of advance.

"You come from X—— Station, I presume?" Parnacute added, mentioning the police station round the corner. He sank deeper into his pillows, conscious that his strength was becoming exhausted.

"From Headquarters — I come," replied the colossus in a deep voice.

The Professor had only the vaguest idea what Headquarters meant, yet the phrase conveyed an importance that somehow was not lost upon him. Meanwhile his impatience grew with his exhaustion.

"I must request you, officer, to state your business with dispatch," he said tartly, "or to come again when I am better able to attend to you. Next week, no doubt —"

"There is no time *but* the present," returned the other, with an odd choice of words that escaped the notice of his perplexed hearer, as he produced from a capacious pocket in the tail of his overcoat a notebook bound with some shining metal like gold.

"Your name is Parnacute?" he asked, consulting the book.

"Yes," answered the other, with the resignation of exhaustion.

"*Simon* Parnacute?"

"Of course, yes."

"And on the third of April last," he went on, looking keenly over the top of the notebook at the sick man, "you, Simon Parnacute, entered the shop of Theodore Spinks in the Lower P——— Road, and purchased from him a certain living creature?"

"Yes," answered the Professor, beginning to feel hot at the discovery of his folly.

"A bird?"

"A bird."

"A thrush?"

"A thrush."

"A singing thrush?"

"Oh yes, it was a singing thrush, if you *must* know."

"In money you paid for this thrush the sum of one shilling *and* six pennies?" He emphasized the "and" just as the bird-fancier had done.

"One and six, yes."

"But in true value," said the policeman, speaking with grave emphasis, "it cost you a great deal more?"

"Perhaps." He winced internally at the memory.

He was so astonished, too, that the visit had to do with himself and not with some of his servants.

"You paid for it with your heart?" insisted the other.

The Professor made no reply. He started. He almost writhed under the sheets.

"Am I right?" asked the policeman.

"That is the fact, I suppose," he said in a low voice, sorely puzzled by the catechism.

"You carried this bird away in a cardboard box to E——— Gardens by the river, and there you gave it freedom and watched it fly away?"

"Your statement is correct, I think, in every particular. But really — this absurd cross-examination, my good man!"

"And your motive in so doing," continued the policeman, his voice quite drowning the invalid's feeble tones, "was the unselfish one of releasing an imprisoned and tortured creature?"

Simon Parnacute looked up with the greatest possible surprise.

"I think — well, well! — perhaps it was," he murmured apologetically. "The extraordinary singing — it *was* extraordinary, you know, and the sight of the little thing beating its wings pained me."

The big policeman put away his notebook suddenly, and moved closer to the bed so that his face entered the circle of lamplight.

"In that case," he cried, *"you are my man!"*

"I am your man!" exclaimed the Professor, with an uncontrollable start.

"The man I want," repeated the other, smiling. His voice had suddenly grown soft and wonderful, like the ringing of a silver gong, and into his face had come an expression of wistful tenderness that made it positively beautiful. It shone. Never before, out of a picture, had he seen such a look upon a human countenance, or heard such tones issue from the lips of a human being. He thought, swiftly and confusedly, of a woman, of *the* woman he had never found — of a dream, an enchantment as of music or vision upon the senses.

"Wants me!" he thought with alarm. "What have I done now? What new eccentricity have I been guilty of?"

Strange, bewildering ideas crowded into his mind, blurred in outline, preposterous in character. A sensation of cold caught at his fever and overmastered it, bathing him in perspiration, making him tremble, yet not with fear. A new and curious delight had begun to pluck at his heart-strings.

Then an extravagant suspicion crossed his brain, yet a suspicion not wholly unwarranted.

"Who are you?" he asked sharply, looking up. "Are you really only a policeman?"

The man drew himself up so that he appeared, if possible, even huger than before.

"I am a World-Policeman," he answered, "a guardian, perhaps, rather than a detective."

"Heavens above!" cried the Professor, thinking of madness and the crimes committed in madness.

"Yes," he went on in those calm, musical tones that before long began to have a reassuring effect upon his listener, "and it is my duty, among many others, to keep an eye upon eccentric people; to lock them up when necessary, and when their sentences have expired, to release them. Also," he added impressively, "as in your case, to let them out of their cages without pain — when they've earned it."

"Gracious goodness me!" exclaimed Parnacute, unaccustomed to the use of expletives, but unable to think of anything else to say.

"And sometimes to see that their cages do not destroy them — and that they do not beat themselves to death against the bars," he went on, smiling quite wonderfully. "Our duties are varied *and* numerous. I am one of a large force."

The man learned in political economy felt as though his head were spinning. He thought of calling for help. Indeed, he had already made a motion with his hand towards the bell when a gesture on the part of his strange visitor restrained him.

"Then why do you want *me*, if I may ask?" he faltered instead.

"To mark you down; and when the time comes to let you out of your cage easily, comfortably, without pain. That's one reward for your kindness to the bird."

The Professor's fears had now quite disappeared. The policeman seemed perfectly harmless after all.

"It's *very* kind of you," he said feebly, drawing his arm back beneath the bed-clothes. "Only — er — I was not aware, exactly, that I lived in a cage."

He looked up resignedly into the man's face.

"You only realize that when you get out," he replied. "They're all like that. The bird didn't quite understand what was wrong; it only knew that it felt miserable. Same with you. You feel unhappy in that body of yours, and in that little careful mind you regulate so nicely; but, for the life of you, you don't quite know what it is that's wrong. You want space, freedom, a taste of liberty. You want to fly, that's what you want!" he cried, raising his voice.

"I — want — to — fly?" gasped the invalid.

"Oh," smiling again, "we World-Policemen have thousands of cases just like yours. Our field is a large one, a very large one indeed."

He stepped into the light more fully and turned sideways.

"Here's my badge, if you care to see it," he said proudly.

He stooped a little so that the Professor's beady eyes could easily focus themselves upon the collar of his overcoat. There, just like the lettering upon the collar of an ordinary London policeman, only in bright gold instead of silver, shone the constellation of the Pleiades. Then he turned and showed the other side, and Parnacute saw the constellation of Orion slanting upwards, as he had often seen it tilting across the sky at night.

"Those are my badges," he repeated proudly, straightening himself up again and moving back into the shadow.

"And very fine they are, too," said the Professor, his increasing exhaustion suggesting no better observation. But with the sight of those starry figures had come to him a strange whiff of the open skies, space, and wind — the winds of the world.

"So that when the time comes," the World-Policeman resumed, "you may have confidence. I will let you out without pain or fear just as you let out the bird. And, meanwhile, you may as well realize that you live in a cage just as cramped and shut away from light and freedom as the thrush did."

"Thank you; I will certainly try," whispered Parnacute, almost fainting with fatigue.

There followed a pause, during which the policeman put on his helmet, tightened his belt, and then began to search vigorously for something in his coattail pockets.

"And now," ventured the sick man, feeling half fearful, half happy, though without knowing exactly why, "is there anything more I can do for you, Mr. World-Policeman?" He was conscious that his words were peculiar yet he could not help it. They seemed to slip out of their own accord.

"There's nothing more you can do for *me*, sir, thank you," answered the man in his most silvery tones. "But there's something more I can do for *you!* And that is to give you a preliminary taste of freedom, so that you may realize you do live in a cage, and be less confused and puzzled when you come to make the final Escape."

Parnacute caught his breath sharply — staring open-mouthed.

With a single stride the policeman covered the space between himself and the bed. Before the withered, fever-stricken little Professor could utter a word or a cry, he had caught up the wasted body out of the bed, shaken the bed-clothes off him like paper from a parcel, and slung him without ceremony across his gigantic shoulders. Then he crossed the room, and producing the key from his coat-tail pocket, he put it straight into the solid wall of the room. He turned it, and the entire side of the house opened like a door.

For one second Simon Parnacute looked back and saw the lamp, and the fire, and the bed. And in the bed he saw his own body lying motionless in profound slumber.

Then, as the policeman balanced, hovering upon the giddy edge, he looked outward and saw the network of street-lamps far below, and heard the deep roar of the city smite upon his ears like the thunder of a sea.

The next moment the man stepped out into space, and he saw that they were rising up swiftly towards the dark vault of sky, where stars twinkled down upon them between streaks of thin flying clouds.

III

Once outside, floating in the night, the policeman gave his shoulder a mighty jerk and tossed his small burden into free space.

"Jump away!" he cried. "You're quite safe!"

The Professor dropped like a bullet towards the pavement; then suddenly began to rise again, like a balloon. All traces of fever or bodily discomfort had left him utterly. He felt light as air, and strong as lightning.

"Now, where shall we go to?" The voice sounded above him.

Simon Parnacute was no flyer. He had never indulged in those strange flying-dreams that form a weird pleasure in the sleep-lives of many people. He was terrified beyond belief until he found that he did not crash against the earth, and that he had within him the power to regulate his movements, to rise or sink at will. Then, of course, the wildest fury of delight and freedom he had ever known flashed all over him and burned in his brain like an intoxication.

"The big cities, or the stars?" asked the World-Policeman.

"No, no," he cried, "the country — the open country! And other lands!"

For Simon Parnacute had never traveled. Incredible as it may seem, the Professor had never in his life been farther out of England than in a sailing-boat at Southend. His body had traveled even less than his imagination. With this suddenly increased capacity for motion, the desire to race about and see became a passion.

"Woods! Mountains! Seas! Deserts! Anything but houses and people!" he shouted, rising upwards to his companion without the smallest effort.

An intense longing to see the desolate, unfrequented regions of the earth seized him and tore its way out into words strangely unlike his normal and measured mode of speech. All his life he had paced to and fro in a formal little garden with the most precise paths imaginable. Now he wanted a trackless world. The reaction was terrific. The desire of the Arab for the desert, of the gypsy for the open heaths, the "desire of the snipe for the wilderness" — the longing of the eternal wanderer — possessed his soul and found vent in words.

It was just as though the passion of the released thrush were reproducing itself in him and becoming articulate.

"I am haunted by the faces of the world's forgotten places," he cried aloud impetuously. "Beaches lying in the moonlight, all forsaken in the moonlight —"

His utterance, like the bird's, had become lyrical.

"Can this be what the thrush felt?" he wondered.

"Let's be off then," the policeman called back. "There's no time *but the present*, remember." He rushed through space like a huge projectile. He made a faint whistling noise as he went. Parnacute followed suit. The lightest desire, he found, gave him instantly the ease and speed of thought.

The policeman had taken off his helmet, overcoat and belt, and dropped them down somewhere into a London street. He now appeared as a mere blue outline of a man, scarcely discernible against the dark sky — an outline filled with air. The Professor glanced down at himself and saw that he, too, was a mere outline of a man — a pallid outline filled with the purple air of night.

"Now then," sang out this "Bobby-of-the-World."

Side by side they shot up with a wild rush, and the lights of London, town and suburbs, flashed away beneath them in streaming lines and patches. In a second darkness filled the huge gap, pouring behind them like a mighty wave. Other streams and patches of light succeeded quickly, blurred and faint, like lamps of railway stations from a night express, as other towns dropped past them in a series and were swallowed up in the gulf behind.

A cool salt air smote their faces, and Parnacute heard the soft crashing of waves as they crossed the Channel, and swept on over the fields and forests of France, glimmering below like the squares of a mighty chessboard. Like toys, village after village shot by, smelling of peat smoke, cattle, and the faint windiness of coming spring.

Sometimes they passed below the clouds and lost the stars, sometimes above them and lost the world; sometimes over forests roaring like the sea, sometimes above vast plains still and silent as the grave; but always Parnacute saw the constellations of Orion and Pleiades shining on the coat collar of the soaring policeman, their little patterns picked out as with tiny electric lamps.

Below them lay the huge map of the earth, raised, scarred, darkly colored, and breathing — a map *alive*.

Then came the Jura, soft and purple, carpeted with forests, rolling below them like a dream, and they looked down into slumbering valleys and heard far below the tumbling of water and the singing of countless streams.

"Glory, glory!" cried the Professor. "And do the birds know *this*?"

"Not the imprisoned ones," was the reply. And presently they whipped across large gleaming bodies of water as the lakes of Switzerland approached. Then, entering the zones of icy atmosphere, they looked down and saw white towers and pinnacles of silver, and the forms of scarred and mighty glaciers that rose and fell among the fields of eternal snow, folding upon the mountains in vast procession.

"I think — I'm frightened!" gasped Parnacute, clutching at his companion, but seizing only the frigid air.

The policeman shouted with laughter.

"This is nothing — compared to Mars or the moon," he cried, soaring till the Alps looked like a patch of snowdrops shining in a Surrey garden. "You'll soon get accustomed to it."

The Professor of Political Economy rose after him. But presently they sank again in an immense curving sweep and touched the tops of the highest mountains with their toes. This sent them instantly aloft again, bounding with the impetus of rockets, and so they careered on through the perfumed, pathless night till they came to Italy and left the Alps behind them like the shadowy wall of another world that had silently moved up close to them through space.

"Mother of Mountains!" shouted the delighted man of colleges. "And did the thrush know this too?"

"It has you to thank, if so," the policeman answered.

"And I have you to thank."

"No — yourself," replied his flying guide.

And then the desert! They had crossed the scented Mediterranean and reached the zones of sand. It rose in clouds and sheets as a mighty wind stirred across the leagues of loneliness that stretched below them into blue distance. It whirled about them and stung their faces.

"Thin ropes of sand which crumble ere they bind!" cried the Professor with a peal of laughter, not knowing what he said in the delirium of his pleasure.

The hot smell of the sand excited him; the knowledge that for hundreds of miles he could not see a house or a human being thrilled him dizzily with the incalculable delight of freedom. The splendor of the night, mystical and incommunicable, overcame him. He rose, laughing wildly, shaking the sand from his hair, and taking gigantic curves into the starry space about him. He remembered vividly the sight of those bedraggled wings in the little cramped cage — and then looked down and realized that here the winds sank exhausted from the very weariness of too much space. Oh, that he could tear away the bars of every cage the world had ever known — set free all captive creatures — restore to all wild, winged life the liberty of open spaces that is theirs by right!

He cried again to the stars and winds and deserts, but his words found no intelligible expression, for their passion was too great to be confined in any known medium. The World-Policeman alone understood, per-haps, for he flew down in circles round the little Professor and laughed and laughed and laughed.

And it seemed as if tremendous figures formed themselves out of the sky to listen, and bent down to lift him with a single sweep of their immense arms from the earth to the heavens. Such was the torrential power and delight of escape in him, that he almost felt as if he could skim the icy abysses of Death itself — without being ever caught. . . .

The colossal shapes of Egypt, terrible and monstrous, passed far below in huge and shadowy procession, and the desolate Lybian Mountains drew him hovering over their wastes of stone. . . . And this was only a beginning! Asia, India, and the Southern Seas all lay within reach! All could be visited in turn. The interstellar spaces, the far planets, and the white moon were yet to know!

"We must be thinking of turning soon," he heard the voice of his companion, and then remembered how his own body, hot and feverish, lay in that stuffy little room at the other end of Europe. It was indeed caged — the withered body in the room, and himself in the withered body — doubly caged. He laughed and shuddered. The wind swept through him, licking him clean. He rose again in the ecstasy of free flight, following the lead of the policeman on the homeward journey, and the mountains below became a purple line on the map. In a series of great sweeps they rested on the top of the Pyramid, and then upon the forehead of the Sphinx, and so onwards, touching the earth at intervals, till they heard once more the waves upon the coast-line, and soared aloft again across the sea, racing through Spain and over the Pyrenees. The thin blue outline of the policeman kept ever at his side.

"From all the far blue hills of heaven these winds of freedom blow!" he shouted into space, following it with a peal of laughter that made his guide circle round and round him, chuckling as he flew. A curious, silvery chuckle it was — yet it sounded as though it came to him through a much greater distance than before. It came, as it were, through barriers.

The picture of the bird-fancier's shop came again vividly before him. He saw the beseeching and frightened little eyes; heard the ceaseless pattering of the imprisoned feet, wings beating against the bars, and soft furry bodies pushing vainly to get out. He saw the red face of Theodore Spinks, the proprietor, gloating over the scene of captive life that gave him the means to live — the means to enjoy his own little measure of freedom. He saw the sea-gull drooping in its corner, and the owl, its eyes filled with the dust of the street, its feathered ears twitching; — and then he thought again of the caged human beings of the world — men, women and children, and a pain, like the pain of a whole universe, burned in his soul and set his heart aflame with yearning . . . to set them all instantly free.

And, unable to find words to give expression to what he felt, he found relief again in his strange, impetuous singing.

Simon Parnacute, Professor of Political Economy, sang in mid-heaven!

But this was the last vivid memory he knew. It all began to fade a little after that. It changed swiftly like a dream when the body nears the point of waking. He tried to seize and hold it, to delay the moment when it must end; but the power was beyond him. He felt heavy and tired, and flew closer to the ground; the intervals between the curves of flight grew smaller and smaller, the impetus weaker and weaker as he became every moment more dense and stupid. His progress across the fields of the south of England, as he made his way almost laboriously homewards, became rather a series of long, low leaps than actual flight. More and more often he found himself obliged to touch the earth to acquire the necessary momentum. The big policeman seemed suddenly to have quite melted away into the blue of night.

Then he heard a door open in the sky over his head. A star came down rather too close and half blinded his eyes. Instinctively he called for help to his friend, the world-policeman.

"It's time, for your soup now," was the only answer he got. And it did not seem the right answer, or the right voice either. A terror of being permanently lost came over him, and he cried out again louder than before.

"And the medicine first," dropped the thin, shrill voice out of endless space.

It was not the policeman's voice at all. He knew now, and understood. A sensation of weariness, of sickening disgust and boredom came over him. He looked up. The sky had turned white; he saw curtains and walls and a bright lamp with a red shade. This was the star that had nearly blinded him – a lamp merely, in a sick-room!

And, standing at the farther end of the room, he saw the figure of the nurse in cap and apron. Below him lay his body in the bed. His sensation of disgust and boredom became a positive horror. But he sank down exhausted into it – into his cage.

"Take this soup, sir, after the medicine, and then perhaps you'll get another bit of sleep," the nurse was saying with gentle authority, bending over him.

*T*he progress of Professor Parnacute towards recovery was slow and tedious, for the illness had been severe and it left him with a dangerously weak heart. And at night he still had the delights of the flying dreams. Only, by this time, he had learned to fly alone. His phantom friend, the big World-Policeman, no longer accompanied him.

And his chief occupation during these weary hours of convalescence was curious and, the nurse considered, not very suitable for an invalid : for he spent the time with endless calculations, poring over the list of his few investments, and adding up times without number the total of his savings of nearly forty years. The bed was strewn with papers and documents; pencils were always getting lost among the clothes; and each time the nurse collected the paraphernalia and put them aside, he would wait till she was out of the room, and then crawl over to the table and carry them all back into bed with him.

Then, finally, she gave up fighting with him, and acquiesced, for his restlessness increased and he could not sleep unless his beloved half-sheets and pencils lay strewn upon the counterpane within instant reach.

Even to the least observant it was clear that the Professor was hatching the preliminary details of a profound plot.

And his very first visitor, as soon as he was permitted to see anybody, was a gentleman with parchment skin and hard, dry, peeping eyes who came by special request — a solicitor, from the firm of Messrs. Costa & Delay.

"I will ascertain the price of the shop and stock-in-trade and inform you of the result at the earliest opportunity, Professor Parnacute," said the man of law in his gritty, professional voice, as he at length took his departure and left the sick-room with the expressionless face of one to whom the eccentricities of human nature could never be new or surprising.

"Thank you; I shall be *most* anxious to hear," replied the other, turning in his long easy chair to save his papers, and at the same time to defend himself against the chiding of the good-natured nurse.

"I knew I should have to pay for it," he murmured, thinking of his original sin; "but I hope," — here he again consulted his penciled figures — "I think I can manage it — just. Though with Consols so low —" He fell to musing again. "Still, I can always sublet the shop, of course, as they suggest," he concluded with a sigh, turning to appeal to the bewildered nurse and finding for the first time that she had gone out of the room.

He fell to pondering deeply. Presently the "list enclosed" by the solicitors caught his eye among the pillows, and he began listlessly to examine it. It was type-written and covered several sheets of foolscap. It was split up into divisions headed as "Lot 1, Lot 2, Lot 3," and so on. He began to read slowly half aloud to himself; then with increasing excitement —

"50 Linnets, guaranteed not straight from the fields; *all caged.*"
"10 fierce singing Linnets."
"10 grand cock Throstles, *just on song.*"
"5 Pear Tree Goldfinches, with deep, square blazes, well buttoned and mooned."
"4 Devonshire Woodlarks, guaranteed full song; *caged three months.*"

The Professor sat up and gripped the paper tightly. His face wore a pained, intent expression. A convulsive movement of his fingers, automatic perhaps, crumpled the sheet and nearly tore it across. He went on reading, shedding rugs and pillows as though they oppressed him. His breath came a little faster.

"5 cock Blackbirds, full plumage, *lovely songsters.*"
"1 Song-Thrush, show-cage and hamper; *splendid whistler,* picked bird."
"1 beautiful, large upstanding singing Skylark; *sings all day; been caged positively five months.*"

Simon Parnacute uttered a curious little cry. It was deep down in his throat. He was conscious of a burning desire to be rich — a millionaire; powerful — an autocratic monarch. After a pause he brought back his attention with an effort to the type-written page and the consideration of further "Lots" —

"3 cock Skylarks; can hear them 200 yards off when singing."

"Two hundred yards off when singing," muttered the Professor into his one remaining pillow. He read on, kicking his feet, somewhat viciously for a sick man, against the wicker rest at the end of the lounge chair.

"1 special, select, singing cock Skylark; guaranteed caged three months; *sings his wild note.*"

He suddenly dashed the list aside. The whole chair creaked and groaned with the violence of his movement. He kicked three times running at the wicker foot-rest, and evidently rejoiced that it was still stiff enough to make it worth while to kick again — harder.

"Oh, that I had all the money in the world!" he cried to himself, letting his eyes wander to the window and the clear blue spaces between the clouds; "all the money in the world!" he repeated with growing excitement. He saw one of London's sea-gulls circling high, high up. He watched it for some minutes, till it sailed against a dazzling bit of white cloud and was lost to view.

"'*Sings his wild note*' — '*guaranteed caged three months*' — '*can be heard two hundred yards off.*'" The phrases burned in his brain like consuming flames.

And so the list went on. He was glancing over the last page when his eye fell suddenly upon an item that described a lot of —

"8 Linnets caged four months; *raving with song.*"

He dropped the list, rose with difficulty from his chair and paced the room, muttering to himself "raving with song, raving with song, raving with song." His hollow cheeks were flushed, his eyes aglow.

"*Caged, caged, caged,*" he repeated under his breath, while his thoughts traveled to that racing flight across Europe, over seas and mountains.

"*Sings his wild note!*" He heard again the whistling wind about his ears as he flew through the zones of heated air above the desert sands.

"*Raving with song!*" He remembered the passion of his own cry — that strange lyrical outburst of his heart when the magic of freedom caught him, and he had soared at will through the unchartered regions of the night.

And then he saw once more the blinking owl, its eyes blinded by the dust of the London street, its feathery ears twitching as it heard the wind sighing past the open doorway of the dingy shop. And again the thrush looked into his face and poured out the rapture of its spring song.

And half-an-hour later he was so exhausted by the unwonted emotion and exercise that the nurse herself was obliged to write at his dictation the letter he sent in reply to the solicitors, Messrs. Costa & Delay in Southampton Row.

But the letter was posted that night and the Professor, still mumbling to himself about "having to pay for it," went to bed with the first hour of the darkness, and plunged straight into another of his delightful flying dreams almost the very moment his eyes had closed.

V

"... *T*hus, all the animals have been disposed of according to your instructions," ran the final letter from the solicitors, "and we beg to append list of items so allotted, together with country addresses to which they have been sent. We think you may feel assured that they are now in homes where they will be well cared for.

"We still retain the following animals against your further instructions —

2 Zonure Lizards,
1 Angulated Tortoise,
2 Mealy Rosellas,
2 Scaly-breasted Lorikeets.

"With regard to these we should advise. . . .

"The caged birds, meanwhile, which you intend the children shall release, are being cared for satisfactorily; and the premises will be ready for taking over as from June 1. . . ."

And, with the assistance of the nurse, he then began to issue a steady stream of letters to the parents of children he knew in the country, carefully noting and tabulating the replies, and making out little white labels inscribed in plain lettering with the words "Lot 1," "Lot 2," and so on, precisely as though he were in the animal business himself, and were getting ready for a sale.

But the sale which took place a fortnight later on June 1 was no ordinary sale.

It was a brilliant hot day when Simon Parnacute, still worn and shaky from his recent illness, made his way towards the shop of the "retired" bird-fancier. The sale of the premises and stock-in-trade, and the high price obtained, had made quite a stir in the "Fancy," but of that the Professor was sublimely ignorant as he crossed the street in front of a truculent motor-omnibus and stood before the dingy three-storey red-brick house.

He produced the key sent to him by Messrs. Costa & Delay, and opened the door. It was cool after the glare of the burning street, and delightfully silent. He remembered the chorus of crying birds that had greeted his last appearance. The silence now was eloquent.

"Good, good," he said to himself, with a quiet smile, as he noticed the temporary counter built across the front room for cloaks and parcels, "very good indeed."

Then he went upstairs, climbing painfully, for he was still easily exhausted. There was hardly a stick of furniture in the house, nor an inch of carpet on the floor and stairs, but the rooms had been swept and scrubbed; everything was fresh and scrupulously clean, and the tenant to whom he was to sub-let could have no fault to find on that score.

In the first-floor rooms he saw with pleasure the flowers arranged about the boards as he had directed. The air was sweet and perfumed. The windows at the back — the sills deep with jars of roses — opened upon a small bit of green garden, and Parnacute looked out and saw the blue sky and the clouds floating lazily across it.

"Good, very good," he exclaimed again, sitting down on the stairs a moment to recover his breath. The excitement and the heat of the day tired him. And, as he sat, he put his hand to his ear and listened attentively. A sound of birds singing reached him faintly from the upper part of the house.

"Ah!" he said, drawing a deep breath, and color coming into his cheeks. "Ah! Now I hear them."

The sound of singing came nearer, as on a passing wind. He climbed laboriously to the top floor, and then, after resting again, scrambled up a ladder through an open skylight on to the roof. The moment he put his perspiring face above the tiles a wild chorus of singing birds greeted him with a sound like a whole countryside in spring.

"If only my friend, the park policeman, could see this!" he said aloud, with a delighted chuckle, "and hear it!" He sought a precarious resting-place upon the butt of a chimney-stack, mopping his forehead.

All around him the sea of London roofs and chimneys rolled away in a black sea, but here, like an oasis in a desert, was a roof of limited extent, and not very high compared to others, converted into a perfect garden. Flowers — but why describe them, when he himself did not even know the names? It was enough that his orders had been carried out to his entire satisfaction, and that this little roof was a world of living color, moving in the wind, scenting the air, welcoming the sunshine.

Everywhere among the pots and boxes of flowers stood the cages. And in the cages the thrushes and blackbirds, the larks and linnets, poured their hearts out with a chorus of song that was more exquisite, he thought, than anything he had ever heard. And there in the corner by the big chimney, carefully shaded from the glare, stood the large cage containing the owls.

"I can almost believe they have guessed my purpose after all," exclaimed the Professor.

For a long time he sat there, leaning against the chimney, oblivious of a blackened collar, listening to the singing, and feasting his eyes upon the garden of flowers all about him. Then the sound of a bell ringing downstairs roused him suddenly into action, and he climbed with difficulty down again to the hall door.

"Here they come," he thought, greatly excited. "Dear me, I do trust I shall not make any mistakes."

He felt in his pocket for his notebook, and then opened the door into the street.

"Oh, it's only you!" he exclaimed, as his nurse came in with her arms full of parcels.

"Only me," she laughed, "but I've brought the lemonade and the biscuits. The others will be here now any minute. It's after three. There's just time to arrange the glasses and plates. We must expect about fifty according to the letters you got. And mind you don't get overtired."

"Oh, I'm all right! " he answered.

She ran upstairs. Before her steps had sounded once on the floor above, a carriage-and-pair stopped at the door, and a footman came up smartly and asked if Professor Parnacute was at home.

"Indeed I am," answered the old man, blushing and laughing at the same time, and then going down himself to the carriage to welcome the little girl and boy who got out. He bowed stiffly and awkwardly to the pretty lady in the victoria, who thanked him for his kindness with a speech he did not hear properly, and then led his callers into the house. They were very shy at first, and hardly knew what to make of it all, but once inside, the boy's sense of adventure was stirred by the sight of the empty shop, and the counter, and the strange array of flowers upon the floor.

He remembered the letter his father had read out from Professor Parnacute a week ago.

"My Lot is No. 7, isn't it, Mr. Professor?" he cried. "I let out a cage of linnets, and get a guinea-pig and a mealy-something-or-other as a present, don't I?"

Mr. Parnacute, shaky and beaming, consulted his notebook hurriedly, and replied that this was "perfectly correct."

"Master Edwin Burton," he read out; "to release — Lot 7. To take away — one guinea-pig, and one mealy rosella."

"I'm Lot 8, please," piped the voice of the little girl, standing with wide-open eyes beside him.

"Oh, are you, my dear?" said he; "yes, yes, I believe you are." He fumbled anew with the notebook. "Here it is," he added, reading aloud again — "Miss Angelina Burton;" he peered closely in the gloom to decipher the writing; "To release — Lot 8 — that's woodlarks, my dear, you know. To take away — one angulated tortoise. Quite correct, yes; quite correct."

He called to the nurse upstairs to show the children their presents hidden away in boxes among the flowers — their rosella and tortoise — and then went again to the door to receive his other guests, who now began to arrive in a steady stream. To the number of twenty or thirty they came, and not one of them appeared to be much over twelve. And the majority of them left their elders at the door and came in unattended.

The marshaling of this array of youngsters among the birds and flowers was a matter of some difficulty, but here the nurse came to the Professor's assistance with energy and experience, so that his strength was economized and the children were arranged without danger to anyone.

And upon that little roof the sight was certainly a unique one. There they all stood, an extraordinary patchwork of color for the tiles of Southwest London — the bright frocks of the girls, the plumage of the birds, the blues and yellows and scarlets of the flowers; while the singing and voices sent up a chorus that brought numerous surprised faces to the windows of the higher buildings about them, and made people stop in the street below and ask themselves with startled faces where in the world these sounds came from this still June afternoon!

"Now!" cried Simon Parnacute, when all lots and owners had been placed carefully side by side. "The moment I give the word of command, open your cages and let the prisoners escape! And point in the direction of the park."

The children stooped and picked up their cages. The voices and the singing in a hundred busy little throats ceased. A hush fell upon the roof and upon the strange gathering. The sun poured blazingly down over everything, and the Professor's face streamed.

"One," he cried, his voice tremulous with excitement, "two, three — and away!"

There was a rattling sound of opening doors and wire bars — and then a sudden burst of half-suppressed, long-drawn "Ahhhhs." At once there followed a rush of fluttering feathers, a rapid vibration of the air, and the small host of prisoners shot out like a cloud into the air, and a moment later with a great whirring of wings had disappeared over the walls beyond the forest of chimneys and were lost to view. Blackbirds, thrushes, linnets and finches were gone in a twinkling, so that the eye could hardly follow them. Only the sea-gulls, puzzled by their sudden freedom, with wings still stiff after their cramped quarters, lingered on the edge of the roof for a few minutes, and looked about them in a dazed fashion, until they, too, realized their liberty and sailed off into the open sky to search for splendors of the sea.

A second hush, deeper even than the first, fell over all for a moment, and then the children with one accord burst into screams of delight and explanation, shouting, for all who cared to listen, the details of how their birds, respectively, had flown; where they had gone; what they thought and looked like; and a hundred other details as to where they would build their nests and the number of eggs they would lay.

And then came the descent for the presents and refreshment. One by one they approached the Professor, holding out the tickets with the number of their "lot" and the description of animal they were to receive and find a home for. The few accompanied by elders came first.

"The owls, I think?" said the pink-faced clergyman who had chaperoned other children besides his own, picking his way across the roof as the crowd tapered off down the skylight. "Two owls," he repeated, with a smile. "In the windy towers of my belfry under the Mendips, I hope —"

"Oh, the very thing, the very place," replied Parnacute, with pleasure, remembering his correspondent. For, of course, the owls had not been released with the other birds.

"And for my little girl you thought, perhaps, a lorikeet —"

"A scaly-breasted lorikeet, papa," she interrupted, with a degree of excitement too intense for smiles, and pronouncing the name as she had learned it — in a single word; *"and* a lizard."

They moved off towards the trapdoor, the owl cage under the clergyman's arm. They would receive the lorikeet and lizard downstairs from the nurse on presenting their ticket.

"And remember," added Parnacute slyly, addressing the child, "to comb their feathered trousers with a *very* fine comb!"

The clergyman turned a moment at the skylight as he helped the owls and children to squeeze through.

"I shall have something to say about this in my sermon next Sunday," he said. He smiled as his head disappeared.

"Oh, but, my dear sir —" cried the Professor, tripping over a flower-pot in his pleasure and embarrassment, and just reaching the skylight in time to add, "And, remember, there are cakes and lemonade on the floor below!"

The animals had all been provided with happy homes; the last cab had driven away, and the nurse had gone to find the flower-man. Parnacute had strewn the roof with food, and with moss and hair-material for nesting, in case any of the birds returned. He stood alone and watched the sunset pour its gold over the myriad houses — the cages of the men and women of London town. He felt exhausted; the sky was soothing and pleasant to behold. . . .

He sat down to rest, conscious of a great weakness now that the excitement was over and the reaction had begun to set in. Probably he had exerted himself unduly.

His mind reverted to his first impulsive eccentricity of two months before.

"I knew I should pay for it," he murmured, with a smile, "and I have. But it was worth it."

He stopped abruptly and caught his breath a moment. He was thoroughly overtired; the excitement of it all had been too much for him. He must get home as quickly as possible to rest. The nurse would be back any minute now.

A sound of wings rapidly beating the air passed overhead, and he looked up and saw a flight of pigeons wheeling by. He fancied, too, that he just caught the notes of a thrush singing far away in the park at the end of the street. He recalled the phrases of that dreadfully haunting list. "Wild singing note," "Can be heard two hundred yards off," "Raving with song." A momentary spasm passed through his frame. Far up in the air the sea-gulls still circled, making their way with all the splendor of real freedom to the sea.

"Tonight," he thought, "they will roost on the marshes, or perched upon the lonely cliffs. Good, good, *very* good!"

He got up, stiffly and with difficulty, to watch the pigeons better, and to hear the thrush, and, as he did so, the bell rang downstairs to admit the nurse and the flower-man.

"Odd," he thought; "I gave her the key!"

He made his way towards the skylight, picking his way with uncertain tread between the flower-boxes; but before he could reach it a head and shoulders suddenly appeared above the opening.

"Odd," he thought again, "that she should have come up so quickly —"

But he did not complete the thought. It was not the nurse at all. A very different figure followed the emerging head and shoulders, and there in front of him on the roof stood — a policeman.

It was *the* policeman.

"Oh," said Parnacute quietly, "it's *you!*" A wild tumult of yearning and happiness caught at his heart and made it impossible to think of anything else to say.

The big blue figure smiled his shining smile.

"One more flight, sir," said the silvery, ringing voice respectfully, "and the last."

The pigeons wheeled past overhead with a sharp whirring of wings. Both men looked up significantly at their vanishing outline over the roofs. A deep silence fell between them. Parnacute was aware that he was smiling and contented.

"I am quite ready, I think," he said in a low tone. "You promised —"

"Yes," returned the other in the voice that was like the ringing of a silver gong, "I promised — without pain."

The Policeman moved softly over to him; he made no sound; the constellations of Orion and the Pleiades shone on his coat-collar. There was another whirring rush as the pigeons swept again overhead and wheeled abruptly, but this time there was no one on the roof to watch them go, and it seemed that their flying wedge, as they flashed away, was larger and darker than before. . . .

And when the nurse returned with the man for the boxes, they came up to the roof and found the body of Simon Parnacute, late Professor of Political Economy, lying face upwards among the flowers. The human cage was empty. Someone had opened the door.

Printed in February 2023
by Rotomail Italia S.p.A., Vignate (MI) - Italy